HOUR OF THE HAWK

A JOANNA HUNTER MYSTERY

JOYCE HOWE

❀ Created with Vellum

To the people of a small mountain village in California, and especially to my family there. Please forgive me for the liberties I have taken in fictionalizing you.

I have invented the eco-terrorism and all the villains of the piece, including the CEO of any large ranch in the area. Any resemblance to real persons is coincidental.

PROLOGUE

The whole thing started at breakfast.

Sitting at the table, I could see the cyclists on the bike path, and people walking their dogs. My laptop was lying to my left, waiting for me as I strip-mined the newspaper for information. It was the beginning of May. The maple trees lining the road had a green mist.

Spring north of Lake Ontario is a little taste of heaven. We sigh and let go of the winter scowls that warded off frostbite. We lift our faces to the long lost sun. For however brief an interlude, it is warm. It isn't freezing like the Arctic or sweltering like a Florida bayou.

The timer rang and I got up and walked into the tiny galley kitchen. I had been cozy enough during the long winter in my first floor apartment, its walls bright with paintings and photographs. But I was ready to sit outside the front door and gossip with the neighbours.

I poured the hot milk into the Pu-ehr tea, and carried it back to the table. I sat it down far to the right of my breakfast, on top of the financial section of the paper. I watched as the mug tipped over in slow motion and poured the milky black tea over the end onto the floor. I grabbed the paper towel and the hand towel and began sopping up the brown liquid. I threw the financial section off the table. Underneath was a small elastic-the villain in the piece. I hung the wet place mat over the chair back. I mopped up the remaining puddles on the table, stashed the wet towels in the sink and started a new cup of tea.

Half an hour later I turned on my computer. Nothing. I tried again. Nothing. It had been acting odd lately, turning off at random. It was just off extended warranty, of course. I had bought an external hard drive to back it up. Now I got the power cord and plugged the computer in. Nothing. No little green light. No orange light. Nothing.

Okay, panic now. All my writing was there.

I phoned the Apple Store, but got only a recording. I couldn't book an appointment on the computer. I tried the iPad. Nothing available. But if I turned up, could they turn me away.

I drove west right out of Toronto to the nearest Apple store-in Mississauga. And yes, a Genius could see me in an hour and a half. I took my trembling self to a coffee stand.

"That'll be $3.80," said the barista, as she handed me my chai.

I fished in my change purse, pulling out a toonie, a loonie and three quarters. Finally, I found a nickel. But wait, it wasn't Canadian. I searched for a Canadian nickel. As I handed it over, I took another look at the American one and exclaimed, "It's a 1936 Indian Head, my birth year!"

So how could this be a bad luck day?

Back in the Apple Store, I found myself at the 'disaster table'. I didn't belong there, of course.

"Yes," said the guy next to me, "my son spilled water on his laptop, it's completely dead and he's just finishing his thesis."

An awful truth dawned on me.

My genius came out of the back room where he had opened my baby up.

"It's full of liquid," he said.

"But the tea spilled onto the newspaper which soaked it up –not the computer," I protested.

"Was the edge of the paper near the computer, say right around the USB port?"

"The paper acted like a wick," I realized out loud, "and siphoned the tea into the computer."

I put my head down. The other three others murmured condolences. The Genius gathered repair figures. Considerably more than a new computer.

Fifteen minutes later, I plugged my external hard drive into a new silver MacBook Air and prayed. Fifteen minutes after that, I turned it on, and there it was my unfinished book, my music, my pictures, my virtual life. I felt as if Lazarus had risen from the dead right in front of me. Cheap at any price, even including the extended warranty.

I called my daughter, Julia, in California.

We considered my bad luck/good luck day. I had lost over a thousand dollars and gained a lucky nickel. It was hard not to read meaning into that, especially if you tended to see things that way. And we did.

"Perhaps someone is trying to get your attention," she said.

I called my sister in Mississauga. "Could be somebody who's passed on?" Georgia suggested. "Or somebody incapacitated. Or somebody in trouble that doesn't want to ask for help. Whoever it is must have a powerful connection with you."

I was not keen on telepathy as a mode of communication. There was too much guesswork involved, but it was not the first time the preternatural had entered my life.

I checked my psychic connections- my brother in Brussels, my ex-husband across the city, relatives in Boston, Texas and Quebec. All these long-distance lines of mutual concern and care seemed to be buzzing along fine. Las Vegas?

"It's Clara," I realized with certainty. She was my opposite number, my daughter's mother-in-law.

I called Clara.

1

TOO MANY BEARS

The bear came down from the mountain in late afternoon. She wasn't hungry. She had eaten well, but she was missing the cub.

She turned at the bottom along the well-worn path, picking up the scent of honey in the distance, and closer up, traces of many other bears, including the cub. The cub was old enough to manage on her own now. There would be a new cub in winter. She was almost there when another darker smell stopped her in her tracks. Blood. Bear blood. She took it in. Not just any bear blood, her cub's blood.

The man got home from work early. He was the boss. He could leave when he wanted. This bear thing had him all upset. All he had wanted to do was help his fellow creatures. They were hungry and starving in this four-year drought.

And cute. You couldn't say how cute. The cubs were black and fluffy. Adorable, his wife said. You just felt like cuddling them, his three kids said- Janey, Tucker and Linc. They laughed at that bad idea. But such good pictures, especially the young ones. The cubs'd hike themselves up onto the tire, and their weight would start swinging it. It was so comical when they lost their balance and grabbed the edge as they fell.

There'd been seven in the yard at one point, four adults. That was all over now. The rangers had cut down the tire swing, and trapped the big old female. Then, oh my God, the next day, they'd come back and shot her cub. The little bear was hungry. Hardly a hundred pounds. She was just walking toward them. How was that aggressive?

And how was it his fault? They'd treated him like he was stupid, like he didn't know what he was doing.

His mother's grandmother was Chumash. He spent summers with her before he started school. She taught him respect for wild animals.

"It's their place first," she'd say. "Always remember that, Tommie."

She would have been proud he got into college. Played for the Renegades, running back. Still had that same fit body.

He caught sight of it in the mirror as he changed into his cut-off jeans and T-shirt. Good to get out of that shirt and tie, his car salesman uniform. He took a good tan in the California sun. Today, though, he didn't care about looking good.

Maybe it would help to go hang a new tire swing for the kids. Without the honey. He shook his head. 'Ruefully', his wife would say.

She was still down working her shift at Kern County Medical Centre in Bakersfield. The school bus would be back up the hill soon. He'd pick the kids up. Save them the walk. But he'd have time to hang the tire.

In the garage, he measured out a new piece of heavy rope, and dragged another used tire off the high shelf over the electric door. He unlocked the door to the backyard. See he kept the bears out of the garbage.

When he stepped out onto the backyard walk, he stepped into the gravel the wardens had used to fill the places where they had dug down to remove the spilled honey.

Once on the dirt–grass wouldn't grow up here- he got busy slinging the rope up over the low pine branch and tying it off. He picked up the tire, studying it for a moment-

I GOT UP FROM THE COUCH WHERE I HAD BEEN READING AN ELIZABETH George mystery. Even with both fans on, the hotel room was unbearably hot. As I took a step toward the open door, my right hip stiffened in non-compliance.

Baby steps, I told myself, and circled the rug in front of the balcony door, until the old hips got organized. I stood looking out. A red-tailed hawk was sitting on a pine tree across the parking lot. Odd. She didn't usually come into the village center. She stuck to the pinewoods near the lake, with its abundance of fledgling red-wings.

It had been an unusual afternoon. Sirens and helicopters had broken the silence of Bear Mountain Place. In Los Angeles, that was normal, but up here, it was scary. Something was happening up on the mountainside.

To take my mind of it, I had immersed myself in *Deception on His Mind.* Not the best of George's work, but long and distracting.

In my blog, I called this place Shangri-La, after the hidden Himalayan village in *Lost Horizon* where no one aged. Bear Mountain Place didn't seem to prevent aging and it was only five thousand feet up, but, like Shangri-La, it was also astonishingly beautiful, with forested mountains, a perennially blue sky and a high desert climate. A village devoted to leisure. It wasn't even a village legally, but an unincorporated adjunct to a country club.

The hawk took flight. I crossed the room to the other door to watch her fly. But when I got there, she was gone.

I went into the bathroom and scooped cold water onto the back of my neck. The mirror showed me that my crows' feet had crows' feet. But only if I smiled. My face still bore the brown blemishes of the early birth control pill. Racoon mask. I had given up on bleaches. Then there was that tendency to moustache. The bones held up, for the time being. A good haircut might help. Ordinarily, I wore it short with *product*. There wasn't enough *product* in town to tame it.

We get the face we earn, I'd heard, but Julia countered that a seventy-eight-year old face should be revered. My wise daughter, Dr. Julia Durant, who lived, like the hawk, in the pinewoods, above the lake.

My face in a mirror continually surprised me. In my dreams, I was always younger, not the child with long dark curly hair, the one who had internalized "What a pretty little girl", but a young woman. My dream self never aged past forty.

This particular face was Joanna Hunter once again. When I gave up being Mrs. Durant, I went back to being one of Rod Hunter's girls. Once upon a time, that meant I couldn't buy property in my birthplace. Now Rod and those who feared him were gone. The Hunter name meant little, but I decided years before that to wear it defiantly.

This defiance went against the family wisdom of "Keep your head down." The old army maxim, "Never volunteer" went without saying. To do so was to lose the cloak of invisibility. Rod's girl children were his cover, allowing him to evade notice as he made his slippery way. A man with two or possibly three pretty daughters in tow was beyond suspicion. Most of all, we knew we must never ever talk to police. For one thing, we couldn't trust them. A surprising number were his buddies. And, if we squealed on him, Rod would take revenge.

After our father died, we uncovered evidence of the extent of his villainy, and did contact police. There was an investigation, involving three police forces and $1,000,000. The patio of our old home was dug up. Nothing. Burned by that experience, I vowed to live by the Hunter code, and never contact the police about anything ever again.

Muddling my way out of this family influence, I studied philosophy. I was the only female in the course by the final year. The male students would quote Hobbes-"Life is nasty, brutish and short", and fall about laughing. It took me most of my life to get it. To me, it seemed straightforward and un-ironic. As it turned out, my life, whatever else, had been long.

Answering Clara's telepathic call at the first of May had led me to this adventure on a California mountain.

Where almost none of the buildings were air-conditioned. I took a few turns up and down the room, moving from one fan zone of hot air to the other. I was anxious and unsettled. People with traumatic backgrounds need structure and routine. So the shrinks told me. Adventure didn't provide that, even if the adventure was in Shangri-la.

I had taught *Lost Horizons* long ago, so I knew about James Hilton's exquisitely beautiful mountain refuge where there were no cares and no one ever grew old. Bear Mountain Place, hidden in a valley, sheltered by pine-clad slopes under a blazing sun seemed like such a place.

Mostly!

Why there were sirens on the mountain and where to get dinner on a Wednesday were my present problems.

All the restaurants, except the Mexican one, were closed. There was definitely no room service at the three-unit Reality Hotel. It was, actually, the Bear Mountain Place Realty Hotel, but my sister misunderstanding an email, had christened it the Reality Hotel.

I tied on a silk skirt and slipped on my sandals. I hadn't heard Clara moving around next door for a while. Either she was napping, or she had already left for El Bruho. Personally, I could not swallow another taco. I hoped she could be roused to let me in to use her microwave. She had the *luxury* suite, two rooms, with microwave and bar fridge. I had one room, and a plastic hot pot from *Bed, Bath and Beyond.*

Clara was a widow of a few years. I had been divorced for over thirty years. We were both waiting. She was waiting for her house in Vegas to be sold. Then she could buy her house here. I was with her when she found it in May. She had made an offer for the asking price. Without a quibble. The seller was also waiting, of course, and not happily. When the purchase closed, I would go to live there with Clara, and continue waiting for my home in Canada to be renovated.

When I phoned her in Las Vegas at the first of May, I found her in despair. The younger friends she had depended on had moved back to Chicago to look after an invalid mother. Clara, who was well up in her eighties, had fallen twice in one month. She hadn't been seriously hurt, but she had been very frightened. She could no longer manage her house, but she was paranoid about hiring help. She was confused about her finances, certain that she was going broke. It was her fear that fuelled her telepathic call for help, no doubt, but, true to her nature, she'd thrown in a joke.

Her son Colin and my daughter lived six hours away from Las

Vegas in Bear Mountain Place, Kern County, California. It became clear as the four of us talked on the phone that Clara should move there. I had come to visit and to help her ease into the new situation.

When I said I was leaving Toronto, my landlady seized the opportunity to renovate my place, so I had hurriedly moved my things into storage in Toronto. But like all renovations, this one hit a snag. It had got to the demolition stage when the renovator got an offer he couldn't refuse. Hollywood North needed a set carpenter. My home stood stripped to the studs at this point, completely uninhabitable. Meanwhile, Clara's house deal was stalled, thus the Reality Hotel, and she was still going to need help getting settled when she did get the new place.

We were both living out of suitcases. Clara had the advantage there. She had driven from Vegas with her Honda CRV packed to the gunnels.

I had flown Air Canada with a 26-kilo bag, generously permitted for an additional $25. I had packed for a four-week stay, but then things hit a snag, and the weather turned hot. Most of what I packed was now too heavy to wear. Fortunately, my daughter had a few loose-fitting, hot weather things that were now mine, including the silk skirt.

It was always a pleasure to open the door to the General Store and step into the cool, quiet place. Today it was far from quiet. A group of seven excited people were gathered at the checkout.

"He's dead,' a large woman exclaimed. "Dead when the ambulance got there."

"But they evacuated him. I saw them load him onto the helicopter."

"No point really."

"They'll have to have an autopsy."

"I heard that his head was crushed in."

They fell silent.

"My God, a fatal bear attack. Black bear at that-"

"Who's dead?" I asked.

"Guy up on Pine Cliff, Tom Braddock, the one who was feeding the bears," the tall, young checkout guy told me.

" A bear broke into the house next door, and wrecked the kitchen last week," offered his short Syrian boss, who had come up behind him. "Turned out what attracted the bear was Braddock had filled a tire swing with honey. The wardens took the swing away a few days ago. That was before they trapped the bear."

""Shot her cub the day after that," said the clerk.

"It's karma," said a thin woman, carrying a yoga mat.

"What a dreadful thing to say," the large, red-faced woman barked as she plunked down her large vodka purchase.

"That cub wouldn't have been shot if that asshole hadn't fed them," said Yoga.

"What's up with all that?" mused a man with a six-pack.

"I told you," said the yoga lady. "Feeding bears is what's up with that. A fed bear is a dead bear."

Everybody started talking at once.

I pushed through the entry bar, and headed for the frozen food at the back of the store. They might come to blows. Voices grew louder as I rummaged for the last Amy's frozen dinner. I tarried in the wine aisle, reading all the white wine labels, and decided on *Barefoot Pinot Grigio*.

Bears, bobcats, mountain lions, dust storms, wildfire, drought, all in a valley rift formed by the San Andreas Fault. Half an hour down a winding mountain road to the nearest drugstore. Over an hour to the nearest city. Ninety minutes to L.A. and a plane home. Now the G.D. bears had started eating people. Shangri-la, indeed!

Clara still didn't answer my knock when I got back. As usual I was knocking on window glass. She locked the screen door so her cats wouldn't escape. That meant she was in, probably napping in her bedroom on the front side. I stood on the second-floor deck staring out at the back of Mad Dog's bar. Yes, there'd be a drink there, but no food. On Wednesdays, the restaurant downstairs was closed. Still the music sounded good, canned though it was.

Why not dump the dinner in the hot pot, get it hot if mushed, eat, and go over to the country club for live music. *The Kentucky Five* would be playing.

Still I stood, gazing between Mad Dog's and the Bear Mountain

Place General store. A few tall pines edged the highway. Across the road six leafy aspens marked the edge of the golf club. The club-house in the distance was brownish-red wood like all buildings at the town center. One pond still held water. A tree leaned toward it. "There is a willow grows aslant a brook". Always and inevitably, willows reminded me of Ophelia, mad with grief and singing as she floated down to death. I walked through a world written by Shakespeare.

I could care about Ophelia, who hadn't actually existed, but not Tom Braddock?

"Oh, Joey," I heard in my head. My conscience had a voice, Aunt Mae's voice. "Where's he got to?"

One Friday evening, many years ago, after a long commute from the city, I struggled through the door, laden with groceries. The phone was ringing. Dropping the bags, I picked it up.

A child had died in a freak accident, a child I loved very much.

"Tell me he's okay. Tell me he's okay!" demanded his distraught mother.

I wasn't sure why she expected me to know, but it was clear what she wanted me to say.

Bad news affects me digestively. In this case, the response was two-fold, both purgative. I held on tight, and heard myself say, "He's all right. He's safe."

I didn't say "in the arms of Jesus". Could be. Maybe. It was more fill in the blanks. What, after all, could be safer than dead?

Unless…..unless …

All those years later, I marched through my room at the Reality Hotel, dropping Amy's frozen stir-fry on the desk. Out on the front deck, I looked off to the left and up. Pine trees and height hid my view of the mountainside where the sirens had ended up. But, in my mind, I saw a confused man alone in his backyard.

"Tom," I thought, gently but firmly. "Tom, can you hear me?" He seemed to be turning to me. "You've had a bad accident. A bear attacked you. Your remains have been taken to Bakersfield. You are in your spirit body now. Look up. Someone is waiting to help you."

Perhaps he looked up. Perhaps a look of understanding crossed his face.

Perhaps. I didn't have much faith in my psychopomp abilities. I just followed the New Age directions, and chivvied the dead toward the clear light. This was the extent of my skill as conveyor of souls.

I arrived a little late at the club. The opening act in the Condor Room was already underway, the Celtic Pick-up Band. I got a glass of Chardonnay at the bar, and sat down at a round table with three women in their fifties, one with an aboriginal face in glittery denim, one in a red tank top, showing generous cleavage, and one in a smart grey jacket she had probably worn to work. They nodded and smiled in greeting. Bear Mountain Place was nothing if not welcoming.

"Did you see what was posted on the BMP website?" asked the businesswoman, passing me her phone. "Somebody's hacked it."

I hadn't seen it, of course, my cell phone didn't work up here.

"*Nature Will Be Avenged*," read the post, backed by a bear standing on its hind legs, long claws extended and its tooth-filled mouth open in a snarl.

"Shocking, isn't it?" she said. And indeed, a shock wave was spreading through the audience as Verizon customers passed their phones around.

"Evie Jackson," said denim jacket, shaking my hand.

"Joanna Hunter," I managed, while the other two ignored us in favour of the smart phone.

The musicians played on. There were more of them than audience members at this point–an Irish harp player with masses of curly white hair and a flowing multi-coloured dress, two men playing guitars, a female fiddle player and several guys playing tambourine, bodran, spoons, bones, tin whistle, flute and recorder. They were in the middle of a set of jigs, but even all that uproar had not quelled discussion.

There was less talk in the next set when Colin took the microphone, and began to sing *Carrickfergus*. It was a favourite of mine-"The water is wide and I cannot swim over/And neither have I wings to fly."

The lover wanted to cross the wide water back to Ireland's County Carrickfergus, only for nights in the town of Bally Grand. He was an exile, in England, with no passage money. It was a heartfelt cry for home-'the long road down to the salty sea'. And those nights in Bally Grand with his love. It sounded like a grand idea.

I saw Clara standing just inside the door, listening to her son.

She stayed there until Colin had finished two more, this time his own songs. One assured us that "everything burns" and another extolled us "to pray for rain". He was a desert boy, no doubt about it.

The band broke up then, several players heading toward the bar, Colin in conversation with the harp player. I beckoned to Clara as she turned away from the bar with her beer.

The table conversation had moved into high gear.

"What does it even mean? *Nature Will Be Avenged*? Is it some sort of conspiracy by one of those ecological groups?" asked the glamorous one.

"You think they've trained bears to kill people?" quipped Evie.

"Your son's a Fish and Wildlife officer. Ask him what he knows," returned Red Tank Top.

"When I talk to him, I will," she said. "Alicia and Monica," she added to me, pointing first to the glamorous one.

"Well, something serious is going on. All those bear incidents in four days!" Alicia whisper-cried.

Monica leapt in, "Now a killer bear on the loose-!

I did a quick check. Tom was no longer in his backyard.

Clara came toward me, resplendent in her latest thrift shop floral top. She sat her light beer carefully on a coaster, and leaned over inquiring in a whisper, "What happened?"

"You missed the excitement," I said and I filled her in, while the argument veered into the relative value of human and ursine life.

Suddenly, we were jolted into silence by the first line of *The Bear Came Over the Mountain*-loud and *a capella*. The *Kentucky Five* had taken the stage.

All that he could see
was the other side of the mountain,
The other side of the mountain,
Was all that he could see.

Silence fell as the last words died away. Then one after another, people rose and left the room. Only half of the audience-about thirty people- remained as the band broke into the Eagles' *Heartache Tonight*. Good thing the audience had grown during the break.

The band pressed on in good form and fettle. Clara looked puzzled. Monica had left. Evie and Alicia looked at each other in alarm, but stayed.

There were, of course, five members of the band. The lead guitarist was Julien Breton, the French chef at *Le Petit Breton*. I didn't know the name of the bass player. He seemed to be Native American. The male vocalist was ex-rocker, Max Rubenstein, a large, shaven-headed fellow with a walrus moustache. The female vocalist, a thin dark-haired girl called Lori, was a waitress at *Le Petit Breton*. The keyboard guy with a silver ponytail was classically trained pianist, Phillip Wilde, whose CDs were for sale in the village shops.

The band swung into *One of These Nights*, then *Lyin' Eyes* before closing the set with *Hotel California*.

In the next interval, Colin came over to our table.

"Sit down, sit down," said Clara, as the rest of us greeted him.

"No, I just came over to say goodbye," he replied, laying his one hand on his mother's shoulder, and the other one on his mother-in-law's-which is to say-mine. He was thin and tanned, with an Irish face and long hair under his black hat. I had a weakness for Irish faces, which I never understood until I discovered on *Ancestor.com* that my biological grandfather was Irish. He had died young so I had never met him, but the appeal of Irish faces was in my genes.

"What did you make of that?" I asked.

He shrugged. Then the band started up again. Colin waved good-bye, and slipped out.

The next set was a tribute to the Band that began with "See the man in the spotlight-"

When they got to the *Rube Goldberg Express* songs, Clara whispered that she was going to go. Did I want a ride? I shook my head.

Once upon a time in Toronto, I had left a club while Max Rubenstein was singing. He had heckled me from the microphone.

"Did the lyrics offend her?" Alicia asked.

I shook my head. Max had trained me well. I didn't dare give a verbal reply.

The words of these hard-driving, Rubenstein blues were risqué, like most blues. Clara hadn't sorted that out. The lyrics were hard to make out even with perfect hearing, and hers was not. She wouldn't have been offended anyway. But she was old enough to dislike loud music.

I left while the keyboard man was doing a solo. Outside, I happened upon Max by the tennis court, smoking pot. We nodded to each other. He didn't recognize me.

Well fine. Why should he? A brief interlude.

There were no streetlights in Bear Mountain Place. Even the LED sign at the entrance was off by ordinance. In the daylight, it told the date, the temperature, the humidity-always less than 30%- and the scheduled events. My eyes adjusted to the darkness, and I could see the vast bowl of the sky with its numberless pinpricks of light. I stopped on the path and leaned back to enjoy the stars.

They were too much. They were always too much here in the Kern County Mountains, well in any mountains, really, the Rockies, the Alps, even my own White and Green Mountains. They were too many. The sky was too vast. I was infinitesimal and yet my eyes contained them. Stars made me dizzy.

I shivered. Something had changed. I had always been alert for a possible critter attack, a fear leftover from my childhood in the isolated Quebec mountains. We were interlopers here as there. But I had been confident that neither large mammals nor snakes would hunt me down. Now I wasn't so sure.

The attack was menace enough, but the hacker's post suggested something more ominous and the Kentucky Five seemed to agree with it.

The next day, being Thursday, the weekly *Mountain Prospector* was waiting when Clara and I made our way down to the bakery. Clara was still chatting with the baker when I sat down outside, tea and croissant at hand, to immerse myself in the headline story: "Bear Attack".

It began, "A Bear Mountain resident was mauled by a bear

Wednesday afternoon and was pronounced dead at the scene. Thomas Braddock, 45, of Pinecliff Rd., Bear Mountain Place." The property was described as next to the fire road leading to the water tower. The story was detailed, running over to the second page. In the last paragraphs the recent history of bear activity was summarized.

California Department of Fish and Wildlife rangers had recently removed a tire swing filled with honey from Braddock's backyard. Later an adult female bear was live-trapped by rangers and transported. Her cub, thought to be 2-years-old, evaded capture. The following day, a CDFW officer, accompanied by a man wearing a vest that read, "Police", shot and killed that cub.

On the next page, an article headed "Bear Killing Raises Big Questions", described the controversy ignited in the community, in particular, the post on the club's website. IT experts were reportedly plugging the gap in the site's security.

Animal rights activism seemed to have died down in recent years, the report said. Was it about to make a comeback? No mention was made of the Kentucky Five's non-PC's choice of music the night before.

Clara had taken her seat across from me and was leaning toward another table in conversation. She had started off with her usual opening question, "Where are you from?" We were nearly all incomers. This was a retired couple from Chicago. Clara had a connection there as she did everywhere else.

I sat, half-listening, gazing at up at Bear Mountain, which rose behind the village.

When the couple got up to leave, Clara turned back to say, "What nice people!"

"Clara," I said. "Do you remember that odd thing we saw when we drove up Bear Mountain on Tuesday?"

We had both been awake before dawn, long before the breakfast places opened. What a great opportunity to watch the sun rise from the peak of Bear Mountain, or as close as we could get, the last two miles being trail, and out of elderly reach.

"You mean the trailer with a big steel cylinder like a culvert on the back?"

"Yeah, a yellow contraption. That was a bear trap. It looked exactly like the thing the rangers trapped the mother bear in on Monday. The *Prospector's* website posted a picture of it on line."

Clara nodded and said, "It had been towed away by the time we left."

"Do you suppose," I said, "the bear came back?"

"*Like the cat came back the very next day. We thought he was a goner, but the cat came back,*" Clara sang gravely.

"This particular cat needed help, I think. Is it possible it was brought back and turned killer? Is that what the Kentucky Five were hinting at, by singing *The Bear Came over the Mountain*?"

2

TOO MANY CATS

I was lying on the hotel room floor, adjusting my back, when Clara knocked on my door.

I had spent too long at the Internet Cafe yesterday, researching bear attacks, specifically black bear attacks. I had found a list going back to the 1800's. There had been more deadly attacks in the 2000's than in any previous decade. Human population growth, and encroachment on bear territory were to blame. Most of the fatalities occurred in wilderness recreational areas, only a small number in villages such as Bear Mountain Place.

Grizzly bears and brown bears were more prone to aggression, but there were certainly cases where a black bear attacked and killed-even several people in a group, or separate individuals sequentially on the same day.

I had read "Living with California Black Bears", a California Department of Fish and WIFE pamphlet, as well as the Bear Mountain Place handout, and I had been told repeatedly not to leave accessible windows open at night. I didn't consider second floor windows, even if they opened onto balconies, accessible, but Clara did. Now she was at my door asking me to come and open her bathroom window.

"It's the one Columbo sleeps on," she clarified.

Columbo was the scruffiest of her six cats, a long haired grey animal that dwelt in its own grey cloud of dander, and never left his windowsill, except for a very short trip to the litter box.

I thought I was over my cat allergy, having been custodian of seven cats at one time. I thought I was over sneezing and scratching. A few days with Clara's menagerie had proven I was not. Everything itched, especially my eyes.

Only one of the six was permitted out of doors, Poirot, a black cat with a white moustache. He was a rescue, who had lived outdoors too long to be penned up now. He had it in for me. He would lurk outside my door, and sidle in when I opened it. Hugging the floor, he would run to hide under my bed. He seemed to want to extend his territory. I would get down on my knees and throw my sandals at him to urge him to leave. On one occasion as I struggled to my feet, he leapt up onto the table, and chowed down on my cold chicken. A cat on a table offends my sensibilities. A cat on a table that eats my chicken is lucky to escape with its life.

There was also Tennison, an elegant Siamese; Sherlock, a tabby; Rebus, an orange Persian cat and finally, Jazz, an affectionate black and white female, the only one that didn't make me itch.

Columbo stared at me dolefully as I leaned over him in Clara's bathroom. I gave the window a mighty upward shove. Stepping back to assess my achievement, I sneezed. It was a wracking, shivering, total body sneeze, followed shortly by another. I sat down on the only available seat and sneezed. I kept on sneezing. Twenty-one sneezes later, my eyes and nose were running. I sat waiting. That was apparently it. Time to change my underwear.

When I emerged from my room in fresh jeans, I called through Clara's screen door, "Do you want to go to the club for breakfast?'

So we climbed on the golf cart, the preferred mode of transportation in the village. I turned the key, pressed the accelerator, and we scudded noiselessly off, one hand on our straw hats and my green scarf trailing in the breeze.

As usual, Clara had a word with the wait staff as we went in, and as usual, we sat at the window, where I could see the golf course.

"Isn't that a nice garden?" she said, gesturing at the side window.

She spoke as though she had just now seen it, but in fact, she said this every time we came.

"Beautiful," I agreed. "So colourful."

Clara was a disarming little old lady, cute, with flashing blue eyes and a lovely smile. She had a great *schtick*. She could seem charmingly helpless-a girl just out in the world, or alternately, a slightly confused elder. The first week she was in Bear Mountain Place, a woman stuck $10 in her purse and told her to buy herself a decent meal.

"Why did she do that?" Clara asked me.

"Generosity," I said. "But next time tell her you need twenty for a decent meal up here."

Financially, Clara was worth way more than me. She owned a house outright and had a better car. Her husband had left her well provided for. And she was careful with her money. I wondered if it was her thrift shop wardrobe that earned her this charity, but her clothes were well chosen and cared for, so I put it down to the *schtick*.

She had been an actor in her youth, and was the most gregarious person I had ever met. When she lived in Vegas, she befriended everyone in her chosen casino on any given Saturday. She had an omnivorous appetite for information and a capacious memory for detail. She had been in town a month, and she knew the point of origin of half the residents. Before winter, she would have the weekenders down pat.

We ordered breakfast–two softly scrambled eggs for her, poached for me. Clara caught up on the news about the waiter's pregnant wife. It was going to be a boy, and they had to pick his name carefully, so that the Japanese side of the family could pronounce it.

When the waiter had gone, I said, "Clara, would you do something for me," I leaned forward so the other diners couldn't hear.

At right of us, the usual five elderly men and one woman were eating their after-golf breakfast. Behind us was a couple, one of them apparently very deaf, given the decibel level.

"You are really good at drawing people out, and I want to know about the people in the Kentucky Five-where they come from, for example."

"Oh, I know about the girl," said Clara. "She waited on me at the restaurant. Didn't I tell you? She actually comes from Vancouver. So does her husband-Tom, no-Ben. He makes furniture."

Whoa! Could be my theory about the Kentucky Five was right.

"I think they live next door to Penny's," I said. Penny was the real estate agent who managed our hotel.

"Oh, yes they do. Penny told me that. And the group rehearses there on-let me see-Thursday evening, I think."

"Hmmn."

"She's called Lori. What else do you want to know?"

"Well, I know quite a bit about the bald-headed guy, Max. He's not from Kentucky either. He comes from Toronto. I knew him thirty years ago. For a short while. He was a rock star in the 60's. His band played all over the world. When I knew him, he slept with a loaded shotgun under his bed."

"I won't ask," Clara said, giving me a look. "Why do you want to know about them?"

"I want to know if they're ecological activists. I know Max used to be. He satirized bad environmental policies. And singing *The Bear Came Over the Mountain* suggests they might be. I wonder if one of them posted *Nature Will Be Avenged.*"

Clara considered this.

"I want to know why they call themselves the Kentucky Five." I went on. What's the Kentucky connection?" I hesitated, but then I gathered my nerve. "There's lots of bear talk, but nothing about that bear trap trailer we saw up on the mountain at dawn."

"I can easily get the chef talking," said Clara. "And the pianist comes to the bakery sometimes, but the native fellow–I think he works down the hill. I'll ask around."

"So," she said beaming. "We have a mystery."

"Maybe," I replied. I felt the frisson of a mystery addict, an addiction she shared.

I had Clara drop me off at my daughter, Julia's. I was due to take their Prius, and drive one of Julia's patients to Bakersfield for radiation. That would be my daily task for the week. I was grateful. It would give me a break from cat dander.

Julia met me at the door with the car key. She had wrapped her small self in a large, indigo robe, the hood up over her long curly, grey hair. She had a classical beauty, like her two French cousins, but her eyes were deep blue.

She was about to join Colin on the deck with her tea. He was wearing his robe and his ever-present black hat. A pork pie hat. It was his signature. He cooked in it, played guitar and golf in it, and slept in it for all I knew.

Julia was working only one day a week at the local clinic. She was still recovering from major surgery. She had given up her medical practice in Los Angeles because of her health. Once news got out in Bear Mountain Place that she was a G. P., she had been pressured to help at the clinic. She needed the money, so she agreed to one day a week. I had reservations about the idea, especially because she got all the seriously ill patients in town. They preferred a doctor to the usual nurse practitioner. The other doctor was half an hour down a hairpin road only recently furnished with guardrails, much to the relief of drivers and insurance companies.

Backing the Prius up in the sandy yard under the Jeffrey Pine, I thought how different mountain life was. People lived on mountain-time. Workmen might be unpredictable in other places; up here they were downright spooky. They vanished for weeks, and no one could tell you where. San Diego, seemed to be the default answer. Skipping L.A., the truants went right on down to San Diego.

The local service station sat with lights on, but no attendant. You could buy gas-if you had a card. Restaurants closed randomly mid-week, and even on weekends had strange, arbitrary hours. You could get pizza from 4 to 7 on Thursday, Friday and Sunday, or until 9 on Saturdays.

But why would you live on a mountain if you cared about time?

On the positive side, if you didn't have a car or you couldn't drive, someone would give you a ride. If you were too sick to cook, people would bring you food.

The mountain demanded cooperation. We survived together or went down together. Empathy was shrewd policy. It was one thing to mistrust wild life, but quite another to doubt each other.

I was on my way to pick up Star Shine Fletcher. She accepted her Stage Four breast cancer, but she deeply resented her "stupid, hippie name". She was waiting in the driveway of her boxcar house when I arrived, smoking one of her three daily cigarettes. She had lived a healthy life, breathing clean mountain air, eating local organic produce, hiking, cross-country skiing, and writing successful children's books. Even the irony of her well-spent life didn't upset her as much as her name. She had given up trying to get people to call her Ellen. It hadn't worked. She was a natural blonde, and even in her tough-girl denims and cowboy boots, she shone.

She settled herself into the passenger seat, and pulled the lever reclining the back fully. She was worn out by daily radiation treatments, and the round trips of two and a half hours.

The S-curves with their precipitous cliff-edge demanded my total attention, guardrails notwithstanding. Julia's yoga teacher still suffered from her crash injuries. As the pinewoods closed in, the road descended in easier loops. I concentrated on taking them well, keeping an eye out for regulars, and pulling over to let them pass. At the turn to Bear Mountain, the highway swung through a long valley. This was where *The Waltons* had been made. It could stand in for Carolina then because it was greener than the mountain. The wooded vistas were still there, but now the houses dotting hillsides spoiled the illusion.

Up ahead, I could see a sheriff's car partly blocking the road and beyond it Black Angus cattle milling about as a two guys on all-terrain vehicles tried to herd them back to their pasture.

I stopped beside the policeman.

"We've got most of them back," he said, when I put down my window. "And the two llamas." He nodded toward the opposite side of the road. "Whoever set them loose cut the fences right down, but they must have driven them out. Cattle would have stayed put, otherwise. Are you from Bear Mountain Place? Did they round up the horses?"

"I didn't know they'd got out," I said.

"Yeah. One of them had to be put down apparently. Thank heaven, they didn't set the goats free."

"Who did it?" I wondered out-loud.

"Some kind of vandals. Drunk kids maybe. You can get around now. Go carefully though."

Evie's goat farm, unlike the more prosperous ranches, sat on a crossroad back from the highway. She had told me that the night the Kentucky Five took the stage to play *The Bear Came Over the Mountain.*

Only a couple of cattle still stood on the side of the road staring as I passed. The rest were back down in the pasture, ambling off toward shade.

Star Shine seemed to still be asleep, so I refrained from audible speculation.

As we neared the throughway, we passed our local metropolis, Douglas Peak. I turned north merging onto the Grapevine, that stretch of the I-5 that wound through Halcon Pass.

Mountain people drove a lot. Julia and Colin did so in silence, no music playing. Julia read, and Colin whistled once in a while. It had taken me a while to get used to that, but it was good preparation for Star Shine's silence. I let her rest until we passed Halcon Ranch. I couldn't stop from observing that this was the biggest ranch in the country.

"Yes, so you've said before," said Star Shine, eyes still closed. "And halcon is Spanish for hawk."

Well, she was very ill, irritable and, also, correct. I did repeat myself.

I turned my attention to the steep hills. They were almost perpendicular, but cattle grazed so far up, they looked like toy creatures from a child's ranch set.

Beside the highway, the parking lot at Fort Halcon was full of yellow school buses. School kids were getting a look at the earliest fortification established by Americans on the west coast. I saw little else, busy getting out of the down-bound truck lane. Large signs set truck speed at 35 miles an hour. Long crash ramps for failed brakes rose on both sides. I hated the one that led to the left. I pictured an out-of-control sixteen wheeler cutting in front of me.

Besides failed brakes, the pass was prone to high winds that pushed big transports sideways. Onto sedans. I always left a lane as buffer.

Half way down, the opposite slope up ahead looked black. It wasn't a cloud shadow. The sun was behind the hill. The sky, flawless blue. I began to smell fire. The enormous scale of the pass hid the source, until curve and descent brought into view police cars, three fire engines and at the centre of it all, a burned out blue Prius. Like the one I was driving.

The car was a blackened shell. Climbing the steep grade, the engine had ignited, and the fire had spread to the scrub-covered hillside. Firemen with tanks on their backs were putting out hotspots, high on the charred slope.

Silent though it was, the drive wasn't boring.

Once we were on flat land, the Central Valley opened out. It lay in the embrace of the barren desert mountains. The colours were an infinite number of shades of blue and grey, like a Lawren Harris painting I had seen and dismissed as unrealistic.

The valley rocked me every time I saw it. I started life as a farmer's daughter, and this was the world's biggest market garden. Mile after mile of green fields and orchards. Its topsoil could be as deep as twelve feet. A third of the country's vegetables and fruit grew here, almost all of its raisins and almonds. The crops flourished under a perpetual blue sky, with a year-round growing season and multiple harvests.

The problem was water. California had been suffering a drought for four years.

As we began passing the almond orchards, I glanced over and saw that Star Shine was still asleep.

We had left the big rigs behind on the I-5. On Rte. 99, the trucks were small and local.

The fields were green, level and stretching as far as I could see. Far off, on a parallel road, workers' cars were parked. We passed a bare field in which a huge machine was ploughing. It must have had GPS to keep the operator on a straight line. There was nothing at either end as a guide, no trees, no fences, and no buildings.

Every so often there were beehives and sometimes workers in white coveralls and head nets, like newly landed aliens. An irrigation ditch ran under the road and a stand of huge pipes rose up on the right, the irrigation control center.

On the other side of the road, a mobile watering device was moving slowly down a cornfield, a giant driverless centipede moving sideways.

"I can't do it. I just want to die." Star Shine's voice jolted me out of my reverie.

She still had her eyes closed.

What to do? As Rod Hunter's daughter, I mastered tough love at an early age. It was how I kept the younger kids safe. My own children softened me up somewhat, but…

I pulled over to the shoulder and turned off the engine. I sat for a moment looking at Star Shine's closed face. I undid my seatbelt and leaned over to put my arms around her. She didn't resist, but began to cry very softly.

I just went on holding her. There was nothing to say, no argument to be made. I had lived long enough to know that. All I could do was be with her as she moved through her despair.

It took a while. I tried to focus all my attention on her without absorbing her anguish. Cars and trucks rushed by, inches away. I worried we'd be late for her appointment.

Finally, she began to grow quieter.

"I just want to go to sleep and not wake up," she said, blowing her nose.

I considered that idea. "We should be so lucky," I said acidly.

She began to laugh. Then we were both laughing hysterically, tears running down our faces.

I got Star Shine into the Kern Medical Centre on time. As usual, however, she was going to have to wait.

"Come back in ninety minutes," I was told. So I got back in the car and drove to Regan's Roadhouse, off the 99 at California Ave.

Bakersfield, true to its name, was 110 degrees Fahrenheit under a glaring sun. It felt like an oven when I got out of the car.

I had parked in the last remaining bit of shade beside a red MGB with its soft top down. I took a minute to admire its red leather interior. A fifty-year-old car, it had been beautifully refitted.

Regan's had a western theme. A mural on the back wall depicted a saloon bar with a handsome cowboy leering at a woman in a low-necked yellow dress. She had a lascivious grin.

I ordered sliders and a Blue Moon beer.

My phone suddenly came to life, pinging to tell me I had an email. How novel! I was back in the world of technology. The email was an ad, but I decided to check the BMP Club website to see if there was news about the horses.

There were two new posts: *Meat is Murder* and *We Are Not Your Beasts of Burden!* The standing bear loomed in the background.

When had I last read those slogans? In the early eighties, it must have been, when my son, Daniel, hung around with anarchists and animal activists in Toronto. Long ago and far away. Why were they back? Were they connected to Daniel's long ago friends? Was it just mischief or something worse?

3

NO GOOD DEED

"I never meant for that to happen," said a man's voice on the balcony of the hotel room next door. "I've never seen Ben so mad."

I was lying on the couch reading, both doors open for the cross breeze, which was finally coming down from the mountain as the light faded.

I knew he was talking to Lori, the girl in the *Kentucky Five*. She had moved into the room on the other side of mine on Sunday. I had some idea why.

Thursday evening, I just happened to be walking Penny's dog for her. She had complained that little Precious was shut in on Thursdays while she-Penny that is-was at a weekly dinner meeting at the club. Clara had said that the band practised there on Thursdays, so I had readily volunteered to walk the Chihuahua. It was what passed for sleuthing on my part. The previous Thursday, I had heard the Kentucky Five rehearsing, but, the second week, as I made my way back down the street, I heard a man shouting. It was Penny's next-door neighbour.

"Find somewhere else to practise," he shouted at the four men loading instruments into two vehicles. "Find somewhere else to plot. I want no part of it."

Listening to Lori and the guy she was talking to, I wondered if the room next door was somewhere the Kentucky Five could plot in private? I certainly hoped they didn't plan to practise there.

"Why don't we go in?" Lori said. I assumed she didn't want a nosy neighbour listening to what it was that hadn't been meant to happen.

The plastic chairs were pushed back on the gravelled balcony floor.

The balcony had an odd and inconvenient floor treatment. It was covered with tiny stones. I presumed they had once adhered to the shingle type floor covering. No longer. Now they got into the track of the sliding door. Having no vacuum cleaner, I had to pick them out with my fingers to close the door. Every so often a tiny sharp pebble made its way onto the carpet, administering agonizing acupressure.

Ben, I remembered, the husband was called Ben. He had seen me on the side of the road just as he said, "Plot." I had pretended I was deaf, but my heart leapt. Bear plotting? Letting loose the herds plotting? Or just wife stealing? I cautioned myself, "One swallow does not a summer make."

Usually the next-door hotel room sat empty. I preferred that. My back door was right next to its back door, and as occupants came and went, they tended to stare through my screen. Maybe, they couldn't actually see me-in tank top and swim bottoms in the dreadful heat.

If Lori was going to leave home, she couldn't have chosen a more convenient spot from my point of view. In fact, it was probably the only available room in town, certainly the only modestly priced one. The more expensive *Bear Mountain Place Hotel* and the *Wild Wolf B & B* would be booked solid in July.

I stood surveying the hotel room. It was an old-fashioned spacious room, decorated with framed flower prints, like grandma's, just not this grandma's. The sitting area was next to the front balcony, with an electric fireplace in the corner, and a Duncan Phyfe drop-leaf table with matching chairs. The couch, I had been lying on, sat on the opposite wall. The bed, with its never washed comforter, stood in the middle facing the purely decorative television set. A white desk, next to it, served as my pantry and water station. An 'antique' dresser, shared a curtained alcove with the clothes rod. The actual closet was padlocked to protect the toilet paper. The bathroom was beside the front door, its window overlooking the stairs. The bathtub had both shower doors, and a plastic curtain, hung wrong way to.

I reached for my Chardonnay.

I was bored and given to idle speculation.

The village was aflame with new outrage. One of its favourite horses had broken its leg while loose. It appeared that like the cattle and the llamas, the horses had been driven out of their corrals. The little Palomino had been found in agony in the ditch beside the golf course. The woman who owned her had had to shoot her.

It didn't seem possible that Lori could be involved in something so destructive. She seemed like one of Clara's nice people. She had been in Julia's yoga class last December, and they had struck up a friendship. They would sit in the club gazebo after class, chatting and drinking their water flasks empty. They were both from Canada, though from widely separated cities. It turned out that they had friends in common-including my son, Daniel. Julia thought they were going to be close, but, suddenly, Lori pulled back. She stopped going to yoga and didn't answer Julia's texts.

I had spent the day at my daughter's, cooking. Colin usually did the cooking, but he had an assignment to write a "silly" song, for a cartoon dog. Silly or not, it was taking all his time and attention

I had a couple of reasons for cooking. The obvious one-I feared starvation. And I hoped I could tempt Julia to eat. She had no appetite, and weighed less than a hundred pounds. Then there was Star Shine. Someone else was driving her to the hospital this week, so I was going to provide meals.

"Fried" chicken done in the oven, potato salad with homemade mayonnaise, and green salad with poached pears had tasted delicious to me. Julia and Colin's dinner plates were still untouched when I left to take Star Shine's meal to her. Colin was deep in concentration, and Julia was going to eat with him. She said.

Star Shine told me she would save her meal for tomorrow's lunch. Clara put her portion in her tiny fridge.

What was this-a no-eat zone?

We did have happy hour.

Clara's Miss Marple role was lending a little zing to her life. Other than talking to everyone she met, napping and reading, she had nothing to keep her occupied.

As readers, we relied on the Douglas Peak library down the mountain, a large and beautiful new building, which had an odd collection. It had all the usual mystery writers, but only their lesser-known titles. I was reading those.

I had introduced Clara to Lee Child's Jack Reacher thrillers, and Ian Rankin's Rebus mysteries. She had enough of those to keep her occupied for months, having bought them for $1 each at the Friends of the Library book sale.

But, really, one could not survive by book alone, thus a little wine in early evening. Tonight, happy hour was late, so we watched the sun setting behind the mountains. The stillness invited me into its embrace. The question was did I want to go into it.

Although I was used to solitude-I lived alone in TO-I was also used to telephone, cable television, the Internet and Netflix. The television in Clara's room pulled in two channels. Mine, a snowy CNN. We never turned them on. Clara had a working cell phone. My smart phone had turned stupid. It couldn't relate to the Verizon cell tower. There was neither telephone nor Internet connection at the Reality Hotel. There was an Internet café a few buildings away.

I knew what my problem with stillness was. I had figured it out camping up here in Kern County years ago. The mountain wilderness forced me to slow down. Way down. My busy mind, in search of distraction, came face to face with itself. Heart of darkness and all that.

In Joseph Conrad's novel of that name, Kurtz had a similar experience up the Congo River. His reaction was somewhat more irregular. His fence posts sprouted human heads. The natives regarded him as a god who could make rain and fine weather. They brought him ivory in tribute, and Kurtz indulged in unsavoury practices to ensure his status. He had discovered the heart of darkness dwelt not within the Congo but within the self.

Next morning, I walked over to find the Internet Café locked. No matter. It didn't have its license yet to serve café or even tea, and I could get a signal on the deck. I settled at a table to have a look at my blogs.

I hadn't posted anything on my blog since I left Toronto at the end of April. Rule one of blogging was you had to keep at it or readers would desert you.

The Café's door opened from the inside, and the real estate agent from the adjoining office greeted me.

It wasn't Penny's office of course. Hers was in the hotel building. Many people in town sold houses. There were four real estate offices in the village, not to mention freelancers who had other jobs as receptionists or sales clerks. The receptionist at the medical clinic was very take-charge, the result, I finally figured out, of being a real estate agent in 'real life'. There were only a couple of thousand houses in the area, but they turned over rapidly. The dream holiday home in BMP proved too far away after all, and too problematic.

The road could suddenly become impassable from mudslides, wildfire, ice and snow, earthquake, come to that. Highway signs read, "Chains may be needed at anytime". Always a chuckle when the thermometer read over 100F.

I moved inside the Internet Café, and checked Bear Mountain weather on the Net. It was going to be very hot. The Café was only a few degrees cooler than outside, but I was out of the sun.

My blog was called *200 Journals*. I was actually only up to Journal 130, but my goal was 200. It was one way of committing to an advanced old age.

Lately, I'd been posting dispatches from *the Septuagenarian Hobbit*, complaining not about my hairy feet, but about these late life adventures. For example, I had spent December in Brussels with my brother, who was invalided by knee surgery. I had had to navigate three languages in the laundry, as well as unfamiliar streets. Now I had ended up on a mountaintop with a certain number of life threatening aspects. My literary conceit was that I preferred a "cozy life", but like Frodo, I didn't get one.

Partly, I wanted to dispel stereotyped ideas of aging, but I categorized most of my posts as "humour". I quoted Samuel Beckett's advice to a young writer-"Despair young and never look back." I liked this riff on Hobbes. Beckett being Irish took a bleak view of publishing and of life, and found it darkly funny. My siblings and I agreed. Today's entry, "The great loneliness", would begin with my flash of despair on the way to Bakersfield.

It came down to this, I reasoned, why are we here? Why are we here battling carnivores and cancer, and Hamlet's "thousand natural shocks"? To be precise-why am I here? Or as my very old grandmother once said, "Why am I *still* here?"

"Do you remember the time Grace got stuck on the high beam?" I asked her then.

"Oh my, yes," she said, and she started to laugh.

Grace was 11. I was 12. The boys had dared us to go out on the high beam of the haymow and jump. Trouble was the new hay wasn't in yet. The old hay lay packed way below the wagon floor. We had inched our way on our bottoms to the middle of the beam. The boys had jumped and been swallowed up. They had to dig themselves out, laughing and spitting hayseeds. Terrified, I had considered returning the way I'd come, but Grace was in the way. She was catatonic. She wouldn't even answer me, much less move. I jumped. I hit the hard hay and bored my way into it. My teeth slammed together and just about popped out the top of my head.

No matter how we pleaded with her, Grace wouldn't move. We three down in the mow sent my little sisters up on the barn floor to get my grandmother, Gladys. She arrived wiping her hands on her apron. She spoke encouragingly at first. That didn't work. Grace was glued in place.

"Gracie Lyn," Gladys shouted. "You get down from there right now or I'll give you such a whupping."

It was evident to the rest of us that there was no chance of that, Grace being out of reach, but fear met fear in her and she jumped.

We dragged her up out of the hay. She was weeping hard. The four of us set off into the loft above the stable and down through trap door to the manger. Grace was still sobbing. As we came up around the granary, we heard a strange sound. There on the ramp, stood my little sisters, staring at their grandmother, her face buried in her apron, her entire body shaking and a deep, rich sound exploding from her. She was laughing harder than anyone I had ever seen laugh before.

Thirty years later as we sat talking, she laughed herself out of despair.

I was writing about the saving grace of laughter when one of our local cowboys came into the cafe. He wore denim, boots and a Stetson. Others, including Star Shine, affected the look, but he was a real rodeo cowboy with the limp to prove it. He sat down behind me, fired up Skype, and started complaining that his cell phone wasn't working again.

"No, I haven't called Verizon yet. They keep insisting it is working and it makes me mad. I tell them I damn well know-I'm the one trying to make a call."

"Of course it's a Verizon. That's the only kind that works up here."

I tried to tune him out.

"Yeah, some big shot up here ponied up a bunch of money to do a fast DNA test on what they got off poor Braddock. The bear left a good deal of spit and whatnot. They compared it to the cub's. The killer bear was the cub's mother."

No matter how I tried, I couldn't shut his voice out. The question was whether she was also the bear that had been trapped. No DNA sample had been taken from the trapped bear, so there was nothing to prove she was the killer.

"Anyway," the cowboy went on, "the CDFW says the trapped bear's been relocated, and they're getting signal from her tag a good distance from Bear Mountain Place.

He fell quiet, listening.

"It's possible. Relocated bears can get back to home territory pretty quick."

"It was a ranger shot the cub. Nobody is saying who he was, but it wasn't Jackson. He did trap the adult, him and his partner. The paper made a big deal about one of the shooters wearing a police vest, but rangers are police."

"Yeah, somethin's fishy in the CDFW. No trust anymore. Half the people up here are terrified of the killer bear-think she's still on the loose-and the other half are terrified of the CDFW. What they gonna shoot next?"

"You're right-Braddock didn't actually kill the cub, but he started it. Honey in a tire!"

"This week's *Prospector*'s got another story about the cub's senseless slaughter."

It wasn't newspaper day yet, so how did he know, I wondered. Mountain telegraph. Up here it seemed as if information leaped from mind to mind.

By the time he got off the phone, I had posted the blog. I turned around and introduced myself.

"Harry," he said, shaking my hand. He was white haired with a long white beard. Younger than me, but not much.

"Tell me, Harry–I couldn't help overhearing–do you know what the bear looked like?"

"Black," he said, as if I had asked a stupid question, but friendly enough.

"Okay. I'd heard that sometimes black bears are cinnamon or even blonde. I was wondering how they could identify the killer bear."

"Beats me. Have to sedate her and get a DNA sample. Could be a mite time-consuming sedating all the girl bears on the mountain. What's her name, that real estate agent bear expert could tell you better 'n me."

"Catching the killer sounds like a long shot," I said.

He shrugged. "'Less she's got a taste for human and kills again." He nodded his head several times. "Know what? I hope that damned bear's in the next county."

Kern County being as large as it was that would be a long way away.

The mid-day heat had set in by the time I left the cafe. Walking back to the hotel, I felt as if I would fall over. When I got there, I eased up onto the golf cart, and set off for the boxcar house. Star Shine would be stifling in it, even with the doors open.

I was grateful for the modest wind the cart's twelve miles an hour produced. It dried the sweat slightly.

A boxcar house, true to its name, looks like a boxcar without wheels. They were some of the earliest houses up here, modular like all the others. In 1970, the oil company, which owned the place, realized there was no oil, and came up with the idea of a vacation town. Now these early houses were some of the cheapest. Like most of them, Star Shine's had sliding glass doors at either end. The only other windows were grouped around the front door on one long side. The other long side, with its amazing mountain view, was a solid windowless wall. The house was surrounded by sandy earth, except for an uneven expanse of pavement near the door. I rang the bell.

"Do you want to spend the afternoon at the club?" I asked. The club was air-conditioned. She was too wasted from her radiation treatments to swim, but she could sit in the game room, and play solitaire on her phone.

"I'll get my bag," she said and returned a minute later with a tightly rolled sleeping bag. When she got tired, she would nap on the carpet.

Dropping her off, I said, "Give me a call at Julia's, and I'll come pick you up when you're ready to leave."

"No need," she said. "Someone'll give me a lift home. And, hey, thanks, but I've still got last night's meal."

I watched her go in the door of the club, as I pushed the golf cart switch to forward. The annoying back-up alarm quit. Only then did I realize I hadn't even asked her how she felt.

How do you think? I asked myself. She's just got back from a radiation treatment. She's due to start chemo. Last week she wanted to die.

Julia had the house closed against the heat. The thermometer beside the fridge read over 90 degrees. Soon the sun would wheel around and shine in the un-curtained windows near the ceiling.

Usually, Julia and I took a short walk down to the pond before lunch, but it was too hot. Peeking into the bedroom, I could see her resting.

I was eating leftover chicken when I heard a knock on the door. It was a Fed Ex guy.

"Nobody home next door and someone has to sign for this. Would you do it?"

"Sure, " I said. "Amazon doesn't usually want a signature for a book delivery?"

He shrugged, took back his tablet, and drove off in a cloud of dust.

Weekenders were not entitled to mail delivery. Year-round residents collected mailed parcels from the post office, but delivery companies delivered only to street addresses.

I put the parcel down on the front hall table, so we would remember to give it to the neighbours when they arrived.

Maybe it was a rare book.

I set about making Gazpacho for dinner. No stove needed. There was homemade bread in the freezer, and cheese in the fridge. I'd put them out to warm later.

Colin appeared briefly from his studio. He nodded to me, but was still working in his head. He filled a martini glass with ice, and bent down to get the gin.

The sun was glaring in the high windows by the time I sat down in the big chair to read.

Julia came out and said, "Let's open the place up. It's a hundred degrees in here. Maybe we can get the air moving."

The fan high above was already on its highest setting. She went to open the bedroom blinds and windows, while I opened the sliding doors.

It was one room, too small to call a great room, but with high-beamed ceilings it felt spacious. The floors were uncarpeted stone collected by the owners, and set in patterns of green, beige and black. It felt soft to the bare foot and cool. But it was liable to have bits of pinecones embedded in it, or pine seeds or worst of all, pine pitch.

The house stood on bedrock, raised on posts over an enclosed crawl space. When the dryer was on, the house vibrated, and reverberated like a drum. In an earthquake, the house would just dance a bit, I told myself. The San Andreas fault-line was just the other side of the pond. As we found out later, and inevitably, the house jolted. Hard.

The houses at the side of us were altogether grander, particularly the one the parcel was meant for. It had no street frontage except a narrow, dirt drive. Marked out by stones, the track wound through pines to the gabled house above the pond.

The owners came and went quietly, a three-generation African-American family. I had seen them, but never spoken to them. The man was in his late fifties, his petite wife, always in pastel golf gear.

I couldn't concentrate. The sun was hitting me full in the face. I was reading *A Long Finish* by Michael Dibdin. It featured Detective Aurellio Zen, a Venetian, stationed in Rome. I got up and carried my book into the bedroom where Julia was watching the food network. I sat down on Colin's side of the bed and settled in to watch a young chef contest. Were these kids even fourteen?

Colin stuck his head in the bedroom door and said, "The people next door showed up and I walked over to give them the parcel."

"Oh, good," I said.

We were eating the cold soup when we heard a siren drawing ever nearer. A sheriff's car pulled up next door. A few minutes later, an ambulance bounced down the drive. The sheriff hustled a man and woman out the house and into the ambulance. We could see him talking on his radio. Colin went out onto the deck, but the deputy waved at him to go back. When he finished talking, he walked through the bushes and onto the deck.

"Just as a precaution," he said. "Stay inside."

"What's up?" asked Colin, through the screen door.

"Suspicious package," he replied.

My heart leapt into my mouth.

An hour later we heard a helicopter coming in for a landing, and the ambulance left. By now there were five more police cars. Another copter came in, and shortly afterward, the ambulance was back. Three figures in Hasmat suits emerged and went into the house.

In the meantime, I joined Colin for a couple of martinis. Julia bare-knuckled it, out of respect for her remaining organs.

I knew I should go back to the hotel. But I was paralysed. The number of police and others, standing around outside, was a clear indication that there was no danger. The Hasmat people stripped off their face protection when they came out of the house.

The light was beginning to fade by the time the sheriff knocked on the deck door.

He stood in the dining area. "Okay. They'll run tests on the parcel for anthrax and ricin, apparently. Let's see," he said opening his notebook. "J.A. Hunter. You signed for the package and took it in?" he asked Colin.

"Well no. My mother-in-law did," he said gesturing me. "I took it over to them when they arrived just before dinner. This is my mother-in-law, Joanna Hunter, and this is my wife, Julia, Dr. Durant."

"Was there any break in the packaging?" he asked me. "Did you see any dust coming off it?"

"No. It was securely wrapped," I said.

The sheriff turned to Colin.

"No, nothing," said Colin, shrugging.

"As a matter of interest," I asked, "what was the book?"

"*The Curse of Tutankhamen*," the cop replied.

"Check it for Valley Fever spores as well," said Julia.

She had answered very quickly, but the sheriff paused.

"Okay, Dr. Durant," he said, nodding thoughtfully.

When he was safely out the door, I observed, "Nice to have 'Dr' in front of your name."

"Well Tutankhamen," she said, shrugging. "Remember we saw that program when I was a kid? It was about the curse of King Tut's tomb and archeologists who entered it dying off *en mass* later. Some scientist speculated the deaths were actually caused by a spore released when the tomb was opened?"

"Huh! Is that where I got that idea?" I said.

"The Valley Fever fungus is coccidioides."

"Easy for you to say."

"It's called cocci, for short. It lives in the soil in desert areas. Around here, about a foot down. It can be released by construction or cultivation. Workers breathe it in. Usually it just produces a rash or flu symptoms. Most people don't even go to a doctor. They just recover."

"Weren't there a bunch of cases of Valley Fever near Bakersfield recently?" Colin said.

"Yeah. Forty or so," Julia recalled. "Two people were very ill, one died. They thought it might be a more virulent strain. Turned out it wasn't. There was just more of it. The spores got blown up from a construction site in a sandstorm. The victims all lived near it."

"Some big box store was supposed to go in there," Colin remembered. "But after the foundation hole was dug, the plan got cancelled. The company had run onto hard times."

"So why did some people get so ill?" I asked.

"They had compromised immune systems." Julia said. "They can go on to get meningitis. I shouldn't say this, but Mrs. King has had a heart transplant. She's particularly susceptible. If it is Valley Fever-it could kill her."

As I rode back to the hotel on the golf cart, dusk was turning to black night. I was shaking. True the night air was chilly, but I was in a state of anxiety, not to mention gut-wrenching guilt, and a cynical voice in my head kept repeating, "No good deed goes unpunished."

4

TOO MANY KIDS

The next morning, a domestic crisis took precedence.

"I still can't find my telephone book," Clara reported tensely, as she let me in.

I pictured a big city directory, and picked the tiny Mountain Community directory from the table.

"No, I mean *mine*, my address book. I remember it was lying on the kitchen counter in Vegas that last day, but so many people were helping me pack. It was 110 degrees-I could barely think. Somebody must have shoved it in a box of dishes or something."

She gestured helplessly at the many bags and boxes she had hauled out from where they had been stashed.

"There are so many people I want to contact, tell them where I've gone to, but I don't have their addresses or phone numbers."

"Sit down. Sit down," I said, propelling her toward the table. "I'll make you a cup of Earl Grey."

I fired up the microwave to heat the water, a piss-poor way to make tea, in my opinion, but our only recourse. When I put the mug down on the little round table, she was almost in tears.

"I've made a mistake moving here," she said, not looking up. "A big mistake."

I sat next to her, gazing out over the general store to the pine-clad slopes. I laid my hand on hers. Mine was veined, wrinkled and brown spotted. Hers was almost translucent.

"Why did you decide to come here?" I asked.

"Well, you know," she took her hand away to blow her nose, "I fell those two times and my friends, Barb and Bob, went back to Chicago. And I'm 85, I thought I needed to be near Colin in case-" she paused. "I'm just so worried. What if I lose the house here? Jane keeps putting pressure on Penny."

"When does your offer for Jane's house expire?"

"I don't know," she was looking at the table and kneading her wad of tissues.

"I'm pretty sure it's the end of August," I said, "but Colin will know. And she's got your deposit. Look, you made the offer before the place was even advertised. You offered what she was asking-you didn't dicker. She's talking about moving back to Washington State. That's going to take at least a month to organize."

Clara finally looked at me. "You think so?"

"Yeah. Let's go to the club for breakfast. The bakery isn't open." I got to my feet.

"Okay," she said.

"I'll get my purse and lock my door. Oh, I brought you this," I handed her a tube of sunscreen. She had developed red splotches on her cheeks.

"Thank you," she said, smiling. "I meant to buy some in Douglas Peak when we were there."

At breakfast, Clara was her cheerful self again, chatting with the priest who read interesting old tomes as he ate. I decided it was all right to tackle the delicate task of telling her about the package.

"Another mystery," she said. "Who would do such a thing? And why?"

"Maybe it's another ecological protest, like letting loose the horses and cattle. Julia thinks it might have contained Valley Fever spores."

I explained that an excavation in Bakersfield had recently released such spores, making people ill.

"You said it seemed to be from Amazon, but of course it wasn't. Hum," she mused.

As we passed the reception desk on the way out, we came upon a group of five people gazing at a tablet screen.

"Did you see this?" one of them asked us.

There on the screen was the familiar menacing bear. In the foreground, large letters read, "*Actions Have consequences. Stop desert development!*"

The woman holding the tablet said, "Apparently, a bunch of Savgo big shots got packages containing a white powder, it said on the news. That was the outfit that got in trouble building the foundation for a new super store in Bako. A lot of folks got sick. Didn't I hear somebody actually died?"

As the others chimed in, Clara and I backed quietly away, and made for the door.

"No point sharing the Kings' business," said Clara, when we were outside.

I dropped Clara back at the hotel, and went to Julia's to get my straw hat. I'd had bad sunstroke when I was young, and the doctor had warned me I would have to protect myself from the sun for the rest of my life. Time had proven him right.

The house was empty. Colin had driven Julia down to see her G.P. I had settled the hat on my head, when I heard someone say, "Knock, knock," at the screen door. I turned to see the tall, shaven-headed man.

"Hi, I'm Justin King from next door. Is Dr. Durant in?" he asked.

"No, they've gone down to L.A.," I said.

I opened the screen door.

"I just wanted to thank her for suggesting it might be Valley Fever. It seems like it was."

"I guess there hasn't been time to develop symptoms," I said.

"No, but my wife's health is fragile, so they're keeping her in the hospital. She opened the package. A cloud of dust rose off the book. Where it settled it looked like a fine white powder, so we thought anthrax, immediately. Well, we should know better than to open something we hadn't ordered, but it was her birthday. We thought one of our family had sent it as a surprise. It was addressed, "J. King"-she's Jennifer and I'm Justin."

"I'm really sorry."

"The sheriff brought me back to get my car. I've got to wait around for the cleaning company-some high end Bakersfield outfit that knows its way around fungal spores. Bonded, highly praised."

"Can I be of help?"

"No, I'll wait and talk to them. Just thank Dr. Durant for me. I'll get back to the hospital this afternoon. We had got attached to BMP, and so we decided to stay in Bakersfield when I took early retirement from *Savgo."*

"*Savgo*? Were they building a big box store in there at the time?"

He nodded and sighed deeply. "I was in charge. I had to resign when all those people got sick. Somebody had to take the fall. Then the whole outfit went under. Retail, these days!" He shook his head.

People here were so forthright. In Toronto, we were more guarded. I liked that openness, of course, being a highly curious person.

"I heard a number of Savgo people got parcels like yours."

"Yeah, so the sheriff's deputy said. One of the others had the wit to call it in. Didn't open it. We were the only ones who did. The cops used my old email list to notify all the Savgo gang not to open any parcel they received. The Sheriff's office thinks there's some sort of eco-terrorism thing going on. "

"It looks like it," I said.

It was the web posts that clinched that supposition. Now there had been two deliberate acts-the poisoned parcel and freeing the animals. Was it also possible that the bereaved mother bear had been returned to the mountain? Was it even possible she had been lured to Braddock's backyard?

Back at the hotel, I opened my room up to let the air in. It was much cooler than it had been, only about 85. I turned on both fans and made the bed.

Cut-rate guests made their own beds. Clean sheets hadn't appeared for me to change 17 days once. My own outside rule was 14. Oddly, clean towels appeared twice a week. Even so, I had to clean the bathroom fixtures.

Clara was out at lunchtime, but I ran her down at the Mexican restaurant, at a picnic table, under a tree. I wanted to tell her about Justin King's job. It seemed like a motive for crazy ecologists seeking vengeance.

"Oh, good, you're here," she said in greeting. "I've been talking to the woman who's taken over the ice cream shop, and I got some information."

Suddenly seven children, four mothers and a father descended on the patio. Four of the children began running around our table. The fifth incapacitated by his stroller howled to get down. Their three mothers settled down at the next table, laughing and tossing their long blonde hair. The other couple sat their two kids down at a third table.

The hilarity of the circling children was rising exponentially. They held arms out to touch the edge of our table, and, inevitably us, as they ran, tripping and howling with delight.

They had just come from Bible camp.

"Please don't let me be one of those grumpy old women," I prayed.

I turned and glared at the oldest, a girl, the leader of the pack. So much for the efficacy of prayer. As each child rounded my corner, I narrowed my eyes and frowned. Their speed decreased. They fell silent. Suddenly it seemed more fun to tip the toddler out of his pram. Half standing, I caught him just in time. The relevant mother got up and picked up the kid. She didn't pause in her animated conversation, or even glance at me. The rest of the kids swerved over to the other family's table.

The waitress had deposited a roll covered in cheese sauce in front of me. A taco? A burrito? A cheese enchilada! My teenaged L.A. grandson regarded me as totally unhip. My jeans were high waisted, and I knew nothing about Mexican food.

A Stellar's Jay had landed on the sluice trough, an authentic mountain artefact, and divider from the parking lot. He was intent on having lunch too. The children's clamour didn't put him off.

"So," Clara continued, finally, "the new ice cream lady–her mother is so nice-she's visiting from Oakland-she says that the cook at *Petit Breton* comes from Belgium. He came here to go to Stanford. He used to work as a-chemist, no- a biochemist up in the Bay Area."

I was drinking my beer and trying to puzzle out who said what, when the significance of what she had just said hit me.

"Biochemist?"

"She–the mother, I mean, knew the mother of his wife. Ex-wife now, I guess. He lives above the restaurant. He used to live with the pianist Phillip Wilde, in his big place up on Pinecliff." Clara raised her hands. "I usually have pretty good gaydar, but I can't say."

Mothers, kids and stroller were making their exit through the wooden gate. We watched their noisy progress, just as a man got out of a white pickup truck with Law Enforcement on the side. It was the bass player and vocalist for the Kentucky Five. He was in the uniform of the California Department of Fish and Wild Life.

I raised my eyebrows.

"Oh my goodness," said Clara.

A CDWF officer and a biochemist! Returned bears and toxic parcels!

What was more, he was very likely the goat farmer Evie Jackson's son. She had promised to talk to her son in the CDFW about the killer bear the night the Kentucky Five outraged the citizenry. Hadn't Harry, the Cowboy, called him Jackson?

"His mother's a goat farmer. Farmers are likely to be long term residents here," I observed.

"And Phillip Wilde," Clara, went on, "he's from Worcester Mass. – studied in Boston. I read that on one of his CD covers."

"So nobody in the Kentucky Five is from Kentucky then?"

"Doesn't seem like it. Well–" said Clara. "I showed you mine-"

So I told her.

5

THE RED TOP-DOWN

Thursday's *Prospector* did not headline the Valley Fever package. It hammered away at the CDFW for killing the cub, implying a cover-up. Why was one officer wearing a police jacket?

I read it on the pool deck at the club, skipping over three more letters about feeding bears, and a long, defensive editorial, justifying the *Prospector's* strong stand.

Toward the back of the 12-page publication, I found the Sheriff's Log. It was better than a checkout counter tabloid.

It began with its usual disclaimer, inviting those mentioned, to present proof the charges had been dropped. *The Prospector* would then print a retraction. A member of a prominent family had been charged with spousal abuse, and unlawful possession of a weapon. Emergency response to specific addresses for unexplained reasons-read-'suicide attempts' were no longer published. Julia's had waged an email battle with the editor to stop that practice. The Log did note that on Tuesday, July 15, the sheriff attended a house on Lakewood for a suspicious package.

I was standing shoulder deep at the edge of the club pool, when I saw Julia come flying up on her bicycle. She leaned it on the low wall beside the pool and waved to me.

For a moment, she seemed thirteen. I expected her brother, Daniel, to come speeding in behind her. He had gone off on a cycling trip around the world, four years ago. He was in Australia when he last emailed. A friend of his I ran into at Toronto told me Daniel had gone on to Malaysia. He was well, and had a travelling companion, a rich girlfriend with a sense of adventure.

Bicycles made me sad.

Julia had settled down in the shade on the lounge chair next to mine. On the other side, was a Chinese woman and next to her a teenaged boy.

"It's lovely once you're in," I said, drying off. "Refreshing."

"This is Theresa Lau," Julia said. "My mother, Joanna." I reached across to shake Theresa's hand.

"This my son," she said, "Xiao Yu. Nineteen." She pronounced the name Shau You, beaming with pride.

Xiao Yu was tall, with a long face and longish dark hair, whereas his mother was short with a moon face. He bowed his head slightly, avoiding eye contact. Then he slid to his feet, and slipped into the pool. The next minute, he was doing the breaststroke, as fast as possible, up and down the pool, splashing wildly as he went.

"Shy," laughed Theresa.

In the shallow end, a young father was yelling, 'Whoopsey' as he dunked a two year old under the water. It looked as if someone should intervene, but when he stopped, the little girl cried out, "Whoopsey? Whoopsey!" until he started again.

Theresa was deep in conversation with Julia. When they paused, Julia turned to me.

"Xiao Yu wants to stay up here for a while, but Theresa needs to get back home to Bakersfield. He's on medication though, so she wants someone to keep an eye on him. I thought you might be able to do that."

"Oh, well-"

"I told Theresa that you have a lot of experience with Chinese boys Xiao Yu's age, tutoring them," she added.

It was true that the most common surname in Toronto was now Li, followed by Smith and Lam. Many Chinese had come before the 1997 repatriation of Hong Kong by China. Sometimes father stayed there, while mother and children came to Canada to establish residency. I had tutored a dozen or so after I retired from teaching.

"Well, yes, and I could do that, but under what pretext?"

Theresa looked puzzled, so Julia tried to clarify.

"If mother say, Xiao Yu do," Theresa replied.

"Confucian values." Julia laughed.

"Is he going to college this fall?" I asked.

"Stanford!" Theresa announced.

"How's his English?"

"Good, good." She waggled her hand. "Could use work."

"Does he read books? In English?"

Theresa shook her head, apologetically.

"Theresa needs to be with her husband. Some trouble about water rights. An ecological group's been picketing their house, " Julia said.

Theresa shook her head sadly. "It's aquifer. On company land!" she added, widening her eyes in outrage.

I gathered that Mr. Lau was the manager of an agricultural company. I remembered reading about a dispute in the Central Valley. Neighbouring farmers maintained that their aquifers were draining because his company was drawing excessive water.

Water was a major issue in the current election campaign, each side accusing the other of favouring water Armageddon, confident that their Christian base knew what the destruction of the world was called. The Bakersfield paper had reported that over the years one farm field had dropped 12 feet from aquifer draining.

"Does Xiao Yu have an iPad, a tablet?" I asked.

"Yes, yes," Theresa said eagerly, gesturing at his backpack lying beside her chair.

Once he had towelled himself off, he seemed willing enough to download *The Great Gatsby* from iTunes, although he was surprised to learn that it sold books. He didn't look his age. He seemed more like sixteen. He was still very compliant, but as Julia implied, that could be a cultural difference.

The problem was that I didn't have phone reception or Internet.

"Oh, I forgot to tell you," Julia said. "Colin found his hotwire. Apparently, you can use it to get onto our Internet connection in your hotel room."

So we arranged to communicate by email. He seemed like one of Clara's nice boys.

Julia rode home with a loose shirt over her wet bikini and I followed on the golf cart. As we put lunch together, I told her my suspicions.

"You know when Daniel was involved with that girl, who was into animal welfare? They had a fundraiser I went to. It was in support of five animal rights activists in Vancouver. They got arrested for writing, 'Meat is Murder' on a KFC outlet-Kentucky Fried Chicken in those days. The graffiti got painted over next day, but they went back that night to write it again. The cops were waiting. The papers called them the *Kentucky Fried Five*. They spent a week or two in jail, charged with every animal rights crime in British Columbia. In the end, most of the charges were dropped, and they got time served. Lori and Ben come from Vancouver. I think that's where the *Kentucky Five* got its name. "

Julia sat staring at me. "And you think they the ones claiming responsibility for the crimes here? You think they sent the parcel?"

I shrugged. "I don't know. Julien Breton used to be a biochemist though. What I do think is someone returned the mother bear that was trapped."

I told her about the bear trap trailer in the parking lot at the top of Bear Mountain. "That was the day the man on Pinecliff was killed." I took a deep breath. "Another of the group works for the Department of Fish and Wildlife- Jackson. Evie, who was sitting at our table when the Kentucky Five last played, is his mother. Her goats were not let loose when the other animals were. Coincidence?"

Julia looked thoughtful. "You know Mrs. King isn't doing well.

The nurse practitioner at the clinic knows a nurse at Kern Medical. Mrs. King's so tired she can't get out of bed."

"If it is eco-terrorism, and the *Kentucky Five* is responsible, they're the gang that couldn't shoot straight. Not even freeing the animals would have been serious if not for chance."

"If it's true, they may have only intended to annoy, but things got out of hand. Are you going to tell the police what you think?"

"Not on your life! Been there, done that, got the hair-shirt."

"It's just a theory-"

"I know. I know. And, by the way, what's this you signing me up for babysitting?"

"Well, you're bored, want something to do-"

"What do you mean? I have a perfectly good job catching eco-terrorists."

She was right really. Colin had finished his song, and was back to baking bread and cookies and rustling up excellent dinners. Star Shine had finished her radiation treatments, and was not yet doing chemotherapy, so no trips to Bakersfield. The altitude and heat on the mountain kept me from walking any distance, and I could read only so many hours a day.

At home, I would have been going to tai chi classes, keeping house, cooking for myself, and enjoying two newspapers, 500 channels, high speed Internet, coffee shops, people-watching in Bloor West Village, etc.

I tried to remember my 'real' life, but it was gone, my apartment stripped to the studs, and all my things wedged into a storage unit.

So this new project seemed promising.

Theresa left on Sunday night. I arranged to see Xiao Yu Monday afternoon. Their house was a few short blocks from Julia's, on a curving street that backed onto a wetland.

Xiao Yu ushered me out onto the back deck, and went into the house to make tea.

I gazed out at the willows and reeds and deciduous bushes. They indicated it was swampy ground, or had been. Deep under ground, it still was.

I first read *The Great Gatsby* on Burlington Beach when I was sixteen. I must have been engrossed. That was the day I ended up with sunstroke. I was invalided home next day from my job in Ladies' Blouses. I went on to teach *Gatsby* to grade twelve students at least twenty times. Probably more. I more or less knew it by heart. Christopher Hitchens said the book "remains great because it confronts the death of youth and beauty and idealism and finds the defeat unbearable and then turns to face it unflinchingly."*, It was the unflinching part that hooked me, although I didn't expect my students or Xiao Yu to articulate that.

Two men and a boy in the next yard caught my eye. They were walking the perimeter of their yard and looking at the Lao's house. Just then Xiao Yu struggled through the sliding door with a tray. He had his back to them. They looked startled when they saw me, but I was more interested in the scent of Jasmine tea.

I got Xiao Yu to talk about himself first. His English was not as clipped as his mother's, and he left out fewer words. His father had come out to California ten years ago, and his mother had followed three years later. Xiao Yu had stayed in Beijing with his grandparents until he was ready to start grade 8 in Bakersfield. He missed his grandparents, he confessed. He usually went back in the summer. Not this year. He was going to Stanford in a few weeks.

I told him about myself, my children, Toronto, my teaching career, about tutoring Chinese students, some from Mainland China. Then I told him about my tai chi and my interest in Taoism.

We stood up and showed each other a few moves. That got us laughing.

"You like Taoism?" he sounded amazed. "Why you like?"

I shrugged. "It's a good way to live."

He raised his shoulders in inquiry.

I felt the way I did the day someone called the tai chi club, and asked me to explain Taoism.

I laughed and he laughed.

"Helping others," I said. "Not taking life too seriously. Keeping the middle ground. Using moderation." I paused. "There is a joke-a mosquito bothers a Buddhist, but he just lets it bite him. A mosquito bothers a Taoist, so he brushes it away. When that doesn't work, he moves to the next room. A mosquito bothers a Confucian, so he kills it."

Xiao Yu drew back, unsure whether to laugh.

"The Buddhist has compassion," I said. "Doesn't kill. The Taoist acts simply. No excessive kindness, only a little inconvenience. The Confucian knows mosquitoes carry disease. So he kills it."

"Confucian kill mosquito," Xiao Yu said, and smiled. It was clear where he stood philosophically.

"So what do you think of Jay Gatsby?"

Well, first, of course, we had to talk about Nick Carroway, the narrator, and get it straightened out that he was Daisy's cousin. It turned out that Xiao Yu had seen the movie on AMC.

"Too much parties," Xiao Yu declared.

"Ah, yes."

In my naiveté, I had assumed an immigrant would identify with Gatsby's longing for the American Dream. I hadn't reckoned with Confucius.

"But why, why does Gatsby have the parties?"

"Not sure yet. Movie confusing. Need to read more."

So we arranged that he would email me each morning with a response to what he had read the day before, and any questions he had.

Rain was forecast, as it sometimes was, but all that ever showed up were a few wispy clouds over Bear Mountain. There was not a drop on Saturday, despite a 60% chance. Sunday grew cloudier and cloudier. Everybody at the bakery talked about rain. They even said they could smell it coming. I went back to reading in my hotel-room, not daring to hope.

When I walked down the deck to Clara's room, the air was heavy with humidity. We were chatting at the table when the first drops hit the windows. Huge drops. They rattled down faster and faster until a veil of rain streamers hung between the golf course and the village centre. It was getting hard to see the bar and the store on the other side of the alley.

Cool, wet air surged through the screen door. The racket on the roof prevented conversation. Then the tumult drew back slightly.

"Oh my God," I said. "Have you ever seen anything like that?"

"That's the way it rains in the desert," Clara said. "Once it gets around to it, it rains in torrents."

I got to my feet to peer out the screen. Streams of water were rushing down the slope of the tarmac. The parking area was one big pond. On the roads, rivers crashed along the curbs, lakes pooling at the intersection. Rushing down the side-road, the runoff actually curled in waves. It had bubbles like white caps.

I like a good storm when I'm inside and dry. It's time to get lost in a book with rain to lull you. This was not that kind of storm. It was apocalyptic.

After forty-five minutes, it began to lose force. It kept on for another fifteen. By then, I had collected myself enough to make tea.

Thursday morning, as Clara and I sat outside the bakery reading the paper, a red MGB slid into the parking spot. A man in his mid-fifties climbed out. He was casually, but expensively, dressed, about 5 ft. 8, with grey hair curling around his ears. I hadn't identified him as the owner of the red MGB's I had seen in Bakersfield, but it was clearly the same car, and I thought I had seen him somewhere before.

"Morning, ladies," he greeted us, and swept into the bakery.

"Now, he looks interesting," said Clara.

When he came out carrying a coffee and a pastry bag, she waylaid him. "What year is your car?' she asked.

"'63," he replied.

I piped up. "I used to have one of those, only in racing green," I said. My children called it the top-down."

It wasn't strictly speaking mine. It was my husband Blake's. I had failed my stick shift test.

"You had it when it first came out," he said. "I've only had mine two years. It's cost me a fortune to get it running, and looking this good. Better than new. Come take a look."

He put his purchases in the convertible and caressed the red leather seat. "Touch it," he said. "Feel how soft it is."

It was indeed. Next thing I knew, he had the hood up. He pointed at this and that, detailing what had been done for repairs, and how long he had to wait for parts. Some had to be made from scratch.

As he gazed at his beloved, I said," I remember my two little children sitting on that little backbench without belts. The slightest collision would have thrown them out. It never happened, but I still think how reckless that was."

"Would you like to go for a ride?" he asked with real enthusiasm.

Clara glanced at me. I was not prone to spontaneous connections. Too Canadian perhaps.

"My mother told me never to take rides with strangers," I said.

"I'd love to," said Clara. There was room for only one passenger.

"I'm not a stranger," he said. "I'm Matthew Greaves." We introduced ourselves in turn. "Let's sit down and get acquainted while we finish our coffee. Then I'll take Clara for a ride."

So we went back to our table. He joined us with his bear claw pastry and coffee. He developed commercial properties, shopping malls, that sort of thing. He had just come back from China where he'd been for six months. His next project was going to be a casino in the Bahamas. His answer to Clara's 'where're you from' question was 'everywhere', and he had been everywhere. If he was to be believed. He had a healthy regard for himself, but despite that, he was charming.

Matthew and Clara drove off waving as they went. I went up to my room to work on my computer. It was about ninety minutes later when I heard Clara coming up the stairs.

"Where have you been?" I asked, in belated alarm.

"Oh, all over," she said. "He's got a place down below Douglas Peak. Real swanky. Gated and all. I met his wife. She's Arta Dietzen-the romance novelist. She's asked us both down some afternoon. Gave me her phone number, well, put it into my phone contacts. I guess you can show me how to call her. Oh, I feel a lot better. I can make friends here."

I saw Theresa briefly that weekend. She was going to the pool as we were coming up from the club terrace.

Then on Wednesday, there was no message from Xiao Yu. I

emailed him, but he did not respond. I felt vaguely unsettled. Even an obedient Chinese boy might sometimes not comply, I told myself. I sent my psychic probe out, but I got a bad feeling back. I went downstairs and got on my golf cart.

There was no answer when I rang the bell, and none when I knocked. Their golf cart was parked in the drive. I assumed that meant Xiao Yu was home. I walked around the deck, and gazed in the back door. It looked into a family room, but I could also see into the kitchen. Water was cascading down through the ceiling onto the granite counter.

I ran back to the front rock garden. How many rocks had Teresa told me? I counted from the walk, the fifth stone in the top tier, seized the rock, and managed to take it apart. Hidden inside its *papier mache* interior was a front door key.

Inside the house, water was puddled at the bottom of the stairs. The treads were wet.

"Xiao Yu, Xiao Yu," I shouted, running up.

There were so many closed doors, six of them. An arc of water, like a child's splash pad, identified the bathroom. I flung open one door after another. Xiao Yu was in the third, lying on his side, motionless, dressed in striped pyjamas. Empty pill bottles lay on the nightstand.

Screaming his name at the top of my lungs, I shook him. He felt cold, but not deadly cold. I stopped yelling and listened. I put my ear near his mouth. I wasn't sure. There was vomit on the bed. I reached my finger into his mouth to clear it, but it was empty. I hit him on the back, twice. Yes, he was still breathing just barely.

His cell phone was on the nightstand. I seized it. Fucking password protected. The fourth bedroom was the master and it had a landline. I shouted into the handset as I ran back to his side.

"No, I can't put him on a hard surface. He's bigger than me. I could drag-"

"Never mind," the operator said. "The ambulance will be there shortly. Turn him on his back and clear his mouth."

"I did. I did already."

"Okay, can you do mouth to mouth. I'll talk you through-"

"Sure," I put the handset on speaker.

One part of my mind listened and did what I was told. The greater part prayed, "Save him. Please save him. Oh, dear God, save him."

"Is the front door unlocked?" the operator asked.

"Yes," I said taking another breath. I could hear a siren approaching.

Heavy boots thudded up the stairs.

"Here, in here," I screamed.

Backing out of the way, I watched as in a dream, the room fill up with big people and equipment.

"What did he take," a faraway voice asked.

I shrugged and gestured at the prescription bottles.

"You his mother?"

"No."

"It's okay. You did good." A cop had appeared and was taking me by the elbow to lead me out. "You did good."

"You go downstairs. See if you can rustle up coffee. I'll turn this water off."

I stood in the kitchen in half an inch of water, staring at the coffee machine. Beside it, was a box of those one-dose pods. I just stared.

I had heard the siren call of despair years ago. It wasn't Hamlet's well- reasoned consideration of "To be or not to be". It was irrational and tried to lure me into overpass abutments. Fortunately, I wasn't a teenager prone to sudden impulse.

Neither was Hamlet, of course. He lived to die *right*. It was Ophelia whose obsequies were stinted because her death was questionable. She didn't try to save herself when she fell out of that tree into the water.

Turned out the cop knew how to use the coffee machine. I didn't even protest that I didn't drink coffee. I sat down and drank it. He sipped his and took out his notebook.

"What's the kid's name and how do I reach his parents?"

When the medics brought Xiao Yu down on the stretcher, the policeman passed the information I had given him to them.

I went to the door to watch them load him into the ambulance. The cop was talking on his car radio.

When he came back into the house, he said, “Okay, his parents will be at Kern Medical when he gets there. He’s going to be all right. Let’s you and me see what we can sort out.”

First we sorted out how I knew Xiao Yu, and why I’d come over to the house.

“Let’s take a look around,” said Deputy Sheriff Jorgensen. “See what there is to see.”

He got up and began walking around, looking at windows. When he went downstairs to the entry level, I followed him. In the laundry room, the heavy wire mesh on the outside of the window had been completely cut away, and the glass neatly lifted out.

“Wire cutters and glass cutters,” he mused. “Pretty small, but I guess a small person could get in.”

“Someone sabotaged the toilet?”

“Seems like it,” he said. “The lid was off and the feeder tube was disconnected, and pointing straight up. All they had to do was flush and the water would keep on running. I’ll get some help up here. See if there are prints.” He turned back to me. “Kid seem like someone who would fall apart in a situation like that?”

I nodded. “He was on medication of some kind. He wanted badly to please. He probably thought it was his fault.”

“Couldn’t just call a plumber? Seems old enough.”

“He could have got me to come. I can turn off a toilet. He wouldn’t know how. Not a practical American kid.“

We went back up through the dripping house, back to our dry spots, where we could drink more coffee, and he could make more notes.

“His father manages a farm in the valley,” I said. “He’s in big trouble with his neighbours for draining the aquifer. It’s been on the news.”

Then it occurred to me. “You have a smart phone. Does it work up here?”

“Has to. Requirement of the job.”

“Can you get up the BMP club website?”

“Sure,” he said, and got busy.

There it was again, the rampant bear. This time it read, “*How Do*

You Like That Water Bill, Mr. Lao?" Smaller letters underneath read, "Ancient aquifer water can never be replaced."

It was 1 p.m. by the time, I showed up at Julia's.

She met me at the front door. "What's up?" she asked.

I walked by her-straight into the bathroom-and threw up the coffee.

6

THE SITTER

The incident did not show up in the Sheriff's Log on Thursday. It didn't need to. It was whispered about. No one actually asked me questions, but I got sidelong glances.

The club's Los Angeles IT company had failed to prevent the website from being hacked. In desperation, the local IT expert, who had lost the bid to the L.A. company, was hired back. He seemed confident he could stop it.

Looking for distraction, I wandered past the real estate office, *The Dancing Bear*-one of three gift stores, the antique shop, another real estate office, and the ice cream shop. The art gallery was open.

Inside, I discovered the wall covered with Max Rubenstein's bright naïve paintings. There was no one behind the desk, so I studied the pictures. For the most part, they were small, 11 by 13 or so. Several depicted the ravages of the drought, a slope of brown pines, and a scorched meadow with a thirsty-looking deer. Max could convey thirst in his cartoonish animal. I was staring at a dead cub and two monstrous, brown uniformed guys with big guns, when I heard, "So, how's Teacher?"

I turned to see that Max had emerged from the back room.

"So, you did recognize me?" I replied.

"I never forget a sitter," he said, with a leer.

"Where's my portrait now?" I asked.

"Still in the collection in Ottawa, I suppose. It was licensed as a book cover some years back."

"Yes, I saw it. Happened upon it in a bookstore. Bought the book. Never read it. Too gloomy-spinster teacher, self-sacrificing, eternally suffering."

"Typically Canadian, but not your cup of tea."

"Possibly too much my cup of tea, minus the spinsterhood."

Max laughed in his easy-going way.

"I suppose the black beast has left this veil of tears."

"My Belle, my *Belle Isle en Mer*? She has, but she had a good long life for a Newfoundland pup, and she still turns up at times. In fact, she seems to be here right now." I looked toward the door.

"Well, for God's sake, don't let her slobber on the merchandise."

"So which of you flooded the Lau's house?"

"When was that?"

"Tuesday night."

"The Kentucky Five were doing a fundraiser at the Blues Café in Santa Barbara, Tuesday night. Young guy tipped over his all-terrain vehicle. Got badly injured. Needs help. In fact we went up on Monday, stayed over and rehearsed. The restaurant was closed and Jackson, well, Jackson's on paid leave."

"Funny way to answer. Shouldn't you start with outraged denial?"

"Why bother? You can see what I think." He gestured at the wall.

"So, do you still sleep with a loaded shot gun under your bed?"

"Want to do a little investigation?" he asked, leering.

"Oh, Max," I said, "be careful what you wish for."

As I turned to go out, a kid about 12 came in.

"Joanna, have you met Zach," Max asked.

"No," I said. "Do you live next door to the Lao's?"

"No," Zach said, with surprising emphasis.

"Sorry," I said, "I'm awful at faces. I saw the kid who lives there the other day. Just for a second. He must have been about your age."

"Zach is staying with his step-father, Ben," Max said. "He's down from Vancouver for the summer. Lori's son. Prefers to live in the Great White North, apparently. Can't imagine why."

Zach made a feeble attempt to smile as I left.

Two summer months in the early eighties. A high fenced backyard, a big bearlike dog, a garden with too many green beans, a portrait of me as Teacher, looking more like present me than age 45, two Polaroid shots of Belle and me, and a painting of an autumn forest on a journal cover. In the Polaroid's, I am an earth mother in a long skirt and a shapeless cardigan.

He was younger, tough, rugged, a biker. He refused to play "Toilets" anymore, bars where people still smoked. He played and sang for me. He was tender when I needed tenderness.

One day, he announced on the phone that we were finished. I drove over to his storefront studio to collect some compromising 35 mm slides–O simpler age. He said, "Don't you want to know why?" I replied, "Can I fix it." "No," he said. "Then I don't want to know," I replied.

He had left another legacy. He had virtually introduced us to Bear Mountain Place on his website, where he was still selling CDs of what he had recorded in earlier days.

It was hot in Bear Mountain Place. Again. The sun shone down from a flawless sky. I was wearing one of Julia's easy fitting dresses–orange, green and fuchsia- with short red boots. Sandals would have been cooler, but my toes hated being impaled by pine needles.

Clara was still wearing light, pastel pants, but I couldn't bear my denim. It smothered my legs. I hadn't worn dresses for years, but shorts were not an option. Apparently clothes maketh the woman, for now I didn't want to wear a brush cut.

I started dropping by the Christian Hairdresser on the off chance of finding him working. Eventually, I did.

"I think I want it longer, to take advantage of the wave."

He studied my head. "It'll be more work," he said.

I doubt it," I said. "I won't be able to blow dry it into a shape. I'll just let it do what it wants."

"All right. Well, we don't want your bangs to be too long. We want to show off these nice eyebrows."

Really? They were dark brown as my hair used to be. My hair was white in the front, grey and black toward the back. My eyebrows were almost as jarring as Martin Scorsese's.

"We'll let it grow out on top, layer it, and trim it short on the sides and back."

We were finished with the wash and were half way through the cut before the conversation turned to the Bible. He had held Bible study that morning, a men's group, he warned, as if I were dying to join. I had a secret advantage, which he did not expect. As a child, I had listened to my grandmother read the *King James Bible*, end to end. I had sung in the children's church choir, and listened to it twice every Sunday. Then I had had the privilege of obligatory Bible study at a Baptist university. It had been defrocked since, so present graduates didn't know as much about St. Paul-the subject of our conversation.

Oddly, he switched to trying to convert me to tennis. He also gave tennis lessons. While I admired his entrepreneurship, I countered that it was no sport for old women.

"I don't suppose Jackson is part the men's group?"

He laughed ruefully. "His mother Evie does go to our church though."

"I hear Jackson's on leave from Fish and Wildlife," he went on. "Very hush, hush." He was blow-drying and artfully twisting a brush to build body in my hair. "Talk is it has something to do with the bear incident. Nobody can say what. We do know that he wasn't there when they shot the cub. He's still on full pay, I hear, so can't be too serious."

I wasn't so sure. The mills of bureaucracy might 'grind slowly' like the mills of God, but not 'exceeding fine'. Besides I was now required to admire my haircut.

I found Clara sitting on the bench outside the real estate office. She was hatless as usual. I took mine off at her command and she admired my new, softer do. I remembered to accept compliments graciously. Then she told me Penny wanted a word with me. The word was Master

Card, no doubt. Clara had paid by check. Would that I could. She preceded me into the office.

"Hello girls," Penny cried. "I hope you don't mind if I call you girls."

"Isn't that what we are?" I asked.

Amidst general merriment, Clara pushed on through the back door to go up to her room.

When she was well clear, Penny gestured at the blonde at the next desk, and said *sotto voce*, "Ginger was just telling me about her bear incident. But I didn't want to alarm Clara." And screw up her pending house purchase, I added to myself.

Ginger launched into a long narrative.

"Last evening, I was folding laundry in our bedroom up on Pinecliff. My husband was in the family room watching a game. I put the sheets in the hall cupboard. Then I turned to the kitchen. There's this enormous bear, its front feet on the table, helping itself to left-overs. It looked right at me. I screamed bloody murder, and ran for the front door. But Mike was really trapped. The bear was between him and both doors. I guess he just stood there. I left the door open and kept on running. I got myself up onto the neighbour's deck across the road. Never stopped screaming. In a few seconds the bear came lumbering out, Mike right behind him with his rifle. He shot over the bear's head. A terrible noise so close up, but the bear just kept on walking. Didn't even turn around."

"It makes me shake to tell it, and I've told it a few times," she added.

"It makes me shake to hear it. Do you suppose it's the killer bear?" I asked.

"No it wasn't," Ginger said. "You know I'm the chair of the Bear Awareness Committee. So I know a little about the bears around here, as much as anyone. I keep a log of sightings with descriptions. This one was a male, bigger than the killer bear. Trouble is people won't believe that. They'll think they're going to be killed in their beds."

"Why do you think you didn't hear it?" I asked.

"Really thick foot pads and they're light on their feet for heavy beasts. And they move fast. You can't outrun them once they get started. Our bear was slow out of the gate. Anyway he wasn't aggressive, just a mooch."

"Do you think it was connected to the other incident?" asked Penny.

"It had been habituated no doubt, by careless garbage handling or feeding. I don't want to blame poor Tom Braddock."

"Could you have prevented it?" I wondered.

"Shut the kitchen door after we ate? I hadn't cleared the dishes, but who would have thought? And it was a hot evening. We wanted the cross draft. The bear just opened the screen door with its hand. Didn't tear the screen. Anyway it's barred."

"Clara's new house has barred screen doors, and she locks her screen door, so she should be safe as long as they haven't learned to pick locks yet."

"The coons do that for them," Penny said, and we all laughed too long and hard.

Julia and I had a lot to talk about as we walked down the horse trail that had been the first road into the village.

"Don't, for God's sake, tell Clara," Julia said.

"My lips are sealed."

Then I told her about my conversation with Max, and the Kentucky Five being in Santa Barbara when the Lau's house was flooded.

"Interesting," she said.

We had come to a ridge in the road, a large pine to our right and a pin oak grove on the left. The trickle of water ran under the low oaks, marking the fault line. A Stellar's jay scolded us raucously. From where we stood, we could look out across the valley to the wetland on the other side, the highway winding through the curves, and above it several peaks that could not be seen from the village.

"I'm going to turn back now," I said.

"I'll join you. I'm still not back to my old strength."

When we got back to the pond, there was a great uproar in the sky.

Dozens of red-winged blackbirds and their brown wives had risen from the reeds, and were chasing the red-shouldered hawk. The hawk was carrying something in its claws. It veered and veered again, the angry blackbirds swarming in to attack. In the end, it made it to a high pine. The black birds kept zooming in, but the hawk was secure in the pine's cover. It settled down to eat the nestling.

We were on the road in the full sun when Theresa came down it in her golf cart. She stopped to talk to us.

"How is Xiao Yu?" I asked.

"Good, good. Still in hospital. You come visit?"

"If he wants me to," I said.

"Yes, yes. Wants thank you. Doctor says."

"Are you sure it's his idea?"

"His too. Ridgeview. I email address."

"It's okay. I know it," said Julia.

"Last week too soon. Ready now," smiled Theresa.

"I see workers at your house," said Julia.

"Floors," said Theresa, "Need work. Also paint." She shook her head. "Bad luck house. We sell. Here not like Chinese."

"That's not why-" I began, but Julia had stepped up onto the cart and gathered Theresa in her arms. She held her for a long time. When she stepped back, we all had tears in our eyes.

"Maybe buy house, Stanford," Theresa said, trying to smile.

After she had driven on, Julia and I continued on up the hot, last leg of our journey.

"Will he be able to start school in the fall?"

Julia shrugged. "Depends, I guess. He'll need to have support up there."

Nearing the driveway, we saw an unfamiliar car parked next to the deck, and a man sitting on the bench. He got to his feet as we approached.

He was at least six feet tall and trim, younger than Julia, probably mid-forties, wearing chinos and a short-sleeved white shirt that showed off his brown arms

"Detective Al Guevera," he said, presenting his identification, not Alberto, but Alvaro.

"Julia Durant and my mother, Joanna Hunter," said Julia.

"Yes, is Mr. Durant in as well?"

"O'Neil, Colin O'Neil, and no, it doesn't look like it. His golf cart is gone and the door is shut. Probably gone to play a few holes."

"Okay, could we talk for a few minutes?'

"Of course," replied Julia, without concern for my cop phobia.

First, we had to open the house up, the windows and blinds. It was hot in there. I took water orders. I poured ice water from the fridge for Detective Guevara, and filled two other glasses with filtered tap water. I handed them around, and joined Julia on the couch.

I had sat in several police interrogation rooms, with my sister and my niece, first-rate lawyers behind us, video cameras rolling, psychologist at the ready. We were there to tell where the bodies were buried. Witnesses to crimes are not criminals, but we had "Signed Undertakings" guaranteeing that we would not be charged. We were in deep shock, in bad shape. If we weren't on meds, we should have been.

This was not an interrogation room of course. It was familiar and comfortable, but I was triggered back to that past terror.

"First, I'd like to talk about the package you took in for the Kings," Detective Guevara began. "This will be repetition for you, I know, but I like to hear things for myself."

So I went back over the few details I had. The detective said he would talk to Colin about the actual hand-over.

"I understand you suggested that the powder be tested for Valley Fever, Dr. Durant. Can you tell me why?"

Julia gestured with both hands, and began to recount the story of watching a documentary about the 1922 opening of Tut's tomb, and the subsequent deaths.

The detective was making notes. We waited in silence.

"And of course when the package was tested, it did turn out to be cocci -whatever," he said.

"Coccidioides, emphasis on the OY."

"As you say," he said.

"I'm sorry to tell you that Mrs. King died on the operating table yesterday afternoon."

"Oh, my God," I cried.

"What happened?" asked Julia.

"Apparently, she had a weakened immune system. She was having a shunt installed to deliver medication to her brain. During the procedure, she suffered a fatal heart attack." He paused. I had closed my eyes and Julia had taken my hand. "I'm sorry to bring you such news. Did you know her well?"

"Hardly at all. She had come into my clinic once, but we haven't been here long. They're weekenders, not here that often."

We sat absorbing the shock. Detective Guevara was turning pages in his notebook. When he looked up, his expression was apologetic.

"We need to get your fingerprints and Mr. O'Neil's for the purpose of elimination. I'll speak to him about it as well. Come into our office in Bakersfield. I'll need to ask you, Mrs. Hunter, about the Lau's house flood as well, but first I need more background."

"Ms," I said, "Joanna. The same perpetrator in both cases evidently, in view of the subsequent web posts."

"In these two cases, there is another common factor," he replied.

"What's that?"

"You."

"Very amusing!" I said. "You and airport security. I get patted down, if not strip-searched every time. A little old lady terrorist!"

"Equal opportunity world," he laughed, getting to his feet and gesturing toward the fridge. "Mind if I-?"

We listened to ice tinkling into his glass.

He sat back down, took a long drink of water and sighed.

"Have you traced the hacker who's posting the warnings?" I asked.

"It's proving difficult. Apparently, it's not as easy in real life as it is on TV."

"It might be a good idea if the hacker carried on until you do," I suggested.

He smiled.

"Was anyone besides Mrs. King ill from Valley Fever?" Julia asked.

He shook his head. "Not so far, Dr. Durant. But we do have three acts of what looks like eco-terrorism-the animals let loose, the toxic parcel and the house flood. In each case, the results were more dire than was intended perhaps."

And a bear that shouldn't be there killed a man, I added silently.

"I'm talking to environmental activists to get their take. I've talked to your friend, Max Rubenstein," he went on.

"My friend? I haven't seen Max for thirty years until lately."

The detective was sitting at the desk in front of a sliding glass door, hard to see in the glare.

He nodded. "Now Dr. Durant, you said you had recently moved here."

"Last fall. I had to give up my medical practice in Los Angeles because of my health. We had to find somewhere cheaper to live."

"So you bought this place?"

"We're renting."

"And your husband, what does he do?"

"He's a musician, a composer."

"Tough times for musicians?"

"Very, but he gets residuals."

"Do you like it here?"

"It's a good place to live, friendly, beautiful, healthful," she gestured at the view through the wall of glass doors, the pinewoods, the slope beyond the lake. A Steller's jay landed on the deck rail and began to yell as if to contradict her. We all laughed, and I felt my irritability diminish.

"Would you call yourself an environmentalist?"

"I sort my garbage."

"You don't have a choice here really," I added. "If you don't get it right, you're in trouble at the transfer station."

"True, but I always have," Julia added, "even when I had to cart my recycling to a depot in L.A. I don't picket or write letters. I love nature because it heals me. My main interest is people though. I guess my philosophy is more humanitarian than ecological."

"And you Ms. Hunter?"

"I'm too worn out for causes."

"Were you ever connected to ecological causes?"

"My son was years ago, and I went to one fundraiser for animal activists."

When would that have been?"

"89, 90."

"Did you know these activists?"

"No, they had been arrested in British Columbia. I was in Toronto."

"What were they charged with?"

"Every animal rights crime ever committed in the Vancouver area. Most charges were dropped. They were found guilty of mischief for writing graffiti on a KFC outlet."

"And your son is in Toronto still?"

"No."

"Where is he, may I ask?"

I shrugged. "He's cycling around the world. He was in Malaysia in April, I'm told."

"Doesn't keep in touch with you?"

"Sporadically."

"Why is that?"

"I don't know."

"So you are here visiting his sister?"

"My daughter."

"An extended visit?"

I explained about the renovation in Toronto and the ever-receding completion date.

"It's cheaper to stay here," I said.

He nodded and turned to a new page.

"Just a few questions about the Lau incident."

I explained about the reading project, and how I had been alarmed when Xiao Yu didn't email. He asked about Xiao Yu's personality.

"He was very much a Chinese son, wanting to please his parents.

He was also a perfectionist, nervous. He was on some sort of medication. What I don't know. Mood stabilizer perhaps. That's why his mother wanted me to keep an eye on him."

We went over the same ground as I had with Deputy Jergensen, Xiao Yu's lack of practical skill at plumbing, and the probability he blamed himself and panicked.

"It seems as if it happened in the middle of the night. His pyjamas were wet," the detective said

"Stands to reason. That's when a break-in would be least noticed. The window they cut was very small," I said. "There's a kid who lives next door."

"Which side?" he asked.

"This side. Closer to us."

He shook his head. "Old couple. Haven't been up in a year or so. It's been empty all that time. Why do you say that?"

"I saw a kid there one day when I was tutoring Xiao Yu."

"What was he doing?"

"Just walking."

"Was he with anyone?"

"A couple of men." It was dawning on me that this could be important.

"What did they look like?"

I shrugged. "One was tall. The other one wasn't."

"Young? Old?"

I shrugged again. "I didn't really pay attention and I have a problem recognizing faces."

He turned back in his notebook. "All right. I think that's all. Have you visited Xiao Yu in hospital?"

"I'm going to next week."

"His doctor won't let us talk to him yet," he said, handing us cards, and giving me a meaningful look.

"Does your husband have his phone with him?" he asked Julia.

"Always," Julia replied.

"Let's give him a call. See if he'll meet me in the clubhouse. Sorry, I kept you from your lunch."

I walked with him to the door. "There are tall genes somewhere in your family," I observed.

"Grandfather, Henry Robinson," he said. "You've seen him sitting on the bench behind the store or up in the Mad Dog Bar. If you go there." He grinned. "He was Kern County Sheriff, back in the day. A great source of information even now."

"Yes, I've seen him." An old white guy, even older than me, sitting on village centre benches.

Julia and I sat at the table opposite each other, a clamshell of prepared salad, a hunk of cold goat cheese and a box of crackers between us. Only the crackers were seeing any action.

"Well, don't that beat all?" I said.

I was a tumult of emotion, still guilty about signing for the package, sad about a lovely woman's death, stupidly scared of being a suspect, and missing my absent son.

"I've got used to people dying," Julia said. "Geriatric patients flocked to my practice. But this was just so-I don't know-unnecessary. She had a second chance at life. Why did they risk putting in a shunt?"

"It was probably a last resort."

"Yeah. You're right." She sat nodding. "You're right."

By the time Colin came home, we had put away the uneaten lunch. He had eaten with Detective Guevara at the club.

"You know tonight's the night they're doing *Son of Frankenstein* in Simi Valley. The Crooks sent us tickets. Their son has the lead. There's only two tickets, but I'm sure we can get another at the door."

"Let's blow this pop stand," I said, springing to my feet.

"What about Clara? Shall we ask her?" Julia said.

"I already did. She says she's tired."

It was a long drive, but worth it, very funny, well produced and performed. I fell asleep on the I-5 and didn't wake up until Colin pulled up behind the hotel.

"I'll wait here," he said. "Lean over the balcony and wave when you've got your door unlocked."

The stairs were dark and just as steep as ever. I more or less pulled myself up by the handrail. As I took the step onto the deck, something cut into my calf. I stepped back down and felt with one hand. Something taut was strung across the stairway.

"Joanna," Colin called. "Joanna?"

I stepped over the wire carefully with both hands on the balustrade, crossed the deck and leaned over the rail.

"You'd better come up," I answered, "and bring your phone."

7

TOO MUCH BAKO

Too bad it was a Friday night. The cops were busy in Douglas Peak dealing with drunken opioid addicts. Uncharitable of me to think so, but I had ugly visions of a different outcome. If I had come out of my door in the dark and made the tight turn to the top of the stairs, I would be lying splayed and broken on the concrete below.

"It was only meant as a warning," Julia said, ever on the alert for my hysteria. "Whoever did it knew you were out and would only stumble."

'Glad you think so," I muttered.

Julia fell asleep on my bed. Colin sat on the deck, smoking more than usual. The smoke drifted in through the screen door. I drifted up and down the room. When I lay down beside Julia, I was so tense I felt levitated three inches off the mattress. I was terrified. Again I was going to talk to the police just what the tripwire was meant to prevent? When did talking to cops ever help me?

The Sheriff's car finally got to the Reality Hotel around 3 a.m. I roused myself to give my brief account. I was somewhat hampered by total body shakes, a dry mouth and a tendency to stutter. I gave a brief account of finding the wire. The two deputies nodded gravely, took pictures, and removed the wire with gloves.

Then Colin sketched out the backstory, and Detective Guevara's involvement. They would let him know, they assured me.

When they left, Julia was still sound asleep, so I lay down beside her again under the two extra blankets and tried to stop shaking. Colin sacked out on the couch.

We were a weary and wary party of four at the bakery next morning. Despite the general policy of not upsetting Clara, we told her about the booby trap.

"It would never have worked," she said. "The elderly watch their feet, even on the ground, but especially on stairs."

Elderly? Really! But I did tend to survey the ground before I stepped. I had to because I also dragged my feet.

The police had asked about other guests and Colin named his mother. I told them the third room had been vacant for a week. Lori had moved out. She was living over *Le Petit Breton*.

The sky was still brilliant blue. The sun still warmed the sandy earth. The hills and mountains embraced the village. The pine trees pointed heavenward. Blue birds flitted ahead of my golf cart. Finches warbled. Sparrows chattered. The people I met still smiled and spoke to me.

I looked on all that beauty through the cold eyes of terror. Beauty carried on, oblivious.

On Monday morning, I pulled the Prius up in front of the boxcar house to pick up Star Shine. She was due to start chemo. There was a big old Thunderbird in the drive. I rang the doorbell, and a smiling Star Shine opened the door.

Her sister, Star Dancing, aka, Dance, had arrived from Lubboc, Texas, in the middle of the night. Dance was a slightly older, fleshier version of Star Shine.

"Dance is going to drive you down then?" I asked.

"Yes." Star Shine was holding her sister's hand all wrapped up in her own. "I'm sooooo glad she's here."

Dance and I laughed. "Well, I'm going down anyway. I plan to visit someone in hospital."

"Maybe we'll see you there," Dance said.

"Different hospital." I hugged Star Shine, and then Star Dancing for good measure.

Driving Star Shine was a silent process, and yet I missed her as I started down the hill.

I had lived mostly alone for thirty-eight years since Blake and I separated. Loneliness had nearly killed me at first. All these years later, I could enjoy solitude. Rumi had helped me get there. A thirteenth century Sufi poet, he wrote that we are like beggars going from door to door asking for crumbs while carrying a loaf of bread on our heads. We ask for drops from other people's water bottles while we stand deep in fresh river water. We already have what we are seeking–companionship, love and connection, but we keep looking for them in all the wrong places.

It didn't take long to shift from outer to inner. If I rummaged around in there, perhaps I would also find the strength to face the fact someone had tried to kill me.

There had been no new post on the club website this morning, but I had no doubt that the same people were to blame. I was also sure that they thought I had information that would implicate them. They were wrong.

I got to Ridgeview Behavioural Health Centre as visiting hours started. I pushed the buzzer, said I was a visitor for Xiao Yu and was admitted to the foyer. The woman at the desk invited me to take a seat until a nurse came out to meet me.

There were two wings. Both doors read 'Locked Ward'. But the ward I was headed for had no window in it. I waited for the better part of fifteen minutes. Then the receptionist noticed me again.

"They haven't come out yet?" She picked up the phone, and the door opened almost immediately.

"You're here to see Xiao Yu?" The male attendant asked. "Good, you haven't brought a purse. Do you have a cell phone on you?"

"No," I replied. I had read the rules.

He took me to the small living room, near the entrance, and waved me to one of the puffy leather chairs. No one else was there. There was a restroom door in the corner, and a door to the outside on the opposite wall. The walls were hung with vibrantly coloured, free form paintings.

Xiao Yu came into the room, followed by the attendant. Xiao Yu sat down in the chair at right angles to me. He had *The Great Gatsby* in his hand. The attendant sat on the other side of the room, and took out his phone.

"Are you eating?" I was totally unable to stop myself from asking this motherly question. He seemed thin and pale.

He made a face. "Food not Chinese."

"And food can't be brought in?" I asked. The attendant looked up and shook his head. "I saw people taking food into the other ward."

"Different set-up," said the attendant.

I translated in my head. This ward had addicts in it.

"Are you reading?" I asked, gesturing at the book.

"A little. Hard pay attention."

"Would you like me to read aloud to you?'

He nodded and handed me the book. He was getting near the end. We found ourselves in a Manhattan hotel room where the five main characters were guzzling bootleg booze against the Manhattan heat. Gatsby quarrelled with Tom. Gatsby and Daisy fled in the yellow sports car. In the Valley of Ashes, on the way to East Egg, a fatal wreck-

Suddenly, there was a terrific thud in the hall and then another.

"Amanda," said Xiao Yu. "She punch holes in wall. Next day guy fix them." He giggled.

"She's allowed to do that?"

"Sure," said Xiao Yu. The attendant had not even looked up.

Several patients stopped at the door, and one politely asked if they could go through to the smoking area.

"I have to be in here," said the attendant.

"Maxine said she would come out with us in five minutes."

"Okay," he said, as Amanda took another pulverizing blow at the wall. He got up, opened the door, and followed the two men and the woman out. As soon as it shut, Amanda hit the wall again, nearer than ever.

I got up and went out into the hall.

"Amanda?" I said.

"Who wants to know?" She was small, smaller than Julia, but pugnacious. Her knuckles were red and covered in plaster.

"I'm Joanna," I said. "I'm talking to Xiao Yu just now. Could you put that off for fifteen minutes?"

Her eyes narrowed and her fist clenched. "Fucking stupid, old cunt," she said.

Holding her head high, she turned on her heel. Before I got to the living room door, I heard her beating her mattress.

Xiao Yu was grinning when I got back. His grin faded and he looked very serious. "Saw small boy," he said.

"When, when did you see the small boy?"

"Flood night. Opened eye, saw small boy"

"How small?"

"Middle school small."

"Did you tell your mother?"

He shook his head.

"Would you tell the police?"

"Yes. When?"

"When your doctor says you're ready."

"Ready now."

"Tell your doctor that."

"Not come every day," he said. "But I tell. Bad mistake I make. Father understand. Flood not Xiao Yu fault."

"Of course not." I considered carefully. "Can I give you a hug before I go?"

He hesitated and then he stood up, arms at his side. I put my arms around him softly. He was taller than me. I had forgotten that. He seemed so young. "Take care," I whispered.

The attendant came back just in time to let me out. As I went, I could hear Amanda screaming obscenities at her mattress, also, apparently, a fucking stupid, old cunt.

Back up on the mountain, I found a note taped to my door that Detective Guevara and Clara were waiting for me at the Mad Dog. I looked across the alley, and saw Clara sitting at a picnic table on the second floor deck, absorbed in her book. Through the bar's open windows, I could glimpse people sitting at the bar. I sighed and decided to give myself a few minutes.

I took off my shirt, soaked a washcloth and wrung it out over my head. Then I sat down to air dry.

Bakersfield had been an oven as usual. The car's AC had cooled me down, but climbing the stairs to my hotel room had over-heated me again. I laid my head on the sink.

Terror was nothing new to me. It was my default setting. I had spent my life until my father's death fearing I'd end up under the patio myself.

Ten minutes later, having put myself back together, I climbed the outside stairs to T*he Mad Dog* and put my head in the open door. Detective Guevara was sitting at the bar, leaning over to talk to Max Rubenstein. They were both drinking coke, and laughing.

"Are you talking to your chief suspect, Detective?" I said.

Max laughed. "Come on, Joanna. Picture wire is the wire of choice for leg traps and garrottes."

"Nice! Now I have to worry about you sneaking up behind me!"

"Not me." He had grown serious. "Would I hurt you?" Indeed his face had softened with some of his old affection.

"You were in town on Friday night then?"

"Actually, no. We went back up to Santa Barbara. Gives us a place to play, seeing as how we wore out our welcome at the club."

"Did the kid go?" I asked.

"Zach? Matter of fact, he did. It was a chance for him to be with his mother for a change; otherwise, he stays with Ben."

"What'll you have to drink, Joanna?" The detective asked.

"Half a Guinness."

"I'll bring it out to the deck."

"Hey, Joanna," Max said. When I looked back at him, he shook his head.

Once we were settled, we sat in silence, gazing over the golf course to the San Emigdio Mountains. Clara had closed her book, after greeting me apprehensively, and rooting in her bag for tissues for me. My red nose and swollen eyes were a dead giveaway. Detective Guevara had his notebook out.

"So beautiful," Clara sighed, gazing out at the view.

When I was torn from my roots in the Quebec hills as a five-year-old, Aunt Mae recited to me, "I will lift up my eyes to the hills, from whence cometh my help." If there weren't any hills where I was, I should picture Mount Hereford. It would remind me of Jesus.

The hills in front of me now had not manifested Jesus, but rather predatory bears, toxic parcels, floods and tripwire artists.

"So shall we go over the details of this latest incident?" Detective Guevara asked.

I repeated how I had discovered the wire.

Then Detective Guevara asked Clara to recount her evening, when she last went downstairs, for example.

"I came up around –oh, I don't know- I never know the time up here. Late afternoon. I had a late lunch at the Mexican place. Then I took a walk. I met Colin coming from the post office and talked to him. He asked if I wanted to go down to Simi Valley to see a play, but I was tired. I dropped in to see Penny in the real estate office. She might know what time. Then I came up to read. I didn't go down to eat supper. I had some cereal and went to bed as it got dark."

"Were you out on the deck at all?"

"Yes, I took a glass of wine out to watch the sunset. Joanna wasn't here for happy hour," she said, glancing at me in mock chagrin.

"You were down, watching the play?" he asked me. When I nodded, he turned back to Clara. "And you didn't see anything suspicious?"

She shook her head. She was decked out in shades of blue and soft mauve.

"Did you hear anyone on the deck later?"

Clara raised her eyebrows. "I'm a little hard of hearing," she said, "and my bedroom's on the front."

"Nobody seems to have seen anything," Guevara said. "The general store closed at 8, along with everything else, except the bar and the restaurant. In the evening, most people park at the front facing the golf course," he said, gesturing at our view. This meant they were not facing the hotel.

"Do you think it was just a warning to keep my nose out of things?" I asked.

Guevara shrugged. "What we know for sure is that the tripwire would have done the job. Somebody knew what he was doing when he rigged it, but, yes, I think it was obvious you were out. Coming upstairs, as you did, tripping would have given you a jolt but it wouldn't have been lethal."

We sat gazing across the golf course to the mountains.

Finally, I said, "I saw Xiao Yu today. He's still in Ridgeview, but he's keen to talk to you. He told me he saw a small boy just before he discovered the flood. 'Middle school small boy'."

"Really? In the house?"

"In his bedroom door, as I understood it."

"Any ideas who it could be?"

"There's a kid about the right age that rides a child's bike to the store. It's way too small for him, but he makes it move."

"Is he white?" Guevara asked.

I shrugged, sighed and gestured, how would I know? "Are you white?" I asked.

"One quarter, so no."

"Then neither is he."

"Actually, come to think, sounds like my nephew, my sister's kid. Hector, Heck or Holy Heck as she calls him at times."

"He's religious?" asked Clara.

"Not very," he laughed.

My social awkwardness had raised its head. "At least Deputy Jergensen's baby blues tell me what colour he is, "I said.

"Despite his redneck?"

"That's not true-"Then I saw Guevara's deadpan cracking into a grin.

"You should buy your nephew a decent bike," Clara said.

"I've got trouble enough buying bikes for my own five," he shot back.

Clara and I widened our eyes, but managed to keep our mouths from falling open.

"I'll get on to Xiao Yu's doctor again. Is he eighteen?"

"I gather he is. His mother said he had protested he was a legal adult, and ought to be trusted to stay alone," I replied. "We were talking about the wire trap-Clara, Colin, Julia and me. Wasn't it a little late to prevent me from telling you whatever they think I know? I'd already talked to you, and I assume everyone in the village knew-there are no secrets on the mountain."

He considered this. "I would have said so, but we don't seem to be dealing with the brightest sparks in the woodpile here."

"Maybe they're just trying to make us terrified," Clara said. "The way terrorists do."

"They're doing a good job," I said.

"Just keep your eyes peeled," said Guevara, heaving his long body up out of the bench. "Both of you. Joanna, don't forget to go in for the finger printing."

The next morning, I was putting away the dishes Julia had washed. She was the dishwasher. Neither Colin nor I got them clean enough for her. She had a special technique. She used about a cup of water because of the drought, and felt each dish carefully, before calling it clean and rinsing it in hot water. 'Wash each dish as if you are bathing the baby Buddha,' she would say, quoting Thich Nhat Hanh.

I was standing on the step stool to reach the shelves. The house was way too small for an automatic dishwasher, but it was high. I spent a lot of time on the step stool.

When Julia came into the kitchen, I spoke from my lofty perch, "I think I need to take something. I'm depressed and anxious."

"Probably," she said. "You should make an appointment at the Debritt clinic."

Just as I feared. She was a purist when it came to treating family. So was her elder son, who practised medicine in Massachusetts.

I sighed.

"You know my philosophy," she said. "I'll make the appointment for you if you like."

"I'll do it," I said. "I'm just not used to paying for doctor's visits." A spoiled Canadian, I paid high taxes instead.

"It'll be about $130," she added.

I was calculating the exchange rate. The Canadian dollar was sinking.

The next day, Colin drove me down past Douglas Peak to the crossroads town of Debritt. At an exit from the Grapevine, it had a huge *Flying J* gas station where truck drivers could stop, eat fast food, shower, get their trucks serviced, sleep in them or walk over to a Motel 6 or the Holiday Inn. A hundred or more big rigs sat in the parking lot that day. There were tourists, as well, headed north.

We made a left at that corner, and found the clinic on the right. It was new and beautiful, with grey stone pillars and a sunburst of white above the entrance. One of the perks of living in California's poorest county was that Federal money provided magnificent libraries and modern clinics.

After I signed in and handed over my credit card, I sat down to read Lee Child's *Tripwire*. Was it coincidence or some cosmic message that I had picked it up last week? The tripwires in the book, however, were not deadly traps but warning devices for the bad guy that the law was closing in.

Colin walked up and down, outside in front, smoking and talking on his cell phone.

A young African American wearing dreadlocks, sat across the room with three children. The oldest, a girl, was holding her baby brother, and playing games with him. He had a delightful laugh. Her other brother was reading *Cat in the Hat*. The father was talking to a woman sitting across from him.

"Yeah, used to live in West L.A., the black Beverly Hills, you know- Baldwin Hills. Now I'm renting in Douglas Peak. Some come-down."

"I know," said the woman." A lot of L.A. people came up here after the crash. Still coming. Where'd you go to school?"

"Hamilton High, my local school, but I was in the performing arts part."

I whipped around to face him. "Really," I said, "that's where my family came from, and my younger grandson went to Hamilton. He was in music."

"When did he get out?"

"Last summer."

"After my time. Were you up on the hill?" he asked.

"No, down below in Green Village."

"Oh, yeah. My uncle lived there. Beautiful. Cars kept to the back. Houses set in a park. So many sycamores, roses, just beautiful."

"'How are the mighty fallen!'" I laughed.

He smiled and put his arms around his kids. "We still have each other," he said.

Then the nurse called them in.

I had been waiting about half an hour and my appointment time had come and gone when a tall man and a kid came in. The boy was bare-chested, and his hand was swaddled in a blood-soaked white T-shirt.

I thought he was Zach, but I'd made that mistake before, apparently. Context helped when facial recognition bedevilled me. The context here was the tall man.

Whoever he was, he was getting more and more exasperated with the receptionist.

"I'm his step-father, Ben Whitehouse. Look, call his mother. He's cut himself on a saw. It won't stop bleeding. Keep the pressure on it, Zach. For God's sake, get a move on here." He gave a phone number. "It's Lori, his mother's Lori."

Finally, the gatekeeper seemed satisfied and escorted them into the inner sanctum. I figured that put me back about an hour, so I walked out for some sweltering air, and told Colin. In the end, it was only 45 minutes. By that time Lori had arrived to wrap her arms around her son. In the fleeting glance I got, it was obvious that Zach would have a sibling in a few months.

"I was cutting a piece of wood to make you a surprise," he said to his mother.

Half an hour later, prescriptions in hand, I climbed into the car and we set off to Bakersfield to be finger printed.

After we had finished that alienating procedure, we went to Mimi's on California Avenue for lunch. I ate a hamburger and French fries, and one of their famous carrot muffins just to soothe my soul.

"Oh, Bako," I said as I finished the last crumbs, "I see too much of you."

8

ONCE, A GREAT BEAUTY

Then, suddenly, there were no more trips to Bakersfield. Paradoxically, I missed the diversion.

On the positive side, the police hadn't been back, there had been no acts of eco-terrorism, and no one had tried to kill me lately. Still, in spite of medication, I was expecting some new trauma to leap out of the clear blue.

I wrote a blog post that began with a line from The Band's *Cripple Creek*, "When I get offa this mountain, I know where I want to go." I was definitely not going straight down the Mississippi to the Gulf of Mexico. I wasn't going to find Miss Bessie, nor end up any more crippled than I already was.

The next weekend, Colin and his mother drove down to Thousand Oaks for a wedding. Julia wasn't up to the festivities. I wasn't up to staying alone in the hotel. Someone might jump out of the shadows with a garrotte. So I packed my PJ's, and went for a sleepover.

She had tickets for dinner theatre at the clubhouse, a comedy called, *Death Trap*.

Life imitated farce.

Two women were already seated at our table. Wendy was dark-haired and rounded, whereas her friend, Elspeth was a typically thin mountain dweller with long grey hair. Down in the city, women cropped their grey hair like me. They didn't want to look like witches. Up here, in hippie land, they embraced their inner crone.

When we had introduced ourselves, Wendy said, "We were just talking about that Chinese home being vandalized. I was saying what kind of an ecological activist wastes water to protest draining an aquifer."

Conversation came to a halt as a tall, older woman protested,

"These are bad seats. I'd have my back to the stage," I don't want to sit here."

"These are our assigned seats," said her companion, a younger woman.

"Well, then get somebody so I can complain."

Several of us interrupted together. "When the play starts, you can turn your chair around."

"Oh," said the older woman. "Well-"

She waited for her companion to pull out her chair, and plunked herself down.

"This is Ariadne," said the younger woman, blonde, short and curvaceous. "I'm June."

Julia introduced herself and me, as did the other two. There were three seats left, but one belonged to Julia's neighbour, who wasn't coming.

Ariadne opened her tiny spangled evening bag and handed some money to June with one word, "Champagne."

I had a wild moment in which I envisaged a bottle of *Veuve Cliquot* and glasses for all.

Ariadne was tall, had a Spanish accent, curly short grey hair and was about my age. The history of South America was written in her face. She was native and Spanish and African. She moved with the hauteur of a Flamenco dancer. She was wearing a long black dress with lights of gold.

By the time, June came back with two tiny bottles of mediocre champagne and two glasses, we had learned that Ariadne was from Venezuela.

"I was an actress when I was young," she announced.

"So was my mother," Julia cried in open-hearted delight.

"I once played Antigone," said Ariadne.

"So did my mother," Julia said, beaming.

"In my time, I was considered a great beauty," Ariadne went on.

I kicked Julia under the table.

"I have lost the love of my life. And so suddenly."

"I'm so sorry," said Wendy. "Was it recently?"

"Ten years," she said, as if it were last week.

"He brought me from Venezuela, so I could have a career in Hollywood, but it was so phoney there. We came up here. He was a flyer, you know. We could get anywhere we wanted."

Shades of Denys Finch Hatton/ Robert Redford, flitted through my mind. I expected her to intone like Meryl Streep, "I had a farm in Af-ri-ca."

"Did he die in a plane crash?" I asked.

"Oh, no. He had heart failure." She sighed. "I miss him everyday of my life. He would do anything for me, spared no expense. But he left me my beautiful home. That's a great comfort."

Blake had left me. Thirty years later, I was living in a cheap hotel. He was the only man I ever loved, but, apparently, he didn't care enough to leave me well off. So, I guessed he didn't qualify as the 'love of my life'.

"You probably don't realize this, but I am sixty six," she added.

"Got you beat," I flashed back, smiling. "I'm seventy eight."

Her eyes widened for a split second. Then she got her face back under control. I wished I were sorry.

Confucian kill mosquito.

At that moment, there was a great stir as a man in a sumptuous suit arrived with three blondes. Two wore their hair long and straight and were in their teens. The other looked like David Bowie, with short platinum hair. She was as tall as her escort and exceedingly svelte.

As they settled at their table, Wendy leaned in to whisper, "Warren Oliver, CEO of Halcon Ranch. The starlet is his second wife. The girls are his daughters."

Clearly, the audience was flattered to have him in its midst.

Conversation broke into smaller groups. Two other women had arrived, Monica and Evie Jackson. I had met them the night the band played at the club. I recognized Evie by her spangled denim jacket. She had brought a container of goat cheddar and crackers, which she sat in the middle of the table. "In case, you're hungry," she said.

"Evie made it," said Monica. "She keeps goats."

It was delicious and timely. Like all the banquets I had ever attended, this one was starting late.

Ariadne was focusing on Wendy and Elspeth. June had gone back to the bar for more champagne. Upon command. Ariadne favoured me with a dazzling smile from time to time, and a flash of her Mayan earrings.

The main course suddenly landed on the table. Julia had pre-ordered halibut and rice pilaf for us. You couldn't get fresh fish on the mountain. You could get what called itself fresh, but that was a different story. Julia reasoned that the club would have made a large order, so halibut could be relied on. It was delicious.

Certain chairs were turned around, and the play began. The 'stage' was on floor level, about six feet from our table. *Death Trap's* clair-voyant neighbour foresaw murder, and rushed over-several times-to try to prevent it. The actress was realistically hysterical. The main character, a has-been playwright, was played a little woodenly. It was unclear who would be victim, who the murderer. It all hinged around a purloined manuscript.

I liked a good mystery.

The first two 'murders', entailed a punch-up, loud thumping, screaming and shouting. I distanced myself by thinking how well choreographed it was. The third 'murder' was less noisy, except for the body tumbling to the floor-an induced heart attack- five feet from our table. My heart didn't like all the noise either. Past history. In fact, I wasn't keen on the idea of death traps at all. Recent history.

As the play moved toward the end, the action moved down stage, until it was beside our table. Suddenly, 'gunfire' erupted.

I came perilously close to a physical response.

I had lost track of the plot twists. I wanted another glass of that second-rate white. Or maybe a large scotch.

I said kind things when it was done. But it hadn't kept my mind off tripwires.

I wanted to go home. I wanted to think about wasting water to protest draining an aquifer.

Julia and I couldn't be bothered struggling with the pull-out couch, so pillow in hand, I took Colin's side of the bed.

"I need to think out loud," I said.

"About the wasted water," she said.

"It's not logical is it? The house was practically a wading pool when I got there. That's a shocking waste of water in a drought."

"Are eco-terrorists logical?"

"Maybe not. My friend, Lea, is so angry at what humans are doing to the earth, that she refuses to give to people charities-the tsunami in the Far East, the earthquake in Haiti, homeless teenagers, none of that. She supports a farm for superannuated donkeys."

"Tree-spikers don't have regard for loggers," said Julia. "Greenpeace takes out its angst on fishermen. Eco-activists do seem to have a different set of values. But would that extend to wasting water to protest wasting water?" She paused, thoughtfully.

"The night of the flood, the Kentucky Five were in Santa Barbara. No doubt that can be verified. The small window the vandal came through suggests a small vandal. Too small for even Lori and anyway, as I told you, Lori is pregnant."

"Actually, I already knew."

"Lori's son is a small 11 or 12-year-old. I met him at the art gallery, and saw him with his stepfather at the clinic. Zach was in town the night of the flood, although not the night of the tripwire. Neither were the Five, so Max said. The thing that makes me suspicious is I asked Zach in the art gallery if he lived next door to the Lao's house. I had seen a kid there one day, but he reacted strangely-too quickly, adamant, angry, as if he were afraid."

"Do you think the Five put him up to the break-in?"

I shook my head. "I can't believe they would, nor that they would make a plan to waste water. It seems unlikely they'd involve Lori's child either. Someone else might maybe."

"Lori doesn't seem like the sort to be involved in a deadly plan, no matter how high minded."

"Neither does Max, obnoxious as he can be," I said. "I think I have to tell Guevara I suspect Zach."

"Have you told him the Kentucky Five took their name from an animal rights group."

"No. I did tell him I suspected Max was involved, but Guevara treated that as a joke, more or less."

"You need to be more specific."

"I got badly stung giving information to the cops."

We sat in silence until I gathered my courage.

"The thing is, Julia, I have a feeling that they–whoever's doing these things-will go on to hurt people on purpose now, not just accidentally. They seemed to be prepared to hurt me."

"Do you think they'll take another crack at you?"

I sighed. "I don't know. I don't feel my life is about to end violently."

"Who else would they hurt?"

"Watch this space. Details at 11."

We sat in silence.

"I think I have to tell Guevara about Zach," I said finally, "and that involves implicating the Kentucky Five. I think I have to take that risk. Otherwise, the kid could find himself in deep water. "

The next morning, I was sitting on the bench beside the front door, reading the Toronto papers on-line, when something fell from the big Jeffrey Pine and landed at my feet. Was it shedding? I was immersed in yet another story when something hit me on the knee. I picked it up. As I did another missile hit the red boards. I looked up. Nothing. I got up and walked to the rail, craning my neck. A series of pinecone bits showered down like well-aimed missiles. I couldn't really see the culprit, but I knew a squirrel was up there eating breakfast. Pinecones, like artichokes, apparently were eaten by pulling off the delectable soft center with the front teeth, and discarding the tough outer part.

I retreated to the wooden chair at the other end, taking my laptop and mug of Yerbe Mate.

Here the deck made a right angle and turned along the back of the house. On the rail's corner, stood a large planter, full of tiny red and white flowers. A small bird was perched at the bottom, bobbing its head through an opening, drinking the drain water. As soon as it flew away, another bird took its place. Meanwhile, two hummingbirds vied with each other over the red flower nectar. Viciously.

The redwings were swooping to and fro among the top branches of the pines, whistling and calling. Soon, they would fall quiet, retreating to their reeds, and the cool of the pond.

The Stellar's Jays used to carry sticks to the beam that jutted out from the house. The twigs fell off, and cluttered the deck. Were they trying to build a nest? No, their nests were always in trees. Nest twigs were always fastened together with mud. Were they making a food cache? The sticks were dry and seedless. Every so often, an adult Jay would land on the deck rail, and scream at the hardworking youngsters. In June, building stopped.

Why was I sitting in this beautiful place, reading about a city thousands of miles away? I closed the computer and sat, watching, listening and breathing the clear air, sharp with pine resin.

A group of finches had landed in the pin oak and warbled at each other. The redwings fell silent. Something caught my peripheral vision.

The hawk made her heavy descent to a high, bare branch, her favourite eating-place. She began to tear bites off the small bird clutched in her claws. The little bird didn't struggle, but its black eyes were open, staring into mine.

Long ago, when I lived on the Scarborough Bluffs above Lake Ontario, a hawk stooped into my backyard and fell upon a pigeon. Reflexively, I opened the sliding door to save the pigeon. Belle, my large black Newfoundland dog, raced by me and sprang on the hawk. I dashed after, waving my arms and yelling. In the mad scramble that followed, the pigeon escaped first, then the hawk. Belle raged at the sky, and I learned my lesson. Do not interfere with the natural order of things. Look away.

Years later, I learned the cry of the hawk here in the Kern County Mountains. Back in my new home in a country hamlet, I heard the call again, across a pasture. As it happened, the young wolves were howling in the woods.

Julia had a special relationship with hawks. When she lived in the park-like Green Village, she could watch a Cooper's hawk eat on a Sycamore's branch. She dreamt of hawks at critical points in her life. To her, they were messengers of change. The Chumash said hawks flew between the worlds.

When Colin was searching for a cheaper place to live than Los Angeles, I remembered Max Rubenstein's website, where he had posted photos of his new home in Bear Mountain Place. He had moved there from Toronto in search of cheap but pristine living. BMP was a well-kept secret, a fresh-air mountain retreat, only 90 minutes from L.A.

The area was familiar to us because we had camped in Kern County mountains. Along with, first one, then two of my grandsons, we had journeyed up the Grapevine, past Bakersfield and Lake Isabella, up the Kern River, to camp at Peppermint Creek.

Once we found a hawk's body partly eaten. Julia said only an eagle could have taken it down.

Another time, I was getting breakfast food out of the car trunk, where it was locked away from bears. Suddenly, something breathed on my neck. "Mauled by a bear," the headline would read. I turned slowly to look death in the eye. There stood a big old white cow, chewing contentedly.

Peppermint Creek flowed through the sequoia pines, and down into a series of cozy granite tubs, before it crashed over a cliff to the Kern River.

The native people used to trek to the creek for sacred ceremonies.

Julia said it healed her.

We always chose the remote, un-serviced camping area, necessitating a trenching tool and water filter. For years, I wondered why peppermint tea tasted like creek water, until I realized the obvious.

The campsite sat at an altitude of over 7000 ft. After I had major surgery, I found that too high. We saw seven rattlesnakes that time, one in our fire pit, and one in the entrance to my tent. I spent four sleepless nights, and we cut the vacation short.

Two days later, wildfire swept through, leaving only the big sequoias.

So we heard. We had not gone back.

Over the years, Julia persisted in believing I had called up the snakes. I thought they had felt fire coming. Maybe I did too.

By that last visit, Colin had joined the party, non-camper though he was. So he understood the sort of place Julia needed to regain her health.

Born in southern Quebec, I had mountains in my blood. I loved those hills and the white pine. I loved the great sighing presence of the vast spruce woods, the big granite rocks and slate ledges. When I was a child, it was a poverty-stricken, hardscrabble place with a brief, brilliant summer, and long, cold, snow-bound winters. Yet, as an adult, I returned there year after year with my children, passing on my love of mountains.

Julia came out from the dining room and walked the length of the deck before she found me around the corner, my Adirondack chair tucked in beside the chimney.

"Don't forget the grand opening at noon," she said. "Did you hear the helicopter come in?"

"No, when was that?"

"You must have been in the shower."

After twenty years of lobbying, Bear Mountain Place finally had a landing pad, and a state of the art fire hall, staffed by firefighters and paramedics.

We walked over, past the village center, and the club entrance. When we got to the fire hall, it was past start time. There were so few people that we were all able to shelter from heat in the short shadow of the building.

Julia was immediately greeted, and I was introduced. Two people tried to wrangle appointments with her, and weren't happy to hear that she wasn't about to extend her clinic hours. Others were just the usual friendly villagers. I found myself listening to a dire tale from Joe who had broken his back years ago, and lived in constant pain. He had given his pain a name-Oscar. Oscar was kept in check by methadone and talk therapy from Joe. Joe was convinced that Julia was just the ally he needed. Unfortunately, Julia was not authorized to prescribe methadone. It wouldn't take much, he insisted. She could easily qualify.

It had always been this way. Julia had carried on treating her elderly and seriously ill patients when she was in more pain than they were. Because she was not in danger of dying, she continued. In the end, she had to sell her practice. Her successor quickly lost her patients. One way or another. That hadn't helped her burnout.

More and more people were arriving at the firehouse. Clearly, things would start on mountain time. Behind me stood a group of booted fire fighters and paramedics.

"Hey, Jackie," I heard one call.

I turned to see Jackson strolling up in his ranger's outfit.

"Good, to have you back, boy," a fireman said, and all his mates concurred.

Jackson just smiled, looking off into the crowd. Following his gaze, I saw Evie. She turned as if she felt eyes on her and, seeing me, she made her way over.

"Joanna, right?" she said. I nodded. "Come down and see my girls someday."

"You mean your goats?"

"Yeah. Nothing like a goat to cure your woes." She smiled and nodded at a woman, coming toward us. "I feel we may have a lot in common."

Before I could ask what in the world that could be, the sound system squealed in ear-numbing feedback. When I turned back to her, she had been captured by the woman, Monica maybe.

A blue ribbon was strung in front of the two fire hall doors, where the microphone stood. Various uniformed officers and politicians, distinguished by being better dressed than most of us, were greeting each other with laughter and backslapping. The crowd of spectators had grown much larger. Things got underway as the sun rounded the building and found us.

The Kern County Fire Chief welcomed the Kern County District Four Supervisor who stepped up to the mike, and described in detail the lengthy bureaucratic process that had led to this moment. I backed up quietly until I found a wall to lean on. The previous Fire Chief provided his recollections, as did the former Sheriff. I had seen him around the village, so I noted his name, Henry Robinson. Then three community leaders who had spearheaded the long campaign came forward. One broke down, describing his dying wife waiting in vain for an ambulance. People near me brushed away tears.

A tall man in a Halcon Ranch sweatshirt was introduced as Warren Oliver, "a friend and neighbour of Bear Mountain Place". I recognized him only because his two beautiful blonde daughters were standing near him, one of them armed with out-sized scissors.

"I am proud and happy to be with you on this momentous occasion. I think I can say that we at Halcon Ranch have contributed, in however small a way, to this achievement. Some of our employees live here in the village, and like you, we lobbied all these many years to bring this about. Thank you for asking my daughters and me to take part in this ceremony."

The girls in their summery dresses stepped forward. One held the ribbon taut, while the other cut it and Warren declaimed, "I declare the Bear Mountain Place fire station officially open."

The editor of the *Mountain Prospector* was front and centre as photographer.

The good news was that we could now go inside to see the beautiful new $6,000,000 *air-conditioned* building.

P.R. had it that it was built to last a hundred years. Two huge stainless steel refrigerators, and two industrial-sized gas stoves engendered envy, even in non-cooks. The equipment looked ready to feed displaced hundreds. There was a regular sized refrigerator outside the lounge. Toward the back, were six small bedrooms, each with its own shower, one outfitted for a differently-abled person. I pictured a wheelchair- bound fire fighter, until Julia said fire halls were refuges for people fleeing abuse. They were also drop-off points for unwanted newborns. No questions asked. One steel-countered room on the other side of the garage area seemed likely to be an autopsy room, but it turned out to be a workroom where equipment was built and modified.

It was nearly 2 p.m. and I was starving. We had taken longer than most for the tour. When we arrived at the barbecue on the club lawn, there was a line-up about a quarter mile long. The fire fighters were at the end, humbly waiting their turn. Julia and I turned as one and made for Ma's Roadhouse.

There was only one person in the restaurant, and that was the editor and, sometime photog, of the *Mountain Prospector*.

"Come, join me," she cried, standing up.

What else could she do? Despite the fact that she and Julia had carried on an email conflict over the Sheriff's Log, a snub would have been unseemly.

"Sydney," said Julia, "this is my mother, Joanna Hunter, visiting from Toronto. Joanna, this is Sydney Akerman, editor of *The Prospector*."

Sydney was about Julia's age, but with blond, curly hair. Her straw hat was lying on the chair beside her. She was shorter than me, but taller than Julia and more bosomy than either of us. She hadn't got where she was by being soft, however.

We ordered the Angus burgers on the off chance that we wouldn't be fobbed off with regular beef.

"I'm glad we ran into each other," Sydney said. "I've been wanting to talk to you."

I was all ears as I took a pull of my Guinness, for she was not looking at our esteemed M.D., but at me.

"I hear that you were involved in some of these recent events."

"Where did you hear that?"

"I have my sources," she smiled, not coyly–she didn't do coy. "You saw Jackson's back in uniform? Well, that's an interesting story! I thought you might like to know."

Our burgers arrived with salad on the side, and Sydney waited until the cook/waiter was back behind the counter.

"Apparently the CDFW investigated whether he had returned the trapped bear to Bear Mountain, but cleared him when the bear's electronic tag started pinging from up in Sequoia National Park."

"I thought DNA showed the killer bear was the cub's mother," I said.

"It did. But the bear that was trapped was never identified by DNA, so there is no proof they were the same bear."

"So," I said, slowly, "let me get this straight. The female adult that was trapped wasn't the cub's mother, even though the cub was with her at the time."

"Aunty maybe," Sydney speculated, with a grin.

We sat absorbing this.

"That's crap," I said before I could edit my language. "I saw a bear trap in the Bear Mountain parking lot at dawn, the day *after* the captured bear was taken away, and the same day Tom Braddock was killed. I don't doubt for a minute the killer bear was the cub's mother."

"Did you tell the sheriff?"

I shook my head.

"Relocated bears travel fast to get back home," Julia put in.

"This one seems to be travelling away from home. Her electronic tag is pinging in from farther north every day," Sydney said. "That was where she was supposed to be relocated."

"If I'm right she was brought back to Bear Mountain," I said, "how did she get from here in Los Padres National Forest to Sequoia?"

"Easy enough," said Sydney, as Julia nodded. "Through an underpass on the Grapevine to the Tehachapi mountain range right there on Halcon Ranch. This year so far, there have been over a hundred sightings of bears in Bakersfield. Then right on north. Look at a map. That's what I did."

Julia was busy bringing one up on her iPhone and in a few minutes, I saw it was so.

"Why would Jackson have returned the bear here?" I asked.

"Probably because of the cub," Julia said.

"The cub had been shot by then and everybody, especially a ranger, knew that," I said.

"Could have been a pig-headed protest," said Julia.

"And then what? Jackson inspires a like-minded group that sets about wreaking vengeance on ecological villains?" Sydney asked.

"Well," I said, "a lot of strong feelings got stirred up. The group he plays with was less than subtle in their song selection that night. They don't play at the club anymore. People were pissed off."

"Yeah," said Sydney, "I can't seem to find out why they call themselves the Kentucky Five. None of them comes from Kentucky and there's nothing on the Net." She waited for me to answer.

I shrugged. She sighed.

"It's just a shame, a fine horse put down, a woman dead of Valley Fever, and a young man recovering in a psych ward," she added, still fishing.

"It certainly is a tragedy," Julia said. "Joanna is going to do her best to help Detective Guevara." Nudge, nudge.

"Yes, I'm a good friend of Al's," Sydney said in a way that made me want to hold up five fingers, five damned kids, lady. Take it easy on the innuendo.

That was about it. We had lost patience with each other. Sydney strode off to pay our bill, and waved in farewell.

Sunday morning, I went to the bakery on the golf cart to pick up croissants for Julia and me. Max was sitting outside with Matthew Greaves and when he saw me coming, he said, "Matthew have you met my nemesis Joanna Hunter? Joanna thinks the Kentucky Five, is responsible for the ecological crime wave in the neighbourhood–returning killer bears, sending toxic parcels–that one would amount to manslaughter or womanslaughter-and flooding houses.

"Well, yes, I have met Ms. Hunter," said Matthew Greaves.

9

TOO FEW BEDS

Suddenly, on Monday, Clara got possession of her house. The papers were signed. The money flew electronically-Vegas to Santa Clarita to Los Angeles, and Penny handed over the key-code to Clara's new home.

I couldn't get the key-code to work; neither could Colin nor the next-door neighbours. Finally, Penny showed up, not very pleased, used her magic touch, and the door opened. Our first task was to find the actual keys and swear off key-codes.

The only items of furniture in the house were a couch and a matching chair; otherwise, it was an expanse of light laminate flooring. We walked around the echoing space and said encouraging things to Clara. Half of her furniture was waiting in a pod in Las Vegas, and half in a storage space in DeBritt. The urgent question was where were the beds.

"I really don't remember," said Clara.

Clara packed up her hotel room, intending to sleep on the couch. Colin showed up to tell me that he had taken the mattress off their pull-out couch for me, and ferried it over to the house, along with bedding for both of us.

I moved at a moment's notice. Even Julia joined in, stuffing things in bags and carrying them to the Prius. Clara had gone on ahead in the Honda.

Clara's new home was on an east/west street called Alaska, one over from Yukon, running off Glacier. It had a small circular driveway. Backing up was not Clara's strong suit. The street ran up a hill, so that one next-door house stood above it and the other below. It had a covered deck along the downhill side. It was a modular house as most of the houses in town were, even the grandiose ones, a huge kit of prefabricated parts, trucked up the mountain and reassembled, in this case in the 1980s. The narrow backyard and the side yard had six-foot high red wood fences that enclosed sandy patches and three scrawny pine trees.

My new room was ascetic, a mattress on the floor. No light, but there were pillows and a fluffy duvet. I closed my door to keep out the cats, and lowered myself onto my mattress.

Ah, shades of the past, when a futon on the floor was cheap and groovy.

You may think I was too old for that. I was. Julia's generation was the futon crowd. But divorce had shaken me out of middle age, and the middle class into youth culture.

The next morning, when I got out of the shower, I heard voices in the kitchen. This guest bathroom had a second door into a utility room that, in turn, opened into the kitchen. Thinking it might be Colin and Julia come for an early visit, I threw on my clothes, and stepped into the kitchen. I found myself face to face with Ben Whitehouse and Clara. They were gazing at the wall and Ben was tapping a steel measure in his left hand. Behind them stood a 12-year old boy with wide eyes and a suddenly white face.

Clara introduced us and we shook hands. Zach's was rather clammy.

"Zach and I met at the art gallery," I said. "Max introduced us."

"I'm going to have Ben build a piece of furniture to put here," Clara said. "He built the cupboard in the club coffee shop. Something along that line. Zach is going to draw it up for us." She beamed at him.

He had a sketchpad, a ruler and a pencil in his hands. He was slowly regaining his color.

"Oh, yes," I said, attempting a smile, but from the look of Zach's face, it wasn't a successful attempt.

I went to fill the hot pot – still no kettle – and busied myself making tea in a Styrofoam cup. I could see that Clara, Ben and Zach had beverages from the bakery.

I took my tea out on the deck where there was a small metal table and chairs, abandoned by the vendor.

I could hear the discussion from inside. Clara wanted a pie rack. Did she bake a lot? Not at all, she declared. Eventually the voices moved over to the kitchen, where I could see Zach at the counter, drawing, as the adults leaned in beside him clarifying specifics.

The deck was a real miracle. Although it was covered, it had three huge skylights, so the interior of the house would not be dark. It faced west and had an unobstructed view because of the slope. It looked across the village, out over the nearer hills, where red wood houses and log cabins climbed and clung to cliffs, then on up to the lower mountains like Timber Mountain, the Molloko Wilderness, and finally to Bear Mountain and its 9000 ft. granite dome. Above all that green was the pure blue sky, not a wisp of cloud to be seen.

Closer to the deck, the pines were alive with bird life, drawn in part by the bird feeder on the deck next door. Bird feeders were *verboten* in the village. Bears eat birdseed. Obviously, we lived next to outlaws.

I was lost in this reverie, when the sliding door behind me opened and Ben came out. He sat down in the other chair and gazed out at the view.

Finally he stirred and said, "You're Daniel Durant's mother, aren't you?"

"I am, Joanna Hunter."

As we reached across the little round table to shake hands, he said, "Ben Whitehouse." He laughed. "We already did that, didn't we?"

"Lori told me Julia was Daniel's sister. I met him when he came out to Vancouver years ago. He was there when Lori and I got married."

"I knew he was out there cycling one time."

"I always thought he had a thing for Lori. She spent time in Toronto before-"

Before graffiti night at KFC, I thought.

"You know I'm not actually Zach's father," he said. "He was born before I met Lori. Anyway not possible, hippie parents, no immune shots, bad case of mumps at just the wrong age."

I was about to say I was sorry, when he went on, "Anyway, I lost touch with Daniel."

"Me too."

"He quit his job at the ad agency," I added quickly, "and started a round-the-world bicycle trip. Last I heard he was in the far-east."

"He doesn't stay in touch?"

"Not lately. I met a friend of his who told me he had left Australia, and gone on to Thailand."

I paused. "Did you notice how Zach reacted to me just now?"

"I did. Pale and sweaty."

"I met him in the art gallery and he was odd then, as well. I had asked him if he lived next door to the house that got flooded. I thought I had seen him there, but I'm not good with faces."

Ben sighed deeply. "Yeah, I've considered the possibility he was involved. I have all the right tools and he hears strong opinions from his mother's friends. He was in town the night of the flood, so it's a possibility. He wasn't here the Friday you found the tripwire at the hotel. I presume that was meant for you."

"Lori had left the hotel by then. Her room was empty. Only Clara and I were there. We assumed it was meant for me, so did the police. I was the one who discovered the flood. And the unconscious boy."

"Even so, why would someone want to kill you?"

I shrugged. "Whoever it is must think I can incriminate them. Maybe it *was* Zach I saw outside the Lao's house. Whoever he was, the kid was with a couple of guys, but I couldn't possibly identify them. I wasn't paying attention and, besides, I have prosopagnosia, a problem with facial recognition."

"They wouldn't know that. These were men?"

I nodded.

"Zach doesn't know anyone except Julien, me and our neighbours." He paused and then went on, "He's decided he doesn't want to go back to Vancouver next week to start school. He wants to go on living with me, and start school here."

"He usually lives with Lori's mother?" I asked.

"Yes, always has done."

"He hasn't seen all that much of Lori this summer," he went on. "She doesn't have room for him at Julien's. It's a pity because Zach seems to want to get to know her better."

"I saw him with you at the clinic the day he cut his arm," I said.

"He's usually pretty good with tools. He was making bookends for Lori, and caught his arm on the saw. The cut's nearly healed up."

"He wants her approval."

"Don't most kids want to please their mothers?'

"At that age perhaps," I said.

"I would have been glad to take him on in the first place," Ben said, "have him live with us, but he didn't want to leave his school, his friends, his grandmother, come to that."

He sighed again, but then he seemed to gather his courage. "I'd prefer it if Zach went back for now. Not that I don't want him, but you know if he's messed up in this trouble-"

There was silence.

"I'm sure the whole village knows about Lori and me separating. About Julien, etc. That doesn't matter where Zach is concerned. Lori's where she wants to be. Where she should be, given the circumstances. Doesn't mean I've given up caring about her or her son."

I was considering how magnanimous that was, when he went on, "This other thing-the eco-terrorism-did you hear about the 19-year old in Coney Creek? Out hunting rabbits and someone got him in the leg. Turned out it was lead shot from a shotgun. You know this is a lead-free zone. It's not allowed on account of the condors. They eat lead-kills, and die of poisoning. So looks like somebody who's a pretty good shot gave him some of his own medicine."

I stared at him. "I didn't hear about the shooting? Was there another post?"

"Yeah, but this time it got taken down quick."

"Guns. That's a worrisome development."

"You talked to Detective Guevara lately?" he asked

"No. You?"

"Not my place," he said.

"A little bird told me you accused the Kentucky Five of plotting," I said.

He grimaced. "Well, you know as well as I do where they got their name."

"The Kentucky Fried Five?" I said. "Avengers of dead chickens. I suppose Lori chose the name."

"I think it was actually Max. He thought it was a good joke."

"But surely they wouldn't start some ecological protest now, after all those years and Lori-" I stopped myself just in time.

"Pregnant. She wouldn't. Not now. Maybe the others wouldn't either. But I've got a feeling Zach is somehow involved, and I think the best way to keep him from getting deeper in is to tell Guevara about the Kentucky Five's connection with the ecological movement. If it came from me, though, Zach would see it as a betrayal. "

"And me, not so much. I will. Talk to Guevara. I pretty well decided I would last Friday. I can't help feeling Zach is involved either, and I'm really worried about him."

"Do it before this gets out of hand."

I was about to say, isn't it already out of hand, when Zach and Clara came out of the front door laughing.

"Such a nice boy," Clara said, as we came back into the house.

That afternoon when I was at Julia's, I called and left a message for Detective Guevara.

Meanwhile, it was taking a few days to find someone with a truck who was willing to move Clara's stuff out of the DeBritt storage locker. It felt like forever.

The only dishes we had were disposable. Ditto cutlery. I had borrowed a desk lamp from Julia, and we carried it from room to room as needed. At least, Clara had a ceiling light not far from the couch. Next to a bed, I missed tables and chairs most. I spent most of my days at Julia's.

The cat tree had been installed in the empty master bedroom, so that it afforded a view through the window. The litter boxes, in the large en suite bathroom. Most of the cats settled in that area, in three cozy basket beds. Some of them made short excursions out to the kitchen peninsula for meals. Columbo had found the windowsill of Clara's bathroom once again, and ate there in the en suite. Only Jazz and Poirot hung out in the living room, although Poirot was often outside. Jazz sat on the window ledge and longed to join him, but while Poirot would willingly tackle a bear, Jazz was not street ready.

These arrangements suited my immune system. Mostly, I didn't itch any more, although I could still muster a seismic sneeze.

Detective Guevara and I played telephone tag for two days until events brought us together.

The third morning as I passed the club entrance, I saw that someone had pasted a red and yellow sign over the LED display glass. It read, "Halcon Ranch Kills Condors". Farther along a cut-down version of the sign covered the 'Danger of Flying Golf Balls' sign. The Bear Mountain Place sign in front of the general store sported two signs. A third partly covered the notice board. The stop sign was entirely covered by a sign that fit.

A club maintenance crew pulled up as I passed. They had their work cut out for them.

I went on-line when I got to Julia's to see if the allegations were true. Twelve years before, a female condor, critical to the survival of the species, had been shot during a hunting event at the ranch. The hunter received a minimal fine. While the shooting was probably accidental, Halcon Ranch had waged a legal war against the reintroduction program, claiming that the new birds were 'experimental and non-essential', rather than an endangered species. Although that lawsuit had been lost, the ranch had been granted an 'incidental take' permit. What you could mistake a condor for puzzled me. A Canada goose?

I was expressing my outrage to Julia, when the phone rang. It was Detective Guevara.

"Have you seen the signs against Halcon Ranch?" he asked me before I could get a word in.

"Yes indeed. They're everywhere."

"The Sheriff has had Warren Oliver, the Ranch's CEO, on the phone, chewing us out for not making better progress on these eco-crimes. He's not satisfied that we've got three deputies up there asking questions this morning. Money talks. I've got orders to start from scratch. I'm re-interviewing everyone. Would you do me a favour and meet me in my office in Bakersfield? "

"Sure. I've being trying to get hold of you. I might have something for you. But I'd prefer to meet you somewhere else," I said. "Do you get a lunch break? Could we meet at Regan's Roadhouse on California?"

"Sure. I could work you in Monday, if that's okay."

Villagers were still working with alcohol and acetone to remove the signs, when the fellow who ran the Mexican restaurant agreed to move Clara's stuff from the Debritt storage locker. He had a pickup truck, and a 14-year old son. And Colin would help. I arrived with a party-sized pizza in the early afternoon to find two boys helping. One was Zach, who was getting along very well with Clara.

The good news was that the beds had been found. Not only that, they had legs. Colin had made mine, complete with a feather bed on top of the mattress. Various small tables had also appeared, so I snaffled one for a night table. There were, apparently, no dishes, although that remained to be seen, since the third bedroom was full of unlabeled boxes.

"We labelled them at first," Clara said.

The pod was scheduled for delivery ten days later.

"Is it true," I heard Colin ask his mother, "That your friend has her dining room crammed with more stuff?"

"Well, only the stuff from the closets and, ah-oh, a few things."

I had heard reports that Clara had weeded her possessions prior to the move. Those reports were greatly exaggerated. I had all my worldly possessions in one medium sized storage locker. True the leather couch was standing on its end. It was dawning on me that Clara had about three times more goods and chattels than I did.

Friday night, Clara and I went to dinner at *Le Petit Breton* and Lori was our waitress. When she took our order, I asked whether it was true Zach was going to stay.

"Yeah," she said, "Suddenly, he can't seem to get enough of the place. I haven't had as much time for him as I would have liked. I've had to do a lot of resting this summer," she said gesturing at the bulge under her apron. "I'm older of course, and I've been battling high blood pressure."

"Should you be working?" Clara asked, full of concern.

"I'm only doing a four-hour shift now, but, yes, if this business is going to make it, I need to pitch in."

On Monday, I drove to Bakersfield, and met Detective Guevara at Regan's Roadhouse. We sat in a booth on the restaurant side for privacy. Fortunately, there was a bowl of boiled peanuts to shell to quell my nerves.

"So what about these signs?" Guevara said.

I shook my head. "I need to talk about the flood first."

He frowned, puzzled.

"I have an idea that Zach Aldano flooded the Lao's house. He's small for his age and would have fit through that small window. He's handy with tools, and every time he sees me, he acts weird."

"Okay," said Guevara, "who is he exactly?"

"Ben Whitehouse's stepson, Lori Aldano's son. She's in the band, *The Kentucky Five*. She's left Ben and is living with Julien Breton, another one of the Kentucky Five. He runs a restaurant in Bear Mountain Place. She's pregnant. Her son usually lives with his grandmother in Vancouver, but he's down here for the summer."

Guevara was taking notes.

"And you suspect him why?"

"The first time I met him, I asked him if he lived next door to the Lao house. I had seen a kid there walking in the yard with a couple of men. He said 'No' before the question was out of my mouth. The next time I met him, he turned white and started sweating. That was after the tripwire thing. Ben is also worried about him. And, apparently, he wants to stay here and start school, something he never wanted to do before."

"Could you identify the men?"

I shook my head.

"So a broken home and prospects of a sibling drove the kid to vandalism?"

"Well, there's a little more to it than that."

Guevara looked at me expectantly, pen poised.

"It has to do with the Kentucky Five."

"Back to that theory. Okay, I'm listening."

"None of them is from Kentucky. In fact, Lori and Max are from Canada. So is Ben." I sighed deeply. "Years ago, Lori was part of an animal rights group that painted 'Meat is murder' on the side of a chicken place in Vancouver. They got caught. The newspapers called them the Kentucky Fried Five. That's where the band took its name from. A couple of weeks ago I overheard Ben loudly accuse The Kentucky Five of 'plotting'. Said he didn't want them in his house 'plotting' and they should find somewhere else to practise."

"I know Max, of course, and he never fails to remind me that you suspect the group, although you've never said why. So Lori Aldano and Max Rubestein. Who are the other three?"

"Jackson, a California Department of Fish and Wildlife officer, Phillip Wilde, and Julien Breton."

"I know Jackson. Worked with him a few times. I've eaten at Petit Breton and I assume Julien is the chef, so I've spoken to him."

"He was a microbiologist before he opened the restaurant. Could he have sourced the Valley Fever spores?"

Guevara took that in and noted it.

"I hear Wilde comes from Maine and is a concert pianist. Clearly, he has money," I said.

"My sister's got that covered for us. Cleaned house for him every week, a while back. Wilde comes from Maine. His father, Tucker, is the latest timber king in the Wilde family. Hated his son's musical tendencies, thought the kid was gay."

"Is he?"

"Couldn't say, but he fended it off as a kid by taking up shooting. Kept his father's interest while his mother encouraged his piano playing. In his late teens he won the NRA championship for his age group. Then he dropped out of the shooting world, and went to Boston to study music."

"So the family money comes from logging? Wasn't there clear cutting up there in the Great North Woods until activists got it stopped?"

"Could be." Guevara nodded thoughtfully. "Did you hear about the shooting in Coney Creek last week?"

"I did."

"Twenty-year old, out hunting rabbits. He made the Sheriff's Log twice for hunting with lead bullets in his 22. Got shot in the leg. Didn't appear to be self-inflicted. And there was a follow-up post on the club website. Beats me why they can't stop that hacker."

"It looks as if the Kentucky Five have the right skill set," I said.

"Well, Wilde's a crack shot and he has a case full of hand guns and rifles, all legal, of course."

"But why does he need so many guns?" I asked.

"You're in the good ol' U. S. of A., now. Most people you meet have guns, perfectly legal, often on their persons. And if you live in bear and cougar country, hell, wild pig county, like here, you might need a rifle. My guess is he keeps them because they're part of his life."

"Do you have guns in a house with five children?"

"I'm a policeman. Of course I do. And I'm a deer hunter. Good to have venison in the freezer for the winter."

Deer meat was what kept the Hunter family fed during the winter, when we were on the farm. I remember a carcass hanging in the woodshed. I was frightened to pass it on my way to the privy. A rifle hung across a set of deer antlers in the kitchen, ready to hand. No gun locker. There wasn't a lock anywhere in the place. If I'd been a boy, I'd have had an air rifle by the time I was five, and a .22 before I was ten. My father called me Jo, but I didn't have male privileges.

"So a skilled shooter and a microbiologist. My sister tells me Lori is pregnant," he said, "and not very well. Seems unlikely she's involved."

"Then there's Max Rubenstein," he continued. "You think he just does publicity?'

"Beats me. He used to keep a loaded shotgun under his bed, but that was for when the Nazis came to get the Jew. I never got the idea he was a marksman. Just paranoid."

"So what's your theory about the fifth member, Jackson?"

"He returned the killer bear."

"He was suspended after the incident, but reinstated when the bear's tag started pinging up in Sequoia."

"I know, but I saw a bear trap in the parking lot on Bear Mountain the morning of the attack."

"Why would he do a thing like that?"

"Maybe he thought she should go back to her own territory even if her cub was dead."

Guevara sighed. "Can you hang on here while I make a couple of calls?"

"I guess so."

He got up and went out the door, where I could see him talking on his phone.

To pass the time, I took out my phone and opened my email. When I finished that I opened *Wordpress*. I was busy reading other peoples' blogs when Guevara finally came back.

He looked at me. "You weren't entirely candid with me. You had met Lori in Toronto."

"I didn't actually remember until Ben Whitehouse reminded me last week. Have you been talking to Ben? What is he saying?"

"As little as possible. He's still protecting his wife, even if she's having another man's kid. He'd been living with her prior to the charges in Vancouver, but he married her so he couldn't testify against her."

"Two weeks on bread, lettuce and water. The system couldn't get its head around vegetarianism, or didn't choose to," I said, only then remembering. "Starvation, time served and community service."

"Ben's been working down in Santa Clarita building kitchen cupboards. He's been leaving home early and coming home late. He admits to having a supply of glue suitable for postering, as well as wire cutters and glass cutters. We decided Zach should sleep over on Julien's couch for the time being."

"So now I'm a police informant, not just a little old lady and possible terrorist."

"Call yourself a lady, do you?"

It took me a beat, before I got a comeback. "I suppose you actually do play poker."

"Yup. By the way, your son Daniel went through customs at the Tokyo airport at the beginning of August. He's still there according to Canadian authorities."

"Oh good, now you've got CSIS following my son."

"You're welcome. Thought you'd want to know. And by the way, CSIS keeps its eye on guys who decide to cycle around the world without my encouragement." He paused. "You've been a good help."

"You met my sister-in-law," he added. "Sydney Akerman. I'm married to Sarah Akerman. Don't know if you've heard of her. Defence attorney. Makes for an interesting marriage."

"Wow, and she's had five children?"

"We certainly have five children, three of them–well–somebody else had them and didn't see their way clear to keeping them. My wife's that sort. She can never leave well enough alone."

For a moment, we were both silent.

Then he asked, "So, as my brand new informant, do you think this may be the end of it?"

"No. I have a feeling something much worse is going to happen."

He nodded more than once as he studied the remains of his BLT. "Me too," he said. "Keep your ears open, you and your friend, Clara, and Dr. Durant, if it doesn't impinge on her conscience-Hippocrates and all that."

"Speaking of kids," he added, "could you put my old bike in the back of the Prius, if I take the wheels off. I'll give you my sister's number, and she can come pick it up for Heck."

Once he had the bike in the back of the car, I heard myself say, "Am I safe now?"

He shrugged and pulled one side of his mouth up. I was not reassured.

On the way home, I came upon a road crew just before the S-curves. They were sweeping something off the road. The flagman came to my window and said, "Tacks on the road. Take it easy and check your tires for slow leaks for the next few days."

10

JESUS, THE CABLE GUY

Guevara's sister arrived to pick up the bike at Julia's. Hector was over the moon, he soon had the wheels back on, and was riding off.

While she was backing her old pickup truck out of the yard, an SUV arrived next door. As soon as it came to a stop, a small boy and girl leapt out crying, 'Papa, Papa". Justin King came out of the house and swept both children up in his arms. They were all laughing.

Standing in the front yard, I felt dizzy, and unanchored, swimming between the long ago past, the unfathomable present, and Japan.

The storage pod had come from Las Vegas while I was gone, and Colin had opened it to retrieve what was easily accessible. When I arrived, he was fending off falling objects.

Clara, seven years my senior, was carrying in boxes that I couldn't lift. Since the third bedroom was jam-packed, the new arrivals were lining the nearest living room wall.

Colin gave up in the interests of self-preservation.

"Who packed this thing?" he asked his mother.

"Friends," she said, "I don't know. It was awful. There were so many people. Everybody just doing what they wanted."

"Well, I'm going to go up to the Internet Cafe to see if I can hire a couple of strapping teenagers."

"With helmets," I suggested.

He found them, but they chose to show up the next day after school. By dinnertime that day the dining area was furnished with table, dish cupboard, dining chairs, two lazy boy armchairs and a great many boxes. The entrance to the living room was lined with walls of boxes two feet apart. There were two alleys of approach to the couch and easy chair. If you walked sideways.

"Your friend, Jose, will bring out the stuff from your other friend's on Saturday," Colin informed us.

"Oh good," she said, "I was so worried. She's having company next week."

Saturday morning Jose and his wife arrived, early, having started from Vegas at 3 a.m. They declined coffee, and began to unpack their rented van.

Just as well. I was still in sweat pants, staring at the newly discovered coffee maker, trying to decode it, when they finished. They retired to the deck, where Clara kept trying to write them a cheque, while Colin stripped hundred dollar bills off a roll.

"Colin has it handled," I kept saying.

I might as well have gone back inside to continue my quest for a French press. Give me a French press, or a good old fashioned filter, a coffee grinder if possible, and I can make great coffee. I had found several packages of coffee, one in a tin, two in full pound packages. Clara swept back into the kitchen, saying, "Oh, throw all that out. It's gone bad by now."

I did as I was told, but I cheated. I threw it, tin and all, into the garbage. Did the guardian of the transfer station have a metal detector?

Then Reg and Doug arrived.

I had managed to put on actual clothes by then.

They were Clara's O'Neil nephews. It was clear they were O'Neils. They were so completely O'Neils, that I couldn't tell them apart. One of them was heavier, and harder of hearing, but I no sooner sorted out who was Reg and who was Doug than I forgot. First and foremost, they were Irish. They spoke with California accents, but their faces were Irish, their boisterousness was Irish and their stories were Irish. One would finish a story, and the other would begin a new one. They never had a better audience than Clara. Her eyes danced and she whooped with laughter.

I myself like a good story, but I couldn't keep up.

Both the men had raised their voices for Clara. Then all three of them raised them further to interrupt and extrapolate.

They had driven three hours north to get here. Since coffee was not possible, and they declined tea, I brought both of them bottled water with ice.

"Sit down. Sit down," they cried. "You don't have to wait on us."

Then Jesus, the cable guy, arrived.

His card read Jesus Morales, Direct T.V. He pronounced it for me, Hesus.

"Hesus, Hesus," I kept repeating to myself. I wasn't used to Jesus as an ordinary name. I wasn't used to Hispanic accents. I could understand Chinese or West Indian accents, and, of course, South Asian, but not Spanish.

He wasn't used to Canadian accents. He didn't understand 'rooof', so I had to say 'ruf'. We kept asking each other to repeat. I held the record. I just didn't get Hesus.

"Sit down. Why don't you sit down?" Reg/Doug called to me.

Clara could tear herself away from them only for a moment. "Joanna can show you whatever you need," she told Hesus.

He turned on the new 70-inch television set. It hung on the wall in front of the couch where Clara and her company sat. We were all jammed into a ten-foot wide space, crowded with unpacked boxes. When the sound came on, Clara cried out, "I'll never be able to hear that." So Jesus turned the volume up and up, until Clara was satisfied. The screen told us the volume was 87. Then she and the 'boys' resumed shouting.

Jesus showed me his work sheet, and began to ask questions. A bald guy on the screen was yelling about the shoddy workmanship on a renovation. Jesus was shouting questions at me. The boys and Clara were splitting their sides at some long ago anecdote. I grabbed the remote control, and turned down the volume.

"It says one box here," said Jesus.

"No, no. We were promised two," I said. "There's another set in a bedroom. Colin talked to the company several times. There are to be two boxes."

Then I moved Jesus over near the utility room, so I had access to the landline.

"Oh, Jesus-with a J-God, I'm going to lose my mind," I thought.

Once I'd got hold of Colin, I handed the handset to Jesus, and locked myself in my bathroom.

It didn't work. I had to come back out into the din. Jesus called.

When I came out, he assured me everything was all right now. The bedroom set was working as well. I dragged Clara away from the boys, explained what had been done, and asked her to sign her name. Suddenly, she decided she should take charge, and began to ask questions that had been answered an hour ago. Jesus tended to mutter in his thick accent.

"Do I have two boxes? Colin said I would get two boxes." She went into my bedroom and came out. "There's just this tiny thing in there, no real box."

Jesus began to reassure her that both sets worked, independently of each other

"You'll have to speak louder," I told him.

He started shouting. I searched frantically for the remote control, found it at last on top of a pile of boxes and pushed mute. I gestured at the boys who were laughing with each other. Now there were only two voices shouting.

"We've settled that problem, Clara," I said. "I'll explain it to you when Hesus is gone."

"But I don't know how to work it," she said.

"I do, and Colin does. We can go over it with you when it's quiet."

"Well, why can't I hear it now?"

I handed the remote control to Jesus and went to my room. I packed my computer and book, and went out to the golf cart. It was parked under the deck overhang and blocked in by Doug's car-or maybe Reg's-on one end of the drive, and Clara's on the other. Colin had arrived on his golf cart meanwhile, and dashed into the house to intervene in the Clara/Hesus debate.

Maybe I could make it if I took a tight enough turn in the golf cart. I had a history of being able to get a small car out of impossibly difficult places. After four tries–reefing with all my strength on the steering wheel-the piercing back-up signal deafening me, I gave up and sat with my head down. I was exhausted. My middle felt as if it had been belted by a heavyweight. When I got to feeling better, I sat up and gazed at the mountains. I soaked up their green beauty. "From whence cometh-" I began to relax and remember to breathe.

"It's too much. It's all too much," a voice in my head began. "You need peace and quiet. You can't be expected to cope with all this chaos. Meanwhile, people are plotting and scheming to kill you, and you're expected to inform on them. You're way too old for this."

"Duly noted," I replied.

I heaved myself off the cart, up the steps and in the door.

"Can someone move their car?" I called.

I stopped at the general store for some *Pino Grigio* and pre-washed spinach. I would make a light lunch at Julia's. First, I was going to lie down for twenty minutes.

When I arrived at the house in the pines, I discovered the boys had beat me there. Reg or Doug was asleep on the living room couch, and the other one was in the big chair. The one in the chair was shouting at Julia who was putting away the breakfast dishes. The ladder to the attic was down, and Colin was up there looking for something. I ducked under the ladder and slipped into his studio. The mattress, which I had slept on at the other house, had still not been replaced on the couch. Mattress-less, the couch sagged in the middle. It didn't invite me. Way too tired to replace the mattress, I closed the door softly, and lay down on the rug. It was a beautiful blue Persian of modern design. It felt like the softest bed. I fell soundly asleep.

I woke up an hour later to find a note on the table, telling me they had gone to the Mexican restaurant, and please join them. Instead I made a spinach salad.

Why not take this brief interval of silence to call my sister Georgia?

I sat on the floor in the studio, and opened my laptop. My brother and I used Skype video calling, but Georgia had tried that once and given up, so I settled for a Skype voice call.

When we had caught up on current events-there was plenty happening back in Toronto-I described my conversation with Detective Guevara.

"Why would he tell you so much?" Georgia asked. "Don't they always say they can't talk about an on-going investigation?"

"In the movies, anyway. I think he is feeding me just enough to keep me on the string, so I'll tell him what's going on up here."

"Doesn't his sister live there? Can't she keep him in the loop?"

"Not right in town. I'm more at the centre of the world here."

"So the kid's still there," she said, sighing.

The teacher in her was speaking. We shared that attitude. Kids did stupid things. But they grew up. They shouldn't necessarily have their lives ruined in punishment.

Nevertheless, I asked, "Was I wrong to delay giving Guevara Zach's name?"

Georgia sighed. "No, not really. I think he needs to get out of there, and go back to Vancouver. If he was involved, his grandmother needs to get him some help."

I paused again. "The move to Clara's house has been a three-ring circus. I feel as if I'm losing my mind. I don't even have time to figure out if I'm still in danger. I keep looking over my shoulder. I don't trust police. I don't trust anybody at this point."

"Well, of course, you don't trust the police."

"I feel as if I've lost my life. I've been dropped into the middle of disorder and chaos. I have no control over anything."

"Are you taking your medication?"

"Of course."

"What are you doing for yourself?"

"Reading. I'm not even keeping up with the blogs."

"Aunt Mae used to say 'Don't take things so to heart, Joey. It don't depend on you. There's lots of helpers.' She told us not to try to change the future. 'Might be you'd make it worse,' she said."

We had talked so long that my Skype account ran out of money and debited my charge card another $15.

"Go for a walk. Can you do that?"

"Maybe. It's pretty hot. This is pathetic," I declared. "I will not be pathetic. I've survived worse than this."

The next morning, my non-pathetic persona tackled the mountain of empty boxes on Clara's front deck. For several days, the wall of boxes had sat undisturbed. I had found a box marked kitchen and unearthed mugs, but it wasn't my place to take charge. Then Clara had begun unpacking. She unpacked the way she packed. In Vegas, she had pulled everything out of cupboards and drawers, and sat things where she could see them. The sight was so intimidating it took her a while to start putting things in boxes. Now, in the reverse process, hundreds of objects sat on every flat surface, and the deck was covered with boxes.

Clara sat on one of two garden swings, pulling boxes apart, and I stood at the round metal table doing the same. I was stuffing the flattened cardboard on its end into a large box. Clara was piling hers beside her.

The sun was shining. Birds were flitting between the pines, happily announcing their territory, dashing down for a dip in the birdbath next door, or a quick snack at the feeder. We were accomplishing something. But it was hard work. I sat down on the other swing for a break and drank from my water glass. I lifted it toward Clara to remind her.

"I always forget," she said. "And it's so dry up here."

We sat staring out at the mountains, Bear Mountain crowning the view. It did seem like a good place to heal.

When the deck was clear of boxes, we loaded them into Clara's Honda and drove to the transfer station, only a few blocks east of the house, and tucked up on a foothill.

A ten or twelve foot fence surrounded it, but the double gates stood open. To the right were big, roofed metal dumpsters with doors. Two had closed signs, and were securely locked. The farthest one stood open to receive our garbage bags. To the left stood a bewildering number of open bins. One was for cardboard. At the far end in the middle was a small booth from which classical music emerged. Beside it were four containers for plastic. Behind these was a fenced area with an open gate with a sign reading, "Employees Only".

I stood in front of the plastic barrels, studying. Each had a sample of the type of plastic to put there, tied to its signpost. The water bottles were easy. We used large bottles of spring water because of the heavily chlorinated town water. I had a box full of flattened bottles. None of the other examples seemed to be precisely what I had.

Suddenly, a fully whiskered man in an overall appeared at my shoulder. He began taking stuff from my box, naming each type of plastic, and putting it in the appropriate barrel. He finished in a New York minute.

Whoa! What happened to mountain time?

I thanked him and headed over to where Clara stood with three of our seven black bags of crumpled newspaper used in packing. Looking into one, the man said one word, "Garbage".

"But it's paper," Clara and I said as one.

"Not recyclable unless it's flat and folded," he said. "Name's Malcolm. Let me know if you need help."

We watched him retreat to his tiny cabin, and swig back half a bottle of water.

We tied the top of the seven bags of paper, and heaved them into the open garbage dumpster. I hoped no eco-terrorist was watching this crime against nature. Beside the cardboard container, an assortment of unbroken boxes lay in a bin. Another chap was pulling out the best and loading them into his car.

"Moving," he explained.

"Will you need more boxes?" Clara asked.

"Oh sure, but I don't want to have to rebuild them," he said, gesturing at our flat ones.

"No, but I'll have a lot more. I could put them on my deck if you want to pick them up."

"That'd be good. Where you at?"

"On Alaska, 4112. You'll know the place, lots of boxes on the deck."

"What's with not taking packing paper?" I asked.

"Oh, Mal, pain in the ass, but I guess he's got his orders. Leave that out in bags too. We can use it."

"Where you moving?" Clara asked, as I walked away.

"North," he said, "getting too uncivilized here."

I was standing with the glass bottle box, in front of three barrels labeled glass. As I started sorting coloured here, clear here, green here, Malcolm whipped up beside me again and pulled out one of my white bottles.

"That one's actually blue," he said. "See here." He held it up to the light so that I could see the faint blue tinge on the thick bottom. He wasn't unkind, just terribly brusque. "That's garbage," he said, taking out what had once held Clara's moisturizer. "No makeup jars."

He walked off, as I stood still puzzling over what remained.

"Better watch yerself," the box man observed. "He's got a loaded rifle in his shed." He got into his car, chuckling.

Clara was standing beside me with a breakfast cereal box. Now where did that go?

"It'll keep our brains young," I said, although, honestly, I felt as if mine was going to explode.

Malcolm was suddenly there a third time, straightening the cardboard.

"Is it true you have a gun? "I asked.

"Sure do."

"Scary!"

"For bears," he said, and laughed. "I don't shoot first timers." Then he sobered up. "Locked up, of course. Say, you've just moved up here. You got an air horn yet? You need one to scare bears off."

"Okay," I said. "I guess they have them at Ace Hardware.

"Yeah." And he streaked off toward someone standing over the newspaper bin.

As I turned to get into the car, I saw Max just inside the gate, studying discarded cans of paint. I walked over to him.

"You're still using house paint for your work?" I asked.

"Why would I change?" he asked.

Looking around, I saw that this was where people dropped off stuff that might be useful. There was a pile of paperbacks on top of a milk crate and I leafed through them - several John Grishams and a few James Pattersons.

"Find anything?" Max asked.

"Not really. What about you?"

"I'll take a few tins." He had five separated out.

Clara had started the car and moved it toward the gate.

"See you around," I said. Then I turned back. "What do you make of Malcolm?"

"Old Mal," Max said. "You think I'm a raving eco-activist! Meet Malcolm.

11

BEAR ALLEY

Next day, when I got out of bed, my body told me I had done too much the day before. It was after 8, and cool in the house. Outside the sun was already warming the deck, so I put on sweat pants and a hoodie and went out. I walked toward the back end, and stood at the rail soaking up the warmth and gazing at Bear Mountain. I noticed a large black garbage bag lying on the bank. Eggshells, fast food containers and avocado shells lay scattered in the sand.

I went down the steps to study it. Certainly, it was not ours. What little garbage we had after yesterday's trip was safe inside the house. And we didn't eat this kind of food. It looked as if it were the remains of a cocktail party. I looked up at the house across the road. It was a boxcar house with a deck and modifications, rendering it less stark than Star Shine's. I had seen a blonde woman in her early forties raking the dirt yard. Had she left her garbage out?

I went in to get rubber gloves and another big bag. Clara saw me and came out to see what I was doing.

"I think the bag's too big to be dragged by a coon," I said.

Clara waded in with her bare hands, too offended to care. We chuntered and muttered and cursed stupid people, weekend people, irresponsible people. We loaded the bag into the Honda, and Clara jumped in to take it to the transfer site.

As she pulled out, the woman across the street came out with an older woman. I crossed over and introduced myself. At first I thought the younger woman was also called Clara, but eventually, I realized she was saying Lara. The older woman was a real estate agent who worked for one of Penny's rivals. I forgot her name as soon as I heard it. It was some days later that I realized she was Lara's mother.

"Oh, yes," said Lara, "there was a bear here last evening. I was out raking when it came down here." She pointed at the space between her house and the one on the next street. "We call this Bear Alley. They're here all the time. Gave me a good scare, though. I was out raking. I yelled but it kept on coming, so I ran around the house and in the back door. I had a twenty in my pocket and it fell out. I've looked everywhere, but it's just gone."

Then the other woman took up the tale. She had talked to the woman in the house behind ours. "They were on their deck when the bear ambled up. They ran into the house and started sounding the air horn. Didn't you hear the air horns going off all down to the club??"

I remembered vaguely, but by then Clara and I had come in off the deck, and I had settled down in my room to watch TV.

I was so revved up when Clara came back, that I blurted out the whole story. When I got to the part about the lost $20 bill, she quipped, "I guess bears have to shop too". She carried her meditation book out to the swing, not in the least worried.

I had no faith in reports that the killer bear was up in the Sequoia Forest. Once animals had tasted human blood, they wanted more. Didn't they?

Did I say I grew up in bear country? When I was 3 or 4, my father took me up into the back country to see a big bear someone had shot. It was hanging from a log tripod. It towered above me, and even above my father.

"It's a big un, an't it Jo?" he chuckled.

I was gripping his hand for dear life. My mouth was dry. I was absolutely terrified. We were standing much too close.

"It can't hurt you," one of the men standing around called out. "It's dead."

They all laughed. They were excited, and drinking something out of soup cans.

It was tied up by its rear feet. Its head hung down at my level. I could see its eye, like my doll's eye, an eye that couldn't see. Worse than that, the bear was speaking to me in bear language. I didn't really understand bear language, but I knew the bear was mad. I was only four, but I knew you didn't want to make bears mad.

When our portion turned up on the table, it was called pork.

Julia and I bought air horns in Douglas Peak. I had no faith in air horns. If you could fire over a bear's head without result, what good would an air horn do?

"Oh, yeah, those dumb people noises!" the ambling bears would think.

At the beginning of May, when I arrived in Bear Mountain Place, we were eating dinner in the club's dining room, one Friday evening. All at once, everyone else ran out the sliding doors onto the deck, cell phones in hand. Our waitress told us that a bear was crossing the golf course. We didn't spring to our feet. Later, I saw Internet pictures of its slow, dignified progress.

When I was old enough to go raspberry or blueberry picking with the women–my mother, my grandmothers and my great aunts-we always carried two pots each, one to put the berries in, and one to bang on it to scare away the bears. At the time, the extra pot made me feel safe.

The only live bear I ever saw, however, was in my grandfather's corn patch. My uncles, younger than me, came running into the house one summer day when their father was haying in the far field.

"There's a bear in the corn," the older one yelled, and they grabbed their .22's off the rack in the kitchen.

"Stop! Stop!" my grandmother cried. "You can't kill a bear with that."

They didn't stop.

Nanny, my young aunt-Grace, and I ran after them. They outstripped us, and went crashing through the corn. We ran to the end of the veranda. Nanny waved her apron up and down, and shouted, "Stop!"

Grant ran down one row, and Owen down another. They were bending low, peering through the tall stalks. Then we lost sight of them. Suddenly, about half way down the patch, two heads emerged facing each other. Eleven-year old Owen was nose to nose with the black bear. Everyone screamed. The two heads disappeared, and there was a great crashing in opposite directions. Owen emerged, white-faced, without his rifle. Grant was fast on his heels. The bear was bound for the hills.

My grandmother bent over double with laughter.

Before she passed on-at ninety-six in 1996-the place was already getting wilder. One day when she was out, a bear crawled through the window over the sink and opened the fridge, and another day, a curious moose tried to shoulder its way in the same small window. She told it to shoo, and waved her apron at it.

I took Belle, my ninety-pound Newfie dog to visit her that summer.

Belle was as close to a bear as a dog could be. She was probably my attempt to tame my primal fear.

I lived in a low cottage in the east end of Toronto then. When Belle wanted to come in, she would unfold her bulk, heave herself onto her hind legs, and flatten her body against the low kitchen window. More than one visitor screamed in terror.

The hills my grandfather farmed produced a reliable new crop of stones every spring. Frost heave, I suppose. He carted them off in a sledge, called a stone boat. He'd plough the garden for Nanny. Put in oats for the horses when he still had them. Then he'd wait for the one meagre crop of hay, praying he could cut it and get it dry before he put it in the barn. Wet hay would spontaneously combust. No barn, no livelihood.

Now the two farmers left, people older than me, were too old to farm. A few fields have been rented out for the hay crop. The others had been left wild, gone back to brush, or been planted with black spruce in straight rows. The sunlit hay fields of our childhood had grown ominous with ever-taller trees cutting off the light. I could see why pioneers hated trees. I thought of how men like my grandfather had cleared the land with such hard labour, how they rose before dawn, and eked out a bare existence. Now the place oppressed me and made me sad.

There was no one left there for us to visit anyway, and the road trip to see the place was too exhausting for Georgia and me.

Deer, moose, wild cats and bear were thriving there.

In my storage locker a one-legged, one-eyed brown bear, as old as me, with a cauliflower ear, injured in the wars of my younger siblings waited patiently.

Colin had a picture of a multitude of bears, enjoying a jazz party in the woods at night. A copy hung in *The Dancing Bear* gift shop. Most of the bears in the picture are standing on their hind legs. Some are curvaceous. Some are playing jazz instruments. There is a conga line. Some are drinking beer at picnic tables. Some are lounging beside each other.

When the bear strolled down Bear Alley, and left its score below Clara's deck, I felt as if my totem animal had paid me a glancing visit.

Still, I wasn't interested in getting within head-crunching distance.

12

BACK WHERE THEY BELONG

Summer was ending. At the transfer station (never say 'dump' to Malcolm), a sign announced that there were no longer extended hours on Thursdays. Longer hours allowed working people to get their garbage out of bears' way before the weekend.

"Does that mean the end of September is the end of bear season?" I asked him.

"Don't know if bears look at calendars," he said. "But it gets downright spooky up here after dark."

"I heard they don't really hibernate this far south."

"Well, they get quieter. They go back up where they belong. Good enough for me.

It got dark earlier and was cold at night. The cold set me up for my own personal muscle spasm pain, while the village fell into a public anguish.

The Prospector added its own angst-ridden voice. How could the anti-Halcon Ranch signs have been plastered on so much public property while the BMP security was on twenty-four hour duty? Was it because the patrol car had been sent down the hill for get pizza for the executive committee meeting that had run past midnight?

And now finally, Sydney Akerman ran a story that linked the freed animals, the Valley Fever parcel, the flooding of the Lau's house, and the shooting of the kid who used lead bullets. She speculated that a group of ecological activists was responsible for those crimes as well as the poster campaign. In an editorial, she called for a village meeting with the Bear Mountain Place executive committee, the security head and Warren Oliver, CEO of Halcon Ranch.

There had been no more widespread postering. It was limited to the car windshields at Halcon Ranch, where surveillance cameras seemed to fail on a regular basis. Then posters appeared again in BMP but only on the homes of Ranch employees. There weren't many of them, but they were loud in their conviction that someone in the Halcon office had leaked their addresses

Going to the village centre or the club was like walking in Athens. People everywhere argued loudly.

Then the LED sign at the club entrance announced a meeting to be held Friday of the following week. The rumour was that Warren Oliver would be there.

Meanwhile, I was never as cold in Canada as I was in California.

When it gets down to 40 F., Canadians turn on the heat, and wake up to 70 F., well, 21 C., actually. We don't throw open doors and windows to 50 F. outside air.

When the inside of Clara's house got down to 55, I made a unilateral decision to turn on the heat.

Nothing. No response. I knew there was propane in the tank. The sale papers said it was half full. I turned the thermostat up. Nothing. I got back in bed.

I tried taking refuge at Julia's. They were in Los Angeles for a four-day weekend. I didn't know how to light the pellet stove, but I turned on an electric heater, piled two blankets on top of me, and read on the couch. It was mid-afternoon before I got warm.

I had a brilliant idea for Saturday. There would be heat down the hill, so Clara and I got in her car and drove down to Santa Clarita. It was indeed warmer. I thought I would get sunstroke waiting for her.

On the way home, my right hip began to hurt. We were well up the I-5, so I pulled onto the shoulder, and adjusted the seat. I had left it where Clara had set it, and she was a few inches shorter than me. Immediately, the pain eased.

The next day, I tackled the heater again. I figured the pilot light was out. I studied the instruction booklet and, stymied, asked the guy next door for help. He didn't have a 'heater'. He had a pellet stove, sitting in front of his fireplace. He came over, kneeled down, and peered at the pilot light aperture while Clara talked to his wife. Watching him, I realized it was dangerous for either of us to attempt to light it. I knew natural gas, but propane scared me.

I called Bear Mountain Propane. The woman who answered was clearly in her own kitchen, taking emergency calls. Someone was sick, so there was no one she could send. We would have to hang on until Tuesday.

Right. We had a fireplace, a huge fieldstone, two-sided fireplace that opened onto the living room and the dining room. We had a pile of wood on the deck - good dry wood. Small pieces, soft, easy to kindle and fast burning. Large pieces, hard and slow burning. We had bags of newspaper, and I knew how to build a fire.

Clara worried it would get too hot. She couldn't stand hot! I thought she coped quite well with hot. She hadn't turned on the AC in 90 F. heat. Anyway no fireplace ever made a place too hot. Unless it was lit mid-summer. A stove, I could get hot, as long as it burned real wood. I went ahead and started the fire.

Clara retreated to her room to read in bed.

I ate my breakfast two feet from the fireplace and began to thaw out. The thermostat read 65 F.

I had begun to limp. My right hip was stiff and painful. So painful that being eaten by a bear felt like a solution. I lay down on the living room rug, and began to stretch. Jazz saw her opportunity, jumped on my middle, and lay down. A few minutes later, Tennison climbed onto my thighs. Okay, cat therapy. Both purred blissfully. It was about 62 F., there on the floor but they had on fur coats. Could they function as a heating pad? Yes, if moved to the right spot. But, no, they wouldn't be nudged. Tennison bailed, and Jazz stood up on my middle, twenty pounds on each paw, stretched leisurely, and strolled back to her mommy.

I limbered up and got up to do tai chi. It was Sunday.

"Let's go to the club for breakfast," I called to Clara.

And behold, the heat was on there.

One solution to the cold and the hip pain was to soak in the tub in the master bathroom. It was as big as the living room of some apartments. It had a large oval tub, a separate shower with a door, double sinks in a very long vanity, and enough additional room for two of Clara's silk palm trees, and a white bench, not to mention the kitty litter boxes. The tub was under the window. The blind could be adjusted for privacy and view.

The only drawback was Columbo. He had taken up residence on that windowsill from which he stared balefully. If I lowered the blind, it hid him, although I could feel his protesting eyes.

I would pour in half a bag of Epsom salts, a few drops of lavender, and get the water as hot as I could bear. All in all, it was a Hawaiian jungle-green, warm and humid.

I would sit reading, topping up with hot water as needed. By the time I got out, I was a sleepwalker.

Wearing my pjs, I did a demonstration of how best to get out of this tub-for Clara, although I wasn't keen on sustaining a concussion while naked either. At home I put a wet washcloth over the side of the tub, turned onto my knees and pushed myself up. Colin had tried a rail attached like a vice to the side of Clara's tub, but the sides were curved and wide. Didn't work. Then he got a short rail with suction cups on the top edge of the tub. When you pulled on it, it let go. Finally, he screwed a rail onto the low wall at the tub's end. It worked for me.

Clara preferred to shower.

In an attempt to treat my hip, I made several appointments with the local acupuncturist. She cancelled each time. A friend of hers was dying of cancer. I took Tylenol, which didn't work. I considered major and possibly illegal painkillers. What if I hung around street corners in Douglas Peak. Would a kindly dope peddler show up? I longed for liquid morphine.

After that very cold weekend, I got back on the phone to the propane company. It had many other emergency calls, of course. As usual, I had to fetch Clara, and get her to authorize me as her spokeswoman. I pleaded with the propane company for help. As I walked the floor with the phone, I heard the grinding of big truck brakes, and glimpsed a Bear Mountain Propane truck outside. I ran to hail the driver.

His badge said that he was Merle. He was so thin that his Bear Mountain Propane overalls hung off his body, and he had a face like a pointed shovel, his features scrunched together to fit it.

"Howdy Ma'am," he said, grinning.

He was a good old mountain boy, a southern mountain boy. He seemed too old for such work, but that may have been because he was nearly toothless. He was completely unselfconscious and, I have to say, charming. It's not often that a man-toothless or not-flirts with you when you're 78.

I described the problem and we both got down on the floor and, leaning our heads sideways, peered into the pilot light works.

"It's deep in there," Merle observed. "My lighter won't go that far."

That startled me, but a glance at him told me he was studying the problem, his face completely guileless.

He tried anyway. He was right. He sat back on his heels. "What've you got for matches?"

As more and more boxes had been unpacked hundreds of tchotchkes had appeared: Buddhas, fine china shepherdesses, old ads and signs, porcelain cats galore, street signs, wrought iron wall hangings, dolls, and framed pictures of Shirley Temple. Somewhere I had seen fireplace matches. I found them beside the fire-tongs, miraculously where they should be.

It took five matches, but finally the pilot light hissed into life. I just about threw my arms around Merle, and kissed him on his widely grinning mouth.

He turned the thermostat up to 90, and soon the heater kicked into life.

"Tacks on the road again," he said, as we waited for the heat to kick in.

"Pardon?"

"You know, tacks scattered on the highway again the way they were last week," he said.

"Are they falling off some builder's truck."

"Not many builders use tacks. Rug guys mebbee."

"You mean somebody's scattering them on purpose?" I said.

"Must be."

"Why on earth-?"

"Too many cars. Too much traffic. Some nut probably thinks." He shrugged. "Be careful. Check your tires after a trip. Slow leak can cause a blowout. Specially in hot weather. Or with a heavy load."

"You're checking yours, right?"

"Sure am."

He turned the thermostat down after the heater had a bit of a workout, but he wasn't finished. Now he had to check the water heater. When I protested that it was working, he said "Safety check".

Evidently it passed. The clothes dryer didn't.

"Was that modified for propane?" he asked.

I had to call Colin who had finally returned from L.A. I passed the phone to Merle.

When he got off the phone, he said, "I told him he has to buy the part. We don't have any o' 'em. I can't do the fix 'til I get the part. If you use it this way, it'll burn your clothes."

Clara appeared. "What?" she said.

I left them to it, and went to my own room.

Call it paranoia but I felt as if Clara thought I was taking over, and wanted to make it clear who was the lady of the house.

When at last, they stopped shouting at each other, and Merle had left, I took the Chardonnay out of the fridge, and poured us both a small glass. She sat on the couch and I sat in the chair at right angles. The sun had moved around to the front, and the deck outside the windows was in shadow.

"How are you finding it here?" I asked.

"I'll give it a year," she said, grimly. "I've promised myself to give it a full year and if I still hate it, I'll go back to Vegas."

I managed not to blow my wine out my nose. Just.

"So, you're feeling a bit down," I said.

"You could say that," she replied.

I moved over and sat beside her. And we sat in silence, occasionally sipping our wine.

"It was a good decision, Clara. You needed to be here near Colin. This is just a transition. You've been doing too much. Take a few days off."

"I want to get my stuff organized," she said.

"I know. I know."

It was a formidable task. I had been working on the kitchen. I cleaned the cupboards first, and washed everything before putting it away. There were about sixty mugs and over twenty dinner plates. She must be expecting company. I hand washed because the dishwasher took two hours, and smelled as if it were about to blow. The faulty dishwasher, and the blonde laminate floors were getting her down.

"Real wood would have put the price out of your range," I said.

"I suppose," she said.

I didn't want to be taking charge, and she didn't want me to, but the hearing problem confused the situation. I had driven her to a Hearing Clinic one day for a test in a hard to-find town, south of Santa Clarita. I asked afterward if she would be getting a hearing aid, "Absolutely not", she said, "far too expensive." Yet when her husband had gone deaf, she kept at him until he got one.

Refusing was just a stage, like adjusting to the mountain.

"Everything's so hard here," she said.

I concurred.

I limped about every morning. Even my entire repertoire of tai chi couldn't keep my hip moving smoothly or painlessly. I was becoming drug dependent, after twenty years of taking none.

It was warmer in the house in the morning, but the evening program on the thermostat cut the heat off at 9 p.m. In the morning, it came back on at 6 a.m. and off at 8. After that I over-rode it, until the sun warmed the place up.

I didn't mention that to Clara.

The dryer part had still not arrived. I took my wash over to Julia's. Clara would wash, and send the wet clothes over with me to be dried.

Julia kept saying that I was doing too much. I couldn't see that.

Anyway, working took my mind off darker matters. Nothing really bad had happened for days. The bears had moved off. Maybe. Still, I was waiting for the other shoe to drop. I was haunted by the idea that we were drawing nearer and nearer to something dire.

The meeting at the clubhouse on Friday ran out of chairs, so it started late. While chairs were being brought in, people got drinks from the bar and brought them back.

Max and Phillip Wilde found seats at the back.

At the head table sat two members of the executive committee, Detective Guevara, the head of the BMP security, and a tall young man in a beautiful suit. Rosalie, who chaired the meeting, introduced the panel, and we learned he was Roger Smith, Warren Oliver's substitute.

Immediately, several people objected that Oliver himself should be there to answer allegations that someone at Halcon Ranch had leaked the addresses of employees. It took a while for Rosalie to restore order, despite her ear-splitting school bell.

Finally, Roger Smith was able to speak. "We are undertaking a thorough investigation. Should we discover the culprit, we will take appropriate action.'

"What does that mean?" several people called out.

"We will notify Detective Guevara, and look at terminating employment, but there are other ways the addresses could have been obtained."

"Such as?"

"It's important for you to recognize that Halcon Ranch is the victim here-"

"You mean poor little Halcon Ranch that wants to build 5,000 homes in pristine wilderness," someone shouted.

"Okay for you to say, you haven't had to scrap those signs of your windshield," shouted another.

"As a matter of fact I have," said Smith.

"One at a time," shouted Rosalie. "Wait for me to acknowledge you." She clanged her school bell for good measure. "Mr. Smith."

"The perpetrators have accomplished exactly what they set out to do," Smith said. "They've turned you against us. It's true that one condor, AC-8 was accidentally and tragically killed during a hunt, but that was twelve years ago. Since then the condors on the ranch have thrived. You see our condors here over your golf course. And the terms we are negotiating with the various ecological groups are generous and protect the species. Successful negotiations are all but complete."

"Why isn't Oliver here?" demanded a man, at the top of his lungs.

Dozens agreed.

"As you can imagine, a CEO of Mr. Oliver's stature has his calendar planned well in advance. This meeting was rather last minute. I believe Mr. Oliver is in New York City meeting with investors there."

Eventually, the audience gave up chewing that particular bone, and moved on to pillory the security chief and the executive committee.

Well, yes, the officers on duty had driven down to the pizza place in Coney Creek. Anyone watching the highway would have known that. Yes, in retrospect it wasn't a very good idea. It wouldn't happen again.

Eventually, it was Detective Guevara's turn. Sydney Akerman, girl editor, took the lead in his interrogation. She managed to sound ruthless.

"Is it true that you arrested a juvenile for the postering?"

"We have questioned a number of people. We have made no arrests."

"Surely you must have made progress on the toxic parcels. What was it, ten copies of the same book sent to the same number of Savgo ex-staffers?"

"That book had been remaindered and could be picked up easily. I can't comment more specifically on an on-going investigation."

"Was the same juvenile questioned about the house flood?"

"No comment."

When Sydney had finished grilling her brother-in-law, various motions were attempted, but Rosalie said this was an information only meeting . She rang her bell loudly when the crowd disagreed.

Each panel member gave a reassuring final statement.

"What about the tacks on the road?" a woman shouted.

Guevara leapt in. "There is no indication that they are part of the campaign. No claim has been posted. But, if you have information, please call. I left a number of my cards on the table, near the door."

As people trailed out still arguing, Detective Guevara waved me over. "Join us in the Mad Dog for a drink?" he said. "Sydney's coming and I'm going to ask Roger Smith."

The weather had changed. It was warm enough to sit outside under the stars.

"I have a feeling Oliver would rather be dragged by wild horses than face that crowd," Guevara said.

"That's why he pays me the big bucks," said Roger.

"Really!" said Sydney.

"No, not really. But he did rescue me from a life in fashion."

"You're a designer?" I said.

"Not even," he said, taking a swallow of his mojito. "A model. Warren convinced me I would be over-the-hill in a wink of Ralph's eye. I think he hired me for my wardrobe."

"Ralph Lauren?" I asked, nodding at his suit.

"Among others. Versace shirt, for a touch of outré."

He downed the rest of his drink. "Okay, now I have to sober up, mind my tongue, be a good little spokesman." He grinned. "What can I do you for, Detective?"

We all laughed. He had gone wildly astray from his Halcon persona.

Guevara shook his head. "Nothing really, unless you know who's making my life so hard. I've got zero, and your boss is standing on my neck. I thought we should get to know each other. Sydney is my sister-in-law. She sees her job as getting the citizenry riled up. Joanna has had the misfortune to be in at the beginning. She thinks the same perpetrators caused death by bear, and is certain something more terrible is yet to come."

"How more terrible?" Roger asked.

I considered for a moment. "Murder, I guess. I mean obvious murder, not just by chance murder, like Jennifer King's death. Maybe more than one murder."

"What makes you think that?" Roger asked.

"It's a premonition, I suppose. There's no actual basis for it, in reason."

"As long as it's not me," he said and sighed. "But how could it be? I'm nobody. I mean I'm Roger Smith, who'd want to kill me?"

"Roger," said Sydney, clearly outraged, "where's your social conscience?"

"Off-shore," he said. "I farmed it out to someone like you." He laughed. Then he sighed deeply. "Look, I don't want anybody to be killed, but these are hypothetical people based on nothing but," he paused trying to remember my name, "Joanna's premonition. I can't take it seriously. I'd like to help out with this crime wave, but I got nothing. No idea. I get sick of people thinking I speak for some higher power. All right if I push off now?"

Guevara nodded.

"Stoned," said Sydney, when he'd left.

"Did a line or two on the way over probably, "Guevara said.

"Is he fit to drive?" I asked.

"He's not driving. He came in the Halcon Ranch limo."

Then it occurred to me. "Listen, I'm Joanna Hunter. Who'd want to kill me? But somebody tried."

We sat considering this.

"Speaking of social conscience-and off the record-what do we want to accomplish?" asked Sydney.

"On the record or off-I want to catch them and put their asses in jail," said Guevara.

"What do you want, Sydney?" I asked.

"I want people to wake up, take an interest in their community and turn the perpetrators in. And you?"

"I want it to stop before things get worse," I said.

"What about punishment?" Sydney demanded.

"I'll leave that to the Sheriff's department," I said.

"Doesn't justice demand it?" she said. "Mrs. King is dead."

"I didn't say I was against it. Of course I want justice."

"Don't tell me-you believe in natural justice," she said.

"For most of my life, I couldn't even tell you what that meant. My history prof in first year assigned that topic to me because I was playing Antigone. I got a B-. When I was teaching English, the students were always saying, 'What goes around, comes around.' My private response was "Maybe, but not fast enough.'"

"So you don't believe in it," said Sydney.

"I do now that I'm older and have for a while. Do you have time for a story?"

Seeing no objection, I went on.

"Thirty years ago, I was living with a crime reporter. He had just finished covering a big trial, and we were in a park, letting our three dogs run.

"The defendant had been found guilty of hiring someone to batter his wife to death with a baseball bat. Connor had had an inside track with this guy, taking calls from him in prison, etc. The murder was clearly a hit. The guy hadn't done it himself. He had a solid alibi, but he got a life sentence with no hope of parole for 25 years. He's still in custody 40 years later.

"Connor was chuckling because the hit man was still at large. He had escaped punishment.

"I was outraged. 'Nobody gets away with murder,' I said. 'Our souls won't allow us to go unpunished. They arrange events so we suffer for the suffering we cause.'

"Connor was a lapsed Catholic, and thought I meant the hit man'd die and go to hell. I didn't - unless our souls create that virtual experience for us after death. I realized as I talked that I could finally write that damned essay. I also realized that Connor and I were finished, or as he said later, 'Quitsville'.

"Who got the dogs?" said Guevara.

We all laughed. "I got the big old Newfie. He got the smaller two."

"But did the hit man suffer?" asked Sydney.

"Yes," I said, without hesitation.

"How do you know?"

I smiled, enigmatically.

"The Santa Annas are picking up," she observed, turning her face to the wind. "We'll get sand."

The next morning around 8, I was out on the deck looking at the brown fog hanging over the mountains. Slowly, it dawned on me that it was also hanging in the air I was breathing.

The Santa Anna winds were blowing off the Mohave Desert.

The house phone rang. It was Star Shine, in a panic. Social Security needed some document or other, immediately, or she would lose her Disability Pension. No one else could drive her. I didn't even have time to shower. It was Wednesday and the office in Bakersfield closed at noon.

I was getting used to the dust, which rose from the unpaved golf cart paths. It settled on the bags I carried, and I had to wipe them down before I took them into the house. I used one of Colin's golf towels to clean the seat each time I got onto the cart. I saw the wisdom of the kerchiefs cowboys tied around their faces, and wished I had me one.

I picked up the Prius, and was at Star Shine's boxcar place by 8:45.

She was so agitated she sat up straight in the passenger seat. I knew she had finished the chemo and that her sister had gone home to Texas.

"How are you?" I asked as I steered through the curves.

"I'm okay," she said. "I'm actually feeling better, a good deal better. The chemo seems to have worked. For now, anyway."

"You look better," I said.

"Yeah, thanks. My sister cooked for me, fed me up. It was easier to eat with her there, especially once the chemo was over."

As we slid into the valley, the air grew denser. Starting down Halcon Pass, I turned my lights on. Traffic slowed. I had experience with whiteouts. I came from the north. This was a sort of beige-out, not blinding, but demanding. Even with the outside vents shut off, the air in the car scoured our throats and eyes.

Once we were down the pass, we were in a kind of tunnel. The wide expanse of the central valley, and the mountains that embraced it were no longer there. Vanished, lost to sight.

Gradually, I got used to it as the traffic thinned.

"Say, Star Shine, do you know Malcolm at the transfer site?"

"Do you mean Malcolm Fletcher?"

I looked at her, mouth open. "He's a relative?"

"He's my father."

"Your father!"

"Yeah, he followed me here." She paused. "So why isn't he driving me to Bakersfield? I'd rather die."

"Okay."

"Growing up, we didn't have a pot to piss in. All because he had to go all commando, live off the grid. Never get a job. My mother fed us making beads and tie-dyed shirts, while he sat in some tree to save it - after he'd spiked it to maim the loggers. She wouldn't have died if she'd seen a doctor. Maybe. She had breast cancer. Died at my age. He could have cared less. Dance and I dragged ourselves up. He cared more for his god damned goat than he did about us."

"Sorry," I said.

"Oh, he's got plenty of excuse–the Vietnam War, killing people, blah, blah, blah. He actually grew up in Wyoming, hunted as soon as he could carry a gun. Came back a hero to the folks in his county. Went to San Francisco to hear Led Zeppelin. Figured out most Americans outside his county hated vets. Met my hippy mother who didn't. Left town when the place got violent. Lived in a backwoods commune. Quite the saga. Then Mom died." She paused.

"Dance and I got out as soon as we could. She got married. I wrote kids' books. Came here. Then he shows up, all contrite, a changed man, actually works for a living. I can't forgive him, even now." She gestured at her wounded breast. "I'd rather count on the kindness of strangers."

"Ooh."

She was crying, but trying not to show it.

"My mother said he'd never talk about the war, but she thought he'd been a sharpshooter. I don't know. Maybe he was at My Lai or something. I don't care either."

"How old is he?"

"Sixty four or sixty five."

"So born in 1951 or so. My Lai was in '68. He'd have been only 16, too young."

"Well, something sure spooked him. He must have had a Jesus moment after we left. He started paying taxes, the whole kit and caboodle, as he used to say."

We were on California St. now and I was looking for a turn.

"Sorry, oh, sorry," she said, head in hands.

"No, no, it's all right."

"No, it isn't. Dumping that on you. It's not all right. I've got family right in town, but I've dragged you out first thing in the morning. His fault. See, I actually want to blame him for that, too. As if I weren't responsible for being such an unforgiving bitch."

I was parking by now and all I could think of to say was "Wow", but I refrained.

It didn't occur to me to worry about cocci spores drifting around with all that sand. I was preoccupied by the petrochemical smell. Little 'donkey' pumps nodded in backyards dredging up crude. The heavy air was holding down the toxic stench.

Star didn't take long. She pulled a high number from the machine, but she was in the documentation queue, and there were only four people in front of her.

We stopped at In and Out Burger on the Grapevine for lunch.

Finally, still in pain, I called Julia's ex-husband, Evan, in Los Angeles He agreed to give me a treatment after he treated Julia on Thursday. I knew this was asking for it. Evan used a combination of deep massage and acupuncture. The massage was so intense that pain just said, "I'm outta here".

He had made good progress treating Julia. He threw in psychotherapy for free. Well, actually, it was all free. We were family.

He looked a lot like Max, bald and large. He too had a motorbike, he had worked oil rigs, been a surfer and a body builder, and had met

Julia at a lecture when he was studying acupuncture. Their nineteen-year old son, Leo, was a heartthrob–tall, fair, handsome-like his father before him, and the same kind of self-taught creative genius.

I had got to know Evan well, when Leo was seven. By then Evan and Julia were separated, and I was living with her. I often did pickups and drop-offs. These handovers proceeded according to kid-time, which is to say, very, very slowly.

To distract myself from the pain of deep massage, I told Evan about the bear, the Valley Fever dust, the flooded house and the posters. Then I offered my theory of a group of eco-activists, possibly *The Kentucky Five* and its sidekick, Zach, as perpetrators.

Evan said, leaning all his weight onto my right hip. "If the Five are in on it, is each one going to take a turn? You think the ranger, the cook and the kid have had their turns. Presumably, the rocker/artist is behind the posters probably with help from the rest. What about the pianist and the waitress?'

"Lori is pregnant, over-worked and hypertensive. I doubt if she's up to a turn. Max would make a better visual than that red and yellow sign. He used to keep a loaded shotgun under his bed. He was expecting another Holocaust. The concert pianist is a champion shooter."

"You did say some hunter was shot in the leg. Some hunter who used lead shot, endangering the condors."

"True, so I suppose that could be his part of the action." It was a relief to realize that murder might be out of the picture. "And Max, he's rude and paranoid, but he's also funny and gentle. I'm sure he's not going to turn murderer. Then there's the question of whether ecologists would waste water to protest wasting water."

"I always had a gun until we had Leo." He remembered. "You know that story about the time I was trying to drive through East L.A. during the riots, trying to get out to the oil rig and got stopped by the cop? He said, 'you can't go through here. It's dangerous for a white man.' Then he noticed my gun on the seat. 'That loaded?' he said. 'Yeah,' I said. 'Go ahead,' he said, and waved me through."

I already knew that story, but Evan liked to tell it.

"How many people you figure have guns up there?" he asked. "Quite a lot - what with hunters, what with folks afraid of bears and folks afraid of folks. The keyboard man isn't the only one who can shoot either. I'd keep an open mind. It may not be one concerted action, or it could be one person with a friend at a lab."

"Jackson, the Fish and Wildlife ranger? There's no doubt in my mind that someone in that department transported the killer bear back."

"Probably, but not necessarily him. Anyway I'm glad the bear got away." He stood up and dusted his hands. "Take a walk around the yard. Loosen things up. Listen to the birds. Then I'll put in needles."

I staggered to my feet and went out of the treatment room, barefoot, moving very quickly from the hot tiles to the grass.

The finches, which had been singing rhapsodies outside the window of the low back house, paused as I passed. High on a wire, a mockingbird took up their melody, and then segued into a robin call, and then a jay's and on and on, until it ended with a car alarm and fell silent.

The next Saturday, I hitched a ride with Colin and Julia again, and got a second treatment, even more painful than the first one. This time Evan spent half the time trying to convince me to cut down on carbs, and the rest speculating about why Daniel didn't communicate with me. Was there method in Evan's madness? Was the CIA using his technique yet? I felt considerably worse for the next few days, and then the pain disappeared and my hip moved freely.

At home, Clara was more settled now that she could watch some of her usual shows. One day, the remote control disappeared, and while mine worked on her set, Clara couldn't rest. All the open boxes, half unpacked, complicated the search, but while I was at it, I found some library books that been missing. After an hour, I gave up, saying I would get back to it when I came home.

Clara felt as if she was losing her mind, but she wasn't. Confusion was just the usual consequence of moving. Mid-afternoon she found it.

One problem was, somehow, the television kept flipping off satellite reception. When I heard the sound of very loud static, I would rush out. I ran because the static made me crazy, and so did having to reset the thing three times a day. The solution was to disappear the television remote. It found a new permanent home behind my television set.

Even with just the one remote control, problems persisted. The television set would not now respond to the remote on a reliable basis. On one occasion, I realized that Clara knew more than I did about it when she touched the screen to silence it. Holy moly! The problem was I now had to walk up and touch the screen to get the audio back. We invoked a no-screen-touching rule, but still the television pursued its own course. I moved the sheet music off the piano. I moved Mozart's bust a few inches right. It took Colin to realize that when we were sitting, the satellite box on top of the piano blocked our signal.

We were too busy to deal with the hearing problem, even though the groundwork had been laid. Volume levels were high. Clara kept apologizing, but it didn't bother me anymore. Except when I was trying to talk to her. Then I would grab the control.

To my surprise, I found myself joining her at breakfast or after dinner to watch HGTV. Once I started watching the *Property Brothers* find a house for some demanding couple, and then renovate it, I was hooked. If I couldn't sit down for all of it, I had to dodge back for the big reveal. Usually the cities in which it, and other shows were filmed were not identified, but I could often tell Clara–east end of Toronto, downtown Toronto, Richmond Hill, Vancouver. Every so often, we were taken to a south sea island or Texas.

Floor plans and renovation interested me. I admired the workmen's ethic and skill, but it was just entertainment. It didn't matter to me that I no longer owned a house, and Clara's house made me feel at home, so I didn't fret as much about my homelessness.

The little Joanna, who had lived through the housing shortage after the war, was still satisfied just to have a place to live, no matter how downmarket. Granite counters were the stuff of legend. Little Joanna watched, astonished, at the sense of entitlement these people had. They rejected perfectly adequate rooms as too 70's, too 80's, even, for heaven sake, too 90's. I had lived happily in rooms that were too 30's.

I had once, in a bold departure, tried to update a country house built in 1889, with Daniel's help. Library books were involved. This was before you could find everything on the Internet. I had made $70,000 by selling the house I had with Connor. The reno took it all. When I retired I had to put the house on the market. I lost the entire $70,000, plus another $18,000. I got enough to buy a leather couch to put in a rental. Ninety-five was a bad year to sell a hundred-year-old house. Like most years.

Since then the greater disaster of the sub-prime mortgage, and the Great Recession had cut an even wider swath through home ownership. Witness why we were in Bear Mountain Place.

I enjoyed the companionship of sitting with Clara, and seeing who could guess what house the buyers would choose. It was an interval of domesticity with no need for first responders.

There were, however, fresh tacks on the highway every time we used it.

13

MT. JOE AND THE K.K.K

I had never heard about the Mount Joe controversy, until I went to Penny's party, a brunch party as it turned out, although I thought for a week that it started at 9 *p.m.*

I had been standing behind the couch near the food table when I heard two women arguing about whether the Mount Joe sign had been stolen because somebody disapproved of the name.

"Joseph Braddock was the Ku Klux Klan leader in the 20's. Why would anybody think it was a good idea to call a mountain after him?'

"Well they did. They called it Mount Joseph. People have got used to that. They like calling it Joe. Nor'wester, what kind of a colorless, bureaucratic name is that?"

"It's what the maps say now."

"Oh Google maybe. Not the ones you buy at a service station."

"Can you even get those anymore?

"Why do people always have to stir things up? If it weren't for the paper, no one would even know, and we could call our mountain by its friendly name."

"We could even have those friendly bonfires with a cross in the middle."

Penny swept in with a plate of tiny sausage rolls.

In the kitchen area, one woman was saying to another, “I saw you scraping something off your windshield the other day.”

“Oh that! I was late leaving for the office and there, stuck to my windshield was another one of those damned signs, ‘Halcon Ranch Kills Condors’. It wouldn’t peel off. I had to get a paint scraper and soak the glass with water. Even so, there were bits that I couldn’t get off. Thank God, the boss sent someone to work on it, once I got to the office. I’m not the only one either. Several other women, who work at the Ranch, had the same problem.”

“What’d they figure?”

“Well, Oliver, the big boss, thinks it’s all part of the campaign against the new development.”

“Halcon Village?”

“Yeah. They’re in negotiation with four or five ecological groups. But Oliver thought things were going well.”

In the dining area, a woman was saying, “Those damned tacks on the highway, and no place to get a tire fixed up here-“

“You can always call that mobile guy, parks his truck at his house near the club-“

“Somebody’s going to have a blowout, if you ask me,” said a third woman, who had just strolled up.

I carried my mimosa out to the back deck. Most of the chairs were taken, so I walked along the deck.

This brought me more or less face to face with Ben, who had been tapping a sprung nail in on his deck. Seeing me, he mouthed, “I’ll come down”. His house was higher and far enough away to require loud voices. He moved to the far end of the deck and undid a gate in the railing.

“Hi,” he said, when he had come around, and was standing below Penny’s deck. “Did you hear the Chinese kid claims he did it?”

“Did what?”

“Caused the flood.”

“He can’t be serious.”

“Seems to be. Guevara says he tried to commit suicide again.”

“How? Is he all right?”

"Not pills this time, but yeah, his mother found him in time. He's back in treatment. At the same place."

"That's not possible? Is that possible? He didn't flood the place, surely."

"A new concept, I guess –suicide plumbers. I hope it doesn't catch on. Seriously, I don't know. I've got wire cutters and glass cutters in my toolbox Zach could've got at. Do you think the Laos do? Seems doubtful and even more doubtful, their kid could use them. But why would he say that?"

"He left a note?"

"An email – 'not small boy, me', something like that."

"Guevara didn't show him just one picture did he?"

"Of course not. He got pictures of his oldest son, and a bunch of his friends as well as Zach's photo. What do they call it? An array."

"Is Zach going to go home to Canada now?"

"Guevara wants him here for the time being. I find that worrying."

"Is he staying with you again?"

"Yeah. I finished that job down the hill. I can keep a good eye on him now."

He started to turn away, "Oh, when the Lao boy recovered, he said, 'Confucian kill mosquito'."

Before I could react, Phillip Wilde wandered over to join us.

"Hey Ben," he said. "Where's your young helper?"

"Up in his room. We were just talking about him, wondering if he picked up some loose talk about aquifers being drained."

Wilde shrugged. "Where would he hear that sort of talk?"

"So, you guys find somewhere to practise?" Ben asked

"We're taking a bit of break what with Lori being *enceinte* and all."

Once again I moved quietly away.

Clara was sitting at a low table with a blonde woman in bright Mexican prints, leaning toward her, and fingering the fabric.

"Of course," I heard Clara say, "I never buy new."

I leaned on the back rail and studied the foliage. Pine, oddly enough.

"Sorry about that," said the man, who had stolen up beside me.

"Childish, I know. Couldn't resist the urge to needle back. I'm Phillip Wilde," he said, extending his hand.

"Joanna, Joanna Hunter."

"Yes, you're Colin's mother-in-law."

"Yes, that's his mother, Clara, over there."

"Oh, I've met her–at the bakery. She introduced herself."

"I can believe it," I said. We both laughed.

"I hear you're Canadian. I've spent a good deal of time there. Performing of course, but I mean on vacation. I fish up in B.C. with my friend David. You've probably heard of him, Suzuki, David Suzuki."

"Our national treasure, the man who's going to save Earth single-handedly. Of course, I've heard of him. I don't watch The *Nature of Things* on a regular basis, but it's hard to avoid his ideas."

"Do you want to?'

"I can take only so much guilt, especially over things I can't change. Elephants, for example, the terrible plight of the African elephant."

"I'm not sure he's done a show on elephants."

"You know what I mean. How has he not fallen into a fatal depression?'

Phillip laughed. "I guess we all have to pick our battles. I'm particularly interested in our California condor. I have a friend who worked with the San Diego Zoo restoring the condor population. He's going to be at my place on Wednesday evening to talk about it. I'm up on Pinecliff." He reached into his shirt pocket and drew out a card. "Seven thirty or so. Have you seen a condor yet?'

"From a great distance. I was on the second floor deck at the hotel. I thought it was a crow over the golf course. Then I gradually realized it was a much bigger bird farther away, way over the meadow, just gliding."

"Yeah, they hardly ever flap their wings. They just drift on the air currents. Their wingspread is nine feet or more. Their heads are featherless, and change color when they're courting. They're making good progress in their come-back, but there are new threats to their survival."

"I've heard about the lead poisoning. Are people still hunting with lead shot?"

He smiled. "So I hear. You're welcome to bring the rest of the family."

"Thanks, but I'd probably come alone. Julia and Clara are home-bodies in the evening." So was I, but I intended to make an exception for this event.

"By the way," I said, "do you know who's responsible for those anti-Halcon Village stickers that are driving their employees crazy?"

"Absolutely not," he said, looking me full in the face. "Not my style."

On Sunday, while Colin was getting an early family dinner. Julia and I were sitting and reading. I told her about Xiao Yu's second suicide attempt and his 'confession'.

"What would make him say that?" I asked.

"Sounds like a break with reality," she said.

"A psychotic episode?"

"You could call it that, although that doesn't mean he is psychotic."

"It seems to me and to Ben," I said, "that Xiao Yu couldn't have cut the security screen or the glass. He wouldn't have the skill or the tools."

Julia sighed deeply. "It sounds as if Xiao Yu is in deep water. I hope they can get his meds right soon."

"I'm not sure I should visit him again. For a while anyway."

Julia considered this, and then she said, "What do you think, Colin?"

"If the Laos want you to visit they'll let you know. They did before. They may all feel a loss of face."

The next day it was full dark when we finished dinner. I had had to take the car home to Clara's, and leave the unlighted golf cart. The unlit street and the driveway made it so dark I had to feel my way to the front door. The motion-activated light gave no hint it detected my stumbling passage. I carried laundry, bottles of spring water, and my computer bag to the porch, banging my left leg in the process. As I opened the door into the light-filled room, I noted two large moths pressed against the screen,

It was Poirot who saw them fly in. He began scaling tall pieces of furniture, and gazing longingly at the ceiling. I thought things would settle down once the lights were off.

I was wrong.

A few hours later, I was awakened by a series of loud thumps at irregular intervals. Noisy burglar? Clara looking for a snack? Phone flashlight in hand, I ventured out of my room. There was the black and white cat on top of the stepladder Clara was using it to hang pictures. The cat was staring fixedly upward. He jumped, sailed across space, and landed on top of the cupboard eight inches from the ceiling. While that was an astonishing feat, he had missed the moth. When he tried to jump back onto the stepladder, I caught him around the middle mid-air, and thrust him through Clara's bedroom door. I closed it very, very softly.

Problem solved.

But no. One moth was now making a pass at my reading lamp. I sat weighing moth murder against patience. The moth vanished. I waited some more. Nothing. I went back to sleep.

In the morning, I felt virtuous. Moths, after all, adore light so much they sacrifice themselves to it. Why, no one knows. There's a theory, they migrate by the moon, and think any light is moonlight. But they don't seem to migrate at all. Perhaps heat draws them, or the light's wavelength, which they mistake for pheromones. I chose to fall back on the poetic and spiritual. Moths, like me, aspire to the light.

That forgiving attitude lasted twelve hours. Next night, it was the same scenario. Both moths revived, one in my bedroom, one in my bathroom. Both flew into my hair. I lashed out. What remained were two pairs of wings and two heaps of moth dust.

'Confucian kill mosquito'.

It had got colder again. I still hadn't reset the heating program. I couldn't figure out how, and I thought it presumptuous to try. My bedroom and bathroom were toasty warm when I woke up, but the main room wasn't. That and what must have been depression–or possibly anxiety-kept me from leaping out of bed.

There came a morning when I woke at 4:45 A.M just enough to smell wood smoke. Someone, going to work at 5, must have put on a stove, I decided. Half asleep though I was, I doubted that.

I was still asleep at 7:45 when a noise started irritating me. Something very loud was thundering overhead, and then whining off into the distance. I considered this in my dreaming state. I would fall back to sleep in the interval, and then come back to annoyed consciousness. I was about to snooze again, when I sat bolt upright and sprang out of bed.

"Idiot," I said.

Wrapped in a robe, I dashed to the door, unlocked two locks and strode to the edge of the deck. There was a fire burning on top of the nearest peak.

Two helicopters were flying along the highest ridge. One veered and headed straight into the smoke. For a moment, I couldn't see it. Then it emerged flying toward the village with a stream of water trailing from behind it.

It turned again, heading away from me, flying lower and lower until it disappeared behind the trees. It was filling up at the pond below Julia and Colin's house.

The smaller helicopter stayed on the ridge, moving back and forth over the blaze.

In a few minutes the bigger one was back in the air, heading directly into the smoke.

No one else was out watching. It might have been an ordinary morning, except for the racket of the helicopters.

"One helicopter is not enough," I said out loud.

My eyes were beginning to sting. Everything was tinder dry. It hadn't rained since May, except for that one downpour while we were still in the hotel.

One summer, in Greece, a fire broke out on the slopes above our campground. It crept steadily down from the heights, until it reached the shrub-covered hill across the highway. Huge bellied planes flew down over the Gulf of Corinth, scooped up water, and returned to bomb the blazing hillside. The flames were so close that we could feel the heat. Ash fell on the campground, and the smoky air was not breatheable. I wanted to get the hell out, but I didn't have a car. My Greek host took a typically Greek attitude. He shrugged his shoulders. We could always walk into the sea, he said. True enough. It was shallow and warm, but cooler than the air. Greek disaster planning did not impress me. In the end, the fire went out, leaving a desolate, blackened landscape, and an acrid smell.

This was not Greece. This was the good old U.S.A.

Enough of this fear mongering. Get dressed.

Once I had got more or less ready for whatever was going to happen next, and had checked the helicopter's progress five times, I got onto the *Mountain Prospector's* website. The report said it was a small, one-acre fire on Timber Mountain, reported at 7:30 a.m., and thought to have been started by a hunter. Deer season had begun the week before.

That made sense. Hunters would be out waiting for dawn when the deer feed. Why should such wilderness know-it-all's care about code reds or urgent signs banning all open fires?

Could I have reported it earlier, if I had roused myself at 4:45?

Now the noise was continuous. Going out I saw that there were two more helicopters dropping water. As one turned back toward the pond, another rose, trailing water as it climbed.

The landline rang. It was Julia. I could hardly hear her for the roar of the helicopters on her end.

"We're at ground zero here," she shouted. "There's always a helicopter filling up at the pond. They put down a hose and suck the water up. How does it look to you? We can't see from here."

"The smoke is less black and more grey. I guess that's steam. The black area is getting smaller and smaller. I'm so glad they sent in more helicopters. One was never going to do the trick."

"No," she said. "It was a losing battle."

I could hear a siren passing her house.

"Here come the marines," she said.

Suddenly, something occurred to me.

"I need to wake up Clara," I said.

It took me a while. I had to touch her arm before she opened her eyes. She joined me on the deck a few minutes later.

"Oh, my goodness," she said, watching the activity above the village.

After a while, two of the helicopters flew off to the east. Only the first one laboured on, dumping water on the dying blaze.

It was still at the job, when I had eaten breakfast. Clara sat on the couch drinking her tea.

I sat down in the lazy-boy chair. "That was an awful racket, but it didn't wake you up." I let that sink in. "You need to be able to hear up here, Clara. How else will you know when there are fires?"

"You're right," she said, nodding thoughtfully.

"I'll worry about you when I'm gone," I added.

She was still nodding.

There was of course, a serious flaw in my argument. Hearing aids are taken out at night.

By 9:30, the last helicopter was gone. As I rode past the fire station, I saw two firemen standing beside a truck with a walkie-talkie. I stopped the golf cart.

"Is it out?" I asked.

One of them shrugged. "We've got seven trucks and 50 fire-fighters up there, putting out hotspots."

"They were able to drive in?"

"Oh, no, it's quite a long hike. There's an old trail across the Molloko Wilderness."

"How do you think it started?"

"Probably a hunter, trying to keep warm," the other guy said.

Around 2 p.m. when I went to the store, I saw five fire trucks in the parking lot. Business would be good for the pizza place, open early for a change.

The Thursday paper gave the size of the burn as less than an acre and the number of firefighters as twenty-two.

14

RAISED BY PUPPETS

Phillip Wilde's house sat high up, just below Timber Mountain, looking down over the village. It was a huge log home with an encircling deck. Two standing bears, intricately carved out of tree trunks, guarded the entrance. They towered over mere humans. But did they keep out bears?

It was actually Max who met me at the door.

"Good, you came," he said. "I suggested Phillip ask you."

"Why would you do that?" I asked.

"Keep your friends close but your enemies-"

"Closer. Is that your own original idea?" I asked, sarcastically.

"Some say Sun Tzu, some say Machiavelli. I say *The Godfather Part Two*."

There were about twenty-five people scattered about the huge room, and outside on the deck, three of them in the hot tub.

Phillip greeted me by name, and poured me a glass of *Pino Grigio*. "Help yourself to food," he said. "Julien got the salmon this morning in L.A. and poached it for us. He can't be here of course and neither can Lori. Busy night at Le Petit Breton."

"Thank you. It looks great," I replied, but in fact, being the *naïf* I was, I had already eaten dinner with Julia and Colin.

I carried a plate of bite-sized pieces to a corner and sat down. My chair was beside a console table, near the sliding doors. The wall of windows rose two and a half stories, and because of the altitude was not yet in darkness.

I was sharing the corner with two Sheba Inus who were snoozing in their rattan bed. I knew these 'bush-coloured' Japanese dogs because my ex-husband has had a series of them. They look like a fourteen-inch high golden Huskie. They say if you feed a dog and give it shelter, the dog thinks you are God. If you do the same for a cat, the cat thinks it is God. Sheba Inus are more catlike. They will honour you with a cuddle from time to time; otherwise, they are self-possessed, and not given to tail-wagging welcomes. Blake's dog stands at the top of the entryway, and watches him come in. They don't bark unless they are alarmed. They are extremely decorous.

Stairs led up to a gallery that crossed over the front entrance. The open plan kitchen was on my right beside the dining room. The two rooms were cosier with lower ceilings. A two-sided stone fireplace divided them.

Everything was on a heroic scale. The great room was so large it made a grand piano seem small. A fieldstone fireplace rose on an angled wall, all the way to the ceiling. On it hung a painting of a condor seen from below and almost life-sized. Beside the fireplace climbed a fieldstone bookcase, a library ladder at the ready.

The books were clearly not decorative. They were every shape and size, and well used.

The couch and chairs in front of the fireplace were beautiful brown or tan leather, the tables, slabs of wood edged in bark. There was another similar seating area across the room from me, with a view down the mountain.

Against the wall near the fireplace, was a large screen, which looked as if it could disappear when not wanted.

Shortly, Malcolm sat down on the other side of the console, with a much fuller plate, and a glass of scotch. He had trimmed his grey beard and looked spiffy in a lime green golf shirt.

"I hardly recognized you," I said,

"Out of the overalls, I'm hard to identify." This idea clearly amused him. "Let's see if I can identify you. Orange, fuchsia and black stripes, black shoulders. I may have to hear your song or ascertain where you nest."

"I nest wherever I can. At present on Alaska, I'm a sort of cuckoo or ovenbird. I share other birds' nests, but I draw the line at kicking out their offspring. As for my song, I could give you a few bars of *O Canada*."

"So a melodious singer."

"More odious at this point, although I still dream I am on-stage singing Carmen."

He chuckled. "Mal Fletcher," he said, shaking my hand. "I'm putting you down in my log book as a fall-foliaged Joanna Hunter bird."

This was not the Malcolm I had met at the transfer site. It was more a Malcolm with the playful spontaneity of two scotches, downed quickly on an empty stomach.

He ate in silence for a while. When he looked up, he seemed suddenly grave. "I feel I owe you an apology," he said. "I am here. I could drive Star Shine to Bakersfield, but she won't let me. She doesn't even want to see me. Has someone bring her garbage to the transfer site. It's my fault. I was a shit of a father. I came here to try to make up for that-especially now she's ill."

"Don't apologize to me. I've got to do something. I can't just take up space."

"Does she talk about me?"

"Only once when I asked, but her answer was a tsunami of words. She said you like Led Zeppelin."

He laughed, back into his initial mood. "That old story of how I lost my innocence in Frisco. You know I didn't actually attend the concert. I heard it free from a rooftop along with a bunch of pot-smoking hippies."

"Do you still listen to them?"

"Sometimes. *Stairway to Heaven, Rock and Roll–It's been a long, been a long, a long, lonely, lonely time.* Since what I wonder."

"Love."

But as if I hadn't spoken, he went on, "When my mind is occupied, most of it just seems like noise. I prefer the classical music I play at the site now. It seems to calm me. God knows I need it. People can't seem to master the simplest recycling rules."

"Simple? Hum," I said. "But I know what you mean about music. I haven't listened to music this summer. I can't even stretch to the classics. I turn it on; then I turn it right off. It distracts me, from what I don't know."

From figuring out who's trying to kill me maybe.

"Downright treasonable not to listen to music, in this community with so many out-of-work musicians, your son-in-law included. He's not here, I see."

"No. My daughter, has been ill too, and he likes to stay in with her in the evenings."

There was a pause.

"So how is *my* daughter?"

"She says she feels better now she's finished the chemo. It's good her sister came. Did you see Star Dancing?"

"Dance? Yeah. Briefly. She brought the garbage up."

I paused and considered. "You know I met a woman who lived for years with Stage 4 breast cancer. It had gone to her liver long since."

He looked at me with interest.

"That's the only thing I learned at that support group. I never went back. Too drear. My own case was as drear as I could take."

"You had breast cancer?"

"Stage 1 tumours, seventeen years ago."

"A real survivor!"

"So they say."

"I know what you mean. I survived 'Nam. Calling yourself a survivor could queer the deal even now." He paused, "In fact, that's maybe what happened to me and a lot of the fellows."

"We're still here."

He sighed deeply. "Hard enough to lose Star Shine's mother at such a young age."

People had been moving chairs around in order to have a view of the screen.

"Fill your glasses and find a spot where you can see," Phillip announced.

Malcolm had one more thing to say, "I feel as if I need to make my mark once before I die."

Then we moved more to the centre of the room. Gradually, the shuffling died down. Phillip was standing beside his grand piano, one hand casually resting on its lid, as if he were about to begin a concert. He was tall, tanned, and attractive. His silver hair fell loose to his shoulders. He smiled and focused on us.

"Before I introduce our speaker for the evening, I want to welcome Warren Oliver, who, as you know, is chief executive officer for Halcon Ranch, and give him the opportunity to say a few words."

Heads turned as Oliver came forward from behind me. He was cultivating an informal look with a beige cashmere pullover. He spoke from the centre of the room, turning as he did so as to take us all in.

"Thank you, Phillip. Phillip and I have known each other for many years, as some of you know, and although we don't always agree, we respect each other. It's possible to disagree and still be friends, although you wouldn't know that from the state of our government." A chuckle swept over the room. "Some things we do agree on, however, and one of those is the importance of the California condor. I'm sure you are as interested as I am in tonight's presentation."

Oliver turned to the speaker, who was older, slight, bespectacled, and clearly uneasy about speaking publicly.

Phillip began, "Some of you will be familiar with the story of how the California condor has made a come-back, although I've made a point of inviting newcomers. My friend, Bert Edwards, had a hand in that recovery. Dr. Edwards studied biology at UCLA, and worked with the San Diego Wild Animal Park to restore the condor population. Retired now, he lives in Coney Creek. Please welcome him."

Bert nodded deferentially at the applause, and flashed his first picture on the screen, a gliding condor seen from above.

"This was taken from a glider, about as close as you can get to a hunting condor."

He was off and running. His shoulders straightened, he had lost all trace of self-consciousness. His grey face grew pink with animation.

"The story of the condor recovery hinges on two individual birds AC 9 and SBF. The 1986 death of SBF, the last breeding female in the wild, finally resolved the conflict over whether to manage the species. Opposition to the recovery program collapsed. Capture of the remaining wild condors began. On Easter Sunday, 1987 the last remaining wild condor, the wily seven-year old male, AC 9, was captured at Bitter Creek. We used a net 'shot from guns'. He was feasting on the carcass of a stillborn calf, one of many such baits we had set for him. I was there watching–in a covered earth pit. It was very moving. If we were wrong, this magnificent creature had roamed the skies for the last time. If we were right, it would come back in larger numbers."

Anxiety rules in the middle of events, I thought.

"This summer the number of condors is over 400, 219 in the wild and 206 in captivity. Here in the village, you can see them soaring over the golf course."

People nodded and began to talk about when and where they had spotted condors.

He went on to correct the notion that the species was a million years old-it was only about 10,000. He indicated that, as a vulture, it thrived around cattle ranches, but not around the native people who killed the *molloko* for ceremonial objects, or around gold rushers, who used their quills to package gold.

Throughout the talk, he had flashed images on the screen, but now he picked up something long made of brown leather and fitted it over his right hand.

"This is one of the puppets we used to rear the young in captivity."

The bare yellow head looked exactly like the condor heads we had been seeing in photographs.

"By 1986, we knew it was not loss of territory that was decimating the population, nor infertility–although the female lays an egg only once every two years. Condors were dying of poison, principally from lead shot in unclaimed kills. Hunting with lead bullets is now illegal throughout the condor's range. They were also dying of ingesting our garbage-bottle caps, glass shards, etc.

He went on to describe taking the one egg laid by a captive female to be raised by puppets. He waggled his puppet arm. "Taking the egg led to double clutching. The female would lay a second egg to replace the one we took. The parents themselves raised the second egg. This method doubled the number of chicks."

Then he demonstrated how the puppet head, every bit as ugly as the real thing, would be used to feed the chicks with the help of a blonde woman, whose hand became the chick.

"At the same time, the young were conditioned to fear humans. One person would edge into view, and someone else would rush in and turn the chick up side down. As my boss at the San Diego Zoo said it was a good day when condors threw up at the sight of a person. They were also conditioned to avoid power lines by getting mild shocks from mock lines."

We couldn't suppress our shocked laughter.

"In the early nineties, the first group of California condors was released at Sespe Condor Sanctuary. In May 2002, AC 9 was returned to the wild after fifteen years. They are now in six different areas, including one flock on the Utah/Arizona border. And they are of course here in Los Padres National Forest."

Phillip stepped forward to thank Bert as applause died down. He added, "You'll see notices in the *Prospector* about a town hall meeting in a few weeks–at the library, town halls being thin on the ground up here. It will be about the proposed Halcon Village on Halcon Ranch property. I notice that you're not calling it Condor Village, Warren."

This got some laughter.

"Our proposal is to build a resort, including two luxury hotels," said Oliver.

"Multi-storey luxury hotels," said Phillip.

There will be helicopter pads…" said Oliver.

"For helicopter playboys…" added Phillip.

"A golf course," Oliver was smiling at Phillip, but not terribly amused. "Homes, some estate-sized…"

"Five thousand houses," put in Phillip. "And all in the middle of the condor's range."

It's a big ranch," said Oliver, "and the condors are getting their share of it. We are nearing the end of a successful negotiation with the major ecological stakeholders. The community will enjoy the benefit of this development in many ways, including access to wilderness areas and Halcon Village amenities."

When it was clear he had finished speaking, Max sprang up. "Just to say we do not support the poster campaign, and we urge you to bring forward any information you have."

The audience began to move, some to the speaker. No one apparently had urgent information about tacks. Malcolm poured himself another glass of scotch. A group retreated to the back deck from which a fragrant odour began to emanate. I didn't want more wine. I was driving. I helped myself to a couple of small dessert squares from the village bakery, and returned to my chair beside Malcolm.

"You know how every last one of those condors has a number on it, like a licence number, clearly visible, back and front, how they're kept on a carcass leash. Their managers leave their food for them. In what way are they still wild?" He asked.

I studied his flushed and pained face for a minute and said, "They've endured."

"Is that all that matters? Does everything have to be tamed?" he asked.

I glanced down at the little dogs, still sleeping beside me. Malcolm wasn't talking condors or over-bred dogs either.

Max sauntered over. "You have to be careful of this one, Mal. She's the enemy. She thinks a bunch of us have plotted and executed a series of eco-terrorist actions. She's got her sights on the Kentucky Five. She thinks we've got the necessary skill set, well us and Zach."

"When did I ever say that?"

"You implied it darlin'. I inferred it. All it'll take is a deadly shooting to cinch the deal."

"Oh you mean Phillip, the marksman," Malcolm was working hard to keep up and beginning to slur his words. "Well, don't count me out. I was in the Fifth Marine Snipers in Nam."

The effort of that speech made him lose his balance momentarily.

"Hey," said Max. "Let me ride you home on my Harley. I'll bring you back for your car tomorrow."

"He can sack out here," Phillip said as he joined us. "He's done that before now."

"Thanks, I'll prob'ly do that," said Mal, trundling off to the nearest soft chair.

Jackson came in the door, still wearing his brown uniform.

"Jackie," cried Phillip. "Let me get you a coke."

"Had a late shift. Couldn't get here any earlier."

"Have you met Joanna, Colin's mother-in-law? Joanna, this is my friend Jackson."

"You're the one thinks I brought the bear back, and sicced it on Tom Braddock."

My mouth fell open. "Al Guevara," he said.

"Friend of yours?" I asked.

'I wouldn't say so. He's trying to shake something loose I guess. I told him what I'd tell you. There may have been a truck with a trap up on the mountain that day, but the bear ended up in Sequoia National Forest."

"A sort of farewell passage, like driving the hearse past the deceased's home?"

"Could be. Anyway there's no conclusive evidence that the killer bear was the trapped bear. And there is conclusive and continuing evidence that the trapped bear is a long way north east, moving farther every day."

I felt exposed, long dress or not, and shivered in the cool evening air.

"Jackie, let's light the fire and close the doors," Phillip said.

"Don't bother for me," I said. "I have to put this old bode to bed."

"Nonsense," said Phillip, "I'm going to play. You choose." He stood waiting an answer.

"Chopin," I said.

He guided me to the softest chair in the room, and went to the piano. Jackson was lighting the fire that lay ready. Phillip's fingers hovered for a minute over the keys and then he began-*The Warsaw Concerto*.

How did he know?

I had learned to love it from my grade one teacher, Miss Graham, who told us the story of the Warsaw Ghetto, and the Jews who were trapped there.

As always, I was swept up in the music, the rising urgency of the beginning and then the quiet simple melody. Even without the philharmonic back up of violins, it tore my heart.

For many years after I left that early school, I seldom heard the piece. Then it came back to me when I studied music in a city school. I loved it as I had loved Miss Graham. It transported me back to a darkened hall in May 1943, and the Red Cross Campaign to raise funds for war relief. The music had a martial passage too, defiant and urgent, calling forth the warrior.

When my grandson, Josh, was two, we visited his Polish grandfather in Queens. He showed Julia and me his tattooed number from Auschwitz. The Warsaw Ghetto had cut short his medical training, and led him on to the camp. After the war, he became a radiologist in the States, but his grandson had fulfilled his dream and become a doctor.

Meeting him then, when Josh was two, I felt as if I had connected with him when I was seven, listening to Chopin's concerto.

Warren Oliver had sat down next to me to listen to the music.

When it ended, he said, "I have always loved listening to Phillip play, especially Chopin. I hoped that one of my daughters would take up the piano, but they both quit lessons. I guess we don't have the musical gene. What about you?"

"I sang. I loved singing, but I never played an instrument. My daughter played the flute in high school, but, no, we don't have much of a musical gene either."

"Do you still sing?"

I shook my head. "And certainly not up here. I can't get enough breath."

"I hope to see you at the library presentation," he said as he stood up.

15

TOO MANY MUSLIMS

There wasn't a single shawarma shop in Bear Mountain Place, but I was about to learn there were too many Muslims.

As I parked my golf cart beside a big maroon Buick, I knew that I was going to have to wait for my hair appointment. There was a Stetson lying on the leather seat. I tried to guess who it was who was going to keep me waiting – a big, old cowboy getting short back and sides?

The cowboy had on beautifully tooled, high-heeled boots, and jeans studded with rhinestones. She had long blonde hair, into which Tony Alvarez was winding tin foil.

"Is that your Buick out there?" I asked her.

"Yaas ma'am," she drawled. "My 1989 Buick Le Sabre. Ain't she a beauty? My last big purchase before we had to take to these here hills. I drove her up when we left L.A."

"Isn't it terrible on gas."

"Don't go anywhere," she said, shaking her head. "Just pick up the mail, do a few errands." Her drawl began to vanish. "Did you see those luscious leather seats? Yum, yum."

"Does it slew on the curves?"

"That baby takes the curves just fine, none of that rocking-over, shit- suspension the cheaper cars had back then. She has deep comfort, rocks you like your mama. You into cars?"

"I own a 2013 Toyota Yaris, two door, which I'd give my eye teeth to have here. But once upon a time, I had a '67 Dodge Charger with a 440 engine. I used to turn heads."

"You've forsaken Detroit," said Tony.

"Well, Detroit forsook me. The Plymouth K car broke down at every family crisis. It needed a new engine before it hit 75,000 K."

"What's that mean?" asked the woman.

"About half as many miles," said Tony.

"I've had four Toyotas. They can go 300,000 K. If you wanted to, you could drive them twenty years," I said.

"I've driven my baby twenty-six," she said, smiling with self-satisfaction.

As Tony washed my hair, he kept talking to Beth Anne. They moved from American cars to offshore manufacturing, and Tony was getting wound up.

"They're killing America!" he declared.

I tuned back in.

They were not the capitalists who had their goods made cheap in China. *They* were Muslims. *They* were coming in hordes, and *they* were coming in order to overthrow the American way of life.

I just about did a head swivel to catch them in the act, but Tony had my hair in a towel vice.

Driving south from Casablanca, singing, "Would you know we're riding on the Marrakesh express', a camel tethered in a field, fragrance of orange blossoms high on a ruined wall, a mother in a hijab pouring boiling water on a big lump of sugar and mint leaves, we four on cushions waiting for tea in a stranger's home, the daily downpour, a soaked and shuddering child, a kindly restaurant owner giving her red wine, cobras charmed in the marketplace, the grace and sway of djellabas, the sudden cry of the muzzein, dust, the heady smell of camel hide and hash.

Rumi, the dervish poet, a drunken lover of God, "Whoever brought me here will have to take me home".

Even the fall of the twin towers could not obliterate what open-hearted Morocco had taught my children and me about Muslims.

Tony started to cut my hair. The discussion grew more outraged. He gestured to Beth Anne with both comb and scissors. I sat very still.

Every single Muslim migrant was intent on ruining the United States of America. In twenty years, they would have destroyed Christianity, and taken over government.

I said, "Have you ever met a Muslim." But no one heard me.

I couldn't stand it any longer.

"You are wrong," I said, "You are wrong." I repeated more loudly.

They stared at me in astonishment. She's not just a head of hair.

"How can you possibly think this country is that weak?" I tried to get my thoughts in order.

"How could you ever think that a few barbaric oddballs, who don't even understand their own religion, could seriously harm this strong, confident, resourceful, resilient, and inventive country? My God, there are three hundred million of you!"

I had no desire to be American, but my reasons were mere nitpicking compared to America's unstoppable energy.

If nothing else, my outburst killed the conversation.

I got the opportunity to show off my new hairdo later that afternoon. I drove Clara down to visit the co-owner of the red MGB.

Arta Dietzen was by no means just the wife of Matthew Greaves. She was the author of fifteen best selling romance novels available in drug stores, for the convenience of the romantically minded picking up medication. Their titles began with *Love at the Aswan Dam*, went on to *Love in Bombay*, *Love in Canberra*, *Love in Denmark*, and had now got to *Love in Oswego*. She published at least one title a year. I definitely had to live long enough to see if there would be a *Love in Zanzibar*.

I stopped the Honda, and pushed the button on the gate's intercom. The gate ground slowly open. The house was not visible until we came around a bend and down a slope. It hugged the earth, totally unlike Phillip's towering wooden home perched on a height.

This house was in the Spanish mission style, adobe walled, not in bright white, but a duskier colour like the sand it rose from. The driveway was paved in brick of a similar shade. Two date palms were the only perpendiculars. A four-car garage stood in its own wing on the left, looking like the stables that adjoined them. It seemed tasteless to leave our vehicle in front, marring the façade.

Arta greeted us as we climbed down from the car. She was blonde, about Julia's age, bosomy and well padded. She had on a wide-brimmed sun hat and a brightly flowered cotton dress.

"So good you could come," she enthused. "You must be Joanna. My husband told me how funny you are, and Clara says you've been such a help to her. I'm Arta. Come in, come in. Matthew isn't here. He's out riding with our friend Warren. They've become BBFs in the last few months."

BBFs?" said Clara.

"Best buddys. I thought we'd just go on through to the back patio." She led us at speed through a room full of heavy, dark chests and tables, chintz chairs and couches.

"What lovely flowers," Clara said, squeezing a word in edgewise. Indeed, large bouquets adorned every surface, all of them white.

"Oh, yes. Today's the day they are flown in, well, one of the two days. The helipad is behind the garages, a little too close to the horses. Imelda!" she called, "you can bring the drinks out now."

The patio was shaded by grape vine, a very old vine judging by the size of its main branch.

"We can move into the sun if you feel cool," she said, as we took our seats in the padded rattan chairs. I had chosen a *chaise longue*, preferring to have my feet up. "Ah, here's the sangria and the iced tea."

Because I was driving, I had decided not to drink alcohol, but I realized I needed a little help to survive this effusiveness.

"I'll have just a little sangria," I said, at the same moment as Clara.

This was deemed highly amusing and we joined in Arta's laughter.

"So do you read romance?" she asked me.

"I'm reading Diana Gabaldon's *Outlander* series right now. I started it after watching the series on television."

"Oh, yes," Arta said with a sniff. "Gabaldon. She insists her books are not just romance novels, but I could teach that woman a thing or two about structure. Her books just slop all over the place. What's her editor up to anyway? Does she even have an editor? What's she written eight of them now? I could show her how to tighten them up, and turn that into sixteen perfectly marketable books."

"She thanks her editor for letting her write as long a book as she wants," I said. "And she says that her books are a study of a married couple's love, whereas romance novels tend to end with wedding bells."

"Whatever," said Arta. "And you, Clara?"

"I mostly read what I can find at the thrift store. I like a good mystery. Joanna has introduced me to a bunch of writers I've never heard of before. I bought a lot of their books at the Friends of the Library book sale. Less that $10, so many I had to make two trips to the car," she laughed. "But I do read a romance book from time to time."

"I'll let you have some of mine when you go."

"You've done very well from your writing," Clara observed.

"Yes, all of this is mine. Of course, Matthew pitches in, and he's done very well himself especially lately in China. He owns the Beverly Hills house. But I'm comfortably placed." She smiled smugly and gazed out and down to the river, or what would have been the river in wetter times. Now it was a ten-foot deep stone-lined gulch. The large stones tumbled about spoke of its past fury.

"I'd love to have rose gardens," she said. "The thing that stops me is how it looks, wasting so much water."

Beyond the bricked patio there was a hedge that smelled like thyme, and then chaparral, wild and drying in the sun, white sage and rabbit bush.

"I try to be ecologically correct. I want to keep my reputation spotless now that I've signed up as the poster girl for the Halcon Village project." She laughed at her self-description. "I've already put my name in for one of the penthouse condos - for guests you know, although it doesn't look as if the thing will get off the ground for years. There's a town hall meeting in a couple of weeks. Things are pretty well settled. The major environmental groups are examining our offer. The offer's so good they can't hold out against it. So this is really an information meeting. I hope you both can come."

Public relations, I thought.

"Yes," said Clara, "Joanna mentioned it. She went to a meeting about the condor at Phillip What's-his-name's, you know the pianist.'

"Oh, Phillip Wilde," scoffed Arta.

"I love this place and it's so important to me to preserve it," she went on. "I bet you don't know why Debritt has a French name."

At last a story.

"Well, seems this French trapper named Pierre De Britt-two words–was killed here, by a grizzly bear in 1868, and the place was named for him. A curious thing-a memorial of the event was carved into an oak tree that stood near the spot. Over the years, the bark grew over the inscription, but a group from Bakersfield eventually removed it, and there was the inscription in reverse on the back of the bark. It's in the Fort Halcon museum now. You can go see it. I believe there's also a plaque near the original site."

We contemplated this as we attended to our drinks. I had switched to iced tea, which should be strong enough if the stories kept coming.

"Fort Halcon was the first military site in the interior of California. That was 1854, but three years later it was badly damaged in the Fort Halcon earthquake. Really the quake was centered some miles farther northwest in Parkfield - 7.9 on the scale- felt as far as Vegas and the Gulf of California. The fort had extensive damage."

Imelda emerged from the house with a plate covered by a white napkin.

"Ah," cried Arta, "some of Imelda's chocolate chip cookies."

Excellent, a sugar substitute for alcohol. The tea wasn't enough to withstand Atra's charm after all.

Arta picked up her phone. "Cammie," she said, "come down for cookies and tea. We have guests. Bring whatever you've got. "

"Where was I?" she asked. "Oh, yes, in the early twenties, when the ridge road was the only highway-"

"Oh I knew the ridge road," declared Clara. "My folks used to drive us up it to my cousins in Monterey. It was a twisty, long road. An accident could close it right down, and there were lots of accidents in those days. We kids would get car sick when we were moving, and bored to death when we were standing still."

"How interesting. You rode the ridge road! Do you remember the big Debritt Hotel, Spanish colonial, very posh. Movie stars stayed there. It must have been at its height when you drove by it."

"It had gambling before Vegas I think," said Clara, "and didn't the Lindberghs used to fly in there?"

"Oh, yes and Clark Gable and Carol Lombard came, even Bugsy Siegel, all the big names. It went down hill later. Got more or less condemned by the county. Stopped paying the bribes that let them have gambling, I guess," she laughed. "Business had fallen off by then. It was torn down in 1968, after only forty-seven years. I feel the hotels in the Halcon Village proposal will bring back that sense of cachet to the area. It will be glamorous again."

"Does it need cachet and glamour? Isn't that L.A.'s role? I asked. "What about the condors?"

"Does it need condors? They're the ugliest creatures! Have you taken a look at that face? Only a mother-" she laughed.

"Have you watched them in flight? They're a magnificent link to the past," I said.

"God damned vultures, you ask me," Arta said, lighting a cigarette. "Sorry, I'll blow the other way. You know, when they rounded them all up, and took them into custody, someone said breeding them in captivity would turn them into 'feathered pigs'. Well now, pigs do fly."

She laughed gaily. I wasn't sure what expression I had plastered on my face. I was never good at concealing my feelings. It didn't matter, apparently, for she was completely taken up by her joke.

"Come to the meeting. I need your support. When Matthew brought Clara here, I thought, here's a chance for me to make contact with the ordinary mountain people, and bring them round to my point of view.

At my age, you could rob banks without being identified. Old people are invisible unless, like Clara, they are cute. Clara should definitely not rob banks. Now I was invisible, and ordinary, as well as a possible terrorist and a police informant.

"Warren, Warren Oliver, the CEO of Halcon Ranch will be giving the presentation, power point and all and we'll be handing out little condor puppets."

"Puppets?" I said. "We'll definitely be there."

It was a rude thing to say, but Arta didn't notice.

A tall, slim, dark-haired woman wearing very short, raggedy cutoffs issued forth from the house, and swept toward Arta bearing a file folder.

"There, you go," she announced, throwing it down, and pouring herself a large glass of sangria.

"Cammie, I'd like you to meet Clara and Joanna," said Arta. "Cammie is my personal assistant."

"Camille," said Cammie, striding over to shake my hand. She had a very firm grip. "Camille Costa."

"Are you also Arta's editor?"

Camille smiled.

"No, my editor is Josephine," said Arta. "She works for my publisher and has her office in Los Angeles. Cammie helps at an earlier stage in the writing. Don't you, dear?"

Camille was wolfing down a cookie, and had making impressive inroads into her sangria. She smiled enigmatically again. "Somewhat earlier," she said.

"A researcher?"

"Among other roles."

Two more dissimilar women would be hard to imagine. Arta was soft and southern, a long haired lazy cat. Camille was taut and electric, a 'cat on a hot tin roof'.

How, I wondered earlier, was Arta able to produce so many books?

The folder, lying on the wide arm of Arta's chair its tab facing me, read 'Q- final'. 'P' was presumably at the printers.

"So what's 'S' going to be about?" I wondered out loud.

"Oh, S!" said Arta, and grinned wickedly at Camille.

"'S' is going to be a bombshell," Camille said, gleefully, "if anybody can figure who *Love at Sequoia Ranch* is actually about."

"It's just a bit of a tease," Arta added. "A good friend can take a tease surely."

Sequoia? Sequoia National Forest, a few hours north, was the site of our old camping ground, Peppermint Creek, and the place where a certain bear was rumoured to be relocated.

Half an hour later full of chocolate chips, laden with bags of books, and vowing to go to the meeting, we climbed back into the Honda.

"Oh, by the way," Arta called, "I'm having a little reception after the presentation. I'd love you to come to that too."

As ordinary mountain people, we promised we would.

She had been holding one of the huge vases of flowers, which she now handed through the open door to Clara. "You can bring the vase back next time you visit. You remind me so of my dear mother."

"Is she still with us?" Clara asked, but Arta shook her head sadly, and stepped back to wave goodbye.

The car instantly filled with the over-powering scent of lilies, the scent of death to some, although Christians saw them as a sign of resurrection. Clara sat apprehensively embracing the crystal vase, the flowers obscuring her view.

I took the first right turn onto the main street of Douglas Peak. Whenever we came down the mountain, we brought a list of things we needed, things the Bear Mountain Place Market didn't have, or which were high priced there. Today there was a police car blocking the road, so I parked in a small lot in front an empty store.

A policewoman was standing beside her car and near her was a daughter of the Mexican restaurant owner.

"Hi, Clara," she said. "The house next door to us is on fire." She drew us toward the sidewalk away from the cop. "They say the guy living there is the one who caused the fire on Timber Mountain."

I could see three fire trucks crowded onto the side street opposite the grocery store. "Is it bad?"

"Really bad," the thirteen-year old said. "He's not going to have a place to live."

"What about your house?" asked Clara.

"It's okay. The firemen hosed it down good. I guess it'll stink some."

"Can we go to the store?" I called to the policewoman.

"Sure, but stay that side of the street."

I couldn't talk Clara out of buying a heavy bottle of spring water. I just hoped I would find someone in the parking lot, to carry it back to the roadblock. It turned out to be Detective Guevara, who made a big show of rushing over to help the old girls.

"Let me give you a hand, ladies," he said, springing to our side. As we walked, he said quietly, "Jergensen called me about this fire. I asked him to, if there were any more ecological events. The rumour's been all over town that this guy was the hunter who started the fire on Timber Mountain, so it could be tit for tat."

"How did the house fire start?"

"Not sure at this point. Arson for sure. Slow fuse, I'd say. The guy left for work around six. His wife's long gone. Separated. Somebody must have got in before daylight, and rigged it up. Fortunately the propane didn't explode. We'll know more when it cools down enough to permit entry."

We had reached the car, and were loading the groceries into the hatchback.

"Your going up the hill? I wonder if you'd do me a favour. The guy's sitting in the patrol car over there. He needs to be driven up to Woodlake Trailer Park, but he refuses to let us drive him. Thinks it will give people the wrong idea."

"Well, sure, I guess." I was looking at Clara.

"Of course we will," she said.

Our passenger emerged from the sheriff's car, clutching a large, longhaired, brown cat.

Guevara introduced us to Ern Dagenais, a thin young man with a tear-stained face.

"This is Tabor," he said. "The firemen got him out." He buried his face in the cat's fur.

When he was settled in the back seat of the CRV, he leaned over the cat's head and said, "Just so you know. I feel really awful about starting that fire on the mountain. I peed on it. I thought it was out. Anybody can make a mistake."

"That's so," said Clara. "You seem like a nice young man."

"I've lost everything except my pickup and Tab here. My wife left last month and took the dog. He was a good hunter."

"I'm sorry," I said. "You'll need clothes."

"My friend, Al's, about my size."

"My son-in-law has a bunch of golf shirts. He could spare you a few."

"I wouldn't mind a few t-shirts. Not sure I could wear golf shirts. Maybe another pair of jeans."

"I'm sure I can pick you up some from the thrift shop," said Clara. "You're about my son's size."

What about a razor, a toothbrush?" I asked.

"Yeah. Gone."

"Let's go over to the pharmacy and get what you need. My treat."

"Hey, do you think we could take a case of beer up to Al? To sweeten his girlfriend up. They live in a trailer, not much room for me."

Clara fished in her purse and handed him $20. "A beer will probably come in handy."

"What about your truck?" I asked.

"I'm not allowed to drive in case of shock. Plus, I had a few beers before they found Tabor here." He teared up, and buried his face in cat fur again.

"Put Tabor down on the seat, and let's go shopping," I said.

Clara was clutching her vase of lilies.

Back in the car with beer, etc. I asked, "What sort of job, do you do, Ern?"

"I'm a flagman with a road crew."

"Were you up the hill the other day, when they swept up the tacks?"

"Yeah."

"You warned me to check my tires for slow leaks. I was grateful."

Oh, yeah. You were driving a blue Prius. This your other car?"

"Neither one is my car. This one is Clara's."

"Joanna is my chauffeur," said Clara, laughing.

"Did you rent that house?" I asked.

"No. My wife and me bought it a year ago. My grandma passed, and left me the down payment."

"You must have had insurance. Mortgage companies make sure of that."

"Maybe. Ellie looked after that stuff."

"You need to get in touch with her," I said.

"No kidding!" He had leaned over between the front seats and was staring like a deer in the headlights. "Wow. Gone just like that."

"Do you have family up here?"

"Just Ellie."

Once we had dropped him, his toiletries and his beer off in the trailer park up the road, we started up the hill again.

"He's sort of nice," Clara said.

When we stepped out of the car at Clara's house, we were greeted by the snarl of chain saws. Two crews were working in the neighbourhood, taking down tall dead trees. A wood chipper whined a stuttering base note, spitting out debris.

Above Coney Valley, whole slopes were rust-coloured, marking out the rain shadow. There was another patch of dead forest this side of our village meadow. Individual trees were dying suddenly, without warning. Alive and well on one weekend visit, dead the next, even if they were ninety feet tall. There was waiting list for tree surgeons, and brush that was supposed to be gone by June 15, still stood, waiting for a spark.

The death of any tree was deeply affecting. The slaughter of a black ash for the sake of a sidewalk turned me into a letter-writing crusader years ago. But I was thankful I was not as sensitive as our friend Peter.

On our last camping trip to Peppermint Creek, Peter had crawled into his sleeping bag mid-day and covered his head with its hood. Some other campers were cutting down a sapling to burn. Peter could hear its screams.

Still I wasn't immune to tree grief. One fall morning on the way to Bakersfield, I had my eye out for the first of the almond orchards as usual, when an astonishing sight greeted me. Hundreds of trees were down, the upturned roots, naked, exposed to the highway. They hadn't been cut. They had been pushed over. Mile after mile, they lay waiting for dismemberment. I was shocked into silence.

I wasn't farmer enough any more to accept the cycle of nature. These trees were old and gnarled. In the next field, almond saplings raised their shiny new branches.

Down the street from my house in Toronto, the parks department did controlled burns under the oak trees, so I understood fire was part of the natural cycle. It cleared the forest floor, letting in sunlight, nurturing the soil and allowing certain seeds to germinate. Ern's fire had burned only an acre on Timber Mountain. Even so, paying for toiletries was as far as I was prepared to go down forgiveness road.

Then we got an urgent call from one of the Kentucky Five.

16

TOO MANY HUSBANDS

I answered the landline when it rang.

"Julia?"

"This is Julia's mother. I'll get her for you."

I handed the phone to Julia who was washing dishes.

"Who is this?" she asked. "Lori, is that you? Where are you? Hang on. I'm coming."

"Joanna," she called, and I came out of the studio, where I had been putting clothes in the washer. "Colin's got the car. Can you take me to the restaurant on the golf cart? I think something's wrong with Lori."

While I was putting on my shoes, Julia got her medical bag. She hadn't got around to mastering the golf cart.

The door to Le Petit Breton was unlocked and Lori was slouched at a table beside it, her head resting on a pile of mail, her cell phone clutched in her right hand. Her bottom was wet.

"Call 911 for an ambulance," said Julia, handing me Lori's phone.

Of course it couldn't be simple. It rang at some distant call centre, rather than at the fire station around the corner.

Julia was busy with Lori, who was conscious enough now to say 'Julia' over and over again, morphing into sobs of 'baby'.

Julia grabbed the phone out of my hand, and urgently outlined the problem. "We need a medevac to Bear Mountain Place. NOW."

"Here, help me, Joanna." She was taking the cushions off a nearby bench. Very carefully, with some help from the patient, we got her lying on them, so that Julia could examine her.

When the medics from the ambulance came through the door, Julia said, "If we get her to hospital, stat, we may be able to prevent premature delivery. She's about 30 weeks."

"The copter's on its way," said the male medic. "Are you her doctor?"

"No, but I am a doctor, and I've seen her at the clinic here."

I watched in a daze as they moved Lori to the stretcher. Julia was calling out blood pressure numbers, and heart rate, although it was clear the female medic intended to take them herself.

When Julia leaned in to speak to her, Lori grabbed her left wrist in a viselike grip. When the medic tried to pry her loose, Lori began to shriek.

"Stay, Julia."

The medics were moving the stretcher at that point, and towing Julia along.

"Get my bag," she called to me, "and meet us at the helipad."

I looked around and began to gather up the blood pressure monitor. Julia still had the stethoscope around her neck. When I had closed the black bag, I looked at the table. An Air Canada ticket and a Canadian passport lay there along with several bills. I scooped them all up and put them in my purse along with Lori's cell phone. I couldn't find her keys. I wasn't going to be able to lock the door.

The helicopter was coming in when I arrived at the fire hall. The ambulance stood open and the stretcher, Lori and Julia still conjoined, sat waiting to be loaded. I handed Julia her bag.

"Can you get Clara's car and drive down to meet me? They'll take her to Memorial," Julia said.

"Sure. Yes. I guess so."

"You've got her phone, haven't you?"

"Yes."

"We won't call Julien or Ben until we know more."

By now the noise of the helicopter and the rush of air ended discussion, and Lori was rushed aboard.

The two ambulance medics were back beside me with the empty, bloodstained stretcher. They had handed the patient over to the two on the medevac.

"You're the woman who found the Chinese kid?" said the man.

"Yes," I said.

"How is he?"

"Oh," I was very distracted. "He's recovering. He had to be hospitalized again."

I tried to focus. "I guess I'd better get moving. It's going to take me a while to get to Bakersfield."

"She's in good hands," said the woman. "Maybe pick up a coffee to go with you on the road."

I made a chai tea at Clara's, and took it with me in a travel mug.

When I got to the hospital an hour later, Julia was in a waiting area near the ICU.

"Lori's been stabilized," she said. "You've got her phone?"

I took it out. Fortunately, it was not password protected. I tapped the Contact icon. The question was who to call.

"Julien," Julia decided.

I handed the phone to her. She walked away down the corridor as she talked, but I knew she would convey the information tactfully.

"He was on his way back from L.A.," she said. "He wants me to call Ben as well."

It turned out Ben was working in Debritt, so he would go by the middle school, and pick up Zach.

"I'm going down to the cafeteria," Julia said, as she put the phone in her purse. "I didn't eat lunch. Do you want anything?"

I shook my head. "I had tea on the drive down."

I sat and stared at the opposite wall. I stared for a long time. Then I came to with a start.

"Okay, okay. Don't just sit here. Do something."

I tried to focus. What was needed here was prayer or whatever it was I did.

"Be present," I told myself.

That took an uncomfortable few minutes. There was a good deal of swirling anxiety that had to be endured. After a while, I was able to focus on Lori and the baby. I thought of my Aunt Mae. She helped me from beyond these days, the way she had once helped me in person. Perhaps, there were other allies there as well.

I didn't ask for a particular outcome. I just sat in the middle of Mae's encompassing love.

Time telescoped, so I was surprised when Ben and Zach came down the hall. Julien was a few minutes behind him.

"What do they say?" both asked at once.

"Nothing yet. She's in there," I gestured at the door to the ICU.

Julien looked as if he were about to rush it.

"What happened?" asked Ben.

Julia appeared at that point and took over.

Julien was walking in small circles while Ben leaned toward Julia as if he intended to shake more out of her. At that moment, the nurse emerged.

"All right, who's the husband?"

Each pointed at the other.

"It's complicated," I said, glancing at Zach, who was hanging back from the fray. "This is Ben, Lori's husband and this is Julien,..."

"The baby's father," said Ben.

"Right," she said, without missing a beat. "You can see her in a few minutes. She's been stabilized."

"Is the baby coming?" Julien asked.

"That remains to be seen. We're doing what we can to hold it off. The doctor will tell you more momentarily."

"But she's all right?" asked Ben.

"The baby's all right?" asked Julien.

"Lori's resting now. The baby's vitals are stable too. Time will tell. Talk to the doctor."

She gestured them to follow.

"Just a minute," I heard her call. "What about Mother?" She was looking at me.

I waved off the invitation.

Julia got Zach to sit down between us. "It's just a question of when the baby will be born," she said. "Do you know if it's a boy or a girl?"

"A girl," said Zach.

"If she's born now, she will be small and need to stay in the neonatal unit for a few weeks. It would be better if she were born later, but either way, she'll be okay, and so will your mom."

"Ben said they flew her here in a helicopter."

"That's right," said Julia. "Me too."

"Was it fun?"

"Not much. I don't like small airborne vehicles," she said. "Besides, I was paying attention to your Mom."

"Oh yeah," he said, realizing his gaff.

"So, you started school here?" I asked.

"Yeah. The cops won't let me leave."

"Oh, that reminds me. I have your passport and Air Canada ticket." I took them out of my purse.

Zach took the passport and opened it up. "This isn't mine. It says Darryl Tanner, but, hey, it's my picture."

I could see it was true. I looked at the ticket. It was made out in the same name. False name! Made sense. Zach Aldano might be small potatoes, but he seemed to be the only link to the eco-terrorists and, as such, had been ordered by the Detective Guevara not to leave town.

"Were you going home?" Julia asked.

"No, I told you. I can't." He looked at us in bewilderment.

"Did you pick up the envelope?" Julia asked me.

I shuffled through the rest of the mail. There was a brown envelope with Lori Aldano's name and Le Petit Breton's post office box number typed on a label. There was no return address. A small piece of paper fell to the floor and I bent to pick it up. When I turned it over, I saw in tiny hand-printed letters, "If you value the kid's life. Get him out of town."

I showed it to Julia and we moved out of Zach's hearing, as he stared at the passport.

"Someone wants him to go home," I said, quietly, "and not a very nice someone."

"I guess we know what precipitated labour," Julia said.

My mind was racing. Someone wanted Zach out of the way. Someone had wanted me out of the way, more permanently. If not the Kentucky Five, then who?

I looked back at the boy, small for his age, leaning forward, the passport on his lap, elbows on knees, his face in his hands. Julia went back and sat down beside him.

She was the most motherly person I knew. She began mothering at age one, when her brother was born. She delighted in it, and that was the key to her success as a doctor. She mothered her patients as they always longed to be mothered, even though they were often much older than she. For all that, she wasn't indulgent. She expected her people to stand on their own feet and take charge of their lives.

I had started mothering my siblings when I was nine. That was when we moved far away from our extended family. My mother's mental health didn't take the move well. I wasn't able to protect the little kids from the cruelty of either parent. So when my children were born, I wasn't a confident mother. I was glad to hand the role over to a tiny Glasgow woman, who mothered them and kept our home immaculate, while I went back to teaching..

"Have you any idea who would have sent this?" she asked Zach.

He shook his head, but did not raise it.

"It's all right," she said, putting her hand on his shoulder. "Don't worry about it."

Ben and Julien had come out of the ICU, and were listening intently to a doctor. Ben came toward us.

"Lori wants to see you, Julia."

When I was alone with the two men, I handed the unopened envelopes to Julien. "I picked the mail up off the table where Lori had been opening it. I couldn't lock up. She had opened this." I handed Ben the note, the ticket and passport.

"What is it?" said Julien, seeing the look of alarm on Ben's face.

"I don't know. I don't get it." He handed them to Julien.

While Julien read, Ben looked at me. "We have to tell Guevara. Zach's life is in danger," he said. "We have to tell Guevara."

We all glanced back at Zach, who still had his face buried.

"One thing at a time," said Julien. "Right now it's Lori we need to be thinking about."

"I'll call Lori's mother," Ben said to me. "She knows me better." He paused. "We don't know how long Lori will be here. It would be good to have Margarita to help out. Keep extra eyes on Zach."

"I think you need to call Guevara right away," I said."

"Somebody clearly wants Zach gone," said Julien.

Or dead, I thought.

Ben shook his head in disbelief. "I've thought from the beginning that the kid was involved in the flood and the poster thing, but I thought…"

"You thought it was the Kentucky Five, right?" said Julien. "I don't know about the rest, but I'm too busy for recreational activism. And surely, you don't suspect Lori."

"Okay," said Ben, pocketing the documents. "I'll deal with it."

"Maybe keep Zach home from school for the next few days," I suggested.

"He can hang around the restaurant," said Ben.

On the drive home, Julia said, "They won't be able to forestall labour. Once the water breaks, a small baby will more or less slip out. It's called PPROM, preterm, premature rupture of the membrane. But a 30-week plus foetus has a good chance of surviving. She would need some time in a neonatal intensive care unit. Five weeks perhaps, until she's able to feed. Getting to the hospital so soon was all to the good."

There was a message from my landlord on Julia's landline when we got home. When I called her back, I learned that the renovation of my apartment would definitely get underway again by the first of November. It would be habitable by the New Year.

I put on my shoes and hat, and stomping off down to the pond I plunked myself down on a stone at the edge of the water, and let my frustration rip. Behind it came a wave of grief. I had no home, no place to be me. Living from pillar to post was stressing me out. Watching for tripwires was stressing me out. Calling emergency services was stressing me out. Being eternally vigilant had permanently stressed me out years ago. Now a child's life was in danger.

A mother coot was teaching her two chicks to dive, and bring up food. They didn't get it. When she surfaced, they swam up to her, calling her to feed them. She dove again and again. No results. Then she gave in, and fed the nearest one what she had brought up. The other one circled back to get in on the action. She fed her too. Gradually her diving took her farther out into the pond, the chicks following.

All summer long a flat-bottomed boat had mowed the waterweed and the cattails to keep the water open. I supposed this had to do with fire fighting, more than the ecology. The reeds on the opposite bank had been trimmed back, and had turned reddish as the sun retreated south. The red-winged blackbirds still nested in throngs there. A lookout blackbird landed in the small tree above me, and whistled territorially. When it flew off, a jay took its place and scolded.

Two brown ducks silently swam around an outcropping of reeds in front of me, one much larger than the other. The larger one tipped itself head-down so its tail waggled above water. It stayed there for a long time and then, suddenly righted itself.

Lori's baby girl was born early the next morning. She weighed in at 3 ½ pounds.

Julia and I went back to the hospital that afternoon. Lori had been moved to the maternity ward. Julien, who was sitting beside her bed, got to his feet as we entered. This time, I noticed how odd it was to see him out of his chef's coat and the white bandana that tied his hair back. His hair was in fact black, his face was distinctly French, and he was a compact figure about five eight.

Lori was lying almost flat, her hair dark against the white pillows. She smiled wanly. "I walked down to see her in the NICU, but they had to get me a wheelchair. I couldn't stay. Too wobbly. Have you seen her yet?"

"Not yet, but we will," I said.

"You don't have to get up," Julia said to Julien.

"Oh no, it's fine. I'll take a walk. Can I get you coffee? I've been here a while."

"You've closed your restaurant for the interim," I observed.

"For a few days" he said. "Ben and Zach have gone down to meet Lori's mother at the airport, so I'll open again day after tomorrow."

As he went out the door, he motioned with his eyes for me to join him in the corridor.

"Ben handed over the note, the passport and the ticket to the detective. Seems the ticket was bought for cash at Bradley in LAX. That's all they know so far. Darryl Tanner was probably a Canadian kid who died young, the cops say. That's usually the case with phoney passports. Who's behind the threat, they can't say yet. Zach's not talking. Not to Ben anyway. He might open up to Margarita, I suppose, but I doubt it. The kid seems traumatized."

"Scared stiff," I said.

"Lori hasn't mentioned the threat. We didn't want to bring it up at this stage."

"It's possible she doesn't remember," I said. "That's one way of dealing."

"You think so?" He looked doubtful.

"I do," I said. "I have some experience of that." Then I went on, "Your daughter arrived safely. That's what matters now."

"It's scary looking at her. She's so tiny."

"She'll be okay. Preemie care is so much better than it used to be."

"And then there's the restaurant! Apparently, it's best if the parents spend as much time as possible with these babies, but I've got to stay on top of it."

"Will it be a serious setback?"

"Well it's not good, but Phillip Wilde has offered to invest in the *Le Petit Breton*. We're thinking of expanding into the empty place next door. The room above it could be the nursery."

As we moved back into the room, he raised his voice and said enthusiastically, "We have some exciting plans once the baby's home.

I've been telling Lori about them. But she is not going to be working." He pointed an admonishing finger at her.

She smiled as well as she could.

"So coffee?" he said, but we both shook our heads.

Julia sat on Lori's right and held her hand. I sat in a chair at the end of the bed.

"I'm worried about the baby, Julia," said Lori.

How many weeks was she?" asked Julia.

"We think 32."

"A 32 week baby has an excellent chance of doing well with today's preemie care. She'll need to be in NICU for a few weeks until she develops enough to go home. My mother was premature."

"Really? How much?"

"Probably 35 or 36 weeks," I said. "I weighed five pounds though."

"How much do 32 week babies usually weigh?"

"Two and a half to three and a half," said Julia. "So she's at the top end."

"My brother weighed just four pounds," I said. "There was no preemie care available, so he was just sent home. He stands six feet tall now, and is a force to be reckoned with."

I omitted my mother's moan that they had sent him home to die. And I didn't mention that I often did the bottle-feeding, two ounces of milk every two hours. My mother was worn out by the night feedings. I had to prod his tiny lips to get him to suck. He kept nodding off. My two little sisters hung over the rocking chair cooing at him.

"Did you sing to him?" said Lori, as she began to relax.

"I always sang to babies." And I began singing, "Hush little baby don't say a word/Momma's gonna buy you a mockingbird/ And if that mockingbird won't sing/Momma's gonna buy you a diamond ring/ And if that diamond ring don't shine…" I gestured furiously at Julia.

She chimed in, "Momma's going to buy you a Jeffrey Pine…"

"And if that Jeffrey Pine don't-"

"Reach," sang Julia.

"Momma's going to buy you a great big peach."

"And if that great big peach don't jell.."

"Momma's gonna be as mad as hell."

Julien came back into the room with his coffee to find the three of us laughing.

"I need to ask you something, Julia," said Lori as our laughter died down.

"Sure."

"It's a favour really," Lori paused. "Would it be all right if we called our baby Julia Ann?"

"I'd be very flattered," said Julia.

"Me too," I said. "I chose that name."

Julien went with us to the NICU and pointed out Little Julia. She wore a diaper and a knitted hat. She was wired into various monitors, and was receiving oxygen through her nose. A plastic tube suggested feeding, but I wasn't sure. She lay on her back with her arms up, her little hands near her shoulders. She was by no means the smallest baby there.

I remembered my first sight of my Julia Ann, an 8 lb. 2 oz. baby, who pressed her left foot against the incubator's side at such an angle, that I was convinced she had clubfoot. This greatly amused everyone in the delivery room.

Grown-up Julia and I treated ourselves to lunch at the Padre Hotel. We sat together on high bench in front of a window. The hotel had been built in 1929 at the height of the oil rush. Above us was a lofty tin ceiling stamped with the portrait of one, Milton *Spartacus* Miller, who bought the place in 1954, and battled bureaucracy over many issues for 45-years. He even mounted a cannon on the roof, pointing at City Hall.

Eventually, the permits must have come through. The Padre Hotel stood solidly on its corner, even though Siri failed to find it every time we asked her to.

We ordered burgers and stout, and settled in for a good conversation.

"The thing I remember best about meals when I was young was the conversation at the table," said Julia. "You and Blake would get going on some topic or other-not just small talk-big talk. One of you would recount what you had just been reading, and off you would go. Blake's ideas usually came from *Scientific American.* Yours would be more from the humanities. Or you'd both take a crack at government or the latest stupid educational reform. I learned more about what made King Lear tick at the table than I ever did in the classroom. You were great intellectual partners."

"And economic partners-as long as I sent out the checks."

She laughed. "You were great parents. You supported us in whatever we decided to do-move to New York City in the early 80s, whatever-even when you didn't agree."

"We didn't always agree with your choice of husband, but we showed up. We weren't much good at the husband and wife stuff ourselves."

"History," she said. "Neither one of you could overcome your history. You were both orphans of the storm. Neither of you could handle the other's neediness."

Julia and I shared a certain view of the world, which we had come to independently after she had left home. (Or home had left her, to be precise.) We thought people came into the world with a clear purpose as a commitment to others. Julia went further and believed that the unborn soul sees its life laid out before it, in the womb, and may opt out in the first trimester. This life contract remains subliminal unless we are lucky, and it works its way up to the conscious level. In spite of a brief period of estrangement after the family's breakup, Julia and I had been steadfast in our support of each other.

We saw Lori and her baby daughter as two souls, who had also made a mutual commitment.

Lori's late term difficulty seemed to us to be the result of an outside intervention, a shock so severe it caused premature labour, rather than lack of commitment.

On the way home, at the Y-intersection, I had to swerve to avoid a carpet of tacks. As we approached the S-curves, we encountered orange cones, and then a sheriff's deputy who stopped us. While we waited for the oncoming traffic, he walked over to our car. It was Jorgensen.

"What's up?" Julia called from the passenger seat.

"Damndest thing," he said. "Propane truck blew a tire, and the front wheels went up over the guard rail. Driver was afraid to move. Called it in and finally, crawled out, I guess."

"Was it Merle?" I asked.

"Yeah."

"Is he all right?"

"I guess he got a good look at the Grim Reaper, but yeah, he's okay. Pretty cool customer!"

"Thank God," I said.

"O'course the fact it's a bobtail tanker made recovery easier. First the fire truck came to spray the tanker with water. Then, after a long wait, the Hazmat guys and the propane expert were 'coptered in. Thank God, there wasn't a leak. So then they had to wait for another tanker to off-load the gas. What can I say? Truck to truck propane loading is not the safest. Nail biting for all of us."

When we passed the accident scene around the corner, the truck was back on solid ground behind a tow truck. Merle and several men in coveralls were studying the under carriage.

When I stepped out of the car at the house, I was in worse shape than Merle, shaking and shivering.

"Is that what you were dreading?" Julia asked.

I shook my head. "I don't think so. I mean, bad as it was-I wish it were- but the dread seems worse than ever."

I fired up my laptop to see if there was a new posting on the club's website, although we had been told it was no longer possible to hack into it.

But the standing bear was there again. "We're not that tacky," it read. "Who's got a hole in their truck bed dribbling tacks?"

That question went unanswered.

Initially, we had gotten hospital news from Ben, but now Julien was also calling us. The first few days were hair-raising despite the baby's relatively good weight.

Margarita was staying with Ben.

I met them, in the General Store. She was a decade or more younger than me, with black hair, thin stature and the same slightly hooked nose as her daughter. Seeing her, I remembered Daniel telling me that the Aldano family had emigrated from Spain, and settled in Vancouver.

She was about to go down to the hospital, so that Julien could come back, and begin dinner prep. I could see she accepted her daughter's choice. I was familiar with that role, having had three son-in-laws. All that mattered to her was Lori and a healthy baby.

"They say the baby'll be off the oxygen any day," she said, "and it seems as though they'll begin breast milk soon. Lori's got one of those kangaroo carriers she'll use-well, we'll all use, depending on who's at the hospital. It's scary in the NICU. Alarms going off. We can't sort out what's a crisis and what isn't."

"How's Lori?"

"Well, she's a new mother, although, thank God, it wasn't a C-section after all. She's tired, a little peaked, and very anxious. She's been staying at a place the Catholic Church has for parents, but she needs to come home, and let the rest of us take shifts with baby."

"Let me know if there's anything I can do. I can spell you off sitting with her. Let you rest."

"We're not ready for a rest yet," said Margarita. "Can't stay away."

Ben turned from the cash register with his purchases. "You might want to visit her when she gets home. I'll keep in touch. As far as the passport and ticket are concerned, we have no idea, and neither does Guevara."

"Fairy godmother?" I speculated.

"Seems doubtful. Fairy godmothers don't cause premature labour," said Margarita.

In the parking lot, we said goodbye to Margarita, who was driving Lori's car. Then Ben turned to me.

"Before all the shit hit the fan, I'd been emailing a friend in Toronto who knows Daniel. He's been in touch with Daniel since he set off on his trip. I asked him what was up with Daniel cutting you off." He paused. "Did you publish a book?"

"An e-book," I said, "a memoir of my childhood."

"So, Daniel's new girlfriend read it, my friend said. Something put her off, and she demanded Daniel choose between you and her."

"Was 'spawn of Satan' mentioned?"

Ben winced. "I take it your father was an evil man."

"He was a mentally ill man. He did some evil things. He certainly abused us, my siblings and me. But he paid in the end."

"I'm not sure whether she doesn't believe the book, or whether she fears an evil contagion."

I stood, looking off toward Bear Mountain.

"I thought you'd want to know," he added.

I nodded again, unable to speak. Ben put his arm around me. He was tall and thin like Daniel, so for a moment I felt as if I were in my son's arms.

For the next few days, I stumbled about, fighting the urge to feel twice the victim. It took me that long to tell Julia, and then Georgia.

I fought not to judge Daniel, not to see it as weakness or disloyalty. He was as fed up with our abusive history as I was. He didn't want it to sour his chances of happiness.

What could I do to make myself happy?

I decided to cook dinner for Colin's birthday. I had missed Canadian Thanksgiving at the beginning of October. This dinner would make up for it.

The hunting and gathering stage meant a trip to Santa Clarita with Clara. First, I hunted for Whole Foods. It was at McBean and Valencia, but which corner?

I seldom got lost at home. What was going on? Was senility knocking on the door? Would I be found wandering like my Bonmama? Would strangers have to fetch me home?

Finally, we spotted the restaurant we had eaten in last time, and I knew the store was on the opposite side of the road.

As I negotiated with the butcher, my resolve to buy two ribs from the small end crumbled under his insistence that I needed three.

I gathered a bottle of *Veuve Cliquot*, the Old Widow's champagne, a *Pinot Noir* from Santa Barbara and Wente's *Morning Fog Chardonnay*. A staffer with a rotund middle under his black apron, his long hair more or less tied back, turned out to be full of information and opinions. After a lengthy tutorial, which went beyond my palate, I escaped with my selection.

The roast was trimmed and ready by then. I staggered when I saw the price sticker. I had done the same many years ago, when the Sunday roast rose to $12. I had lived long enough to see it cost ten times as much. Whole Pay Check, indeed!

I had a small breakdown over Brussel sprouts-to buy or not to buy. Would Caesar salad suffice? My neurosis would carry over to the next day, when I decided I needed them after all. Colin would get some when he picked up his cake at Suzie Cakes in Manhattan Beach. He was going down anyway, and such are the compromises of mountain living.

I loaded up on root vegetables for a mash-up, luxuriated in the cheese counter, adding Humboldt Fog to Parmesan, and chose six, large brown eggs. The Humboldt Fog, a wine wrapped goat cheese, reminded me of Evie's invitation to meet her goats. I should definitely do that.

I had a brief moment of contentment.

Clara met me at the checkout, took one look at my cart and offered to pay half.

"Oh, no," I said. "My birthday treat for Colin."

Clara was careful with her money. I was prodigal with mine. The sticker shock in this case might be too much for her. I didn't want to risk a third 911 call, certainly not in the middle of the checkout line at Whole Foods.

I found my way back to the mountain without a problem, but at the Y-intersection, I lost my confidence again, despite the daily 'sweeps' the BMP security was now doing for tacks. I didn't relax until I reached the village.

The birthday dinner was a two-house project. One had fridge space, the other had equipment.

Saturday, I wasn't on my game at first. I hauled out the root vegetables and began peeling. Clara had said she would help me, but she had disappeared before I got up. I had been looking forward to that companionship. I like a good work party.

As I peeled and chopped, I remembered chicken pie and oyster stew suppers at the church hall. The women came with their fruit pies already made, stoked up the wood stove and worked together, happily gossiping, to make the main course. Meanwhile, we children slid around the dance floor on wax pucks.

I had borrowed Julia's big blue ironware pot for the root vegetables. Once I had covered them with water, I could barely lift it onto the lowest fridge shelf where the rib roast was enjoying maximum cool.

I had my head in the fridge, and nearly jumped out of my skin when Clara came through the door.

"You started without me," she exclaimed.

Clearly, she didn't know how much work this was going to be.

"I went to the thrift shop," she said. "The woman there phoned to say there was new stuff to fit the kid, Arn, Ern, the fire kid. I took it to him. He's got his own trailer now, and his wife's come back. With the dog. They'll get money from the insurance company. They think they'll be able to rebuild." Her voice trailed off as she left the room.

So much for being judgemental.

I had the house in the pines to myself. As I made the Caesar dressing, I listened to Colin's music on my iPhone. The only usable counter space in the tiny kitchen was the breakfast bar. I had to stand on the step stool to drip the olive oil into the food processor. When it was done, I sat down at the table to pull apart a baguette for croutons, the oven ticking up to toast them.

The sun was shining brilliantly. It was absolutely quiet. The birds were on siesta, and the pines were still.

I felt at home. I had the rump end of my own family here, and had been drafted into the family that was the *Kentucky Five*. I liked the four I knew, despite their musical *faux pas*- singing about the bear that came over the mountain.

The next day, everything went wrong. The mash was watery; the Brussel sprouts were the size of small cabbages; the digital meat thermometer would not rise to 120 degrees; and Julia used all the drippings for the Yorkshire pudding, leaving none for gravy.

Didn't matter.

I downed some more wine, and *ad libbed.* The roast told me when it was medium rare. I put the mashed veg back on the heat, added butter and recooked it until it was fluffy. I sliced the sprouts thinly, cooked them in chicken stock, and sautéed them in bacon fat. I used olive oil and beef stock to make a huge batch of gravy, and Julia's Yorkshire pudding, baked in brioche tins nodded over, plump and crusty.

There were the four of us mountain dwellers and three flatlanders for dinner, Leo, my grandson, his father Evan and Leo's friend Jamil. There was not much conversation, however, except 'Pass the gravy' until we got to the pineapple cake.

"So I hear a propane truck nearly took a header down a cliff," said Evan. "Accident or conspiracy?"

"The scuttlebutt at the general store is that Merle had checked the tires after they filled the tanker," I said. "As he drove up he ran through a bunch of tacks at the Y-intersection. Ten minutes later a front tire blew just before the S-curves. He lost control, and climbed the guardrail. There's an eighty foot drop there."

"The activists posted a denial on the club website," said Colin. "But so far nobody's come forward to admit their truck's leaking tacks."

"And I hear you don't think it's the musical five anymore," Evan said to me.

"It doesn't seem as likely to me now," I replied.

"If they're good guys, who're the bad guys?" asked Leo.

"You mean who are the terrorists?" said Jamil. "Got any Muslims up here?" He laughed.

"Eco-terrorists," said Julia. "Supposedly."

"Maybe that's just what they want you to think," said Jamil, with mock menace.

"So Joanna," said Evan, "you still think there will be something worse?"

I sat for a moment at the end of the table, looking out through the window where the light was fading.

"I do," I said, finally.

"Could just be your nerves," said Clara, "after everything."

Jamil said, "My mother gets feelings like that. She's usually right."

I looked around the table.

"Could be," said Colin, "stranger things-"

"Let's wait and see," said Julia. "Sometimes these feelings are just a manifestation of fear."

It was time to toast Colin and wish him a Happy Birthday, and then, of course, Clara, who had been an integral part of the process. And finally, baby Julia Ann.

Terror closed the heart. Thankfulness opened it. Rumi was right. The heart is an immense river bearing the world in its current.

17

TOO MANY PUPPETS

The baby grand from the library's auditorium had been rolled out into the library proper, and Phillip Wilde was playing something light and melodic. I gathered from the fact that his back was to the entering crowd that it was his idea, not part of the program.

On a table at the back of the auditorium, sat a model of the proposed Halcon Village, an upscale version of the flour and water models we made in grade seven. There were tiny trees lining the tiny roads and a shimmering lake of mirror. The hotels had been sited on lower ground, and all of their infinitesimal lights pointed down. The helipads and golf courses were on higher ground. There were homey looking houses that you could almost believe might be yours. Then there were Spanish villas set in acres of land. The facilities were so tastefully included that you would be hard pressed to find the cop shop, or the fire hall, or even the gas station. Wait-gas and tires and other smelly necessaries would be down in Debritt, along with the garbage transfer site.

A sign indicated that all aspects of the plan were subject to change.

Sales people in blue blazers were handing out pamphlets and shaking supporters' hands. Arta didn't have time to shake mine. She was having a breakdown in the lobby. When the door opened every so often, I could hear her hysterically declaring that Warren *would* be there. No matter what they thought. He had promised her he would be, and he would be. She got on the phone, but evidently didn't get through. The man beside her finally took her elbow, and practically dragged her past the piano into the Children's Room, and shut the door.

By now the auditorium was full and newcomers were standing against the back wall. The screen was down at the front for the power point presentation.

Camille Costa was conspicuous by her absence. Evidently, she drew the line at shilling for Warren Oliver.

I caught a glimpse of Arta charging into the restroom near the entrance. We went back to waiting. Phillip had long since joined Max in the audience.

Two sheriff's deputies were trying to be inconspicuous near the door. The Sheriff himself entered and strode to the podium.

"How're y'all? " he asked cordially. There was a murmur of good, fine, Sheriff. "Now you are my people and I've made an undertaking that this will be a civilized social event. Why they've even laid on milk and cookies." We laughed obediently.

"The main ecological difficulties, incidentally, still have to be settled. El Halcon Ranch is negotiating with five groups. By Halcon's proposed terms, you residents will all stand to benefit in terms of public access to the land, support for community infrastructure, and most of all by protection of the condor, the spotted owl, the kit fox and all the other endangered or rare species that live on the ranch. After all, this is private land and we Americans believe a fella can do what he wants with his own land," he paused, "so long as he obeys the law and don't tick his neighbour off too bad." A few joined his chuckle.

"Now I believe Ms. Arta Dietzen, our local wordsmith, is ready to introduce our speaker."

Matthew Greaves at the end of the back row smiled encouragingly at his wife as she came in the door. She was dazzling in a filmy sky-blue dress, her blonde hair up with a few cascading curls. Her heels were so high they scared me. She reminded me of why I don't watch award shows. They make me feel inferior. And Clara wasn't there to buck me up because the altitude was bothering her ears.

"Good evening," said Arta. She was speaking directly to me, warmly, just short of taking me in her arms. Of course, everyone else was having the same intimate experience. "I'm soo glad you could take some time out of your busy lives to support me here. Thank God for PVR's." And we all laughed a little too long.

"Now first thing, I know I'm going to disappoint you. I promised y'all that Warren, my good friend Warren Oliver, the CEO of El Halcon Ranch, would be here. He isn't. Just wait till I get my hands on that no-good, low-life critter." She screwed up her face and hunched over so that she looked like the bad witch in *The Wizard of Oz*.

Whoops of laughter. Howls of laughter. Tears of laughter. The audience had been well and truly salted with supporters.

She straightened up, did a resigned face and said, "He has sent Roger, dear Roger, in his stead, like Abraham sacrificing Isaac. I only hope God and this audience will appreciate his willingness and not demand his death. I give you Roger Smith, Public Relations Officer for El Halcon Village. I'm just a shill, a poster girl if you will." She withdrew to the seat in front of the podium that had been reserved for her.

There he was young and good looking as ever in a grey suit this time. "Calvin Klein," the woman next to me whispered. He was calm and self-possessed despite the *contra temp* with Arta. He paused for a moment to let his smiling eyes sweep over us, raising his eyebrows in greeting when he saw me. He took a look at the notes he had laid on the lectern, but then he spoke without them.

First, he outlined the generous settlements that his company proposed to make with the ecology groups. His face said that we all knew how unreasonable those groups could be–at least one with an office on prime real estate on Santa Monica Blvd. Over 1000 acres, nearly half of the Ranch would be a publicly accessed conservation area. More than enough to support the condors. He went on at some length, detailing a gift of this or that sum of money for fire fighting education and other community programs. It seemed small beer, to me, considering the millions and millions they stood to make.

From time to time, hands were raised with questions, but these would all be answered at the end of the presentation.

We saw artists' paintings of the buildings and the two golf courses. The hotel amenities-pool, massage, exercise facilities, restaurants-were depicted, all available to the general public for a small membership fee. (It seemed unlikely the folks in the Woodlake Trailer Park would be joining.)

I had to make a trip to the rest room after an hour of this. As I came out, I met Phillip putting away his phone.

"That's strange," he said. "The BMP security called to say the dogs had got out, and were wandering the street, but I dialled into my security system, and they're asleep in their bed." He took his phone out to show me. Truly, they were lying nestled together in their wicker basket.

The Sheriff was also in the lobby on his phone. He walked into the auditorium and, interrupting the speaker, he announced in a loud voice, "Ladies and gentlemen, I'm going to close this meeting now. I ask the audience to remain seated until Ms. Dietzen and Mr. Smith have exited the building. Please come with me," he said to Arta and Roger. He gestured to one deputy to go ahead, and the other to stay at the auditorium door.

Phillip and I moved to let them through. They paused in the vestibule while one of the deputies went to tell their driver to bring the car to the foot of the stairs.

Matthew Greaves had followed, and was urgently appealing to the Sheriff. Finally, the little group set off down the outside stairs. Phillip and I moved out into the vestibule.

It was 8 p.m. and dark, but the parking lot was ablaze with lights.

The four of them were half way down the steps, the Sheriff in the lead, Arta and Roger behind him, and Greaves last, and higher on the stairs. Suddenly Arta fell, pitching forward with her own momentum. The Sheriff turned and caught her in his arms. Then Roger fell, crumpling straight down, his upper body coming to rest on the step above.

Phillip and I moved as one through the doors, paying no attention to cries of 'Get back. Get back'. The limo driver, who had been holding the car's back door open, jumped in, and gunned the car out of the parking lot.

Phillip came up behind Arta and took the weight of her body off the Sheriff. Together, they laid her down in her filmy robin's egg blue. She had a bloody hole in her forehead. Roger's head was turned toward me and had the same precise, red aperture. I finally saw Matthew Greaves, huddling behind a brick pillar at the top of the stairs. The deputy was shouting into his two-way radio.

It had happened quietly-the only sounds, the revving car motor and the deputy's shouting. The shots had been silent.

Phillip was checking for pulses, but clearly, they were both dead. The rest of us raised our eyes to the height of land that rose straight up from the parking lot, a thirty feet high wall, cemented in a cut stone pattern. Several houses stood on the top. None had lights on.

"Get down," shouted the Sheriff, suddenly coming to.

I didn't, neither did he nor Phillip, and Matthew Greaves hadn't got up,

The sniper wasn't interested in us.

Two patrol cars rolled up almost immediately. The Sheriff's office was just across the main highway, less than two blocks away. One parked blocking the road. Another tore past the T-intersection in the opposite direction, making for the road up the hill. The Sheriff conferred with his deputies and two of them came up the stairs toward us. Phillip was standing helplessly over Arta's body, and I was sitting on the step above Roger Smith's.

"Stop with the irony," I wanted to shout. "Do-over. Do-over."

One deputy gestured to Phillip for us to precede him, and took my arm as he passed.

Inside, we could hear the restless alarm of people who didn't know what had happened, but felt unsafe.

Phillip and I were escorted into the Children's Room. The deputy closed the door. Through the glass, we could see him joining the two others at the door to the auditorium.

My phone had no bars.

"Can I borrow your phone?" I asked Phillip and when he handed it to me, I called Bear Mountain Place.

The deputies had a table with two chairs set up across the double doors of the meeting room, and one of them was speaking to the audience. He was shouting so we could hear him telling them there would be a wait before they could go. When they did, names and contact information would be collected.

Phillip and I roamed the room, trying to stay out of each other's way. He was walking between the rows of bookshelves. I was doing circles in the reading area.

"I suppose we might as well relax," he said, and lowed himself onto the cushions on the floor. He gestured at the rocking chair.

It was a remarkable chair, designed in Mission style, but with a wooden glide mechanism, soundless and smooth and responsive to the slightest touch.

"You're not going to call your dogs?" I asked.

He chuckled. "I actually can, you know. I'll check on them from time to time and if they get unsettled, I will. I think you and I are going to be here a looong time."

"No doubt."

I rocked in silence and he opened a book he had picked up in his wandering.

"How do you feel," he asked, suddenly.

"I don't feel anything," I said, gesturing helplessly. "I'm dissociated. Trauma does that."

"Dissociated! Yeah. Me too. Shock, I guess."

His phone rang, and he answered it.

"Yes, I see," he said. "You'd better tell her yourself." And he handed the phone to me.

After the call ended, we fell silent. Phillip read *The Wind in the Willows,* and I rocked. I could see people restlessly moving about the auditorium. Then the Sheriff came through the lobby, and entered the auditorium. He turned in the direction of the front and was lost from sight. He spoke in a strong voice. I caught Arta and Roger's name and the sudden gasp of the fifty people in the room. Then he appeared back at the door and came toward ours.

"Sorry about this. I've told the rest they will be allowed to leave now, once they've given their contact information. I'm going to have to ask you two to stay longer. Detectives as well as crime scene investigators are on their way, some from L.A. County, some from Bakersfield. All of us on the scene will be asked for statements. Oh and I've asked for juice for you. I'll have someone call for coffee if you want."

"Have the bodies been moved?" I asked.

"Not yet. We've put up screens, tough job on stairs. We're going to let people out the back way and have their cars brought out to them up the road. It's not disrespect, God knows. It's necessary."

"Where is Matthew Greaves?' asked Phillip.

"He's been taken to the Debritt clinic. He may need to be taken to Bakersfield. We'll see. So juice first. I've had mine. Get the blood sugar up for the shock. Put in your orders for coffee or whatever when it comes. Anything else?"

"Could we have a couple of blankets?"

"Sure. And don't talk about it. Keep your individual memory clear."

"We haven't," I said.

"Good."

"Before you go," I said, "can you tell us why you ended the meeting, and hurried them out?"

The Sheriff sighed deeply. "Anonymous phone tip."

None of us said the obvious. He had delivered the victims to their murderer right on cue.

Gradually the crowd filtered past the deputies taking names, and went down through the library to the fire door. We could hear the cars being driven out of the lot, and stopping on the road above us. Then we began to hear helicopters.

"They got the screens up just in time," said Phillip. "The press is arriving."

"Can they land here?"

"In Debritt? Oh, yeah and have done many times. In the early days when the club in Bear Mountain Place was being built all the employees had to be coptered in from here. The club came first. It drew the vacationers. The highway up the mountain hadn't been built. Went as far as where the Y is now, so you could get to the track to Bear Mountain, but nothing after that. A trail here and there, I suppose. So yes, you can land a helicopter down the road. You could probably land one at the intersection out here, come to that."

He was trying to distract himself as much as me.

"I knew that something really bad was going to happen," I said.

"You do the future."

'Not in a reliable way. Nothing specific. Oh, maybe what's in the mail. I'm good at that. Or some vague feeling, like this one. Very helpful." I sighed. The juice hadn't perked me up much. "Anyway, sorry to have suspected the Kentucky Five."

Phillip laughed. "You're giving up that easily? But if not us, who?"

"Just so."

"Okay, let's be frank. It looks like Zach was a bit of a bad boy."

"Did he confess?"

Phillip grimaced. "Good one. I shouldn't have said that. No, I haven't heard him say he flooded the Lau's house."

Since Phillip had abandoned *Wind in the Willows*, I took it up. I looked up the chapter about Toad's infatuation with the motorcar.

When I chuckled aloud, Phillip said, "Read it to me."

I was off and running. Twenty minutes later, we were both surprised when the door opened. It was Al Guevara.

"We're ready to take your statements now." He gestured at a man and a woman outside the door, deep in conversation. "Detective Fred Trantor will be taking yours Joanna, and I will take Mr. Wilde's."

"Phillip, please."

"They killed Roger Smith!" I said softly to Guevara.

"Yeah," said Guevara, putting his hand on my arm. He left it there for a moment.

"Can't I please talk to you, not a stranger?" I asked. I was on the point of turning wimpy.

He shook his head. "This is big now. I've got my orders. You'll be all right," he said, ushering us out of the Children's Room.

Fred was more the typical middle-aged Kern County detective. He hiked his trousers up under his overhanging belly. The woman with him was short and solid, and had a way of settling her weight firmly on first one foot, then the other, as if establishing herself. She was wearing plastic thongs for shoes, a black skirt and a white shirt.

"We'll use the library tables," said Guevara, ushering us out.

Turning out of the Children's room, I caught my pant leg on the edge of a cardboard box. It was full of sock puppets, each with a yellow and red plastic condor head.

I caught up with Guevara and quietly asked, "Was there another web post?"

"Yeah. It said '*You Were Warned'*. Plus the usual standing bear. The club's website was immediately taken down."

I found myself seated at a library table near the fire door. The woman I had seen with Guevara clumped toward me. When she arrived, she did that characteristic thing she did, an in-place two-step. When she sat, she settled her hips the same way.

"Right," she said, brusquely. "I'm Detective Fred Trantor, Freda as my mother called me, but to the boys I've always been Fred. I've been seconded from the Los Angeles County Sheriff's office. And you're Joanna Hunter, retired teacher, from Toronto, Canada, living in Bear Mountain Place temporarily while waiting for your apartment in Toronto to be renovated." She pulled back her mouth in a wide, close-lipped, I-gotcha smile.

"Yes."

"Tell me about your dealings with Detective Al Guevara."

I stared at her. Was she a stickler for rules?

She tilted her head in inquiry, and grinned again.

What the hell! What did I have to lose? And Guevara had deserted me. I began at the beginning with that first interview at Julia's about the toxic package. AND house flood. Every so often, she stopped me to ask for more detail and made notes of my answers.

"You seem to have a good deal of detail that normally the Sheriff's Department would keep private."

"Mountain telegraph-the mountain communities have their own instant communication. As soon as something happens, everybody in town knows it, down to the last detail. Sometimes, I hear stories back about things I was involved in, and I hear more detail than I remember."

She nodded thoughtfully. "But you have met Detective Guevara privately in Bakersfield?'

"That's true. That was after Warren Oliver started putting pressure on the Sheriff's department about the poster campaign."

She nodded again, pressing her lips inward. "I think we're ready to move on to this evening. Let's begin by talking about your relationship with Ms. Dietzen."

"I had met her husband at the Bakery in BMP–Bear Mountain Place. My friend Clara met Arta though him, and then Arta invited Clara and me to visit her. While we were there, Arta asked us to come to this meeting."

"Despite the fact that you are not a permanent resident and would have no vested interest."

"She didn't know that. She called Clara and me ordinary mountain residents."

"Was Clara here?"

"No, she wasn't feeling well."

"Tell me why you came."

I gestured helplessly. "Amateur sleuthing? I wanted to keep my eye on people, see who was a likely activist and maybe responsible for the recent spate of crimes."

"You were heard to say that you expected something worse to happen. What made you think that?"

"Things seemed to be escalating."

Now she had pulled her lower lip together with her fingers. Either she didn't have a poker face or this was it.

I went through the list of disasters, omitting only Lori's emergency.

"Well, if you count the bear killing Braddock, as you do, it started out serious," she said.

"I'm fairly sure the bear wasn't trained to kill Braddock."

Then we went over the very few details I had about the shootings at least three times.

"What else did you see or hear from the sniper's position?'

"I assumed it was one of the houses on the cliff above the parking lot. But nothing-no sound, no movement."

"No car? How do you think the sniper got away?"

"On foot or on a golf cart, maybe even a Prius, I suppose. They're quiet. But probably he made for the mountain, off into the Los Padres forest."

"Who do you suspect?"

"No one. All my suspect shooters are accounted for."

"Clarify."

"Phillip Wilde, championship shooter, was here. Malcolm Fletcher, sniper in Vietnam, was passed out cold in his living room in Bear Mountain Place. I got interested in marksmen when the kid from Coney Creek got shot in the leg."

"How do you know where Fletcher was?"

I called his daughter. She went over and found him there."

"Time?"

"When were they shot? About 15 minutes after that."

"Didn't the Sheriff tell you not to make calls?"

"No."

All right. I'll verify that. The daughter's story, I mean. Now I need to talk to you about your views on ecology."

"I can't do that."

"You want your lawyer?"

"I want to rest. I'm seventy-eight, thirty years you're senior. I'm tired and my nerves are shot."

"I guess it is 3 a.m.," she said, looking at her silver man's watch.

"Exactly. And I'd rather talk to Detective Guevara, so I won't have to repeat everything I've already told him."

"I know you'd like that. That's why you'll be talking to me. You're a mystery fan. You know the drill–repetition is the name of the game."

I sighed. "Do you also know my shoe size?"

"I read Detective Guevara's notes on the way here. But I'd say"-she glanced under the table-"8."

"Very funny."

"You okay to drive yourself home?"

"Sure."

"You need to come down to the Bakersfield office 'as soon as' to put your statement about tonight in writing. Perhaps you and Mr. Wilde could come down together."

Now I smiled insincerely. I wanted to get huffy about being able to drive there myself, but I remembered I had played the pity card. "Thanks for the suggestion."

"I'll have your car brought out to the road, if you give me your keys. You can leave by this fire exit. The alarm's been turned off."

I kept the high beams on all the way home. The car moved in the tunnel of that light. The heights and chasms were lost in utter darkness.

In the morning I waited until I knew Colin and Julia would be up, then I woke up Clara.

"I've got croissants already," I told her. "I need you to come over to the house with me, so I can tell you about the meeting. I'd like to do it now, and shower later."

Clara looked alarmed, but I didn't explain. I went out to wait on the deck.

We took the car. I needed to get there quickly, and have this over with.

At the house, I put the baked goods on the table and filled the kettle. Colin ambled out of his studio with his coffee, and Julia had her Pu-erh mug in her hand.

"Last night, the Sheriff broke the meeting up early and escorted Arta and the speaker–not the Halcon Ranch CEO, but the PR guy Roger Smith- escorted them out of the library. I was in the lobby when they were leaving and so was Phillip Wilde." I paused. Then I began to cry. It took me a while to speak again. "They're dead, Arta and Roger. They were shot on the library steps. By a sniper."

I sat down at the table in my usual place, crying. The kettle began to whistle. Julia moved to take it off the heat.

Clara sat down heavily in the chair opposite me. "Arta's dead?" she said.

I looked up and nodded. Now my head was shaking, doing a little bobbing motion.

"Can I have some of your Pu-erh?" I asked Julia. I needed the caffeine.

She stood dumbstruck at the news. Then she pulled herself together. "Of course. And Clara, you want Earl Grey?"

Colin joined us at the table. "Why didn't you wake us up last night? You saw them die?'

I nodded again. Really it was just a slightly bigger head bob. "I didn't want it to be real. If I didn't talk about it, it wouldn't be real."

"You must not have slept all night," Clara said.

"No," I said, head bobbing. "I slept like the d…"

That started me crying again.

"I actually knew Roger too, a little anyway. He went for a drink with us at the Mad Dog-Guevara, Sydney and me-after the meeting at the club."

"Have you taken your meds?"

"Not yet. I will when I've eaten. I have them here." I drew the two bottles out of my hoodie pocket.

"Shall we heat the croissants?" Colin asked.

No one answered, so he got up, and put them on a baking sheet. He had turned the oven on after I called.

Julia brought us our tea and sat down. "Tell us everything from the beginning," she said.

I closed my eyes for a moment and then began. I described the model of Condor Village at the back of the auditorium, and the blue-coated sales people, Phillip playing the piano with his back to the arriving crowd, the Sheriff's introduction, the no-question policy during the address, and so on.

Colin brought breakfast to the table. I paused to put jam on my croissant. Then I took the story up again. Twice, I fell to crying, once when I mentioned Arta's frothy blue dress rucked up beneath her, and again, when I came to the box of condor puppets. Still, I went on until I got to the point where Fred Trantor dismissed me. I paused, and then I described my surreal drive up the mountain.

I had been tearing off bits of pastry and eating between details. The crust lay there, crying out for more jam. I finished the roll off while the others pulled themselves together.

"I should have gone with you," said Clara. "She was my friend."

"Well," Julia said, kindly. "You hadn't had time to form much of a friendship. Take it easy on yourself."

"Arta was self-centered and condescending, and she wore silly dresses," I said. "And she had every right to be that way, and live to be old like us." I was looking at Clara.

I had a flash of Arta as a very cute baby with her delighted young mother. Then I realized I would never learn if Z was for Zanzibar. Without a beat, I saw her happily shopping in a heavenly mall with the young woman who had been her mother.

But where was Roger? Hanging out in a gay bar in the beyond?

I wanted very much to get my part over with, so Colin said he would drive me to Bakersfield. Julia decided to come with us, and drop in to visit Lori who was at the hospital with the baby.

18

THE GIRL FROM ARKANSAS

The receptionist at the Sheriff's department on Norris Rd. asked me to wait. Only a few minutes passed before Fred Trantor showed up.

"I assumed a deputy would take my statement," I said as I stood up.

She gave me one of those Cheshire cat smiles and led me down a hall. When she opened the door, I found myself not in an office as I had expected, but in an interview room, a standard right-out-of-television interview room–four chairs at a table, camera up in the corner, bare walls and a small audio machine on a low shelf.

"What can we get you? Coffee? Water?"

"I've brought my own water, thank you."

"Good. Here we have paper and pen. We need you to write down what you told me about last evening's events in as much detail as possible." She gestured me to sit down and took a seat opposite me.

"Okay. And you're just going to sit and watch me?"

She nodded. "I've brought some reports to read." She opened a file I hadn't noticed she was carrying at her side.

I took a deep breath. "Where shall I start?"

"Begin with the circumstances of your being invited, briefly. You might want to mention why your friend Clara O'Neil didn't go. Tell what happened after you arrived at the library, but give most attention to the actual shooting, how you happened to see it, for example."

"Right."

I began. I have a few quirks: I can identify voices, although I suffer from a degree of prosopagnosia-difficulty recognizing faces. It made life as a teacher challenging. On the other hand, I have always been capable of writing down every word of an hour-long lecture while listening to it, an ability I had passed on to Julia. My memory is spotty, so I have kept a daily journal. I can remember details of the previous day long enough to record them.

I put the last two skills to work now. The task absorbed me completely, although from time to time, Fred Tranter turned a page over, reminding me that she was there. When I finished, I estimated that forty-five minutes had passed. Another of my useless talents-I keep time in my head.

She read through it quickly.

"Okay. Please sign it."

I did so, and handed it back. She signed it in turn and looked at her heavy watch. She wrote the time and date down.

"Now, if I may, I have a few more background questions."

I clenched up, internally, despite the Ativan. I smiled and nodded, noting that she had failed to give me her usual insincere grin.

She went over the same ground as Guevara had weeks before until she had established that the only contact I had with ecological activists was through my son, many years ago. I had to establish that Daniel had friends who were into animal rights. This inevitably led to a discussion of the Kentucky Fried Five, and the musical group in Bear Mountain Place.

Daniel's whereabouts were duly noted.

"There's something very remarkable here." Trantor said. "You claim to have seen a CDFW bear trap, which you assume was returning a bear to the mountain, you took in a parcel, which proved to have Valley Fever spores in it, you called 911 for an attempt suicide, and you were not only present in the building when Dietzen and Smith were shot, you actually witnessed it."

"Yes," I said.

I let the affirmation ring in the air for a while.

I added, " I also called 911 when Lori Aldano went into premature labour."

"You don't deny this remarkable list of coincidences."

"I don't deny the facts."

"As I understand it this is not your first time helping the police with inquiries."

There it was-what I had been waiting for. The other shoe had dropped.

"I reported my suspicions that my deceased father was behind the kidnapping of two children in separate incidents over twenty years before."

"Yet, after an investigation by three police forces at a cost of $1,000,000, nothing of the sort was proven."

"Much to our humiliation."

"Our?"

"Three other family members had gone to the police with me."

She sighed. "But several members of your family did receive compensation from your province's Criminal Injuries Board?"

"Six of us."

"I understand this was to offset psychiatric therapy in part."

"Yes."

"So you have received such treatment? What diagnosis was made?"

"I'm sure you already know. It'll be in the file. We were deemed to be sane, but suffering from post traumatic stress disorder."

"Mmmm."

"Do you always demand that witnesses to crimes have perfect mental health? Or do you believe that you can trigger me into an emotional collapse, which will somehow elicit different answers? That I'll be more use to you that way? Or are you alleging that I suffer from Munchausen Disease and cooked this all up to make myself look good to the police?"

She was actually looking at me and not the report now.

I went on, "Finding a sniper is beyond my skill set. I'm a middling authority on *Hamlet* and *King Lear*, not even an expert there. I have no connection with labs capable of isolating cocci spores, and no scientific training. I was Xiao Yu Lau's tutor, and thank God, I realized there was something wrong with him. Lori called my daughter, Dr. Durant, and I went with her to help Lori. As for the bear trap, Clara O'Neil saw what I saw."

She pushed her bottom lip out and said,"Mmmm."

"Is that all you can say?"

She tilted her head, seemed about to say 'mmm' again but relaxed her face instead. She took a deep breath. "No doubt Detective Guevara will be in touch with you-again. I may have some additional questions. No point in giving you my card. You have Guevara's number."

"Please do, nevertheless."

She fished in her shirt pocket and handed one over.

I called Colin to come get me once I was outside where I could enjoy the luxury of shaking uncontrollably.

As I stood waiting to be picked up at the front of the low building, Phillip Wilde drove up in his grey Ford Bronco, parked, and pulled a long gun case out of the back.

"Are you after big game?" I asked, as he approached the entrance.

"Pretty big," he said. "Guevara asked me to bring in my M24 for purposes of elimination. Might have known the shooter would choose a gun I have."

"I wonder how he knew?"

"Well, it's not a secret. I talk about my guns from time to time."

"So they'll be able to tell the bullets weren't from this gun?'

"Oh, yeah. The rifling has already told them they were fired by an M24. Now they do a comparison between a bullet from my gun and the fatal bullets."

I stared at him for a moment. "Was the bullet still in Arta's head?"

"No," he said, "a head shot like that-the bullet doesn't slow down when it hits bone. In a body shot, there'd be no exit wound but in a head shot, there is." He paused. "That's why the cop got my jacket off the back of my chair in the auditorium. My shirt was-uh, stained." He paused. "I'm glad you didn't notice. And that neither of our bodies slowed the bullet."

"Me too. All I saw was the small perfect red circle on their foreheads."

We looked into each other's faces. Then he sighed.

"I'd better get on with my civic duty," he said. "See you later."

Colin arrived as the door was shutting behind Phillip, and we drove farther east to pick up Julia who was waiting outside the hospital. Then we drove back to Mimi's Restaurant for a late lunch.

Julia reported Lori was holding baby Julia next to her skin, and giving her breast milk. Lori said she was more relaxed now that she was getting used to the NICU and sleeping in her own bed. The four of them had worked out a schedule, and the baby was alone for only a few hours at night. True the commute tired them all, and Lori's old Honda was getting a real workout.

There was no further news about the fake passport and the air ticket.

I was glad to listen to Julia. I wasn't ready to talk about brain-covered shirts at lunch.

On the way home, I took score. Four people dead, if Braddock were counted, and another triggered into serious mental illness.

Xiao Yu's admission to Stanford had been deferred. He was in a private mental health facility in the Bay Area. Teresa was living in the house they had bought there. She was renting rooms to two first year Chinese students. She cooked for them, and took food to Xiao Yu as well. Her church in Bakersfield had handed her on to a church there, and so she had a ready-made community.

When I arrived back at Clara's house, her car was not in the drive. I unlocked the screen door with the key we kept under a pot, and then the door itself. I shut the heavy metalled screen door, but left the inner door open to the warm air.

Jazz was lying on the window ledge snoozing, and barely looked up. While I was getting a drink of water, I noted that three cats were perched on various levels of the cat tower in Clara's bedroom window.

Poirot would be outside prowling. Columbo, creature of habit, would be on the windowsill of the en suite bathroom.

I took off my shoes, went into my room to the left, and threw myself down on my bed. I let the tension drain out of me. At least, I tried to. Trying to relax is always a contradiction in terms. I listened to the ticking of the tiny garden windmill Clara had stuck in the flowerbed. I let my mind go blank. The next thing I knew I was waking up. I lay there for a while, gathering my wits until I decided to make tea.

As I emerged into the entryway, I saw the screen door was open. There was no cat on the window ledge. I rushed out, calling "Jazz, Jazz." Not on the deck. I cornered the front of the house. No cat. I ran out to the road. No cat there either.

"Oh God, oh God, oh God."

I rushed back into the house. Closed the screen and locked it.

"Jazz," I called. "Jazz."

When had she ever come at my call? When had any of them ever come at anyone's call?

I started a systematic search, well systematic as possible when driven by terror. I searched Clara's room first. No mean feat. There were still eight boxes of clothes half unpacked, and the immense closet had its sliding doors open. Inside, there were yet more boxes on the floor. I lay on my stomach to look under the bed. The three cats on the climber watched me with detachment. I reeled dizzily into the big bathroom. I peered into the cupboard under the vanity. Columbo eyed me suspiciously.

I was still reeling when I emerged back into the living area. Not in the broom closet. Not in the dining area. Not in the fireplace or up the flu. Not on top of the kitchen cupboards. Not in the cluttered utility room. Not in my bathroom. Not as far as I could see in the box-filled third bedroom. I checked under my own bed. Not there. Not in my closet, which was closed anyway.

I tore into the living room again. Not behind the chair. Not behind the couch.

Could I call BMP Security? Was a lost cat a sufficient emergency?

I sat on the couch and pushed the heavy coffee table out of the way with my feet. I lay down on the rug and peered under the couch. Not there. I was pushing myself up to my knees, when I stopped. The underlining of the couch was hanging down. It needed to be tacked up. We had talked about doing that. But why was it bulging at the end that wasn't hanging down?

I lay back down and stretched my arm under awkwardly. Something heavy and soft, something vibrating slightly.

"Jazz," I cried. "Get out of there." I gave the weight a shove, but it was going to take more than that. In for a penny, in for a pound, I thought, and ripped the lining down until a black and white cat fell out. I grabbed her by the front legs and hauled her out. She windmilled trying to escape me, and I was glad to help her go. She landed a few feet farther away than she expected.

I was leaning against the coffee table pushing it back in place when Clara unlocked the screen door. Jazz was the first thing she saw.

"How's my Jazz baby?" she called out.

All summer, we had been the 'mothers'. Living in the centre of town made us visible. It was 'cute' how we looked out for each other. Clara looked the part. I took that with a grain of irony. I had never been that kind of nurturer.

Neither had Arta's mother.

The biographical notes on Arta's books had few clues about her mother. Her website described her life growing up in Hot Springs, Arkansas, her father, a high school English teacher, and her mother, a part-time librarian, and gourmet cook, specializing in southern cuisine.

Hot Springs brought to mind Franklin D. Roosevelt and Bill Clinton, but also my granddaughter-in-law, so I called her in Massachusetts.

"I assume you heard that Arta Dietzen was murdered." She had, of course. "When you were growing up in Hot Springs did you hear about her," I asked Kirsten.

"Sure, but that's not her real name. She was Kelly Brown as a child."

"Did her father teach you English in high school?"

"No way. Her father Ken Brown died young, and her mother Marlene went to jail for manslaughter. Apparently, he beat her, so one night when he was passed out drunk, she dragged him into the bathtub, and drowned him."

"So she wasn't charged with murder?"

"Mitigating circumstances downgraded the charges. It seemed like an impulsive act as well. She wouldn't have been charged if his family hadn't pointed out that they had never known him to take a bath. She probably did kill him, but there wasn't much real evidence, no bruising."

"How old was Arta-Kelly?'

"Not in school yet. I'm not sure."

"What happened to her?"

"She had no other family, and couldn't be adopted. Her mother wouldn't allow it. She went from foster home to foster home. Before the mother, Marlene, had finished her sentence, she died in jail. Tragic story. She overdosed on smuggled drugs. Kelly was in her teens by then, and she vanished from sight. My grandmother recognized Arta Dietzen's picture on one of her early novels and told us the story."

"Arta names Hot Springs as her birthplace. Yet, the story hasn't got out."

"I'd attribute it to southern pride, or possibly venality," Kirsten said. "Every copy of Arta's books is a little ad for Hot Springs. Why mess with that when your town relies on tourism? And honestly, you have to feel sorry for her, having such a bad start. I'd like to think people are just kind."

"She was certainly beloved by her readers," I said, and then I changed to subject to catch up with her and my grandson, Josh. They were both just finishing their residency there in a Massachusetts hospital.

I was very impressed with the way Arta had reinvented herself. The real Arta was way more endearing than the false one. I spent my life trying to live down my own childhood. No one now remembered it, not even my siblings. I was the eldest. It had vanished from sight, except in my heart.

A part of some of us would always be a child with a shameful secret.

None of my online searches gave any hint of the Brown saga, not even on the twentieth page of the Google search list.

I wondered how much Matthew Greaves knew, or Camille Costa, or Great Day publishers or Arta's editor Josephine. Had Arta ever opened her heart to any of them?

On Monday, Clara decided we absolutely had to return the crystal vase to Arta's house because they were going to need it. I was pretty sure that the house had crystal vases aplenty, but I didn't argue.

We were buzzed through the gate and I parked in the middle of an otherwise flawless *Architectural Digest* photo. Matt Greaves was polishing a beautiful black car, and hailed Clara to come see it.

"Is that new?" called Clara.

"No, no!" he replied, gazing at the shine. "I had the Benz brought up from the city. It seemed more suitable for the occasion. Come and get in the driver's seat."

Clara handed me the vase and moved toward the car saying, "Oh, my!"

I stood staring. His beautiful wife's body was lying in a morgue somewhere, having been carved up by a pathologist. Meanwhile he was happily simonizing.

Imelda answered the door, and I said, "We brought back the vase. Clara thought you might need it."

Imelda began beckoning me to come in and when I did, she took me by the elbow and hurried me through the living room, shaking her head and tut-tutting all the while. We moved speedily along a corridor until we came to an open door from which a terrible sound of grieving was emanating-a sobbing, fist pounding keening worthy a hired mourner. Imelda gave me a slight push into the office. Camille sat at the desk facing a window with her back to us, rather to me, for Imelda had fled.

I stood, immobilized, thinking, "What the fuck? Who named me mother of the world?"

I took a deep breath and hauled a chair over so I could sit beside her.

"Camille, it's Joanna. We met the other day–here-at the house-before– you know-" I put my hand softly on her shoulder.

There was enough Canadian in me to find touching a stranger painful.

Camille turned her tear-lined face toward me, and threw herself at me. I fielded her with outstretched arms. She proceeded to weep in great heaving spasms, soaking my shoulder. I hitched my chair forward to get a better purchase on her long thin body. Her chin bobbed up and down on the ridge of my shoulder bone. Her fists beat a light tattoo on my back. I was pretty sure her nose was running. I muttered, "There, there", from time to time, or "It's okay". I must have meant 'it's okay to cry', because nothing else was.

I held her firmly, but she clenched me. I wanted to take a deeper breath. I remembered holding Star Shine on the shoulder of the 99 as she said she wanted to die.

Gradually, Camille began to run down, or the grief did. She grew quieter, her fists and hands began to slacken. She gave little spasms from time to time, and wiped her face back and forth on my shoulder like a child. Slowly, she began to pull back, mopping her face with her hands, back and front. She turned back to the desk, looking for tissues. She blew her nose, wiped her eyes, and turned back to swab my shoulder.

"Don't worry about it," I said.

"You see I loved her," Camille said, clenching her face against a new onslaught.

"Of course you did."

"No! I mean I *loved* her and she *loved* me!"

I saw what she meant.

"*He* doesn't even cry for her." She pressed the balled up tissue to her mouth.

"Can I get you something?" I asked.

She pointed to the tiny fridge in the corner. "Gin," she said, "with ice. Have one yourself."

Don't mind if I do.

I reached the bottle, and two highball glasses down from the shelf. I filled them with ice from the bar fridge. As I poured generous portions, I realized that this was Colin's recipe for a martini, and that Clara would have to drive home.

"He came back from China in the middle of the night. We didn't expect him, not for another two weeks. A big surprise, it was supposed to be. Actually he wanted to catch her at it. He thought she was getting laid by Warren Oliver. But-surprise! He would have challenged Oliver to a duel at forty paces, out under the live oaks, but it wouldn't look so good taking a few rounds out of a skinny bitch like me. He woke us up roaring at the top of his lungs. Then he split, tires squealing. Apparently, he went right to Warren. Woke him up. So Arta heard from Warren's wife."

"I wonder why he would go there," I said. "A minute before, if you're right, he thought Oliver was his rival."

"He doesn't know anyone else up here," she said, shrugging. "Wanted an ally, a shoulder to cry on, perhaps."

"You certainly misled me. Arta dissing you, calling you Cammie, ordering you around."

"That was our game. I loved her calling me Cammie in the bedroom."

"So I suppose you know the real story of her childhood."

"Oh, God, do you? Who are you going to sell it to? Have you told anybody?"

"No. Of course not."

"But you don't even like her or her books." I refrained from asking how she knew. "Anyway, who told you?"

"Someone from Hot Springs. Nobody there is going to spill the beans. Too much to lose, Kirsten says. She's my grandson's wife. From Hot Springs. She lives in Massachusetts now. She's a doctor, if that's any guarantee."

Camille began to relax. Her eyes were red and swollen. She was the picture of misery.

"So am I right that this will not mean the end of Arta Dietzen's *oeuvre*?" I asked.

She nodded. "She outlined them all, all the way up to Z. There were a few locations that need to be visited, but when there's enough background material available that isn't always necessary."

"And am I right that you've been doing the actual writing?"

She shrugged and made a face. "She got tired of it. All the detail bored her. She did all the first ones up to *Montreal*. Then it became more of a partnership. So no, this is not the end of the brand."

"I hope she left you protected."

"Oh, yeah, she worked out a new contract with Great Day Publishing, this summer, while Matthew was in the Caribbean. The royalties are divided 60/40. I get the smaller share." She paused and seemed to switch gears. "The other share is held in trust. It and this house were to signed over to a company she incorporated for the production of future books. Two are already in the pipeline. So I will still be able to work here." She ended on a softer note, the girl friend once again.

She gazed out across the stands of dried rabbit bush and white sage toward the dry riverbed.

"Does her will say that as well?"

"Oh, yes. She had the same lawyer make the changes. There's a board of three to manage the corporation, Josephine Barker, Warren Oliver and me."

"So Greaves doesn't get a look in?"

She shook her head.

"You could sell that story as well," she added.

"I'm not going to sell-or even tell-any story. But did you tell the detectives all this?"

"I told them, her, Fred Trantor, that Arta and I were lovers. I probably left the impression that the other eight books are already written, but I also told her about the new contract."

"It gives him a motive."

"It bloody does," she said. "Wounded male ego, wounded macho ego."

"How long ago did he find out you were lovers?"

"March."

Time enough, I thought, to make a complicated plan to frame unnamed eco-terrorists.

"Does he know about the royalty split and the new will?"

"I don't know, but if he doesn't, he will soon."

We considered this in silence.

"I like old Fred," Camille said. "I think she can get him."

She didn't say 'get the murderer'.

"I assume Fred is lesbian," I said.

"Her? Oh no. She's got a boy friend, also a cop, came with her. Looks like a good old boy with his gut hanging over his belt."

She was gazing out the window again.

"I'm very sorry, Camille."

For the life you won't get to live, for the pain you will have to bear. And I was very sorry for Arta, who had finally been living the girlhood she had missed.

Camille gave me a wan smile.

19

IN OTHER NEWS

Before last Friday, we pretended that Bear Mountain Place was the Centre of the World as Chumash legend said. Suddenly it really was.

The shooting death of the famous romance novelist, Arta Dietzen, had made the news worldwide. Television crews descended on Douglas Peak.

Warren Oliver was interviewed on every channel and by the L.A. Times. The logo of the ranch-a hawk in flight-was in the background each time. He was eloquent in his grief and his defence of the Halcon Village plan. His passion for the project made it seem as if he were offering to re-house the homeless, rather than the luxuriously housed upper class. The networks didn't ask why he hadn't been at the library meeting when Arta was killed.

What gave the story even more legs was the ecological angle. The sniper was clearly trying to prevent further damage to a precarious environment. He thought he was taking out the CEO of Halcon Village. Roger Smith had just been unlucky. We caught a glimpse of his grieving parents, and then no more.

I took to disappearing into my room when the news came on, more news-phobic than ever.

I didn't watch news at home in Toronto. Day-old print news, I could handle. The Toronto Star and the National Post had had a meltdown when I stopped the hardcopy subscription. Now I was paying a company in NYC to access the websites of my Canadian papers. The New York Times and the L.A. Times gave limited free access.

By the time I had a copy of *The Mountain Prospector* in my hands on Thursday, a week after Douglas Peak became world famous, there was little to add.

Later that day, we got a hand-delivered invitation to Arta's private interment on Halcon Ranch. Camille had enclosed a note saying that we were also welcome to the public funeral at the Hollywood Bowl. According to the news, Elton John was going to fly in. It didn't say whether he was bringing another song 'dedicated to a dead blonde', as Keith Richards once put it. It wasn't just the rich and famous that were coming. Readers were flocking to Los Angeles, romance readers that is.

The funeral was scheduled for Saturday, two weeks after Arta's death. The interment, for Sunday afternoon.

"Why were we invited?" Clara wondered. "I mean it's thoughtful, but-"

I called to accept. It was Josephine from Great Day publishers who answered. "Oh, yes, let's see. Clara O'Neil and Joanna Hunter. Camille put you on the list. I'm glad you're coming. Can I put you down for the reception back at the house as well?"

"I'm not sure," I said.

"Just drop in for a moment. I believe Camille has something of Arta's for you."

On Friday, a week after the shootings, I parked the Prius under the only tree in Regan's parking lot. I had to kill time again while I waited for Star Shine to get a check-up by the radiation oncologist.

At least some good seemed to be coming of my suspicions about local marksmen. Star Shine was reconciled to her father-more or less. She had moved in to supervise his drying out. She said that she still wasn't speaking to him. When I dropped her and her bags off at his place earlier, I saw that he was ready to trade in booze for his daughter.

Once again, the red MGB was parked against the restaurant wall. I rolled down the window so I'd be able to breathe with the A.C. off-it was still over 80 degrees in Bakersfield.

I sat remembering Camille's conviction that Matthew Greaves was behind Arta's assassination. She was convinced that Fred Trantor agreed with her. Certainly the field was open now that it was clear that someone had tried to frame the Kentucky Five, and Greaves had motive. Should I take the risk of embarrassing myself by calling Guevara?

Surely, if I had learned anything in the last few months, it was to trust my instinct. I took out my phone and selected his cell phone number.

"I'm not sure if you're interested, but I'm here at Regan's Roadhouse on California, and it looks as if Matthew Greaves is here too."

"That could be interesting," said Guevara. "We're just spinning our wheels here. Going over everything again. What say I meet you there? If he's in the bar, sit in the restaurant and vice versa."

There was no hostess at the front of Regan's as usual at 11a.m. I glimpsed Matthew Greaves at the otherwise empty bar with a tall, dark man, wearing a ball cap backwards. I sat down in the first booth on the restaurant side, facing the door, and tilted my cowboy hat down on the bar side.

I was studying the menu when Guevara slid silently into the seat across from me. He had on a ball cap, right way round, and an uncharacteristic denim jacket. The partition came up to our shoulders and a beer ad further obscured his face.

As he picked up the large menu, a burst of male laughter came from the bar. Guevara and I widened our eyes at each other over the menus.

"Well, you know," he said, flippantly, "a whole week, time enough. Don't order breakfast. Order lunch. You're going to have a glass of beer later."

"I am?"

A small dark waitress appeared and I ordered sliders and fries. Full price, it wasn't happy hour yet. The detective ordered ribs.

"So tell me what you told Trantor about Malcolm Fletcher," he said.

I went over the story of how I had called Star Shine from Phillip's cell phone. She had borrowed her neighbour's car, and driven up to her father's place. He hadn't answered the door, but it was unlocked. He was passed out, sprawled in a lazy-boy, with *Blue Bloods* blaring on the television.

When I mentioned what I had learned about Arta's early life, Guevara said they had already traced it, by starting with her name change when she was twenty-one.

After we had been eating a few minutes, Guevara caught the eye of the blonde, curly-haired bar waitress, and gestured with his head for her to come over.

She arrived beside our table and said, "You're not with Sapphire martini today."

"You mean she comes here with other men?" Laughing, he lowered his voice. "Don't say my name, but do you know me?"

She nodded.

"I need you to leave those glasses on the bar when they're finished," he said, softly, turning his head fully toward her. "Later I'm going to ask you to describe the younger guy to a police artist. I'm sure you won't give the show away."

"The sniper shooting?" she said, equally softly. "You can count on me. I'm good at faces. Right?" she asked me.

"Unbelievable at faces, unlike me."

"Can't say what it's about," he said and then in a slightly louder voice, "So, bring a half a Guinness for my aunt here. She needs cheering up."

When she was back at the bar, getting my Guinness–out of a can-she called cheerily to Matthew and his friend, "Another scotch, gentlemen?"

They waved away the invitation and the younger man headed for the restroom. Matthew stood draining his glass. After a few minutes, he headed for the front door with his hand moving to the inside of his jacket. Then the younger man walked swiftly by us, and out the door.

"Does he look like military to you?" Guevara asked.

"That or police."

"Too erect for a cop."

"So I gather the Dietzen/Greaves marriage was less than ideal," said Guevara.

I told him about my conversation with Camille Costa. "But I take it you already knew this from what Camille told Detective Trantor."

"Yeah," he said. "Do you think Greaves knows about the new royalty deal?"

I shrugged. "Camille wasn't sure when I talked to her."

Guevara got up to go into the bar.

I followed him. "You have to tell me what you find out," I said.

"Strictly speaking, I shouldn't."

"Strictly speaking, you shouldn't have told me most of what you have. Anyway, the sniper won't have left prints at his perch."

"No, but we may be able to identify the guy. See if he's a likely suspect. You might as well go now. I'll take care of the bill. I'm going to try to get the waitress to come to the station right away. If I can round up a sketch artist."

"I'm going to be so mad at you if you don't keep me in the loop."

"Okay, Auntie. I'll see what I can do."

I was still sitting in the Prius when Guevara came out of the restaurant carrying a takeout bag, no doubt with the glasses in it. I got out of the car and walked rapidly toward him.

"What if it was never ecological?" I said.

He stood looking into the distance, nodding gravely.

Early the following week, Guevara called Clara's to say that he would be dropping by the bench behind the general store the next morning, about 8. I drove over in the Honda a few minutes to, and found him deep in conversation with the elderly ex-sheriff.

"This is my grandfather Henry Robertson, Joanna Hunter, Pop."

He stood beside his grandson to shake my hand, and I could see clearly where the tall gene came from. He held his felt hat in his hand, revealing a full head of rumpled white hair. He was clean-shaven. His face was weathered and lined, but he was as lean as his grandson.

"I was just telling Pop that we got interesting results from the fingerprints on the bar glasses. The unidentified man is Morris Russell, a Darkstone *employee*, shall we say. He was a Marine initially, but now he works contracts for Darkstone Security. He's worked for them in North Africa, Iraq and Afghanistan. His special talent is long distance shooting, so he's invaluable in protecting other Darkstone workers who are dismantling mine fields, etc."

"In other words, he's a sniper."

"Told you she was smart, Pop."

"Very funny!" I said.

"The other interesting thing is that Matthew Greaves also worked for Darkstone in, shall we say, a managerial position."

"Hum," I said and recounted the bare bones of the plot of *Love in Kigali*, the hapless American writer falling for a mercenary commander.

"Russell's probably long gone, but let me know if you see him."

"You know that Camille Costa thinks Greaves had his wife murdered," I said, "and given the fact that she's going to get a good deal of money he thought was his, Camille may also be in danger."

Guevara considered this. He looked at his grandfather, who shrugged.

"Makes sense," Robertson said.

"I'll drop by the house on my way down," said Guevara. "Have a word with her. Maybe I can convince her to stay in the city for a while."

"The funeral is on Saturday in L.A., so it would be logical. She could be helping Josephine with the arrangements."

"I'll try to get some idea of what Greaves' plans are after that," he said.

"Don't trust him," I said and knew right away that I hadn't needed to.

"Speak to Henry here if you see him, "Guevara said. "I really won't be able to talk to you directly anymore. We're getting extra officers in to go through the whole thing again. They're going to canvas the ecological groups to see what the chatter is, who might be radical enough to mount this campaign. The ones assigned to the Valley Fever package may be up to see you again. I'll be busy organizing things. Besides Fred's not keen on my talking to you."

When I got back to Clara's, I told her that I was going to be shut out of the investigation now, and I didn't like that.

That didn't mean I had to stop thinking about though. If Greaves was behind the eco-activism, how had he managed it? Was he capable of hacking into the club website? Had he personally shipped the King Tut books laced with cocci spores? Had he ordered the posters? Let loose the animals? Hired or cajoled Zach into breaking into the Lao's house, and plaster the village with signs? Zach wasn't going to talk apparently, but Greaves would have left some kind of a trail surely. Hiring a friendly marksman seemed easy for him, given his background, but how had they managed to secure the sniper site? Whoever was responsible was clearly ruthless. The incidental body count was no obstacle. And how did the killer bear figure into all this?

A few days later as Clara and I got out of the Honda at the supermarket in Douglas Peak, she observed, "Oh, look there's that little dog again and no one around. It seems to make a habit of getting loose."

"I wouldn't worry," I said. "It seems to make a habit of getting found as well. It's well fed."

I turned right toward the frozen food, and Clara went off into the main store. I was pulling out Amy's Dinners when a tall man asked, "Any good, those."

I turned to him. Puzzled for some reason. "Not bad, better than some, if that's what you have to eat."

He laughed, reaching in to grab two. He had a baseball hat on backwards.

What if…?

I was coming out with two gallons of spring water, when I saw him at the cashier. Was it Russell? Guevara had shown me the police drawing of him only the day before, but I had that facial recognition problem.

If there are two blondes in a movie, I'm lost. I can't tell which is which. Once my students were in the hall, out of their regular desks, names clearly marked on my seating plan, I didn't even know they were mine. I grinned at one and all. If they stopped to talk to me, I prayed for some identifying comment.

In this case, I didn't dare stare. Only one checkout counter was in operation, so I stood behind him. He pocketed his money clip, picked up his groceries and went out.

When I emerged into the glare of the parking lot, Clara was asking him if he knew whose little dog that was.

"Couldn't say," he said. "Sorry ma'am." He gave her a toothy smile and swung himself into his black Rav4. He had excellent teeth.

I was weak kneed as I climbed into the driver's seat of the Honda.

Clara's cell phone had a signal, so I phoned Guevara, and gave the first four digits of the licence number, all I'd been able to memorize. As we passed the Sheriff's office, two cars were heading off in opposite directions.

If it was Russell, why was he still here?

It wasn't until I ran into Henry Robertson behind the BMP general store that I felt reassured. The RAV4 and the man with the backward baseball hat were not to be found anywhere in Douglas Peak.

"Al says not to worry. Camille is still down in L.A and he'll talk to her before she's due back."

"Presumably, she'll be back for the interment on Sunday."

"He'll know that," said Henry.

I realized I thought of him as Henry, not Robertson. As I climbed onto the golf cart, I also realized that I didn't have to suppress my attraction to him. He was age appropriate and single.

"Well, sure, Joanna," I said to myself. "As if you didn't have enough troubles."

Friday was Halloween. When I asked about trick or treating, Colin said that was a thing of the past. Too dangerous now. People had parties instead.

The clocks were due to fall back to Standard Time that weekend, but Daylight Savings Time surprised me in the middle of a Hallowe'en hot dog and French fry dinner at Julia's.

"Oh, look," I cried. "It's dark already."

I gathered my gear together while Colin packaged up dessert for Clara and me.

"There'll be more light once I get out of the woods," I reasoned, "and once the time changes, it will be lighter at night."

Both my conclusions were definitely questionable.

I sped away on the golf cart–at ten miles an hour. Turning right, out of the street, I expected to find light, and it was true that the aspens at the edge of the golf course were florescent yellow against the grey sky, but the sun had vanished behind the heights. The mountains on either side loomed ominously. Over rocky Bear Mountain, a rack of black cloud hung, and over the San Emigdio Mountains, grey and black cumulous promised a storm.

I hit the dusty trail above the golf course where I usually slowed down, but the atmosphere made me speed up. I began to hear Mussorgsky's *Night on Bald Mountain* in my head, full philharmonic version.

I imagined Russell lurking above me on one of the village center's balconies, his night vision rifle trained on my head.

I bounced up off the trail and crossed the drive to the golf club. As I passed the bus shelter, I met a couple with two children, decked out for the party at the club. The father was in a top hat and cloak, carrying a cardboard scythe, while mom was a witch with a broom. The little girl was a ballerina and the son wore a Guy Fawkes face, now more easily identified as Anonymous.

I waved and pressed on.

"One hundred percent chance of rain by eleven," Clara called out gaily, as I locked both doors.

I fell asleep with deep thunder rolling in from the west. Waking up an hour later, I heard either high wind or heavy rain. I sought oblivion once again. Time passed, I presumed, before I was jarred awake by a bone rattling crash of thunder, followed instantly by a great glare of light. I covered my head. A second identical thunderbolt made no dent in my dissociated state.

"That wasn't much rain," said Clara as she stepped out onto the porch the next morning. "Oh, look," she cried. "Snow!"

And indeed, there was snow on the tops of all the mountains.

Saturday was All Saints Day, the day that the Hallowed Eve ushered in. This was the day the religious honoured those souls who had made it to heaven. Then in a spirit of generosity, they celebrated Sunday as All Souls Day, to honour all the dead, no matter where they found themselves.

Saturday was also the day of Arta Dietzen's public funeral at the Hollywood Bowl, which was only half full, if that. In other words, about 3000 people had turned up. LAX had been almost as busy as Oscar week.

The service was all show biz with three of Arta's favourite female vocalists, two of whom had songs at the top of the charts, as well as Lyle Lovett. Elton John did not perform. Perhaps he did not even attend. A number of Arta's friends, including Hollywood notables, spoke of their friendships with her. The late night host who acted as master of ceremonies, noted that her husband, Matthew Greaves, was too overcome to speak.

Booths, set up by various booksellers, a generous gesture by Great Day Publishing, sold an astonishing number of books. Most of the sellers ran out of stock, and resorted to taking orders. A new print run was in the offing.

So Clara told me. I resolutely avoided listening to any of it, so I couldn't be critical of the lack of specific detail. Rihanna? I wondered.

20

BURIAL OF THE DEAD

The interment was entirely different.

It began as a hayride. Following emailed directions, I drove to the corporate center of Halcon Ranch. I parked the car in the large lot, and Clara and I reported to the staging area. We were offered a cold drink, and told that the wagons would be returning in a few minutes. Declining refreshment, we sat on a bench. When they appeared, the 'wagons' had benches on both sides, seating five people a side, and were drawn by an all-terrain vehicle.

We were helped aboard and once the wagon was full, we set off. There were three men and five other women. The women all wore hats. Out of respect, or fear of skin cancer?

Two of the women speculated in whispers about why Arta was being buried at the ranch. A third piped up in an outraged tone that Arta was not only a member of the Halcon Ranch Board; she was also the public face of Halcon Ranch Village. After that silence fell as we hung on to the sides, and bumped over the trail.

The journey to the grave site was longer than the ceremony itself. We wound our way over hill and dale. I began to see why Halcon Ranch could advertise itself as a location for every kind of movie. We passed through desert, hills of olive trees, orchards, forested creeks, and chaparral until we finally ended up in a grove of pin oak. We still had to walk a few hundred yards until we came to the open grave sheltered by oaks. Here the view opened up to a vista of valley and hills.

Someone said, "She has a nice view."

"We have a nice view," I wanted to say. Arta had gone on ahead.

The modest granite gravestone stood aside looking as if it had been chiselled off the dome of Bear Mountain. The inscription was simple, 'Arta Dietzen' and the date of her death. Above it a hand-sized hovering angel was rough-cut into the polished stone.

Granite is older than the metamorphic and sedimentary rock of the San Emigidios. Bear Mountain arose earlier than these facing hills. Formed by fire, it is hard and tough. As a child, I played house on a great granite boulder we called the Big Rock.

Whether Arta had such a connection with it, I didn't know. I knew very little about her really, but neither did most people. She was an enigma of her own making. I did know that both our characters were formed in the fiery crucible of unhappiness. The church taught us that this was the purpose of life–to polish our souls through suffering. Arta would have known that, having been Catholic. She had attended St. John's school in Hot Springs.

Folding chairs sat on three sides of the grave in two rows. Clara and I found seats in the back on the left. The grave was covered with a green carpet of fake grass, which contrasted markedly with the brown ground cover. I studied the program we had been handed. It was a Catholic liturgy but familiar to me as an Anglican choirgirl, and from my parents' interment.

Camille sat in the middle of the front row beside a woman I assumed was Josephine. She looked to be as tall as Camille, but she wore her dark hair long and straight, whereas Camille's had been shorn since I last met her. It stood in spikes, shorter than mine used to be.

On the right three empty chairs in the front row had been reserved. Matthew Greaves, Warren Oliver and the priest arrived last. The priest stood hands folded in front of his cassock beside the grave. Greaves and Warren sat in two of the reserved chairs.

Shortly afterward, a wagon arrived bearing the coffin, almost hidden by white floral tributes, many of them lilies. There was a flurry of activity as the flowers were lifted off and placed near the headstone. Then the serious task of rolling the coffin off the wagon began. Six pallbearers received it, two of them, young and sturdy, probably employees of the ranch.

All of this was accomplished in silence, except for the sigh of the wind.

Once the coffin had been placed over the grave, the priest began, "We are gathered here to commend our sister, Arta to God, and to commit her body to the earth."

The coffin was polished oak, not so very different from the one we had chosen for our father. His just deserts dictated a plywood coffin, but we got uppity, and honoured him out of sheer intractable love. Since his second wife refused to pay for it, we ended up eking out the money by claiming minor policies and selling his old Thunderbird. Wife #2 got everything else our mother had helped him earn.

Then the priest told us that nothing is lost through death, and that we would rise up on the last day. He blessed the grave itself, since of course it was not on hallowed land. According to the church. He called down an angel to watch over it. Clearly, he didn't get the picture. The angels had preceded him.

He invited us to say a silent prayer.

I bowed my head, closed my eyes, and felt the breeze and the dappled sun warming my face. I felt Arta there beyond and yet vividly near. She was happy and excited, chatting, quite unaware of the sad group gathered around her remains. I wished her well.

"I know that my redeemer liveth," said the priest.

"And in my flesh shall I see God," we responded.

"Into your hands, Father of Mercies," the priest began, and now the coffin was lowered into the grave.

A sharp cry, immediately stifled, arose from the front. Camille buried her head on Josephine's arms.

I looked at Greaves. Truly, he was ashen, but his face was stiffened into a mask.

This was that final awful moment of letting go, the moment when people threw themselves into open graves–people like Laertes and my mother.

My mother was restrained by her burly brothers, all five of them. But she took the opportunity later to fall into a rage, and then a fugue state. She was mourning her father, dead of lung cancer at seventy-eight. The doctor made a house call. Sedatives were administered. I was assigned to check on her every hour. She snored deeply all night.

We mourners were prayed for, and then we were dispatched with my favourite piece of liturgy: "May the peace of God, which is beyond all understanding keep you hearts and minds in the knowledge and love of God and of His son, Jesus Christ and of the Holy Spirit."

I didn't doubt that life persisted, but that was no compensation for the loss of Kelly Brown. She had made herself into Arta Dietzen, a successful novelist, whose books I couldn't read, and who didn't actually write them anymore. She had fallen for a dashing military hero as a young writer, and then for dark-haired Camille Costa. What else would she have added to her story before it came to a natural end?

Murderers had no curiosity.

The reception was to be held at Arta's home. The drive was full of cars by the time we got there. Entering the house, I heard Gabriel Faure's *Pavane*, and was surprised to see that Max was playing it on his guitar. Phillip took up the melody on his keyboard.

The summer that I knew him, Max had vowed to teach himself classical guitar, and he had succeeded well enough. Jackson stood with his bass ready and waiting.

Caterers from Halcon Ranch were uncovering plates of tiny sandwiches in the dining room. I went through the kitchen door with my two tins of cookies. Colin had sent cowboy cookies and his famous peanut butter cookies. I expected to find Imelda in the kitchen, but I was surprised to see Fred Trantor, Sydney Ackerman and a woman I didn't know, cutting chocolate and lemon sponge and loading plates with cookies.

"At least the dessert is down-home cooking," Sydney observed, licking her fingers. "Oh, hey, Joanna, this is my sister Sarah."

"I'd shake but-," said Sarah, whose fingers were yellow.

"The plates are up there," said Fred, "And no, I bought it, but from a very good bakery. None of that Costco slab cake for this gourmet." She flourished her coconut cake on its cake stand.

Imelda chuckled as she took my tins.

Through the door, I could see Clara talking to Matthew Greaves, her head tilted to one side, the picture of consolation. Matthew was nodding as he placed his hand around her shoulder and guided her toward the bar.

"You're wondering how we co-opted the party," said Sydney, holding her knife in front of her. "I claimed my on-going friendship with Arta of course." She winked. "Well, I had been summoned on various occasions- new book, news release on Halcon Village. I just phoned and asked Camille. I suggested the women of the community would bring dessert, so here we are in our glad rags."

I had already noted that Fred's sandals had rhinestones on the toe thong.

"Happy to see you," said Imelda, carefully and smiling broadly, as she finished heaping Colin's large cookies onto plates.

"And there is music," I said, throwing out my arms.

"Indeed," said Sarah, "and my husband is lurking in the underbrush, keeping an eye out."

"Are you going to let Camille stay here?" I asked Fred.

"Greaves is leaving once this reception is over. He's taking the Mercedes. He had somebody drive the little red thing down already. He's off to the Bahamas. Urgent business. I doubt if he'll show his face here again now he knows the place is held in trust."

I watched her as she washed her hands at the little sink on the island. She no longer seemed like an ogre, and her smile no longer struck me as false.

"I know," she said looking up. "Phillip has offered to have her stay at his place. But she won't go. She wants to be here in Arta's house." Fred was looking for a towel and not finding one, wiped her hands on her skirt.

"It's hard to think that the 'perps' would try anything more at this point," said Sarah.

Sydney scoffed. "Doesn't being a defence attorney teach you anything? They're on a roll here. Might as well finish the job and get Camille out of the way."

Imelda had a platter in both hands, and was moving into the dining room. The main table was covered with sandwiches, the buffet was serving as the bar, but there were two side tables, one at either end of the room that held coffee with space for these platters. The rest of us passed the other dessert plates in to Imelda.

Then we stood around the island, looking at each other, all except Imelda, who was rinsing off the knives.

"Camille is not safe here," I said.

"See if you can talk to her," said Fred.

So I took myself out into the living room, wine glass in hand. The *Kentucky Three* were playing *Let it Be.*

Warren Oliver and what looked like the board of Halcon Village were seated together, deep in conversation. I wondered if Arta had been replaced yet.

Greaves was talking gaming to a couple in a corner of the room. Several women were looking at a display of Arta's novels and trying to remember when they had started reading them.

On the patio, the smokers were lounging in several groups, the catering people moving among them, taking drink orders.

I prowled down the wing where Camille's office was, passing its open door and several closed doors, which I presumed were bedrooms. Between the doors, white cabinetry lined the walls, so that each doorway was recessed. One door stood open into a narrow room fitted with similar built-in storage, some tall like clothes closets, some drawers and some shelves packed with linen, all in white woodwork. Imelda was kneeling at a linen shelf, pulling out white napkins all tidily folded. She was too absorbed to notice me. The next door was open and I availed myself of its facilities. It had a large shower as well as a tub, not the facilities I needed.

I knew that the master suite was in the wing on the other side of the house, along with Arta's study. At the end of the hall, I came to a sun porch with a billiard table and a fireplace. Camille and Josephine and two women I hadn't met were seated around the fireplace. There was a small fire burning. Camille waved me over, and one of the women joined the other on a floor cushion, so I could have her chair.

"I've been trying to convince Camille not to stay here alone," said Josephine.

"Fred sent me on the same mission," I said. "How are you doing?"

"Badly," said Josephine. "One part grief, two parts bloody-mindedness."

"It's my home," said Camille. "Arta left it to me. Well, more or less."

We nattered on at her, to no avail. Then I got up and went to get food. It was dinnertime.

Clara called me over to where she was chatting with the priest, the same priest who read Thomas Aquinas every morning as he ate his breakfast at the club. Could I believe it? She demanded. No, I couldn't. I hadn't recognized him.

As I was picking up sandwiches, Clara came over, carrying the crystal vase, apparently now hers, and said she needed to go home. She was tired, but she had called Colin, who was just coming up from the city, and who would pick her up in fifteen minutes. Did I mind?

I wanted to leave myself, but Fred Trantor, who had overheard Clara, gave me a look, which told me I should stay. I assumed that once the crowd thinned, we would make a concerted effort to change Camille's mind.

The Halcon Ranch board had broken up, and its members were making a perfunctory effort to mix. A woman still sat talking to Warren Oliver. I sat down at one of the chairs beside them, and we introduced ourselves.

"And how do you know Arta?" asked the woman, a sleek blonde in black silk jacket and trousers.

"I live up the mountain," I said, "in Bear Mountain Place, and met her through my friend, Clara. I haven't known her very long, but apparently Clara reminded Arta of her mother."

"Oh, yes," she replied and that seemed to bring our conversation to a halt.

"And you?" I finally said.

"I met Arta through Warren here," she nodded at him and smiled sweetly. "And of course I'd read her books. Aren't they wonderful, so absorbing, a girl's daydream?"

I smiled broadly and checked Warren's expression. But he was a businessman and had on his game face.

"Perhaps you're not a reader," she went on. Her tiny nose tilted skyward.

"Oh, very much so," I replied. "But I only just learned about Arta's books. Somehow I missed them. Fortunately, she gave Clara a number of them last week."

How civilized not to have resorted to the gag reflex, I thought, broadly smiling.

I presumed that not speaking ill of the dead included damning their life's work.

At that point, Greaves approached Warren Oliver, and the two of them walked out the front door. There I could see them in deep conversation in the entrance.

I hated parties. I liked half a dozen people talking together over a good meal. But my social awkwardness was at its worst in these fluid situations, where you had to seek out a place to be, and some stranger to talk to. I made a trip to the cookie table, and got a cup of hot black tea.

I drifted into the kitchen, which was spotless and empty. I tried the patio where the smokers had filled all the chairs. I took a stroll through the chaparral in the direction of the riverbed. The temperature was beginning to fall as the sun slid behind the hills. I came back by way of the corral on the other side of the helipad. The three horses came over to greet me at the fence, but didn't stay interested when they figured out I was empty-handed. I could see a stable guy at the other end. When I arrived back at the patio, Matthew Greaves was doing what looked like a farewell circuit, thanking everyone for coming. People, especially the women, held his hands and gazed into his eyes with deep sympathy. He soaked it up.

Back inside, I found the musicians had slid into slightly less sober music, Leonard Cohen's *Hallelujah*. Max was mouthing the words, but not actually singing. I wished he would. When they finished, they looked around at the dwindling crowd and decided to take a break. As the three of them moved toward the dining room, I realized that Max and Phillip were the only people there that I knew even slightly besides Fred and Sydney. My relationship with all of them had been adversarial, but at least I could talk to them.

I left my teacup on the kitchen counter, and went to refill my wine glass in the dining room. Phillip, Max and Jackson were standing there with plates of sandwiches.

"So what's the thinking now amongst conspiracy theorists?" asked Max.

I shrugged. "This conspiracy theorist thinks it was never about eco-terrorism."

"So what was it about?"

"Personal animosity?"

"It does look," said Phillip, "as if somebody planned a frame-up, quite possibly with the Kentucky Five in mind."

"So who was the real intended victim?" asked Jackson. "Arta Dietzen? And poor Roger Smith was just part of the frame-up?"

"Seems like it," said Max, "and the frame might have stuck, if Phillip had left the meeting, to answer that bogus lost dog call."

Phillip nodded. "Somebody didn't do his research."

"Not on your security maybe, but otherwise not bad," I said. "Still not many people have dog nanny cameras."

"Really!" said Phillip, in mock astonishment.

Fred came into the room through the door to the other wing. "Bring your plates and join us in Arta's study," she said.

We trouped after her down the side hall, and arrived at the first door on the left where Guevara, Sydney and Sarah were standing. Arta's desk stood against the window looking out on the corral where a golden horse was tossing its head. Fred perched on the edge of the desk facing us. She pushed the desk chair in my direction with her foot. I fielded it, and rolled it to the side to sit down. Guevara offered the only other chair to Sarah while the four men stood. The walls were lined with glass- fronted bookcases. What had Arte read?

"Do we all know each other?" asked Fred and seeing a general affirmation, went on, "It seemed only fitting, that those in the frame should be drafted as allies. Joanna, Sydney and Sarah have followed the story from the beginning. I'll let Al Guevara outline the situation."

"Greaves has left. Once the guests are gone, we're going to change the security code. We've already done a walk-around to check whether the perimeter is safe, inside and out."

"We're not making any allegations here," Fred interrupted, "but conceivably the perpetrator, having discovered that this house is now the property of a trust, favouring Camille Costa, and that royalties now go to her, may have designs on her as well. Phillip has offered to have her stay at his place in Bear Mountain Place, but she has declined. She has also refused to allow an officer to be stationed inside the house."

"We will have a car outside," said Guevara. "But the property is very open and remote."

"I'd like Phillip and Joanna as well to have another go at Camille. You don't necessarily need to be specific about who may be a threat to her," said Fred.

"I'll stay," said Max. "Like to see anybody get past me."

"Me too," said Jackson.

"Well, I suppose you could plead too drunk to drive," said Fred.

"Doesn't work very well for teetotallers," I observed. I knew Max never drank, and Jackson didn't seem to either. I didn't add that while Jackson was in his forties, Max was nearer my age, a bit past a physical fight.

"Re alcohol abstinence-I have a secret weapon at my disposal," grinned Max.

"Please, don't go on," said Guevara.

"That's fine for tonight, but what about the future?" said Phillip, who had noticeably not volunteered to put his body between Camille and danger.

Fred sighed, "One day at a time."

As the meeting broke up, Guevara pointed out that there were two master bedrooms opening farther down the hall, with a joint master bathroom on the corral side of the house. The hallway itself looked out on the patio, as did the hallway on the opposite wing.

Max's secret weapon turned out to be brownies. By this time only six of us remained-the Kentucky Three, Camille, Josephine and me. Josephine had stayed the night before and intended to stay tonight. The two women were still sitting in front of the fire, which was all but out. Jackson worked at getting it going again, while Max produced his brownie tin. I had had Max's brownies before, as well as others, although not for years. I was extremely tired by now, so I helped myself as the tin went round. We took turns trying to convince Camille to leave, but so far as I could see neither the brownies nor our arguments were having any effect.

Then I stood up.

"Oh dear," I said. "Those were awfully strong."

"No they weren't," Max protested. "I halved the magic ingredient."

"Beg to differ," I said, trying to get my balance. It wasn't even a nice stone.

Of course it was amusing. At least it drew Camille out of herself for a moment.

"The two bedrooms and Imelda's cot are taken, but you can sleep in Arta's room. If you don't mind."

"Don min," I said.

O God, what an awful stone!

Not for the first time, I found myself sleeping in the bed of a recently deceased person. That's the sort of thing that comes with age. I was just straight enough to be thankful that I related well to dead people.

I fell asleep with my phone clutched in my hand. It was two in the morning when I woke up, hearing what sounded like a toilet flushing. Which reminded me. I managed to get up, find the door to the bathroom, and even to turn the light on. The water in the toilet was not quite still.

"I hate that," I thought. "One of those malfunctions where a toilet sets itself off. Unless one of the guys had taken Matthew's room, next door and used it." Then I forgot about it.

In the morning, I went into the kitchen, where I chatted with Imelda and drank a lot of water.

"I didn't know you lived here," I said.

"No," she said. "Live *me esposo* Carlos."

Declining breakfast, I passed Max and Jackson sleeping on couches and fled to Clara's Honda.

When I arrived back home, Clara was sitting on the deck swing, in her coat, reading her meditation book.

"You went out already?' She asked.

"No, I'm just getting home. I didn't think I should drive. A few of us stayed over."

"I just assumed you were still asleep in your room," she said.

"That's the good thing about this house. Your room is on one end and the guest rooms are on the other."

I never missed a chance to see the positive side of the move from Vegas.

Back to normal, I thought, as I showered and ate breakfast. Out of the spotlight. The police would handle Camille's safety.

I did some housework at Clara's, and took my wash to Julia's where I got back to my blogs. When the temperature rose at mid-day, I walked with her down the horse trail. She was able to hike farther now, so I walked back by myself. An enormous racoon crossed the path in front of me as I neared the lake, and disappeared into the reeds, headed for some daytime fishing. Obviously it didn't know it was supposed to be nocturnal. The ducks and coots were still there, despite advancing autumn. Like the red-winged black birds and the Stellar's Jays, this was as far south as they needed to go.

Where did the coon live I wondered. Somewhere down in the 'wet-land'. Now I was envying a racoon. Think of yourself as a wandering Taoist, I advised myself.

Before dinner, I sat outside with Colin while he had a martini and smoked a cigarette. The hawk was sitting on her dining branch. Dinner was a good-sized mouse. It hung limply from the bird's claws-much to my relief.

After dinner, I went back to Clara's and watched HGTV with her. Then I retired to my room to watch *Death at Pemberly*. I slept soundly in absolute darkness. The moon was down behind the mountain.

Next day, Clara and I breakfasted at the club, and I let myself stretch out emotionally. I began to relax from the trauma of the last week. Camille was not my problem.

Julia and I were devouring Diana Gabaldon's *Outlander* series. Julia was reserving through the public library, and picking up at our ill-fated Douglas Peak branch. I was downloading them on my iPad. We were usually reading the same book. Basically, *Outlander* tells the story a WWII nurse just after the war. She has gone on a second honeymoon with her husband from whom she was separated all the years of the war. While she is visiting a ring of standing stones in the Scottish highlands, she falls through the circle into the eighteenth century.

In the third book, *Voyager*, I came upon a delightful section in which Claire, now a surgeon-yes, she leaps about in time-picks up a romance novel called *The Impetuous Pirate* in the doctor's lounge. Gabaldon includes a few pages of this novel. The lady in question, a prize of war, finds herself reluctantly drawn to the dastardly pirate, who has just killed a hundred men, and is making bold advances on her person. Suffice to say nipples come into play. They usually do in a Gabaldon novel. But this is a rape fantasy writ large. Rape fantasies are quite *other* than rape reality, and Gabalon's rapes are serious matters, not that there isn't-never mind.

In these few pages of *The Impetuous Pirate*, she is saying, "This is romance. It is not what I write". Here the characters are stereotypes, and there is none of the rich historical and natural detail of her main book nor her readable style. If T*he Impetuous Pirate* deserved a 2, Arta's books would merit a 5, whereas Gabaldon's might rate 8.

That afternoon, I was at Julia's standing on the step stool to put away dishes when there was a knock at the door. Colin was playing golf, so Julia opened it. I heard Guevara's voice asking if I was in and I climbed down.

"Leave your shoes on," Julia was saying.

"And track in pine pitch?" I thought.

Fred Trantor appeared from around the corner. "We need a word," she said.

"I'll leave you," said Julia, turning back toward her bedroom.

"No, no. Stay, Dr. Durant," said Fred. "Another brain will help."

Guevara took the desk chair again; Julia sat in her big, reading chair with its immense ottoman, while Fred and I shared the couch.

"At 2 a.m. this morning, emergency services received a call for an apparent attempted suicide," said Fred Trantor, "And Camille Costa was transported to hospital."

"That's why she insisted on staying there? She intended to kill herself?" I said.

"Not exactly," said Guevara, and he waited for Fred to go on.

"It appeared that she was in the process of cutting her wrists in a half full bathtub. Only one wrist had been cut. Curiously, Camille was unconscious when Imelda found her. They're running blood tests, but we are fairly sure that they will find Rohypnol in her system, and in the gin bottle beside her bed."

"Imelda found her before she lost much blood," Guevara went on. "She had heard the water running from her cot in the storage area. It woke her up. She knew Camille never took baths. As she went to look, she was nearly knocked down by a tall person rushing past her."

"We've examined the data from the security system. None of the doors or windows were opened after 5 p.m. Imelda's husband dropped her off just before that. He was about to pick up his truck at the Flying J for a long haul up north. Imelda doesn't usually sleep at the Dietzen house, but when she does, she always bunks on a cot she pulls out in the storage room," Fred added. "In fact, so far as we can tell the doors were opened only for Camille or Imelda all day. Camille at least had the sense to keep the place closed and the alarm on."

"So, we believe her assailant was in the house somewhere and had been since Sunday afternoon."

"You slept there Sunday night, we've heard. Did you see or hear anything that might help us?" asked Fred.

I was shaking my head, absorbed by shock. I realized I had put my hand to my mouth. It was like a replay of the news of Mrs. King's death from Valley Fever, delivered in the same place, weeks earlier.

Fred had started talking again, to Julia, about the effects of Rohypnol in terms of the time line.

"Just a minute," I said and recounted the story of the running toilet.

"Someone could have been hiding in Greaves' room," said Guevara.

"Pretty risky," said Fred.

"Otherwise how could he have slipped the drug into the gin bottle at the right time?"

"No one would have expected me to sleep in Arta's room, or Imelda to sleep there Monday night," I said.

"We think Greaves' accomplice is an experienced sniper and black operative. Wouldn't such a person be more careful?" asked Fred.

"That house is like Clara's," I said. There are bedrooms on opposite sides of the house. Of course, in Arta's house the separation is much greater because the place is bigger, and maybe we need to factor in arrogance."

"We know that whoever it was left the house after Camille was transported to hospital. Imelda followed in Camille's car, so the place was empty by then," Guevara added.

"We may find finger prints that match Russell's, but I doubt it," said Fred. "Of course we'll find Greaves' prints everywhere. Someone like Russell would have worn gloves throughout."

"Maybe he splashed the toilet seat," I suggested, but the laugh I got was very wan. "Does urine have DNA in it?"

"Not actually unless it has epithelial cells, and healthy urine doesn't usually have those," said Julia.

"Exactly," Fred agreed. "Fecal matter can determine animal species, but that's about it."

"What about the killer bear identification?" I asked.

Guevara grimaced. "Saliva, digestive juices."

We considered that for a moment. I was sure all of us had come up with a bodily excretion which would provide DNA, but that seemed like a long shot.

"What I need to ask, Joanna," said Fred, "Is whether you would be willing to take Camille under your wing? She doesn't want to go to Phillip's. Allergic to dogs, she says, and Phillip admits Sheba Inus shed constantly. Allergic to the Y chromosome, ask me. Anyway, we can put her in a fairly secure room at the inn, and provide an officer out in front. But she'd really need someone to act as gofer and support."

We could do that," said Julia, "but are we sure the sniper isn't still in the vicinity?"

"He may have been," said Guevara. "Russell does own a RAV4, such as Joanna reported seeing, but we've scoured the area and found no sign of him or his vehicle, even from the air. Seems he's cleared out."

"Not sure I agree with the Sheriff's decision to put her up here," said Fred. "He thinks it's the least likely place Russell would expect. And there's always cost to consider."

I blew out a big breath. The village hadn't felt safe to me for a while.

"We don't think they'll make another attempt on Camille's life anyway," said Guevara.

21

BARISTAS AND THE BOTTOM LINE

When I arrived at Bear Mountain Inn two days later, Detective Guevara and his grandfather were in the room setting up a collapsible table, borrowed from the golf club.

The Inn was a cut or two above the old Reality Hotel, and correspondingly, more expensive. It looked like an Alpine Ski Chalet, and sat at the other end of the village centre, nearer the post office than the general store. Like the Reality Hotel, however, the second floor rooms were accessed by outside stairs. The Inn had stairs at both ends, accessing two rooms each from a shared balcony. Of the four rooms on that floor, the front two also had private balconies. Camille had been booked into one of those. The room that shared the side balcony would be kept empty.

"If the little desk could be stored somewhere else, we could put the table where it is," Camille said. That was in front of the sliding glass door to the private balcony, through which the astonishing mountain light was streaming.

"We can move it," said the landlady. I recognized her from the inn's website. She was Donna Haynes.

"Am I in the way?" I asked.

"No, no," said Fred Trantor. "Glad to have you aboard."

Guevara and his grandfather were moving the small desk onto the side deck, and the landlady was following them out.

"Let me know if there's anything else," she said as she left.

The two men came back in, and Guevara shut the door.

"As I've explained to Camille, it's best if she lies low for a while, until we have some idea where Russell is," said Fred Trantor. "We do know now that he's using the alias of William Morris. That's the name he used to rent a mailbox online, in L.A. It's one of those with an actual street address. We think he's got a place in Venice Beach. I'm hoping we'll have more information shortly. Meanwhile, we want Camille to keep her head down."

"There's a small fridge here," Guevara said, gesturing toward the bathroom vestibule, "and we'll provide a microwave, but food will have to be brought up. Henry will be gofer for pizza or deli stuff. We're hoping we can count on you to help out with meals, Joanna. I know Dr. Durant offered to help as well."

"Colin does the cooking and we've shared his meals before. One of us will bring food over," I said. "He's a good cook," I assured Camille.

She was sitting in a desk chair, which had been brought up from her office. Her face was white and as she drew her hands through her cropped hair, I saw the bandage on her right wrist.

"Okay," she said. "I'm going to follow instructions to the letter. I can do with the rest. No distractions."

"Oh, we'll get a television set in for you," Fred began. "We can connect to the inn's satellite dish."

"No need. I have my computer."

"Talk to Donna about that," Guevara put in. "The internet connection is slow up here, no cable of course."

"I've got a bunch I haven't read on my tablet, and I've got writing to do."

"We're over-extended at the Sheriff's Department in spite of the seconded officers," said Guevara, "but Henry here and a couple of retired deputies will do shifts keeping an eye out. He'll introduce them to you. The village center is small and easy to observe. The guys will do sweeps randomly to keep track of what cars are here. Bear Mountain Place Security will also be helping out. We've told them it is a witness protection issue, but not who you are."

"Of course there's the famous mountain telegraph," Fred chuckled. "Ideas springing from mind to mind."

I smiled insincerely.

"Something like that," said Henry. "Don't worry, Ma'am," he said to Camille. "We've got your back."

"I think that's it," said Fred. "Tell Henry what you need."

"Could Imelda bring me what I might have forgotten?"

"No," said Fred, "Too easy for someone to follow her. We'll see to that for you. Tell Henry what you need."

When they were gone, the room felt a little bigger, but not much. Beside the door, a stone fireplace was wedged into the corner. On the other side of the door was a small comfortable-looking couch covered in orange and yellow silk. The fire had to be enjoyed from the sleigh bed apparently. There was kindling and wood in a basket. There was also a wall heater. An antique dresser stood guard next to the bathroom foyer. The folding closet door there was open, revealing the bar fridge with Camille's shirts hanging above it and pants beside it.

It occurred to me that clothes would need to be washed in a week or so. She hadn't brought much.

Camille sat at the table staring through the window. I sat down on the love seat.

"How are you doing?" I asked.

She started as if she had forgotten I was still there. "I'm okay, I guess. It occurs to me that Russell, whatever he's called-Greaves' assassin-may have had the right idea."

"Are you suicidal?"

"No," she shrugged, "not really, just really, really sad. I'm right off gin, so something good came of it. A little wine for my stomach's sake, but no more hard stuff."

"Do you want me to pick some up?"

"I brought a couple of bottles from the house, the best there was. I intend to ration them."

"How do you think you will manage here?"

"I feel like curling up in a ball for a few days. Well actually, I feel like curling up in a ball for the rest of my life, but that isn't my way."

"Nor mine."

"Kindred spirits." She sighed deeply. "I'll get back in the saddle momentarily. I'm writing my own book as well, as you probably don't know."

"No, I didn't. What sort of book?"

"A bit hard to explain. Economics really."

My astonishment showed.

"Well, I did my degree in economics at Yale. You had me down as an airhead."

"Did I?"

"Maybe not you, but most people. They label-labelled-Arta as feather-brained, so what did that make her assistant? My book's along the line of Yanis Varoufakis's *The Global Minotaur*, which he aimed for ordinary readers. He was explaining the cause of the Great Recession of 2008, and how we should be dealing with its fallout."

"I liked that book," I said.

"The Minotaur metaphor grabbed the imagination," said Camille. "But the simpler one was more important. Here is a mountain of debt. Here is a mountain of savings." She used her hands. "How do we get the savings to flow into the debt? In other words, there's more than enough wealth. We just have to get it circulating."

Varoufakis had yet to become world famous that summer as the abrasive Greek Finance Minister who almost broke up the Eurozone.

Reading his book I came to see that Canada and America work because there are mechanisms that facilitate the flow of money to Have-Not areas, and people within those countries find it easy to seek work outside these areas. Europe does not have these self-correcting aids. Language being one major obstacle.

But even in America, it did not always work. There was enough wealth to deal with the debt caused by the Great Recession. Money flowed from the government to the banks, but not to the people, whose income disappeared and who lost their homes.

"He's very forthright in denouncing bogus economic theory and false presumptions," I said.

"I started my book during the Occupy Movement, and my audience will be that 99%, as they called themselves. Like Varoufakis, I don't believe austerity and budget cuts are the answer."

"It will sell well on the mountain," I said. Half the people here have fled one economic downturn or another-Julia and Colin included. A few years ago they were making a solid six figures a year." I thought for a minute. "Blake, Julia's father, thinks the downtrodden are going to rise up in riot and revolution. He lives in hope of it." Then I added, "And a guaranteed income for all."

"Certainly the bottom-line business model isn't working. It's everybody for himself."

"No pensions, no benefits, no job security, no real attachment, no sense of community at the job."

"If consumers don't get paid fairly, they don't consume. They can't consume. What happens to the economy then?" said Camille.

"The book's finished really, but I'm working on references and so on. I'm calling it *The Barista and Henry Ford.* Ford paid his employees enough so they could afford to buy a Model T."

"And you don't think Starbucks pays enough, so its employees can buy a latte?"

"Very funny," she said.

"I suppose you have the contacts to get it published."

"I've already got a publisher. Great Day is part of a big German publishing conglomerate, one of the three or four big houses still left."

"So was Arta feather-brained?"

"Pretty much," Camille replied, smiling up at me.

I went out the door humbled. I had disliked the simple-mindedness of Arta's romances, and had been outraged that Camille was actually writing them, but now I saw why. Love had come into it of course, but it also allowed Camille to do her real writing. And she was writing about ideas I could barely understand.

When I came down the stairs from the second floor deck, I saw Henry sitting on a bench in front of a real estate office and joined him.

How did they figure out Russell's alias? Do you know?" I asked.

"He's pretty smart, but we got the jump on him when you and Al saw them in the Bakersfield bar. He didn't expect to be identified that quick. If at all. Then the deputies working on the Valley Fever parcel found out that a dozen copies of the book had been ordered from Amazon, and sent to a Wilshire mailbox store. The box had been rented in the name of William Morris. The guy behind the counter there remembered who picked them up. He had a crush on her. She was a barista at the nearby Starbucks. When they showed her a photo array, she identified Russell. He picked the books up from her at the coffee shop. Turns out a William Morris owns a house on the canal in Venice Beach. A neighbour identified him as Russell. Some ultra modern place behind a high cement wall, way beyond Russell's pay grade. The tech guys are still looking at the money trail. Seems it's going to take a while."

"Do you think they'll get a search warrant for the house?"

"Yeah, but Russell's not stupid enough to keep the gun. They're already talking to gun dealers. Too expensive to trash-for Russell anyway. Apparently, he's careful with his money. Seems unusual for a risk-taker, but he also seems to be-what do they say-OCD. Wants to control every last detail."

I sat absorbing this information. "Thanks for telling me," I said.

"Here's something else." He stared off to the mountain northwest of the village. "Hector, my great grandson 'fessed up that he and Zach went for rides in a red sports car this summer. The man, who owned it, bought them pizza and ferried them up Mount Joe. He talked to them about environmental issues, especially how farmers were draining the aquifers. He pointed out to Zach that his mother cared about the water issue. Hector thinks Zach met him alone as well. After the Lau's house was flooded, Hector was pretty sure Zach had done it, but Zach avoided him, so he never got to ask."

"Wow!"

"Looks as if the passport and flight ticket were meant to get Zach out of town before he spilled the beans."

"I'm surprised Russell didn't just shoot the kid," I said.

"From what Hector says Greaves really liked Zach. I doubt if he would have sanctioned that."

"Still, Zach should get out of town before one of the villains changes his mind."

The next day, Ben and two helpers moved Clara's new sideboard into her kitchen. In two pieces. That's how big and heavy the Craftsman-style, oak buffet/ cabinet was. Ben screwed the top on, while the other two held it in place. One side had a wooden pie cooling rack below a glass-fronted pie safe. The other side had open shelves. It filled the end wall of the big kitchen.

"I'll put the fine china in the dining room display cabinet. The simpler pieces will go here." She gestured at one of her brightly plumaged roosters, and several Mexican pieces of red and orange.

"It's beautiful," I said.

Ben stood back and nodded, smiling.

"I think I'm going to like living here," Clara said, as she put the rooster on the buffet.

When the job was finished, Ben found me on the deck doing tai chi.

"We're going to do an intervention with Zach. The three of us, and Margarita. Guevara is going to bring his nephew Hector. Lori's going to ask Julia to be there. I guess she's afraid we may need a doctor. I was wondering if you would come too. I figure you can never have too many grandmothers in a situation like that."

Julia and I joined the family on Tuesday night. The restaurant was closed as usual on Tuesday, but Julien had made dinner for the family. We arrived just as they were putting dishes in the dishwasher. Tables had been pushed together into one long dining surface. Urns of coffee and hot water for tea sat on the counter. Zach was searching for coke in a cooler.

"Bring a couple," Ben told him.

"You mean I can have more than one?" asked Zach.

"Not necessarily," said Ben.

"I take it little Julia is on her own tonight," I said, as I sat down with my herbal tea.

"Our favourite nurse, Debbie, is on tonight," said Lori. "Besides this is a two-child family. Tonight's Zach's turn."

"What?" said Zach. "It's not my birthday."

At that point, Guevara came through the door with Hector.

"What are you doing here?" Zach demanded.

Hector answered by raising his eyebrows and grimacing, as he took the coke Ben was handing to him.

Julia had been seated next to Zach, and, by arrangement, she began. "You don't have to worry, Zach. You're not in trouble, but we do need your help. Hector, can you tell us what you told your Grandpa Henry?"

Hector squirmed in his chair, looked at his uncle, Al, and took a deep breath. "Don't be mad, Zach. I told him about Mr. Greaves taking us for rides in his sports car, and talking about how farmers like Mr. Lau were draining the aquifers. I told him I thought you broke into that house and caused the flood." He stopped and looked at Guevara.

Zach's eyes had opened wide, but they didn't seem to be focused.

"It's all right, Zach," Julia said, laying her hand on his arm. "You're not going to be charged. We just need to hear from you. Is this true?"

Zach turned to look at his mother. "He told me you cared about the aquifers. I thought you would be proud of me. It was stupid. I was stupid." He lowered his head to the table and began to sob.

Zach was wailing about that Chinese kid, who tried to kill himself, and anyway, the sniper would kill him now that he'd told.

"He already tried to kill that lady there," -he pointed at me- "cause she saw him the day we scouted that Chinese house."

For once my prosopagnosia had let me down. I had actually recognized Zach, stranger though he was, when I saw him a second time at the art gallery. By asking him if he lived next door to the Lao's, I laid myself open to the tripwire. I hadn't recognized Greaves, although I had met him several times before. I might have if I had seen him in the context of his red MGB, just as I did when I saw him in Bakersfield. I had yet to encounter Russell when I saw the three of them. My facial recognition deficit made it unnecessary to eliminate me, but they didn't know that.

A game of musical chairs had erupted, so that Lori could embrace Zach from one side, and Margarita from the other.

When things quieted down, Guevara said, "Nobody outside this room is going to know."

Zach looked at him doubtfully. It made sense, I supposed. With first- degree murder charges pending, the lesser crimes would likely not be prosecuted. Zach would never have to testify against Greaves.

Lori and Margarita went upstairs with Zach.

"I would like to get a fuller statement from Zach," Guevara said. You seem to be able to calm him down, Dr. Durant. Would you be willing to carry on?"

"I don't mind doing it, but I'm not sure I'd know what to ask."

"We can go over that now before the others come back down," said Guevara. "I can sit at another table while you talk to him."

"Do I need to stay?" Hector asked.

"No. Grandpa Henry can take you home." He paused, "How do you feel about blowing Zach's cover?"

"I don't know. Not good, I guess, but those guys are murderers. I want you to catch them. And Zach wouldn't talk to me anymore anyway."

After Hector had left, Guevara and Julia worked together while Julien went to the wine cooler. When they were finished, Zach was still upstairs being consoled, so Guevara brought us up to date.

"So it looks as if it was never eco-terrorism. Seems like personal revenge-the scorned husband and all that." There were puzzled looks from some of the listeners. "Arta was having an affair. Greaves discovered that when he returned unexpectedly from China." He paused. "That's when the conspiracy began. Greaves got involved at the beginning, recruiting Zach. Had a bit of fun. Not a bright move. The rest, he seems to have left to Russell. The spores came from a Level 3 biosafety lab in Arizona. We know who got them out. Sad story there. The spores are microscopic, of course, and laced into powdery white flour. It seems unlikely Russell packed them under the same rigid conditions as the lab worker. So the search of his Venice place will entail Hazmat suits."

"During the Second World War," he went on, "Minter Field just north of Bakersfield had a big problem with Valley fever. That's when the military got interested in it in the 50's, and actually developed it as a bio-chemical weapon."

I wondered out loud, "Freeing the animals, the flood, the Valley Fever package, the wounding with lead bullets, the arson in Douglas Peak and the shootings – was the bear part of it too?'

Guevara replied, "Some bright spark said it was doubtful the bear was trained to kill."

I hadn't seen Clara since the morning. When I got back to her place at around 9:30 p.m., she came out of her room with Jazz at her heels.

"Is it too late for happy hour?" she sang out.

"Never," I said, fishing the wine out of the fridge door.

Clara's wine glasses were so small that could be true, and still not make us alcoholics.

"Well," she said, taking her glass. "I want to hear about your intervention, but first, I've got news of my own." She took a sip of her *Barefoot Pinot Grigio*. "I feel as if I've let you down on the detection front, I've been so busy, but I've got something now. I got to talking with a woman in the thrift shop in Douglas Peak. She closed the place up and went for lunch with me at the Mexican restaurant. Seems she lives in one of those houses above the library next door to the sniper house. They call that a 'hide', she said. Turns out the people were away because they won a trip to Hawaii, all five of them. They couldn't even remember entering the contest. A travel agent contacted them to say the tickets were good only for one certain week in October, airfare and adjoining rooms at a hotel in Maui. This was the end of August. I mean that's when they were contacted. So the parents took the week off in October, and pulled the three kids out of school. Who can blame them?"

"So the house would be empty the night of the town hall meeting."

"When they came home on Sunday, they found the ladder to the attic pulled down and the attic window still open. Those poor people, they're just devastated."

"I can imagine. I wonder if the travel agent met whoever arranged it."

"Yes. It seemed fishy so the agent insisted on it. Seems it was a woman, turned up with $7000 cash. Said it was actually her sister's family, but the sister would never accept charity, so they would need to make out it was a prize she'd won. At least, that's what my thrift shop friend had heard."

"I wonder who the woman was."

"Not a sister. The so-called winner was an only child. Anyway, she's Filipino and barely five feet tall. The 'sister' apparently was six feet."

"Did she have long black hair?" I could feel my own hair wanting to stand on end.

"She wore a newsboy's cap, so she might have tucked it up."

"Another barista perhaps," I said.

When Clara looked uncomprehending, I told her about our séance and its aftermath.

"Well, you know," Clara observed, "all those baristas have degrees and half them are really actors. Tom and I were pretty classy secret shoppers when we were between gigs. We checked up on how well the sales staff was doing. Never once got *made*." She was clearly delighted to use that word.

I recalled my own days behind the counter. A '*Shoppe*r-in-the-store' rumour would run like wildfire down the floor from Perfume and Cosmetics, to Jewellery, to Scarves and to me in, Bargain Blouses. Then I would find an urgent need to go upstairs for change. There I would spread the news to the second floor: Better blouses, Dresses, Coats and Lingerie. I did not, however, disabuse Clara of her notion that she had been invisible.

Clara appointed herself breakfast provider for Camille. She'd phone her early, take her order, and bring her breakfast from the club or the bakery, when it was open.

I took dinner to Camille. One night I brought two glass containers - main course and apple crumble, a Ziplock bag and an insulated cup with a double espresso.

She had to get up from her worktable to let me in. She had drawn the drapes against the dark, and pools of lamplight gave the room a cozy feel.

"I'm cross-eyed," she said. "I need to stop."

"You'll probably want to warm this up in the microwave." It was shepherd's pie, one of Colin's specialties. From eating out in good L.A. restaurants several times a week, he had switched to gourmet cooking on a budget.

"Not a chance. Too hungry," she said, digging into the container.

"The desert is non-gluten, but excellent," I said.

"Really! I didn't dare say that I'm non-gluten. I thought I'd just motor through the gluten experience for the time being."

"There's a Ziplock bag of non-gluten bread here as well. Enough for breakfast anyway. Colin will be making more shortly. It's also tasty. But you don't have a toaster."

"Donna said she'd loan me one. She's got a spare."

"So are you okay here?"

Camille sighed. "Henry dropped up and made me laugh. I sat out on the deck with him. And later Donna came up to see how I was doing. I guess I'll take Detective Guevara up on his offer of a TV set just so I can rest my eyes from the computer screen."

"Good idea. Do you hear from Josephine?"

She shook her head as she spooned up more mashed potatoes. "It's *verboten*. I've been instructed not to contact anyone at Great Day. If there's anything urgent, we have to go through Detective Trantor. Seems odd."

"I guess they have their reasons," I said, and sent up a little prayer that I was wrong in my assumption.

"Josephine has been a good support for you. You must miss that."

Camille made a face. "Well, of course, but still-" She shrugged.

I raised my eyebrows.

Camille took a deep breath. "It seemed as if she was-you know, making a move on me. Which would have been okay, but not so soon after Arta passed. I could be wrong, but it felt creepy to me. When I stayed at her place in L.A. before the funerals, she'd show up in a filmy nightdress to say goodnight, oozing sympathy, but there was more to it."

"I guess it's traditional-using sex to obliterate grief."

"Not for me, apparently. Or not with Josephine anyway. She's such a bony, angular opposite to Arta. My beloved, feather-brained love." She shook herself out of her dreamy state. "And listen, a feather-brained woman could not have established such an empire of romance readers. Arta adopted that role with me. It was like semi-retirement. She could let me carry on as breadwinner. She thought she'd found a white knight in Greaves. Didn't turn out that way." Camille sighed. "I might have gone the distance for her. We'll never know now." She sounded infinitely sad.

"I used to dream, " I said, "when I was married, that Blake and I would retire from teaching and sail our *Northern Twenty Nine* to Greece. I actually met a couple, recently, who did just that, in a *Northern Twenty Nine*. It's a sailboat designed for the kind of short, choppy waves the Mediterranean kicks up. They spent a year there, sailing from port to port - three months in Turkey –Istanbul etc., grilling fresh fish on their deck. Living in the place, not just touring. I told them they had lived my dream."

Camille was listening attentively.

"Blake kept the boat. It's called *Sirocco*, red-hulled with a lead ballast to right it if it capsizes. He spent time in the South of France and in Spain, but not on the boat. He only sails it around Toronto Island now." I paused.

"I wouldn't have been able to do it anyway. Not strong enough. And if I had stayed with him, I wouldn't be the person I am now. Not that any of that is a consolation for you, I know. I guess what I'm saying is that the death of a relationship means the death of a dream."

"How long did it take you to get over it?"

"Much too long." I wasn't going to say it took seven years. "But my mental health was not the best and my children left the same summer."

"Whose mental health is?" she said. "Well, at least I still have our children." She gestured at the box of novels that stood open on the floor beside the table.

"How are you different than you would have been if you were still married?" she asked.

"Hard question." I took a minute. "I'm my own person now. I've always been prone to repressing my self, subsuming myself in those I'm close to. There's much more to it. I think I'd have to write a book to explain it."

"I suppose I'll have to wait and see how I change," she mused.

As I started to go out the door, an idea struck me. "That 'S' book you are going to write. Who's the friend Arta said she was teasing?"

"I shouldn't really say. There's a hint in the title, I guess. But it also involves a politician. Arta got the idea when we dropped in on a friend of hers who was on holiday. She had cleared the book with the lawyers, who said it was okay to go ahead, but only if we changed the politician's gender. We had to do that anyway. Arta's readership isn't ready for a gay romance."

"Did the friend know she was going to write that book?" I asked.

"Arta didn't tell him, but Matthew knew, and I worried he'd spilled the beans."

I more or less reeled downstairs.

22

TOO LITTLE DOPAMINE

"I did try not to involve you," Detective Trantor was saying over Clara's landline, "But that woman doesn't have a single friend, except Josephine Barker, who is not a viable alternative. Can you meet me in Camille's hotel room in an hour and a bit?"

"Sure," I said.

"I have to convey some news to her that she may find hard to take."

Seventy minutes later, Fred swung her car into a parking spot, before I climbed off the golf cart, and I followed her blue plastic thongs up the stairs. As we waited for Camille to unlock the screen door, Fred gave one of those grimaces.

"I'm not sure you should leave your door open like that," she said as we went in.

"Bloody hot in here when the sun comes around," Camille replied.

"Let's all sit," said Fred, plunking down on half of the couch. I joined her, and Camille returned to her desk chair.

"Josephine Barker has been helping us with our inquiries. She's handed us Matthew Greaves on a platter. But she'll be charged as accessory to a double homicide."

Camille stared at her, open mouthed.

"I know it's a lot to take in."

"Josephine helped in Arta's murder?" Camille said.

Fred nodded. "I'm afraid so."

Again we sat in silence, Camille trying to make sense of it, whereas I was having my suspicions confirmed. Fred glanced from Camille to me, and then back to Camille again.

"I don't understand. Arta was her big earner," Camille said.

"Wasn't it more likely that you were her big earner?"

Camille hesitated. "Well, maybe, but Arta was the brand, the public face."

"What usually happens when an artist dies?"

"Sales *have* soared in the last few weeks."

"And likely to go on doing so now word is out that Arta left many unpublished books. In your head apparently."

"But Josephine was our friend!"

"That's as may be," said Fred. "We'll have to get a statement from you about the changes Arte made to her publishing agreement and her will, but that'll wait till you've got your head around this."

"So am I still in danger?"

"Not from Josephine. Never were. And she's enjoying the hospitality of the Kern County Sheriff's Department, so you're not now. Greaves and Russell are still AWOL of course, so you still need to be protected."

"I can't imagine Josephine agreeing to help them," Camille said.

"Try harder," said Fred. She grimaced again. "Listen, I'm sorry. I'm such a hard ass."

She sighed deeply. "I need to get back down." She looked at me, inquiringly.

"Sure," I said.

"Walk me down," said Fred. "Joanna will be right back, Camille. Take it easy." Camille was staring into space.

On the way down the stairs Fred said, "That Josephine is a hard-hearted bitch. When we picked her up, she agreed to help us get 'those bastards' to save her own skin. They didn't actually become bastards in her mind until they went after Camille, if that's any consolation to her. Still Josephine didn't turn herself in."

"I doubt it will be a consolation. I take it Josephine was the one who booked the Hawaii trip."

"Why am I surprised you know about that?"

"Mountain telegraph," I said, glumly.

I watched her walk to the parking area and get in her black Camry. Then I sat down on the stairs. I could feel it coming-the great loneliness, like a herd of bison stampeding toward a cliff.

It's not your story, I told myself. Don't get caught up in it.

Then I considered my own story. I was homeless. My things were wedged into a storage locker on Toronto's Keele St. My son was on the other side of the world, and wouldn't speak to me anyway. My daughter was ill, unable to work, had lost her home and savings, and I had nothing to give her. Cursed by God, I had heard Julia say in moments of despair.

And no decent television.

A Steller's jay alighted on the deck above me and called loudly. I would have preferred the hawk, but needs must. I got to my feet and climbed the stairs.

Camille was lying on the bed, gazing at the ceiling, holding a small white bag in her left hand.

"Here," she said, gesturing with the bag, and I walked over to take it. "I've taken out enough for a week. I want you to keep the rest. Please."

Oh, good, she was handing a depressed person a bag of pills. I dropped them into my purse.

"Feel free to join me," she said, gesturing to the other side of bed.

We lay there staring at the ceiling.

"How long did you say it takes to get over grief?" Camille asked.

"A year. You'll feel a lot better in a year."

She sighed. "Okay. A year. I can do that."

From what I knew of grief, a minute was unbearable and eternal, but I had given the answer she needed.

At least it made a change from asking her how she was doing. I was tired of that role. I had been playing caretaker all summer. I felt very satisfied with this lie, and vowed to use the technique again.

Usually, I wracked my brain about such questions, coming up with a truthful answer. Really, that wasn't what was needed. I didn't need to figure out how to help Camille. All I had to do was respond to her.

"It's my fault," she said.

"What?"

"I flirted with Josephine. I led her on."

"Really! A conniving husband, a coldblooded sniper, and a woman out to kill off her best client, and it's your fault?"

"When you put it that way-"

There was a knock at the door–the five-knock code of Henry and his crew. I got to my feet and went to peer through the peephole. I could see an eye peering back at me.

"It's Max," said the eye. I opened the door. "I've come to carry you off for a Max Rueben spaghetti dinner. Cancel all other plans." He had two helmets in his hand. "You'll have to follow in your car, Joanna."

"Did you clear this with Henry?"

"I am Henry. He couldn't take his shift, so I stepped up. I figure this helmet's a pretty good disguise, and Camille can wear my jacket." He had put the helmets down on the table and was taking the leather jacket off. Underneath he had a heavy denim shirt.

"Well, what's the hold up?"

"I'll just call Julia to say I won't be back for dinner," I said, going to the phone beside the bed.

The jacket would have held two Camilles.

I followed the motorcycle out of the village center, left onto the highway, and eventually left again onto a street that wound its way up and up, until we came to small log house perched above the pine forest. Max bumped the bike down from the road and parked next to the front walk. I parked on the side of the road.

The front yard was bare earth with several stumps on which sat a chamber pot, a milk can and a hand-powered, black sewing machine. A pair of skis was fastened diagonally on one side of the door and crossed snowshoes on the other. They looked as if they had been there pre-Max. There were various pieces of harness hardware gathering rust on the floor of the small porch, really a step with a roof. The rust would have been pre-drought.

Stepping in the door, I saw that Max was living, as he always had, amid clutter. The place was small, but its high ceiling offset that. A ladder directly ahead led to a central sleeping loft. Hooks on either side held his entire wardrobe, one garment over another. To the right a tiny kitchen emanated a delicious tomato and basil fragrance. Every available surface was covered with stuff-herbs and spices, packaged food, bowls and pans. On the other side of the kitchen and open to it, was Max's studio where the light of the setting sun poured through the windows. The door that led out to the deck had police tape across it.

When Max saw me looking at it, he said, "You might not actually fall to your death if you went out, but it's possible. The deck posts are subsiding down the hill."

We all moved to the window in the door. The floor of the deck was pulling away from the wall of the house, and slanting at an alarming angle over a drop of forty feet.

"I have to get some heavy machinery to put in some big old posts, big, old, long posts."

"Have a seat," said Max, taking us back to the living room on the other side of the entrance. On one side, its window looked out over the inclining deck. Standing at it, I could see the meadow across the valley and a large area of dead pine trees.

"Rain shadow," I said, pointing.

"Yep," said Max. "Natural process I guess, but every time I look at it, I think global warming."

Camille went to the other window.

"This deck's still in tact," she said.

"It's sitting on solid ground," said Max, "But the only access now is from the outside."

I remembered a one-act play I had taught to my grade nines, the title of which was lost to me. The family wastrel returns home after years away, to extort money from the old folks. After scaring them half to death, he is interrupted by the arrival of visitors and rushes out the back door. Trouble is the river has eaten away at the land back there in the years he has been away. The last thing we hear is a muffled scream.

"How do you heat the place?" I asked Max.

"You're looking at it," he said, pointing at the fieldstone fireplace in the corner. " And I have a small stove in the studio. I can get it above 60 degrees. Plenty warm enough."

I shivered.

"There's a heater and a propane tank if you happen to be a millionaire. Which I ain't."

Heavy maroon, velvet curtains on rods were pushed back at the sides of the windows and in the doorways.

"I bought them from the Kirk Douglas Theatre in Culver City, cut them up and made them into curtains. You probably forgot I'm a dab hand with a sewing machine."

"I certainly did not forget."

"Can I get you apple juice or water?"

We opted for water. Foolishly. It was unadulterated Bear Mountain tap water. Surely it must be illegal to use so much chlorine in potable water.

"Eight minutes to lift off," said Max. "Well, a little more. First I have to get the water boiling and that takes a while up here."

"Do you mind if we change our minds and have apple juice?" I asked. "I can get it."

"Go ahead," he said.

I poured the water into the pail where Max was saving grey water. "For my trees," he said. "They say next summer will be even dryer. By the way, in tribute to the phenomenal green bean harvest you had that fall, I've found the last of the yellow beans from the valley. From now on, we'll be beaned from Mexico. I plan to dump them in with the spaghetti for the last two minutes."

I carried the apple juice back to Camille who was busy inspecting Max's artwork, including one of his penis-nosed politicians. She widened her eyes at me.

"Max is actually a great cook," I said, loud enough for him to hear.

Then I lowered my voice. "And he makes a mean Italian pasta. Non-gluten would be an anathema to him."

I had found that you had to let go of your preconceived notions around Max. He was unpredictable, rude, and deliberately obnoxious, and yet, once I relaxed, he made me feel safe.

We ate our spaghetti, yellow beans, and tomato sauce on our laps in the living room, a real balancing act. Fortunately, dinner was in large soup bowls. Or small serving bowls. Hard to tell which.

Camille started to fill Max in about Josephine, but he already knew.

"What makes people do such things?' Camille cried.

"The usual seven deadlies," Max replied. "Greaves-pride, anger and greed, Josephine-lust and greed, Russell-greed and pride."

"Pride in a job well done," I said.

"Sure," said Max. "He's really good at covert action and long range shooting. He'd probably do it for nothing if you pointed him in the right direction. Haven't you done things for no more than the satisfaction of doing them well?"

"I have," I said.

In fact I had a long history of such folly.

"Some of us are suckers for excellence," said Max, gathering our dirty dishes.

"I suppose that's why I was willing to write Arta's books for her-pride," said Camille. "And lust and greed," she muttered.

When we got back to the Bear Mountain Inn, Camille unlocked the door, and I rushed in to find my purse, which I hadn't missed until I was leaving Max's place.

It was sitting on the worktable. Beside it were its contents, neatly arranged in order: Camille's two pill bottles and one of mine, my credit and debit cards one above the other, my licence, car ownership, and car insurance, assorted membership cards, reward cards, and two pictures, all carefully sorted. Bills lay in denominations, Canadian and U.S. separate. Even the coins were organized into a stack of quarters, dimes, nickels and pennies. My Canadian loonies and toonies were safe at Clara's. My day planner and chequebook lay side by side near two pens, nail clippers, my extra car key, my flash drive and a small blue dispenser of dental floss.

"Oh, my God," cried Camille.

A Sheriff's deputy arrived 10 minutes later, followed by two more in quick order.

"Where," I wondered, "had they been lurking?"

The room filled up with men. Pictures were taken with a cell phone. Calls were made out of our hearing. Camille and I were escorted down to reception where Donna was all aflutter. She opened a bottle of red wine and poured some into three juice glasses. The deputy stood outside the door, which he had firmly closed.

"I didn't hear anybody go up," said Donna. "Max dropped in to tell me he was taking you out to his place. I was listening for you to come back, but I didn't hear anybody. How could I not hear?"

"We think this guy is a trained military operative, gone freelance," I said.

Camille had been sitting wide-eyed and silent. Now she spoke up, "I don't suppose you have any gin, do you?"

Forty minutes later, the deputy came in, followed by Max.

"You can go up and get your things ma'am," he told me. "A female officer will be here shortly to help Ms. Costa pack hers."

"You're taking her away?" I said.

"Detective Trantor is making an alternative arrangement for Ms. Costa's safety."

Despite the gin, Camille sprang to her feet in alarm.

"It's okay," said Max. "It's okay. He's just toying with us, but better to move you."

I knew that was true, but I wanted to cry out, "What about me?"

So Camille vanished. There was a rumour the FBI's witness protection unit had taken her under its wing.

Clara felt as bereft as I did.

"I feel useless," she said. "It's all got too big for me."

"Me too," I said.

I set about bleaching Clara's mugs to get rid of the baked-on tea stains. Clara was still making tea in the microwave oven. I started off by using steel wool and white vinegar, but as the stains resisted me, I resorted to chlorine bleach. Why Bear Mountain water didn't do the job by itself beat me.

At the house in the pines, I emptied the cupboards, and scoured away the white mineral deposit from the humidifier.

Saturday morning, Colin, Julia and I left for Los Angeles. We would meet my grandson Leo for lunch in Culver City Center, as was our custom. We always went to Ford's where the wait staff pampered us, and the bartender made Colin's Sapphire martini without being told. That terrible day, we found it closed forever. Mr. Ford was putting his efforts into new places, one at the Staples Center and one at the airport.

"Why didn't Kate tell us?" mourned Julia.

"Non-disclosure agreement. Break it and lose your job," I said. "But remember she gave Colin a free martini last time. That was her way of hinting at it." Their martinis cost $15.

Julia phoned Leo and we met at *City Tavern* a few doors away. We still had the same view of art deco downtown Culver City, and good food, but it wasn't our place. Ford had a lot to answer for, even if his father was Harrison.

Leo arrived, taller than ever, with curly light brown hair, anybody's idea of cute. He and Colin went back out, so Colin could have a smoke.

"We can't keep doing this," said Julia. "We'll have to eat somewhere cheaper in future. There's that Thai restaurant near Evan's."

"This is my treat," I said.

"Thanks, but still, we have to tailor our life style to suit our means."

"Gone are the days," I said and the rest of the lines echoed in my head, 'When my heart was young and gay/Gone like our friends from the cotton fields away'. Only a white man, like Stephen Foster, could have written that. Old Black Joe kept on wailing in my mind.

"Song writers have a lot to answer for," I said to Colin, as he sat back down.

"You've got another ear worm," he replied.

"Oh, God, yes."

"Try singing it out loud. It works for me."

"Possibly not for those around," I said, glancing at the full table a foot away.

We brought Leo up to date on the on-going crime wave in Bear Mountain Place.

"That stuff in the hotel room, " Leo said, "that is really creepy."

I agreed. "It reminds me so much of being a kid when my father thought it was a hoot to scare us shitless. You do know that your great grandfather was a sadist and a child abuser?"

"So I've heard, but not really, know what I mean?'

I summoned up a relatively innocuous story about the time, I had asked him to drive my ten-year-old sister, Georgia, and me to my high school one Friday evening, so we could see *The Pirates of Penzance*. I had been offered a lead in next year's operetta on the condition I see this year's. My father refused adamantly.

"I won't let you be in another play," he shouted. "You're to stay home and help your mother."

"Shall I quit my job?" I yelled back. "Do you want to pay for my clothes and books and bus fare?"

"Don't answer you father back," my mother put in.

"Besides that, I also do my share of housework. I pull my weight and I get top marks. I'll do as I please."

"Not while you live in my house you don't."

I took Georgia by her arm. "Get ready," I said. "We'll walk."

"Rod, you can't let them walk. It must be three miles-in the middle of winter-at night," my mother cried, hysterically, but he had stomped off down to the basement.

"So Georgia and I got dressed and started to walk, first an unlighted mile to the highway. It was a new housing development-partly built and unlit–homes for War Workers, even though World War II was over and World War III not yet begun. Then we walked through the even darker apple orchard until we reached the Queen Elizabeth Way. Instead of walking along the shoulder, we turned along the railroad track. I didn't want our father to drive up behind and scoop us up. It was pitch dark as we stumbled along, and we had to keep sharp for trains. We were about half way to Brant Street when suddenly a dark figure wailing like a banshee rushed up behind us.

"I grabbed Georgia's arm and dragged her off toward the Queen E. We managed to cross at a run just in front of speeding westbound cars. We caught our breath briefly on the grassy median, before a break in the eastbound traffic let us through. Rod Hunter still stood at the shoulder of the other side. Laughing!

"We arrived at the school, out of breath, just as the band started butchering the overture.

"As we got up at the end of the operetta, my $12 Timex said it was 10:30.

"'I'm a-scared to walk home,' Georgia said.

"'We won't have to. He'll pick us up.'

"'How do you know? He won't. He'll kill us.'

"Sure enough he was there, sitting in the old black Dodge. No mention was made of earlier events. As it happened I didn't get the lead. I could sing, but I failed the audition. I couldn't sing the sight part. Funny about that. I had faked my way through Vocal Music for two years. Damn Gilbert and Sullivan!"

"What was up with him?" asked Leo, when I finished the tale.

"Some form of mental illness," said Julia.

"I gave up speculating long ago,' I said. "But he always worked, at two jobs when necessary, so he wasn't schizophrenic probably. Are there high-functioning schizophrenics?"

"His brain chemistry was unbalanced," said Julia, " probably low on dopamine. Gamblers' brains lack dopamine. That's why they seek the adrenal rush of risk-taking. Dopamine triggers the reward center, and makes people exuberant. It helps a stressed-out body feel good. People, who lack dopamine, create situations where the body goes into overdrive and produces it. Rod was doing that. Today a psychiatrist could get him the right drug to even him out."

"Whatever," said Leo, "I hope it's not genetic."

Of course we laughed. But I thought of Morris Russell while Old Black Joe went on whining 'I'm coming. I'm coming, for my head is bending low.'

After lunch, Colin went grocery shopping, while Leo and I dropped Julia at Evan's for a treatment. Then we set out to get Leo a haircut.

Since it was a Saturday, he parked a few blocks north of the beach, and we walked to *Rock, Paper, Scissors*. I used to take my older grandson, Josh, there twenty years before, and later young Leo. It was a rock and roll sort of place.

We had the usual banter with Katsu, remembering, for example, when seven-year old Leo had insisted on having his hair dyed bright blue.

When Leo's curly hair had been reduced to stubble, we walked down to the boardwalk, but we took one look at the swarms of people-skaters, cyclists, strollers, joggers, performance artists, not to mention dogs of every shape and size, winding their leashes around unsuspecting legs- and I said, "I've got another idea. I found a place for sale there that I think belongs to Morris Russell, the one we think's the sniper. Let's scout it out."

As we walked up the south side of Venice Blvd, I was catching up with Leo's musical career. Having a bankrupt musician stepfather had not discouraged Leo. Electronic music was different. He didn't say that, but I knew from experience that an artist is not easily deterred by crass reality. Meanwhile, Leo had a day job, which he stumbled to after working all night on his music.

The real estate listing on Zillows showed a stark, cement-walled house on the south side of Venice Blvd. bordering a canal. I knew I had seen the interior of it in *Architectural Digest* years before.

I could see a *For Sale* sign ahead hanging on a metal post. As we got closer, a man came out of a high gate and put a handful of flyers into the sign's holder. Straightening up, he turned toward us-a tall figure in a Speedo, an unbuttoned Hawaiian shirt, and a sombrero, with a cigar clenched in his mouth. He doffed his hat, removed the cigar and gave me a maniacal grin. Then he took a flyer out of the sign pocket and handed it to me.

"I'm not in the market," I said, as I made to go around him.

Leo took my arm and steered me out onto the road to get by.

I set a fast pace to the car. Then I took out my phone and brought up a picture. Guevara had sent it to me, but I hadn't been able to open it until we were half way to L.A.

"Is this who we just saw?" I asked Leo.

"Looks like."

"I think he's the sniper."

"Wouldn't you recognize him?"

I grimaced. "I've seen him twice–I think-well, at least once, but I have this thing-I don't recognize faces very well."

"I'm Leo," he said. "Your younger grandson." And he cracked up laughing. "Sorry, sorry. This is too serious for jokes." But he was still giggling as he pulled away from the curb.

I texted Guevara, "Russell saw me as I walked past his house in Venice Beach."

"Why were you walking past his house?" he texted back.

"Looking at real estate," I replied. "He's selling the house."

"We know," he texted. "Not enough to arrest him on yet. Stop looking at real estate!"

"He wouldn't know who I am."

"You want to bet your life on that?"

Figuring that was a rhetorical question, I didn't answer.

We started home a little after 3 p.m. Sitting in the back seat, I sank into a reverie about Russell's antics.

Had he identified me or was his goofy act accidental? Even if he did know who I was, would he still see me as a threat? I wasn't even an incriminating witness. But how would he know that?

When Imelda saw Russell fleeing after his attempt on Camille's life, Greaves and Russell knew their cover was blown. Greaves had flown to Bahamas, while Russell went into hiding near Bear Mountain Place.

It was the sort of adventure he thrived on. It got boring, so he spent time watching the village through his scope. Snipers were used to lying in wait. Then he discovered that Camille had been moved to safety there, and couldn't resist the challenge. Not that it mattered. His cover was blown. It was no longer the story of ecological terrorism and a despondent lover. Now all he and Greaves could hope was they had left no tracks.

Looking out the car window, I saw that we were cresting the Sepulveda Pass.

Julia turned around and asked, "Why don't they arrest Russell now? They know where he is."

"Guevara said they didn't have enough on him yet."

"Well, they could at least arrest Greaves, or would the Bahamas resist that."

"I looked it up. The U.S. has had an extradition treaty with the Bahamas for almost twenty years. With Josephine's testimony they should have enough on him, at least."

We were all silent for a few miles.

"They have their own code, you know, these men." I said. "Rod didn't leave scars on us, not visible ones anyway. He wouldn't have a gun in the house, not a real one. He did have an air pistol that looked real. Russell has a code as well. He only kills for a good reason. He's not a madman."

"Ya think?" said Julia.

"He kills the 'enemy'. In this case the enemy was defined by Greaves, and probably included Warren Oliver who was supposed to be there with Arta. Tough on Roger Smith. Russell's proud of how well he does his job, and it never causes him grief."

"Sounds to me as if Zach could be in danger," Julia said. "Russell has no way of knowing Zach has already spilled the beans, and Greaves isn't here to stop him. And how do you know so much about snipers?""

"I downloaded the book *American Sniper.* That's how Chris Kyle described it, even shooting his first kill, an Iraqi woman about to throw a grenade at a convoy of Marines."

"That movie should be out soon," said Colin. "They finished it without him."

"Why?' asked Julia.

Colin turned to look at her. "He was shot. He died last year along with a friend of his, killed by a vet they were helping to rehabilitate. They had taken him out for shooting practice."

"I don't follow the news," said Julia.

"He held a record for sniper kills, they say," Colin added. "A hundred and sixty or so."

"Verified kills," I put in, "possibly more. That was his job and he was good at it. He made no apologies. Fascinating to get a glimpse into that warrior mind. I swear the training alone could give a person PTSD."

"I believe that," said Julia. "I've seen it depicted. They even water board them."

"Those guys must be seriously dopamine deficient," mused Colin.

I took up walking in the cooler November weather even when Julia couldn't join me. She was at the clinic as usual on Friday, so I set off alone, past the lake where ducks and coots were still in residence, but the reeds were dying back. There were no fisher folk today. I unclipped the chain across the side gate, and went through onto the paved path. There were no golfers at the green beside the lake. I approached the archery range and turned right down the horse trail–the Ride, the English would call it.

The plants at the edge of the path were dying back. I was glad to see signs of autumn. Seasonal changes here were too subtle for a northern eye. Certainly, the sun did not know it was fall. It was blazing down through the thin mountain air. I noted other small changes in the bushes and trees as I walked. The pin oaks were evergreen, but some of their leaves were darkening. There was still a muddy line on the left, suggesting a stream, and marking the fault line. The trail grew sandier as it came to the top of a steep incline. I spread my feet to avoid the ruts and keep my balance. At the bottom, I checked the rabbit bush, a blaze of yellow now. There was a good deal of it in the village flaring by the turn up to Clara's. Then I turned toward the meadow to look at the Texas sage.

My scalp itched so I took off my hat. I held it in my left hand and pushed my hair back. Suddenly, the hat flew out of my hand and landed twenty feet away in the sage bush. Astonished, I stood for a moment. Then I raced toward it. As I picked it up, I saw a hole through the crown. A bullet hole.

I turned fully around toward the steep wooded hillside, my hands out at my side.

"Asshole," I shouted and then I elaborated, "Fucking asshole."

I stood there offering the best possible target, and distinctly heard the sound of distant laughter.

Of course, I still had no working cell phone, and it was an uphill slog back to the house. I knew I had to go easy. Between rage and exertion, my heart was racing. But I felt no fear. I was not afraid. I could feel the shooter's eye on my back, even when the trees made it impossible. All it did was further enrage me. I trudged on.

Wasn't this a stupid and unnatural reaction, I asked myself, but I knew it wasn't. I was back to being Rod Hunter's daughter. When he moved to the city, he became a predator without prey–no bear, no deer-just his children. More than once I had found myself in a dark, deserted place pursued by a black figure, and more than once I had heard such laughter.

"It's only a game," he would say at the end of the chase when I berated him for frightening us.

"You did what?" yelled Guevara when he finally arrived. Apparently, it was inadvisable to stand and shout insults at an armed man.

The Rangers and deputies were off scouring the woods. At least ten cars were parked along our street. One arrived within fifteen minutes of my call, another two in the twenty minutes, along with the ambulance. The medics were surprised by the harridan who presented herself. I clearly did not need resuscitation.

I did not want kindness either. Basically, I wanted to kill, preferably with my bare hands. Meanwhile, those hands were gesticulating wildly, still holding my cowboy hat as I repeated the story to new arrivals.

Colin led me up onto the deck and put a glass in my hand. Absentmindedly I took several large swallows. As it burned its way down, I looked more closely. Gin. I swallowed the rest. Guevara joined me where I sat in one of the wooden chairs.

"He's gone," I said. "He's been living in the Wilderness Preserve. He can move through the woods like the wind and leave no trace. He's better than the ancient Chumash."

"You think?"

"No, I absolutely know it. He moved across the valley from Bear Mountain after Camille left the inn. Sometimes I can sense things."

"Well, at least you're not speaking in tongues," said Guevara.

He listened to me tell what had happened again, made a few notes, and went back down to the roadside where I could hear him talking to several other officers.

When Julia got home, she already knew what had happened.

"Why don't you go on back to Clara's? Colin's will pack up one of those pork tenderloin meals he froze. It wouldn't hurt to take 1 mg. of Lorazepam."

"Trying to get me out of the house?"

"No, of course not, but there's no sense in you being here in the middle of things. Are you worried about being safe? Detective Guevara says he'll have a deputy drive you over, and stay to keep watch on the house."

"I'm not afraid. If Russell wanted to kill me, he would have. I'm pissed off. But you're right. I need to get away, and deal with myself."

Back at Clara's, I let myself in the locked screen door, using the key under the plant pot. Clara was watching HGTV.

"I thought you came in earlier," she shouted above the roar.

I carried my bag into my room, ready to throw myself on the bed. And stopped dead in my tracks.

All of my underwear was neatly folded and lying fanned by type on the bed. One row was white underpants, one was black and the shortest fan was beige. Matching bras were cupped above them. Camisoles were arranged in a rainbow of colours, white at one end, black at the other, with green, purple and pink in the middle. The tights being all black, were divided into footless and footed. T-shirts were near the bottom in a graduated stack so the neck of each shirt showed. The colour order was tasteful. A rolled red scarf, green floral scarf and purple wool scarf lay at the bottom.

The books on the dresser were arranged alphabetically by author. They were standing between a small plaster bust of Walt Whitman and another of Thoreau. Both of these objects had been in the third bedroom, which was still crowded with boxes and objects that hadn't found a home.

I walked closer to examine a pile of paper. The receipts I had stashed in one of the narrow top drawers were lying on top, stapled together in order of purchase. It must have taken half an hour to accomplish this artistry.

I went back out to the living room.

"Clara," I said loudly. I walked over, picked up the remote and put it on mute. "Thanks for tidying my room."

"I haven't been in your room," she said, looking at me as if I were nuts.

"Take a look," I said. Then I went out the door to get the deputy sitting in his car.

"Who did this?" Clara asked, as I came back in.

I opened the closet door. The plastic bags I used for laundry and threw haphazardly on the floor were all folded into ten-inch squares and stacked in the hanging shoe rack. My shoes, which had been higgledy-piggledy were now side by each on the lower shelves. My clothes were hung in order of length.

The television remote, the satellite remote and the living room remote control I had hidden behind the set were lined up on the edge of the round, red-metal TV table. My night table stuff-almond oil, tear gel, muscle ointment, skin cream and chap-stick-were lined up behind my travel alarm, the tallest nearest. As the tallest was the hand cream, it was conveniently placed. Of course, in the dark, I would have knocked it over reaching for the lip balm.

"Oh, there's my TV remote," said Clara.

I sank down in the blue velvet rocker in the corner of the room as the deputy came in.

"I had the screen door locked," Clara said to him, bewildered.

So then we had to wait for Guevara to arrive, along with two deputies, one with a camera, and another with a finger print kit. We all knew that Russell's prints would not be found this time either.

Eventually, we gathered in the living room to bring Clara up to date, and to enlighten her, as gently as possible, about her recent visitor.

"That settles it," she said. "I'm getting a hearing aid." Then she added, "And I'm going to see about my eyes."

"Good idea," I said. Eyes and ears could prove helpful, but I wasn't sure what I could do about facial recognition.

It turned out Russell had picked the lock. They could tell by the scratches.

Once they had left, I started shoving every item of clothes into the laundry bags. I wasn't going to wear anything he had touched until I had washed it in the hottest water possible. Then I took the receipts, put them in the fireplace, and burned the lot. I carried the shoes outside where I would clean them and give them an airing. I opened all three windows top and bottom. I got a pan of water with soap and bleach and began to wash every surface. I threw the plastic hangers in the laundry tub and let them soak. I stripped the bed and put new sheets on it. I took off the duvet cover and put the duvet back on without its cover. I took the quilt Julia had loaned me out of the linen closet and threw it on top.

I now had four bulging bags of laundry and I wanted very much to go back to Julia's and wash it. Instead I gave the room a spray with the bathroom deodorizer. I took a look around. Whitman and Thoreau were back in the other bedroom, still homeless.

That was about all I could do and it didn't erase his presence. That of course was what he wanted.

"I've got sage," Clara said, standing in the door.

"Perfect," I said.

We lit the tightly wrapped bundle of sage and began wafting it into every corner of the room, even into the empty drawers and the closet.

"That'll do for now," said Clara. "But we'll do it again tomorrow."

And the day after and the day after and-

"Should I go?" I asked.

"Where?"

"Away, back to Canada. I don't know."

"Of course not," said Clara. "We don't run. Ef 'em as a friend of mine would say."

Well, not precisely what your friend would say, I thought, but close enough.

I'd had it. I was ready to put a hex on Russell. Aunt Mae had told me that of course I could. She just didn't recommend it. Once you got that sort of energy going, it might boomerang.

Okay, fine. I decided on a moderate hex. Not a mild one like holes in his hiking socks in the middle of a trek. Something more inconvenient, but not lethal. And indeed I may have released nastiness that would come back to bite me.

23

TOO MANY COYOTES

That night I dreamed that my father was sitting in the blue velvet rocker in the corner of my room.

"What are you doing here?" I demanded in my dream.

"Looking out for you," he replied.

"Since when?" And I fell back asleep.

On Sunday and Monday, I worked on washing Russell 'right out of my hair', which is to say my clothes. On Monday, it was warm enough to put the clothes racks out on the deck. Like Julia, I preferred to line dry, especially in clear mountain air. Clothes smelled so good.

As I picked up the empty basket, I remembered my dream, and turned to tell Julia who was drinking her tea on the deck.

"How long since he passed?" she asked.

"Twenty-six years," I said, once I had done the math in my head.

"Time enough to do some learning."

"Learning or healing?"

"Aren't they the same?"

I sat down on the chair beside her, holding the empty wicker basket in my lap, and gazed out at the pines and pin oaks beside the road. I was crying.

Parents are supposed to make you feel safe. Mine didn't. Feeling safe and feeling happy was the same thing to me, and both were fleeting.

When I told the dream to Clara, she said, "Do you want me to send him packing?"

"Georgia certainly would. She won't let him near her. I'll let you know if I need help."

Detective Trantor called Clara's to arrange for me to talk to a profiler. As soon as possible! Phone or meet, I wondered. Both as it turned out.

On Wednesday, Detective Trantor arrived at Julia's with a younger woman in jeans and a tailored jacket, whom she introduced as 'Agent ' Rita Salvador. The identification Ms. Salvador presented was FBI. Fred had asked me to bring my passport, which I presented. Then we went over the story of my extended stay in Bear Mountain Place. I gave my Canadian address as well as my sister's and my cell phone number. They already had Clara and Julia's numbers.

Fred took a look at my face and interrupted, "Joanna thinks you are going to deport her."

Whoa! Sensitivity lessons from Fred Trantor.

"Not my job," Agent Salvador said, still entering information on her laptop. Then she stopped and looked up. "Sorry. No, we're not interested in that. Anyway, you don't have to leave until-" She checked my passport. "December."

I did not say that I would be over-limit by the time I went.

"Now Ms. Hunter, my purpose here is to build a profile of the suspect, Morris William Russell."

"Call me Joanna," I said. "With all due respect, you know who he is. Isn't that enough?"

"A profile will help us to apprehend him."

"Why don't you just walk by his house in Venice Beach? He'll pop out and greet you."

"We did go to arrest him Monday and there was no sign of him," said Fred.

"Well, I certainly saw somebody," I said. "Did you have enough to arrest him if he had been there?"

She shook her head. "Not really. We've got a couple of eye witnesses, one in connection with the Valley Fever parcel, and one in connection with the arson in Douglas Peak. Purchase of incendiaries." She looked at Rita. "And according to the Canadian boy, you saw him, Russell and Greaves behind the Lau's house. You were sitting on their back deck."

"I didn't recognize either of them."

"Let's go back to the beginning, Joanna," said Rita. (I had decided to call her that in my mind, *in lieu* of picturing her naked.) "The first time you got a look at Russell was-" She checked a notebook lying beside her computer. "Friday October 24th at Regan's Roadhouse in Bakersfield. Tell me about that."

So I did. She didn't interrupt me, but didn't look at me either, too busy typing.

"Describe his demeanour."

"Standing at ease at the bar, open, jovial, not concerned about being seen or heard. So far as I know he had only one Scotch. He may have had more before I arrived, although it was only 11:30 in the morning."

"And you are sure he was with Greaves?"

"Yes. Detective Guevara will confirm that."

She nodded.

"When did you see him next?"

"In the Douglas Peak supermarket, I think."

"Did you see what he purchased?"

I shook my head. "Clara might have." I stopped to think. "Well, maybe I saw him at the chest freezer."

"So you didn't see him the night of the Town Hall meeting."

"No."

"Let's talk about last Saturday."

So I described the bizarre appearance of a tall, sparsely clad, sombrero-wearing, cigar-chomping man, with a crazy grin, who thrust a real estate flyer into my hand.

"And you can identify him as Morris Russell?"

"Not really."

"Why is that?"

So I told her about my prosopagnosia, but I couldn't remember the word, so I called it my 'inability to recognize faces I was unfamiliar with'.

"So what makes you think you saw Russell?"

"My grandson, Leo, was with me. I showed him the picture of Russell that Detective Guevara had sent to my phone, and Leo identified Russell."

She turned to a fresh page in the notebook and handed it to me. "Write down your grandson's full name, address and phone numbers."

Then she went on, "I'm curious, given this- ah -disability, how you can be sure you saw him the other two times."

"Detective Guevara was with me the first time, and got his fingerprints. But you're right, I might be wrong about the general store sighting. You could ask my friend Clara, who spoke to him that day."

She nodded. I had a feeling that someone else in the store had identified his picture.

"Tell me about the two intrusions, the first…into Camille Costa's room at the inn, and the second into your room at your friend's house. By the way, Detective Trantor, I want to take a look at both. It would be good if you would come as well," she said to me.

"Sure." I said, raising my eyebrows, but only Fred noticed. Had Rita not grasped that one of these places was where I lived?

"Let's start with the inn episode," Rita said, looking up with what was supposed to pass for an inviting look. "Begin with why Ms. Costa was out of her room."

"Presumably, she was not actually incarcerated there," I said, but if Rita recognized irony, she gave no sign of it. I went on to describe dinner at Max's and the return to the room. The arrangement of objects in both cases was etched in my memory. Rita kept her eyes down and took notes.

"I should talk to your friend Clara," she observed at the end.

"Since we are going into her house that goes without saying," I said.

"Right," she seemed dazed when she looked up. "I need to understand what made her think you had come in earlier. Obviously, she heard something of Russell's movements in spite of her hearing difficulty."

She studied her screen for a moment. "Do you think he is obsessive compulsive or just pretending to be?"

"Both," I said, surprising myself. "I think he has OCD, but he has it under control. He just let it off the leash for the fun of it. Clearly, he has a sense of humour."

"Or thinks he does," said Fred.

"He's a trickster," I realized out loud. "Like the Chumash coyote figure of legend." I paused, realizing something. "He's counting coup."

"What is he counting?' asked Rita.

"Native Americans, Indian warriors, instead of just killing their enemies outright, sneaked up on them, and touched them with their coup stick. It was considered a great achievement to do that three times."

I thought of the tricksters in my life-my father, Max Rubinstein, Leo's father Evan. Evan's stepfather had a native connection. He had taught Evan to track and introduced him to shamanic skills.

"Does Russell have any aboriginal blood?" I asked.

"His military record might say," said Rita. There was a long pause while she searched. "One quarter Chumash," she said, at last.

"Was his mother's name Jackson?" I was clutching at straws. Jackson was the only aboriginal family name I knew.

After a few seconds, she said, "Looks like it."

Some straws, apparently, could hold weight.

"Jackson," I said to Fred. "Could they be cousins?"

"Not the bloody bear thing," Fred exploded, holding up her hand like a traffic cop.

"Bear thing? Jackson?" Rita was clearly lost.

I shrugged. "Detective Guevara can fill you in," I said. "Detective Trantor doesn't want to add a seventh dimension to the investigation. Jackson is a Fish and Wildlife officer. Of the Chumash nation."

"Seventh dimension?" asked Rita.

"The release of the horses and cattle, the house flood, the Valley

Fever package, the wounding with lead bullets, the arson and the sniper murders add up to six. The bear thing would be the seventh," I said.

"I see," said Rita, but, of course, she didn't.

"The so-called eco-terrorists did post "Nature will be avenged" after the bear attack," I said.

"Seems to have been a dry run," said Fred. "The hacker had to prove to his employer he could hack the website before the main events got under way."

"You know who it is!" I said.

Fred grimaced. "Let's say he had a thorough understanding of that particular site."

The IT guy at the club let go after an L.A. company made a lower bid, I concluded. Then when the company failed to prevent further hacking, they hired him back. Who better to get past a firewall of his own making?

There was no one booked into Camille's room at the Bear Mountain Inn, so Donna Haynes let us in. I pointed out that the desk in front of the sliding doors stood where Camille's worktable had been and added that was where Russell had arranged the objects from my purse.

"Pictures were taken of them," I added, "by the police, I mean."

Rita looked around and nodded as she did. "Was the door locked when you and Camille came back?"

"I don't know. Camille put the key in and didn't appear to notice it wasn't locked."

"Did she unlock the deadlock as well as the door knob lock?"

"Yes. So far as I could see. I was worried about my purse at that point."

"Was anything taken?"

"No. There wasn't much money, about $100 Canadian and less than sixty American. It was all there. I haven't missed anything else."

When we had finished, I started for the door and then turned back.

"Why wasn't Warren Oliver at the Town Hall meeting?"

"Yes," said Fred. "We're looking into that."

"Camille is writing the 'S' book, *Love at Sequoia Ranch.* Whose love story is it based on?"

"I can't talk about an on-going investigation," said Fred.

"But you think Camille's life is still in danger?"

Fred didn't reply. She turned to Donna to thank her for her help.

Rita was already waiting at Fred's Camry when Fred and I started down the stairs. Donna was still in the room, fussing over pillows.

Fred muttered to me, "Oliver was in an acute care unit in Santa Monica suffering ketoacidosis, a potentially fatal condition. And we have advised Camille to skip 'S' and go on to 'T'."

The next stop was Clara's.

I knocked on the outside safety screen, loudly. The television was blaring. There hadn't been time yet to see about the hearing aid. There was no answer. I went to the table and got the key from under the pot. Rita started and began to speak, but I shook my head.

"He picked the lock," said Fred.

Once inside, I called out to Clara, who was not, in fact, in the living room watching television. I walked across to her bedroom door, and found her organizing boxes on the floor of the room-wide closet. I walked toward her, calling as I went, but she jumped when I came up beside her.

"I'm a sight," she said, smoothing her hair.

"You're fine," I said. "Your shirt picks up the lavender in your pants."

Clara swept back out into the big room, a smile on her face. "Welcome to my humble home," she said, with a laugh. "I'm Clara O'Neill. I haven't had many visitors yet. You're some of my first."

I introduced both of them. When Rita produced her badge, Clara brushed away that formality.

"Sit down. Sit down," she insisted, while I turned off the TV.

"Now where are you from?" she was addressing Rita.

"Dallas," said Rita, as if she were wondering how she had lost control of the situation?

"Oh, my grand daughter lives just outside of Dallas in Greenville. She's almost a daughter to me. Well, there was a little trouble. My son was separated from her mother. She came to live with us. She has two boys and a beautiful daughter. Such bright children. Do you know Greenville?"

"Well, yes. Most people from Dallas would."

"And where did you study this FBI business?"

"I went to the University of Texas at Dallas, criminology. Then I trained at Quantico."

"Yes, it's always mentioned in the TV shows. Do you still work there?"

"I have a place there, but my work takes me all over the country." She sat up straight, ready to get down to business.

"And where are you from?" Clara turned to Fred.

"Long Beach. Californian born and bred."

Clara laughed delightedly. "We lived in Torrance." She was off - describing her neighbourhood. "And where did you live in Long Beach?"

Clara loved to situate people geographically. I could understand why since I was geographically specific myself, but I couldn't make a personal connection with American places unless they were in New England. I took a rest. I was stressed out.

Rita just had to wait it out as well, but she was rendered human in the process. Very few people could resist Clara's charm, or had the nerve to over-ride her enthusiasm.

Just as Rita saw her break and started to speak, Clara turned back to her.

"And what does your mother think about you working at this kind of job?"

"Well-she's proud of what I've accomplished. I guess she's glad I'm not actually working in the field. I probably won't get shot doing a profile."

"I've never actually understood what a profiler does," said Clara.

"We build a picture of a suspect, based on the information we collect about the crimes committed. In this case, we know the suspect's identity, but we are trying to predict where he might be hiding now he appears to have left here."

"What an interesting job! Maybe you should use Joanna here as bait. He seems to find her." Clara laughed merrily.

"Yes," said Rita attempting a smile. "Perhaps we could get down to the task at hand. You told her that you thought she had come in earlier. What made you think that?"

"I thought I heard her cross from her room to her bathroom."

"Did you look up?"

"I don't see very well. I need to get my glasses changed."

In fact, we would learn later that week that Clara had cataracts in both eyes.

Eventually, we did move on to my room where Rita went over where my clothes had been arranged, and where the receipts had been.

"Where did he get the stapler?" she asked.

I turned back out into the short hallway to the other bedroom, still half full of boxes In front of the windows, Clara's desk had a disarray of items, including a stapler and the busts of Thoreau and Whitman.

"So you didn't find the stapler in your room?" Rita asked.

"No, I didn't. He must have brought it back here."

"How many receipts do you think there were?'

I shook my head. "Maybe thirty."

"And he took the time to arrange them chronologically."

"Apparently."

"I wish you hadn't burned them," she said, but more to herself than me.

By now, Clara had waylaid Fred in my bathroom and was debating what colour to paint it. Fred seemed the least likely person to consult about interior design.

Finally, it was over. Fred's Camry vanished down the hill, carrying Rita to Bakersfield to write her report and, thence, God willing, back to Dallas.

I went back to village life. It wasn't quite the same now. For one thing, I had given up walking down the riding trail. For another, it was colder. We didn't sit outside the bakery in the morning, although some hardy souls in ski jackets did. We brought our croissants back to one of the houses. Colin would have the pellet stove going and the little house warming fast, although you did need your fuzzy slippers on the stone floors. At Clara's, my bedroom retained the heat after furnace switched off, so I could wrap up and read there. Or I could wear three layers and get busy in the big room cleaning the floors or washing dishes.

For many weeks, now, I had felt something dark hiding inside the dazzling light of the mountain valley. I had looked at its beauty with anguish.

The one new thing was that every time I turned around I felt my father off to the side, in his grey fedora and his dark suit. Like me, he always wore a hat. He got skin cancer in spite of it. He used to wear a suit only on Sundays or when visiting. It wasn't Sunday, but he was visiting.

His presence didn't alarm me. It emanated, "Just looking out for you", but it was annoying nonetheless. I'd made it this far, why show up now? What was a ghost going to do? Throw his protoplasm between the bullet and me. Scare the guy to death. No explanation was forthcoming. In death, Rod Hunter was a man of few words, and he had said them.

Even so I didn't take up Clara's offer to drive him off.

Then the centre of the world fell apart.

On Sunday, Zach, Hector and two other grade six boys were fooling around on their bikes at the bus stop near the club driveway. Zach popped a wheelie, and the Plexiglas on the shelter exploded. The kids stood staring at it with wide eyes. Then Hector yelled, "Gun!" All four leapt on their bikes and pedalled for the club. The BMP Security arrived minutes later. When I chanced by on the golf cart, a woman in a Security uniform filled me in. Several Sheriff's deputies were trying to reconstruct the scene. Other squad cars could be seen on the street high above. Zach was sitting in the back of a cop car looking white-faced and forlorn.

I scudded on by and phoned Ben when I got home.

"Oh, my God!" he said. "Why haven't the cops called?"

"Maybe they called Lori."

"I hope not. She just brought the baby home yesterday. Oh my God!" The line went dead.

I stood at the phone desk, looking out at the shrubbery that screened next door. Margarita was still in town to baby sit, so I wasn't needed, and I didn't believe in gawking at a crime scene. I tried checking on the paper's website, but found nothing. Surely now, Guevara would have to let Zach go back to Vancouver. But wasn't Russell capable of going there as well?

The trouble with having post-traumatic stress is that you are easily triggered back into the original terror. I trembled and shook and sat down in one of the leather chairs hugging a pillow.

Something worse was going to happen. I just knew it.

Julia was summoned to minister to Lori. It was a difficult task, given that she was nursing Baby Julia. Treatment ended up being a cross between yoga and hypnosis.

When things died down, a Sheriff's car was posted outside Ben's house where the family gathered around Zach. Patrons looking for Sunday dinner found Le Petit Breton closed again.

On Tuesday, rumour at the general store was that Zach had been seen boarding the school bus. Did this mean the police had picked Russell up?

I knew Zach had been agitating to go back to school. Later we found out what had happened. He hadn't got the okay, but he saw an opportunity while Ben was on the phone to grab his bag and head out.

At 8:45 a.m., somewhere between the school bus and his homeroom, Zach vanished.

24

TOO FEW KIDS

It was immediately clear that this was a targeted kidnapping. An Amber Alert was issued. Zach's picture and description were distributed, and finally, pictures of Matthew Greaves and Morris Russell hit television screens and newspapers.

All of Greaves' cars were present and accounted for at his L.A. home, although he was not.

He was no longer in Bahamas either to answer to extradition. Since he had apparently not left by any commercial airline, he must have hitched a ride on a private jet. The F.B.I. was on that trail.

It seemed to me, and many others in BMP, that Greaves had taken Zach. Not so much to keep him from talking as to keep him safe from Russell. We wanted to believe Greaves had that much goodness in him. This didn't square with the fact that he had had his wife shot, but it did help to calm us down.

Russell didn't seem like the type to take hostages.

Detective Guevara was dropping his own kids off at their schools in Bakersfield when Zach vanished. He instantly became the Sheriff's go-to man for placating the family, and explaining why the deputy hadn't been guarding the house. The family was too distraught to care.

School officials wrung their hands, and declared the middle

school's security up to standard. If it was anything like a Canadian school, it was all but inaccessible. No one, staff or student, reported seeing Zach once he got off the bus.

Local communities organized searches by residents, under the direction of the Sheriff's department and BMP security. In our village, this involved phone calls to owners of vacation homes. Many of them arrived to open them for Security, while others directed officers to neighbours who held their keys.

After search helicopters had done several sweeps of the wooded slopes, the more athletic citizens searched on foot under the rangers' direction. That search was most frightening because it implied that Zach no longer had need of shelter. At least that search established that Russell was no longing lurking in the forest.

Fathers and grandfathers, travelling with a boy, found themselves surrounded by cop cars. These encounters were always fraught. How many twelve-year-olds travel with identification?

Wrapped in a coat and blanket, Clara continued to meditate on the chair-swing on the deck, but for twice as long.

Lori lost her mind. Any mother would, but it turned out Lori was more vulnerable than most.

Zach's disappearance had plunged her back into the bipolar disorder, which had prevented her from mothering him in the first place.

Julia went with Lori to the Douglas Peak mental health unit to hand over her treatment. The consultation proved to be a video call. As it progressed, Julia found the psychiatrist knew less than she did about potential side effects of drugs on a nursing mother and baby. Julia inquired about the doctor's qualifications. The doctor replied that she was a nurse practitioner, qualified to prescribe under supervision. Julia asked Lori to leave the room, and demanded to speak to the supervisor. Immediately.

Immediately involved a two-hour wait during which Lori walked up and down in front of the clinic frightening arriving addicts. Meanwhile Julia harangued mental health officials.

The actual psychiatrist appeared on screen at 6 p.m. much to the chagrin of the receptionist who usually left at 5 to take up her real estate job. Having satisfied himself that Lori was not suicidal, the doctor came up with a combination of drugs. She said she was "out of her mind," but not so much that she would desert her newborn. Not after all that trouble.

Julia concluded that she could have prescribed after all, given her experience and access to the Epocrates app.

I got down to the last of my Lorazepam. If I wanted a renewal, I had to submit to a full roster of blood tests and a complete physical, both of which I had done less than six months before, back home, and which were going to cost more than I wanted to spend. I had a renewal on file in Toronto. I called it in, saying a friend would come in to get it. Blake picked it up and mailed it to me. Legal, schmegal!

Still Zach stayed missing. The wait was bearable, we told ourselves. Zach was safe. He would be found. Day after day passed, and it was no longer bearable. It was harder than ever to find a restaurant open in Bear Mountain Place, and, anyway, who wanted to eat?

I envied Clara, who went on calmly meditating.

I was thrown back into my fundamental self. That was a state of dissociation, of invisibility. I disappeared myself.

What I couldn't shut down was the picture in my head of a red convertible at the bottom of a cliff.

25

JUST ENOUGH GOATS

I floated the idea to Clara.

"You know me," she said. "My family put a lot of stock in that sort of thing. Far-seeing, we called it. But then, we used to levitate tables."

"I'm just not sure it's the sort of clue the police could act on. Anyway, there are a lot of cliffs around. And the red MGB is in its garage."

Outside the general store, I found Henry Robertson back on the bench. "Did you hear that Darkstone cut Russell and Greaves loose?" he said.

"No," I said. "Will that make them easier to catch?"

"Could be," he said. "Depends on whether Darkstone was helping them with ID."

"I suppose there's more than one way to get false papers."

He nodded, ruefully. "Their pictures are out there now. Someone somewhere is going to recognize them."

"Russell's mother's name was Jackson. I'm wondering if he might be related to Jackson."

"Jackson had a cousin about his age. Spent summers up here with the old folks. Called him Will. Might have been Will Russell. I called him bad news. He tried to make the village a rabbit-free zone. Not too keen on jays either. I had more than one word with Eveline Jackson, Evie, trying to keep Jackson out of trouble. His old man was gone by then, living a drunk's life on the finer curbs of Bakersfield. Next summer, Will was sent off to Texas for school holidays. His folks were up in Kernville, I think. Might've been a Russell. Not called Morris though."

"I've met Evie a couple of times. She even invited me down to meet her goats. Do you still know her?"

"Sure. You don't stop knowing people up here. She's mostly down in Coney Valley now where she has her goats. Makes a great goat cheddar. "Still comes up here for church. Still has the old Jackson home. Jackson lives there. Up on the highway, real old-time place."

"So it must be Evie's sister-in-law who was a Jackson," I said.

"You like goat cheddar?" he asked.

"Very much."

"Why don't we go visit her? You could buy some cheese and we could ask about this Will."

"Well sure. You mean now?"

"When better?"

Why not?

Henry's pickup knew the hairpin curves intimately and took them at speed. I had to slow down to 35 in the Prius, but the truck never dropped below 50.

Henry chuckled when he saw me glance at the speedometer.

"Flatlander," he said.

"Too true."

He did stop at the T-intersection up to Bear Mountain. We were bound down.

"Too dry up the hill for goats," said Henry, "Even if they are browsers, not grazers. I guess even goats draw the line at pine needles."

"I thought they'd eat anything."

"A myth, but they do enjoy a woody snack."

We took the first right off the highway, down a winding road. We passed a saltbox ranch house, which always struck me as an anomaly out here in the west, and slowed at the next driveway. A sign held by a grey goat standing on its hind legs read, 'Fresh Goat Milk and Goat Cheese'.

"That'd be a Nubian," said Henry. "Jackson made it. Pretty lifelike. Evie has Nubian and miniature Nigerians. She likes their sweet milk."

The goat pen had come into view as we neared the house, and I could see that some of the goats were smaller than others. The house was low and white, more or less. It had got sandblasted over the years.

"Evie'll be inside now, working on the cheese probably. The goats will have been milked hours ago."

It was only 9 a.m., but I supposed goats, like my grandpa's cows, would get raucous if they had to wait.

Henry led me around to the side door, tapped lightly, and opened the screen without an invitation.

"Evie," he called.

"Henry," she called back. "Aren't you a sight for sore eyes?"

"I've brought along a city girl. This's Joanna, Joanna Hunter, Canadian. Loves goat cheddar."

"Oh, I know Joanna. Been trying to get her to visit. Have a seat. I just have to cut these curds."

There was very little counter space and her cheese pans, one inside the other, were sitting on the table on a big, thick, cotton pad. We each took one of the wooden chairs that sat randomly, having been pulled away from the table. Evie had a long thin knife, and she was cutting the curds, first one way, then another, and then diagonally in swift, deft movements.

"There," she said. "I've got five minutes. I'll make you an espresso, Henry."

"A double?"

"Oh, well make it yourself then and make me one. And you, Joanna, I'm going to take a shot in the dark and say you're a tea woman."

"I am. How did you know?"

"You're not the only one who can do that," said Evie. "What'll it be?"

I got up to look at the tea drawer she had pulled open. It was all loose leaf, no tea bags for this lady.

I pointed at the chai.

"I'm going to make it with this morning's milk. Now don't pull a face. My goats give sweet mild milk. I keep the buck out there in the other pasture with his buddy, Bud, the old horse."

I hadn't had time to pull a face actually, but she had read my thoughts. Again.

"You watch the milk," she ordered. "Don't let it boil."

I stood over the small pan on the electric burner. From there I could see the horse grazing in the distance and the Billy goat lying near him, thoughtfully chewing. Or re-chewing, I supposed.

"Jack and Charlie," I said.

"Bud isn't blind. Not yet, anyway, but they are devoted to each other."

"Jack and Charlie?" Henry asked.

"Charlie was a blind horse in an animal sanctuary and Jack, the seeing-eye goat who guided him into the woods each day to his favourite grazing ground," I said.

"My friend, Alice, and I planned a trip to see them," said Evie, "but Charlie died before we went, and then, of course, a little while later, so did his seeing-eye goat. We did do a road trip to Oklahoma afterwards–one of Alice's daughters lives in Oklahoma City. We went to Wild Heart Ranch to talk to Annette Tucker and see her other rescues."

"Do you think Jack, the goat, felt compassion for Charlie or just wanted the companionship?" I asked.

"Beats me. I do know goats can be very smart," said Evie. "Are you keeping watch on that milk?"

I snatched the pan off the burner just in time.

"There's the diffuser," she said, pointing to the table. "You know a goat's pal has to be hoofed. A dog won't do, nor a kitten, come to that. A cow might, but maybe too placid."

She was busy. She had set the curd pan in the sink and was adding hot water to it, while checking the curd's temperature. "It has to be a gradual rise to 100 degrees.

I'll have to resort to boiling water from the kettle. My tank doesn't get very hot. Fortunately, the dishwasher reheats the water for the power wash."

"Hand me my coffee, Henry. I'll have to attend to this. Twenty minutes, half an hour, but we can still talk while I stir and monitor it."

Evie was in her mid-sixties, tanned and robust, about 5'5" and solidly built and she was wearing a very white cover-all that looked like an old-fashioned nurse's outfit, tied in the back. Her long grey hair was pinned up in a bun under a hairnet. A health department pass hung framed beside a doorway.

"So what really brings you here, Joanna?"

I glanced at Henry, who grinned and shrugged.

"What's driving everybody around here these days? Who's got the kid? Is he safe?"

She turned away from the stove and looked at me gravely.

I went on, "I've been questioned by police about this crime spree more than once. The last time by the FBI. I made a leap in the dark and discovered that one of the suspect's mother was a Jackson."

"You mean Russell. He's my nephew, well my late husband's blood nephew. Will's mother was Ed's sister."

"Will?"

"He hated being called Morris, hated Moe even worse. Said it made him sound like one of the Three Stooges, so he went with his middle name and we called him Will."

"Do the police know he's Jackson's cousin?"

"Why wouldn't they?" she shrugged. "It must have come up. You knew they were looking for my nephew, didn't you Henry?"

"You know, I didn't. I hadn't put two and two together. I always assumed the pain in the ass who stayed with your in-laws in the summer was Will Jackson and the one they're looking for is Morris Russell."

"You mean your detective grandson doesn't know either?" she asked.

"Well, he may now that Joanna has mentioned it to Detective Trantor. Probably, he worked it out earlier himself. I don't always know the latest scoop, especially not when it involves my grandson looking like a fool. I know kids stick to their own group, but Al is about the same age as Jackson, and they must have hung out together some."

"Maybe," said Evie, "But your daughter kept a close eye on your grandson, Henry, and the Jacksons were *wild* Chumash."

I pictured them in loincloths and feathers dancing around a fire.

"So Jackson and Will were playmates in the summer?" I said.

"Oh, yes," sighed Evie. "The two of them ran rings around Henry and any other deputy that ventured onto the mountain. Old man Jackson just laughed and said, 'Boys will be boys'. And God knows, Will needed civilizing. Not sure that Bear Mountain Place was much better at it than Kernville though."

"Henry said he came from Kernville."

"His folks ran a tavern there. Doubt if they made any money though. They drank up the profits. It was good the kid could get away."

"I wonder if Jackson has seen Russell recently. I mean before they started looking for him."

"I wouldn't know. Jackson helps out when I need him too around here. And of course, he's sunk a bunch of his salary into getting me up and running–equipment, licences."

She pointed to a piece of stainless steel equipment sitting on a metal rolling island. It was pushed out of the way against the wall. Beside it were two small fridges-a wine fridge with cloth wrapped cheeses visible through the door, and a half size fridge, with 40 written on it in black marker. The kitchen fridge was a big white enamelled one beside the other two. They took up that end of the kitchen.

"But we're not real *confidants*." She said the word in a show-offy way and laughed. "A son is not a daughter."

Seeing me glance at the wine cooler, she said, "Had to buy that-the only way to maintain a steady 55 degrees to age the cheese. A real fridge is too cold. Then I had to get the little apartment-sized fridge to keep the milk at a steady 40 degrees. The regular fridge fluctuated. All of it cost us, but fortunately, Jackson can live cheap in his grandparents' house, long since paid for."

"So did Jackson bring the bear back to Bear Mountain?" Henry pressed on.

She shrugged. "He's got a sentimental streak, but mostly, he keeps his nose clean and the damned bear is up in Sequoia now."

"Okay, that's it," she announced, stripping off her latex gloves and untying her cover-all. Underneath, she had on short shorts and a tank top.

"Let's go see my girls," she cried. "You can thank them for your delicious chai."

"I will. I mean it was delicious. Thank you."

"Teasing, just teasing," she said as she breezed out the door.

As I followed her, I realized, here was a woman who could wear shorts in mid-November, and who celebrated veiny, well-padded thighs. Clearly, she had a lot to teach me.

"The bigger goats are Nubian, like the buck," she said. "Although you can get dwarf Nubians.

The buck was standing in the farther field, staring at us. His body was white. His tail seemed to be cropped. His large dark brown head, with its Roman profile, long ears and curved horns, scared me.

As a child, I had been chased by a bull and his herd. I knew how touchy the lord of the harem could be.

"We'll see you later, Jake," she cried. "I couldn't very well call him Jack-so I settled on Jake. Bucks stink, especially around does, and then the females produce pheromones that gives the milk a musky taste. That's why we keep them separate."

She opened the gate and we went into the pen. On one side was a fairly big shed with stalls, open to the pen, and facing southeast. At the other end a large gate stood open to the pasture. Several goats, including two kids, were in the pen, but most were out in the pasture.

"The kids are seven months old now, and most of them will be leaving us in another month when they are weaned. We had a good crop of girls this year. People will add them to their milking herds. I don't sell my kids for meat. Some of the boys will become wethers, castrated, you know. And I'm keeping a couple of does. I want to get my herd up to 21."

A small grey goat with a prominent nose and floppy ears nosed up to me, and began to investigate my shoe laces.

"Daisy, leave the lady's shoes alone!" cried Evie. "She likes to untie them. Nubians can be naughty. They have been compared to Jersey cows-for their milk. I doubt if Jersyes are mischievous."

"According to my grandfather, they are just ornery and stupid and prone to step on your foot, like all cows," I said.

Henry was busy loving up a little white and black goat. "This one's a dwarf Nigerian," he said.

"So you bring in a buck for them?"

"I do trades with a guy-my Nubian for his Nigerian. The boys have no objection to the extra work. It'll be coming up soon. End of November and December."

By this time, Daisy was licking my hands and submitting to caresses. Her fur was short and glossy.

"When are the kids born?"

"We dry the does out by the end of January, and the kids start arriving in April. Jackson takes a week off then and when he's not here, a teenaged girl up the road helps out. They're not troublesome birthers like sheep. Pretty straight forward, but there can be up to five kids."

"So you have a slack time in February and March when you're not milking?"

"That's when I get the girl to feed my critters, and go up to Frisco to see my daughter. She's a paediatric nurse up there. Of course, I never stay long. Farmers are homebodies."

By now most of the herd surrounded us. Evie moved toward the shed with goats tailing behind her. "Here's the milking stand," she said. "Jackson made it out of the pallets the stove pellets came on."

The milking stand was raised off the ground and a low stool sat beside it.

"Some people just sit straddling the back of the stand," she said, "But I'm short-legged."

There was a stanchion for the goat's head, which could be locked around the neck, and a pan filled with food attached to the outside to keep the goat occupied while she was being milked.

Evie pointed to a leather loop hanging on the side brace. "I don't have any kickers just now. Sometimes the new milkers kick for a while, stand in the milk pan, get wound up in your clothes, and just generally make you curse the day you got into goats."

"Here Daisy," she called, and Daisy leaped onto the stand, put her head through the stanchion and began to nosh on the pellets.

"Goat treats," she said. "Take a handful and make a goat happy."

The goats pushed and shouldered each other to get to us. Henry dipped his hand in the bag as well.

"So, did you milk your grandpa's cows?" Evie asked.

"Tried but never succeeded."

"The trick is to pinch the nipple near the udder to let down the milk-that's called a *let*, and then to start pulling. Come back this evening around six and try it."

I didn't reply. I was overcome with my self-consciousness. I blamed my WASP background, my Toronto-ness. This was way more generosity than I could cope with. And I wasn't sure I wanted to subject myself to a potentially embarrassing experience.

"They don't butt?" I asked.

"No, not these girls. Jake does, of course, but I can deal with him."

I was back up in the village by 11 a.m. and no one had missed me. The amazing thing was not that I hadn't thought about Zach while I was there, but that I hadn't *obsessively* thought about Zach.

Julia was certain that I would be transformed by milking a goat, so I borrowed the Prius, and arrived back at Evie's by 6 p.m.

Evie got Daisy, the dwarf Nigerian, back up on the stand, sat me down on the stool, and showed me how to clean the udder and teats with a baby wipe. Then she told me to do two squirts from each teat into the air to clean out the duct. I had seen my grandfather do the same when he milked his cows. She handed me a shallow stainless steel pan

It took a few tries before I got the hang of it. Even then I kept backsliding and having to tighten my pinch to produce another *let*. After fifteen minutes, my hands were about to fall off, and there didn't seem to be any more milk. Moreover, at this rate, we wouldn't be done until deep dark.

"Let me have a try," said Evie.

She sat down, made a fist and punched the udder. She pinched and started to pull. Daisy gave no sign she noticed, and as it turned out, gave as much again before her withered udder told us she was done.

Getting up, Evie handed me a jar. "Rub this balm into her teats while I empty this milk." She poured it into big stainless steel pail with a lid.

The balm was lovely and moisturizing for my mountain-dry hands as well as Daisy's teats.

I stood back to rest, balm at the ready, and watched Evie get on with the job, her two hands flying.

The herd was gathered waiting-black and white, brown and white, beige, and grey, emanating a not unpleasant goaty odour and an animal ease that drew my milking anxiety out of me. When that was gone, my anxiety about Zach began to ebb as well.

The peace of goats, 'which passeth understanding', I thought. Did it also lead to the knowledge and love of God? I was pretty sure it did. Domestic animals had a way of doing that.

I leaned on a post, between stints of applying the balm, until Evie got to the last goat, a grey Nubian.

"Want another try?" she asked.

I shook my head. "Not this time," I said. What did I just say?

Our eyes had got used to the gathering dusk, but I knew I had kept Evie late.

"How long does it usually take you?"

"Twenty minutes, half an hour."

We started for the house. Evie looked back to check that the gate to the pasture was secured. She was carrying the covered pail and I had the shallow one.

"I've got a frittata ready to cook. You're welcome to share it. Jackson's coming too. Thought you might want to meet him. Are they expecting you up on the hill?"

"Not really. Colin may cook. He cooks enough for all four of us, but he doesn't care if or when we eat it."

Once we were inside, she handed the cooking of the egg dish over to me. The ingredients were already mixed and waiting in a big, black, iron skillet.

"Ten eggs. Should be enough for two women and an outdoor man. This is how I cook it. I put the oven on to 350. Then I cook it on a medium hot burner until the egg just starts to set. It'll need ten or fifteen minutes in the oven after that."

"Zucchini and potatoes and cheese," she went on. I usually add some cheese to the top for the last few minutes," she said. "I trade my milk for Jessie Frank's eggs. She's just up the road. Supplements her pension that way. A fresh egg is a thing of beauty."

She was straining the milk into quart mason jars and covering them with white plastic lids. "The metal lids discolour and rust," she said, when she saw me notice.

"I have a-changing the subject," I said, "I have a persistent image of Matthew Greaves' '63 red MGB at the bottom of a cliff."

She transferred the steel filter to another quart-bottle. "Have you noticed that sometimes you *see* something that turns out to be true in general, but not in detail?"

"Yes."

I had had an image of walking alone with a child in an alpine meadow. Later, I found myself walking with Julia, Evan and four-year old Josh in just such a meadow at Sawmill Campground in Yosemite.

"If Greaves is back in the country, he's probably not driving a '63 red MGB convertible, and yes, he took me for a spin in it too," said Evie.

"No, the MG is in its garage in L.A and he's not in his Lamborghini either."

'He's got one of those too!"

"So Detective Guevara says. I guess you're right. He'll be driving something black, probably the Mercedes."

"But if you just *saw* a black car, you wouldn't identify it with him."

"Do you think he's going to escape justice?" I asked.

"Legal justice maybe, not natural justice. I've had that bottle of Pinot Grigio open since we went to milk. Pour us each a glass." She gestured with her head to the small tumblers on a cupboard shelf."

"Don't tell me – a little old lady up the road has a vineyard and you trade equal with her."

"Evie laughed. "This little old lady is up Napa Valley way, and I trade at the Douglas Market, green backs for bottles."

I set the table, while she cut the frittata. We would start, she said, since you could never tell when Jackson would arrive, but just as she said that, he came through the door.

"Hi, Joanna," he said.

"Oh, you've met," said his mother.

"Now I'd love to serve this with a salad, but this many miles from civilization, you'll have to make do with bread. Which another neighbour made. Real wheat, not the crap wheat you city folks can't eat."

In fact, I have found on the mountain that I could eat many of the foods my body usually rejected.

I got up to get a glass for Jackson, but when I picked up the bottle, he held up his hand.

"It's in the fridge," said Evie, and he came back with a pitcher.

"Fruit punch, this time," she said. "Funny he doesn't tuck into a large glass of goat milk," she teased.

Apparently, Jackson, like Max never drank. Perhaps, the wild Jackson gene made it ill advised.

As we polished off the egg dish, Evie said, "Tell us about the bear, Jackson."

He turned white, and cast a glance at me before looking back at Evie.

"Don't worry about Joanna. I'll turn you in myself if you've been working with Will Russell."

"I haven't," he protested. "Well, not intentionally. I was so pissed off when they shot the cub. I had already arranged the transport of the mother bear up north, but the night before I was so outraged, I decided to drive her back to Bear Mountain. I don't know? Stupid. I wanted 'closure' for her. What does a bear know about 'closure'?" He considered that. "Unfortunately, I guess, this one did."

He took a rest to pull himself together. "What are the odds," he cried, "of Braddock being out there just as she arrived in his backyard?"

"Well, *she's* long gone now," his mother said.

"Fine, unless she's got a taste for human flesh," said Jackson.

We pondered this.

"Any loss of life up Sequoia way?" asked Evie.

"I'm going to quit anyway. Warren Oliver has offered me a game warden job on the ranch."

"Don't be hasty," Evie and I said as one.

"I don't trust him," I said. "It was very convenient that he wasn't there when Arta and Smith were gunned down."

"Really?"

"Don't quit your day job, son," said Evie.

"I heard he was in hospital that night," said Jackson.

I shrugged.

"So you don't think it stops at Greaves?" asked Evie,

Shrugging again seemed redundant. "Maybe. Arta's next book was supposed to be called *Love at Sequoia Ranch*, a teasing expose of a friend's affair. I'm sure Sequoia Ranch is a pseudonym."

"Maybe not. Oliver has a ranch on the edge of Sequoia Forest," said Jackson. "He bought it from Phillip Wilde a couple of years back."

"You've been there, haven't you?" asked Evie.

"Yeah. Before. Not since Oliver owned it. It's not a working ranch, but the grazing rights are leased. It just has a two-bedroom house, great for getting away. And we've hunted from there."

"Sounds like a good place for a clandestine affair," I said.

"Phillip has flagrant affairs; he can't be bothered otherwise," said Jackson.

"Do I have to worry about you?" Evie quipped.

Jackson gave her a nasty look. Then he went on, "I was up at his ranch one October when Oliver was there. This was before Phillip sold the place."

"Was Oliver with anyone?" I asked.

"Some guy, politician from L.A. County. Didn't know one end of a gun from another. Almost as good-looking as Roger Smith. Was. I thought good for you, Oliver. He'd just divorced, and I thought he was about to come out of the closet."

"Halcon Village will actually be in L.A. County, won't it?" I asked.

"Just south of the Kern County line," he said.

I knew this boundary. The Flying J charged for plastic bags, but across the road in Kern County, they were free.

"Arta's next book, *Love in the Sequoias*, was supposed to be written by Camille Costa, although she was going to change the gender of the lover," I said. "The cops have suggested she skip the S plot for now."

"So it's true the romances are just going to keep on coming?" said Evie.

"Apparently they've been planned out all the way to Z," I said. "And Camille has done the actual writing for some time. The P book is at the printers and the Q book is in its final edit."

"But Arta tied up the royalties somehow? Greaves doesn't get them?" said Evie.

"Seems like it, and the house in Douglas Peak was left in trust so the books could be written there."

"Well, I guess Greaves has his own money."

Jackson said," So he wants us to believe, but there's rumours he got screwed over in China, and the Bahamas plan may not come together. Maybe he had Arta bumped off for the money."

"Maybe," I said, "but what I'm beginning to think is that someone wanted to prevent *Love at Sequoia Ranch* from being published, and thought that with Arta dead it wouldn't happen. Then news broke that the books were going to be published anyway."

"That's when Camille's life was endangered," added Jackson. "She planned to write the Sequoia book, which likely would have caused a scandal for Oliver –Hollywood reporters being what they are-and she stands to get most of the money, leaving Greaves out in the cold. Do you know where she is?"

I shook my head.

"What are the odds," Evie asked, "of the two men teaming up though?"

"The night Greaves found out his wife was sleeping with Camille, he made tracks for Oliver's place," I replied, recalling what Camille had said. "I wonder if he stopped to get the Love in Sequoia notes first."

"How would he have even known about it?" asked Jackson.

"Arta thought it was a big joke," I said. "She crowed about it. She honestly thought her friend Oliver would see it as a joke."

"Could she be that naïve?" said Evie.

"Could she be that narcissistic?" I countered.

We sat in silence as this sank in.

"And all this bull crap about ecological terrorism," said Jackson, rousing himself, "who did what?"

"Russell had the package dosed with Valley Fever," I said. "He got the cocci spores from a contact in a lab, a single mother in a jam, in a bigger jam now."

"And the flood at the Lau's was Zach's work, guided by Greaves," said Jackson. "So I heard from Henry."

"Both Russell and Greaves knew how to rig a tripwire, I guess," I added.

"Wouldn't take much know-how," said Jackson.

"They've found out that Russell bought cotton cord and paraffin candles from the Douglas Peak supermarket," I said. "That kind of home-made fuse was used to burn down the house there. 'Revenge' on the hunter for causing the wildfire on the mountain."

"Which brings us to the *piece de resistance*," said Evie. "The shooting of Arta and Roger Smith. I was there in the library auditorium."

"Were you really? So was I," I said. "Well, not actually in the auditorium. Phillip Wilde and I were in the foyer. We actually saw Arta and Roger fall. Phillip was answering a call from BMP Security saying his dogs were loose."

"As if,'" said Jackson. "Those dogs are so good mannered they wouldn't leave a burning building. Fortunately, Phillip didn't fall it, plus he was in plain sight when the shots were fired. So expert rifle man or not, he couldn't have been the shooter. At least, then, people," he gave me a look, "let the Kentucky Five off the hook."

"I'm really, really sorry, but you know-"

"You were right about the bear," he finished.

"The thing that cracked it," I said, "was the attempt of Camille's life. Imelda saw the assailant fleeing, even if she couldn't identify him. And Camille had Rohypnol in her system."

"So," asked Evie, "what can they prove at this point?"

"Russell can be identified as the receiver and sender of the Valley Fever package, as well as the one who paid the lab worker. There is circumstantial evidence in the arson case. Greaves hired Josephine," I said, "to make sure the house above the library was empty that Friday night, so it could used as a hide. She sang like a canary about that. So Greaves is in the frame. If they catch him, he might implicate Russell."

"Marines?" said Jackson. "Aren't they *Semper fidelis*?"

"Darkstone contractors for years after that. Maybe they black-oped their way free of honour," I suggested. "I don't think the cops've found a money trail yet to really nail Russell."

"One or the other has got Zach," observed Evie.

She went to pour me more wine, but I protested, "Oh, no, I have to drive back up." I poured myself some of the fruit punch. "So you agree it's possible that *Love in the Sequoias* was actually going to be about Warren Oliver?"

"And his politician friend from Los Angeles County?" said Evie.

"But Arta had been told to change the friend's gender. He's married again and acts the family man," said Jackson. "And even if the truth came out, isn't it a little late in the day to worry about being outed. This is the left coast, after all," said Jackson.

"Maybe not, if it was also political," said Evie. "A scandal like that might put the permissions for the development into question."

"Two strikes against Halcon Village," said Jackson, "a closeted gay CEO and political corruption. So Oliver could have thought he had cause to join Greaves in the conspiracy."

"Joanna keeps 'seeing'," Evie drew air quotes, "Greaves' red sports car smashed up at the bottom of a cliff."

Jackson regarded me solemnly. Then he stood up. "I've got Oliver's home number here. Maybe I'll just give him a call." He strolled off into the living room.

Evie and I sat at the cluttered table. "I should pick up these dishes," she said.

"I should help you," I said.

Neither of us moved.

Jackson came back, phone in hand. "Oliver isn't home. I said I was an old hunting buddy back in town, and the woman who answered, laughed and said, 'What a coincidence. Oliver had gone up to his hunting cabin.'"

"In Sequoia National Park," said Evie. "Lot of nasty drop-offs on the way up there."

We digested this information.

"I've got some time off coming to me," said Jackson. "What say we scout around up there? See if we can find us a 12-year-old?"

"Shouldn't we call Guevara?" asked Evie.

"On the grounds a hysterical female is having visions?" I said. "Can we start now?"

"It's dark already," said Jackson. "I'll pick you up in BMP at 6 A.M., and we'll pick my mother up at 6:30. We need light to look for car wrecks and lost kids. Mom, you'd better arrange with what's-her-name to look in on the goats, in case you don't get back to milk them in the evening."

Jackson followed my car up the hill in his Fish and Wildlife truck.

I reported the day to Clara, who was already in bed reading, but not averse to a little Pinot Grigio. When I finished, she kept nodding.

"I'd like to be there, but I'm too tired."

"Do you think we'll find a wreck?" I asked.

She cocked her head. "Stranger things…" she said.

Tucked up in my bed, I couldn't sleep. Of course I couldn't sleep. I fired up the Internet and spent the night with Warren Oliver. Virtually.

I found pages of information, on line, much of it related to Halcon Ranch and the proposed Village. There were publicity photographs of him and Arta, of him and other board members, of him and his two beautiful, blonde daughters, of him and his movie star wife, and in older posts, of him and his first wife. She was about his age, in her fifties, attractive, and on the board of LACMA. The second wife was whippet thin, with cropped platinum blond hair. Her own website included pictures of her in black leather–stills from one of the recent Marvel movies. In one interview, she bemoaned the way the tabloids questioned her gender identity. "She was," she declared, "all girl. Why I'm even named for a princess." Ariel, I assumed, must be a Disney princess, Ariel Flyte-Oliver.

I uncovered an article in *Vanity Fair* about the man himself. It concentrated mostly on what designers he favoured, but did give his background briefly on the last page. He was an Angelean, and a Harvard School of Business graduate, thanks to a generous uncle in the 'business'. The business meant only one thing in Los Angeles. Oliver had started there, but soon made a move to property management. He was aggressively ambitious, but he paid his dues. He had done a crash course in agricultural management, before he got his job at Halcon Ranch.

Eventually, I fell into a semi-sleep – I was aware I was trying to sleep. At a certain point, I either fell into REM sleep or woke up.

My father was sitting in the blue velvet chair.

"Hey Jo," he said.

"What the f…?" I replied.

He laughed, the way he always had. "Hey, I'm here to help."

"You help me?"

"I told I was sorry before they killed me."

"Okay, help me then."

"Go get 'em, Jo. You can do it. You got me in the end, brought me in."

"In where?"

"To the light, to the love, whatever you hippies call it. Go to sleep. I'll keep watch."

When Jackson arrived to pick me up on in the morning, I had the headache and burning eyes of an insomniac.

26

STANDING BEAR

"What if I'm wrong?" I said, as I climbed into the cab.

"Don't worry," said Jackson, "I've been on these expeditions before. We'll call it an outing, and have a burger at O'Brien's."

What troubled me even more was that I might be right, and that Zach, as well as Greaves, might be in that smashed car. My mouth was dry and my heart was racing.

Evie was waiting outside with two thermoses when we arrived. I climbed down, so she could sit beside Jackson, who was wearing his brown winter CDFW jacket. Evie and I were wearing down jackets as well. Up on the mountain it had been down around 40 degrees, and we would be climbing again before we reached our destination.

Early as it was, the truck traffic on the Grapevine was already heavy, and commuters were heading north to their Bakersfield jobs. Jackson drove in the fast lane, passing the steady, sleepy regulars.

We were silent as we swept by Halcon Ranch and down the pass. Cattle still grazed on the almost perpendicular slopes, and a hawk hovered, hunting in lazy circles.

In the valley, the downed almond trees still lay, their crowns pointing east, their roots exposed to our prying eyes.

"Next year's firewood," observed Evie, "Lovely and fragrant."

In the fields beside the 99, crews were already at work picking whatever got picked in November. Not green beans, so Max had told me, but the other leafy greens. And not zucchini, which also came from Mexico now, and cost more accordingly. In a Toronto winter, you got sticker shock when you bought zucchini.

We passed the exit to Tehachapi, the one I usually took to the hospitals, and took the exit to 178, toward Lake Isabella.

"We're headed to Kernville," I realized out loud.

"Yup," said Jackson. "That's where Oliver's place is. Well, farther up the mountain."

"I know that area. I used to anyway. We camped up there at Peppermint Creek."

"The place of taking off, the way west to the Spirit World," said Jackson. "And more than a few unwary tourists have done just that."

"Do you suppose your bear is up there?" Evie asked.

"I sincerely hope so," he said.

As we drove, I felt worse and worse, ready to vomit.

When I was living with Connor, I had had an urgent prompting to help people with AIDS. Those were the bad early days before the drug cocktail when gay men were dying in droves. I attended several evenings of instruction. The men running the workshop deliberately tried to gross out us do-gooders. I wasn't offended really, but I found it juvenile. I was ready to quit when Connor got word that his gay brother had been found dead, a suicide. Could Connor see to the arrangements? And, by the way, his brother had had AIDS, and had been dead for weeks before his body was discovered.

Connor handled it, including the surreptitious burial of the ashes on his parents' grave in a Catholic cemetery.

I went on to know two men with AIDS, one a good friend, who is keeping pace with me as we age.

But my call to minister to dying AIDS patients gave me had good reason to doubt my ability as a seer.

"It's just an outing. Right?" I said to my companions in the front seat.

Evie patted my arm. "So, what's Warren Oliver like?" she asked Jackson.

"Well, you can imagine that he's intelligent and driven. I met him when Phillip and I went up to the ranch to hunt as I said. He was aggressively macho then. Had to be the best hunter. Pretty hard when he had a world-class shooter, and a CDFW officer along. Wanted badly to impress his friend, who only cared about getting back for Happy Hour. Oliver bought the ranch from Phillip shortly after that, but we were never invited back. A couple of years passed, and I heard he'd married a starlet. Maybe, he figured out he needed his straight image to sell Halcon Village."

"You don't admire him then?" I said.

"Who am I to say? Country folk, you know-not very open-minded, not in Kern County anyhow. I guess he thought that's what it would take to get the go-ahead for Halcon Village. I wouldn't mind working at the ranch."

"Even if Warren could be a major bad guy?" asked Evie.

"The ranch is still going to be there. Somebody else's going to be CEO, and they're going to need game management. A game warden would have a close up view of the Halcon Village development, and might be able to help with conservation."

"Maybe," said Evie. "And maybe you'll finally find a girl there."

"O Grandma," he said, grinning. "Your second sight doesn't work on some."

She widened her eyes, concluding he had already found one, I thought.

We were approaching Lake Isabella. Twenty years ago, the sight of it had filled me with dismay. It had already been tamed into submission. I dreaded what it would look like now after years of drought, all sandy bottom and no water to speak of.

When we caught a glimpse, Jackson said, "It's down to 8% of capacity, about 40,000 acre feet. Full it's over 500,000. The outflow has to be kept at a certain level to preserve the fish downstream and, of course, there's been a bigger draw on the reservoir in this drought. The water's warmer now it's low, so cold water fish like trout aren't doing well. With less snowmelt, the Kern River doesn't support much white water rafting anymore. Companies have gone under."

Years ago, I wondered why anyone could regard Lake Isabella as a vacation destination. I came from the Great lakes after all. I thought Lake Isabella was low, hot, ugly and dry. Yet others regarded it as beautiful. The river itself was a different matter, white water most of the way up. Damming the river had created the lake, and inundated the old town.

Evie said, "I read that Old Kernville has come to the surface and you can see the outlines of the drowned buildings, the saloons and the rails where you tied up your horse. Some of the buildings escaped the flood. They were moved up to the new site of Kernville."

"The dams are sixty years old and leaking now," said Jackson. "The Army Corps of Engineers has begun work to strengthen them, making them higher, believe it or not, in case of a flood event. We had a bad one back in 1860-a forty three day storm."

We had just passed a sign detailing the flood alert signal and escape route.

This is actually the Bakersfield city limit," said Jackson, as we climbed into Kernville.

I remembered the Kernville grocery store, and the restaurant where the cook came out of the kitchen, and menaced us when Julia complained about the coleslaw. He was carrying a cleaver.

On the other side of the highway, was the upscale restaurant that looked out on the river canyon. We had eaten there as consolation when my insomnia cut our vacation short.

According to the sign, the number of river deaths had climbed to 269.

The road had been winding most of the way, but now we moved into serious hairpin curves and steep grades. My '92 Tercel always threatened to over-heat, as I got farther up the mountain, even when it was new. Jackson, like Henry, was an expert, playing the gas pedal and cornering precisely. I wasn't sure whether I felt like throwing up because of the motion or the terror. I hung on and tried to concentrate on not being sick.

"Please let Zach be safe. Please let Zach be save," I heard myself saying over and over in my head.

At times, we could glimpse the river slicing through the canyon, still frothing over boulders and rocks and pooling in depths. The cliff at the road's edge grew steadily higher and the shoulder narrower, guarded by nothing but naturally occurring rocks in places.

Then we swayed around yet another blind curve and saw skid marks in the down-bound lane, leading to the edge. Jackson slowed, drove on to a relatively straight part, did a U-turn and came back. He had to drive past the skid marks to find a place wide enough to park on.

"Stay here," he ordered, grabbing something out of the glove box, and leaping out.

We didn't have a choice really. There was no room to get out on the passenger side. We turned to watch him run back, and peer over the edge. He raised binoculars to his eyes. He took his radio out of his belt and made a call. Then he turned and walked back as he talked.

We heard him say, "It's a mountain rescue, but I don't think it's a survivable wreck."

He answered a number of questions, turning away so he was hard to hear.

"Well, it's not a red sports car. It's a red jeep," he said. "Can you crawl out this side?"

I found that I could follow Evie out over the gearshift, but once there, I couldn't seem to stand. Both of them reached out to steady me.

"Sit down," said Jackson, so I sat on the running board.

Evie put her hand on the back of my neck and pushed down, so that my head was between my knees.

Jackson was getting something out of the back of the truck. He handed several orange cones to Evie.

"Go up the road to where we turned and set these across the road. I'll go down." And they both set off leaving me to my low blood pressure.

When they arrived back, I sprang up and said, "Is it Greaves? Is Zach with him?"

Jackson was rummaging in the back of the truck. He jumped down with a coil of rope. He hooked it onto a guardrail post. It looked as if the vehicle had swerved suddenly, and actually jumped the rail.

Jackson hefted his weight against the knot, put on gloves and began rappelling over the edge. Evie and I stepped over the guardrail, so we could see. It was a long drop, but not too long for Jackson's rope. He hit the ground, steadied himself, and began walking toward the wreck.

From where we stood, we could see only the back half of the Jeep. The front half was jammed against a huge boulder bigger than the vehicle itself.

In the beginning, when I started *seeing* the wrecked sports car, I had assumed it would be found on the S-curves outside Bear Mountain Place, down at the bottom of the eighty-foot drop. This cliff was barely half that.

Jackson was peering into the jeep, training his flashlight inside. He walked around to the far side and studied the interior a long time. Finally, he turned and walked a few steps toward us. He held up one finger, and pointed to the driver's side.

The cold, clear water of the Kern River rushed on, oblivious. I turned and threw up my breakfast. By the time I'd pulled myself together, Jackson was back up the cliff.

"It may be Greaves," he said. "Hard to tell. Pretty banged up. But he was alone."

Back at the truck, I pulled my water bottle out of my backpack and rinsed my mouth.

"How far are we from the ranch?" I asked.

"Less than 15 minutes," Jackson replied.

At that moment, a silver SUV came down around the corner. The driver took in what was happening, stepped on the gas, and disappeared around the next curve. I could hear the cones bouncing and clattering away.

"Was that Russell?" I said.

"Let's go," said Jackson, waving us back into the truck, me first.

Before we could do up our seat belts, he was making a U-turn and gunning the engine up the mountain. I grabbed the overhead grip, while Evie gripped the dashboard. The tires screamed as the truck veered around the tight turns, without regard for lanes. Then, it slowed and crept along until it settled behind an outcropping of pine-covered rock.

Jackson put his finger up to shush us. "Get out very quietly," he whispered. "Leave the door ajar."

We climbed out, and he pointed to the right. As we began to walk up the road, we heard a shot, but Jackson gestured to caution us and we moved on. He had a rifle slung across his back, and he had drawn his handgun, which he held down at his side.

We came to a driveway, which wound through the woods. The ranch house was still out of sight. As we walked its interminable length, we heard a second shot and, after a long pause, a third.

"Target practise," whispered Jackson.

When we finally came into sight of the house, Jackson stopped. We listened. We were away from the rushing noise of the river here, but the pines were sighing in the wind. Although we strained our ears, we couldn't make out where target practise was taking place. Then there was another loud crack. It came from behind the low house on the right.

"Stay here," said Jackson.

He ran quietly toward the left of the house. I looked at Evie. Then, as one, we set off running to the right. Jackson was younger and faster, but we had less distance to cover.

There they were-a man and a boy, the boy holding the rifle, and the man correcting his stance.

"Zach," I cried, turning my ankle and falling to my knees. "Zach, it's me, Joanna, your mother's friend," I yelled as I struggled to my feet.

Zach lowered the gun and gawked at me. The man suddenly wasn't there.

"Drop the gun," yelled Jackson, from the opposite direction.

Zach dropped it. "I was just learning to shoot," he said, plaintively.

Jackson swept up the rifle. Evie and I converged on the kid, weeping. Jackson handed the gun to his mother. That left me to wrap my arms around the boy.

"I was learning to shoot," he said, pulling away.

Jackson was moving around the house to the door. "Get him into the truck," he yelled.

We stood for a moment.

"I guess we'd better," I said, after weighing the odds of disobeying a law enforcement officer a second time.

Evie clearly wanted to stay as second gun. But I could see that she also knew Zach might still need protection.

As we started back, we could see Jackson at the door, on his radio.

"Stand down. Stand down," we heard. "Wait for backup. Are you clear?"

Turning away, Jackson mumbled an acknowledgement.

When we were half way back to the truck, we heard a shot. We stopped in our tracks.

"A rifle," Evie said. "Not a side arm. Inside the house, I'd say."

"Who was in the house?" I asked Zach.

"Nobody. Well, Warren, maybe. I don't where he went. He was coaching me. Matthew went to the store first thing to get bacon, but he took too long. Russell got sick of waiting, and went to find him."

Would Jackson go in against orders?" I asked Evie.

She looked at me, and shook her head. "I don't know. I doubt it. I mean we've got the kid. There was no hurry."

I pulled the corners of my mouth down, and she responded with a grimace of her own. Zach looked from one to the other. "What are you saying?" he asked.

"We'll have to wait and see," said Evie.

As we waited in the truck, I was probably not the only one saying the mantra, "Please let Jackson be safe." Every third time, I threw in, "And thank you for Zach."

A Tulare Sheriff's car arrived fifteen minutes later, and Evie climbed out to update the officer. Somewhat hysterically. He got out and came to the window of the truck.

"Is it true you are Zach Aldano?" he asked.

"Yeah," said Zach, obviously frightened.

"You're not in trouble kid," he said turning away. We could hear him on his radio. Then he came back. "Seems like the CDFW guy is holding, outside the house. If anybody's hurt, it's inside."

Evie let out a breath, and leaned her weight against the truck.

"Can you drive the truck, Ma'am?" the deputy asked.

"Sure," said Evie.

"Take it back down to the accident site. There'll be people there can give you any help you need."

As the cop pulled away toward the ranch house, two more cruisers came up the hill and joined him.

As soon as Evie stopped the pickup, Zach leapt over me and out of it. He had seen the first responders on the other side of the guardrail, and could not be restrained.

Evie and I looked at each other and shrugged. We watched Zach's back as he caught sight of the accident scene. His shoulders slumped. We got out to go to him.

"It's Matthew's jeep," he said to us. "Is he dead?" Getting no answer from us, he went over to a fireman. "Is he dead? Is the guy dead?"

The fireman nodded.

"What happened?" demanded Zach.

"Well son, looks to me as if a bear might have been on the road." He pointed his toe at a large bear turd beside the verge.

"He was my friend," said Zach.

Holy Stockholm Syndrome, Batman!

Evie and I towed the weeping child back to the truck, where we broke out the thermoses. The chai had honey in it, that might work, but then a medic arrived with two cokes. He and Zach sat in the back seat behind the wire mesh, drinking them.

When Zach grew calmer, the medic asked, "Are you hurt? Do you have any injuries?"

"No," Zach protested. "Matthew wouldn't hurt me."

"What about Russell?" I asked.

"Matthew wouldn't let him. Neither would Warren."

I wanted to say, "So you were just on a little unscheduled hunting trip?"

I bit my tongue. Evie took hold of my hand.

Now Kern County Sheriff cars arrived. Two deputies approached the truck. The younger one said, "What say, Zach? How'd you like a ride in a police car? If that's all right?" he added to the medic.

"Seems okay. Doesn't need an ambulance."

"Are you going to take me home?" asked Zach.

"We're going to take you to meet your mother in Bakersfield. Do you want one of these ladies to come with you?"

"No," he said, without hesitation. Climbing out, he added, "Can we turn on the siren?"

"Hmm, maybe for a minute or two," the deputy said, grinning.

The other deputy stayed behind for a minute. "Detectives Guevara and Trantor are right behind us. They'll talk to you. I guess we owe you a big thank you, along with Officer Jackson. You don't seem to getting one from the victim," he laughed.

It was a good result. It was an excellent result. People were happy. So far.

Then the ambulance pulled away and started uphill. Evie and I drank our beverages, sitting side by side.

The outside lane of the highway was completely blocked with emergency vehicles. We saw another Kern County car arriving in the up-bound lane. Guevara was driving. We sprinted out of the truck.

When Guevara stopped, Evie demanded, "My son, the CDFW officer, is up there. What's happened?"

"Officer Jackson is fine. He's done a great job."

"And Oliver?" I asked.

Guevara shook his head.

Dead! Oliver dead. I didn't see that coming.

"I'm going to send Jackson back down," said Guevara, "And have him take you to O'Brien's to wait for us. It'll be a while before we get there."

Fred Trantor nodded to me from the passenger seat.

Retrieval of Greaves' body was proving problematic. Firemen and tow truck drivers were debating the possibility of lifting the big, hardtop Jeep Wrangler up with the body still in it. They had put out a call for a wrecker complete with boom, and more than capable of lifting the load. Once it was up on the road, firemen could get busy cutting Greaves' out.

Meanwhile, the ambulance that had been waiting for him had gone up to the ranch house. There were five or six Sheriff's vehicles up there by now. I wanted to walk back up, but the Tulare deputy had ordered us to stay put. Then the ambulance returned, and paused so Jackson could get out. He conferred with the officers in charge of the recovery, and walked over to see how things were going down the cliff.

"So, is it Matthew Greaves?" Evie asked when he got into the truck.

"He rented that vehicle," said Jackson. "So the Tulare deputy told me up at the house.'

"And Zach said Greaves started down for food early this morning."

"Not a pretty sight," said Jackson. "Speaking of which...." He heaved a big sigh, "neither was the ranch house."

"What happened, Jackson," asked Evie.

"You probably heard the shot on your way to the truck. "I'm glad you didn't turn back. I was still outside waiting for backup. When I heard nothing else, I moved in closer. I couldn't see much through the windows, but it was deadly quiet. I kicked in the door. Oliver had shot himself."

I shivered.

"There was a scrawled note beside his cell phone, 'Check the videos.' I couldn't do anything for him. Half his head was gone. I called it in. Then I checked the videos, four of them, documenting meetings with Greaves, and one with both Greaves and Russell."

"How did you bear that?" Evie asked.

" Hell, Mother, you're a farmer."

"I think I saw Russell pass us just as you came back up over the guardrail," I said. "And Zach said he went down after Greaves."

"I remember you said that. I figure he must be driving Oliver's Lexus SUV," said Jackson. "His own RAV4 is parked in the wagon shed at the ranch. I called that in as well. The Tulare Sheriff may have stopped him."

Zach was safe. That was what mattered most. Each of us was absorbing what had happened. We rode in silence.

About ten minutes later, we came upon two Sheriff's cars, blocking a gravel track. Jackson pulled in just down the road. As soon as he turned off the engine, we could hear a helicopter, very close and very low. Out of the truck, we found a roadside clump of pines blocked our view.

Jackson approached the two deputies standing beside the cars.

"What's up?" he shouted as he approached.

"There's a silver SUV parked behind the cabin in there. Apparently, it may be the sniper we've been looking for. Copter's pinning him down. The SWAT team's on its way." One of the deputies shouted back.

We had to stand in a tight knit group to hear, even so.

"I'm hoping they get a move on," shouted the other deputy.

"They've got a sharpshooter in the copter, but the goal is to get him out alive."

"Me too," said the other guy. "I mean me too-alive."

"You got a rifle too?" asked the deputy in uniform, nodding toward Jackson's sidearm.

"I do."

"Get it and hang around at least until they get here."

"Do you think Russell's armed?" I asked. "He was just going for groceries."

"He was going down because Greaves was AWOL," said Jackson, coming back with his rifle. "He knew something was wrong, so, yes, I'm sure he's armed." He turned back to the deputy. "How'd you find him?"

"We were on our way up to the accident site. It's a pretty straight stretch here, and I guess the guy saw our cars. He turned in here at old Dawson's cabin. Well, I knew Dawson died last summer, so I stopped and called it in. The fire truck went on ahead. We were told to block the access while they sorted things out. There's no other way out, except through the woods. Half an hour later, we got word that Russell was driving a silver SUV down the mountain."

"Yeah, I called that in," Jackson said.

"Maybe he's made a run for it," Evie said.

"Don't think so. We got our eyes on the place pretty quick. There's only the one door. No windows on the back."

"I tell you," shouted the other guy, "I expected him to crawl out the chimney and get us in his sights." He laughed. "I was glad when the copter came, and we could step back."

"I hope you walk a better walk than you talk, Kern County," said the other deputy.

It was only then that I realized that they were from different Sheriff's, one from Tulare and one from Kern. That made sense. Kernville was just down the road.

"You gotta keep laughing," said Kern. "What've we got so far? Kidnapped kid, fatal accident, suicide and deadly sniper standoff. What're the odds? What are you guys doing up here anyway?"

"Day off," said Jackson, coming back with his rifle. "Bit of an outing."

"In November?"

At that point, a SWAT truck roared into view. In a split second, eight heavily armed officers jumped out. The one in charge sent the deputies to block the road in both directions with their cars.

"You stay here," he told Jackson. "Have you got a vest? Park your truck across the driveway. And you two," he meant Evie and me, "take shelter in one of the units."

Jackson handed us our backpacks, and we set off southward, Evie stumbling as she tried to see whether her son did have a Kevlar vest. As we rounded the corner, we could see him behind his truck-in a vest-with his rifle at the ready. The SWAT team had melted into the woods.

Having lived in L.A., I was familiar with the noise of a helicopter circling, circling just above the trees. Sometimes for hours. It ground me down then. Green Village was solidly middle class, patrolled by its own security, but the neighbourhood around it was rife with crime. If I had been the pursued, I would have given up just to stop the noise. This was worse, much worse. The noise was engulfing, all-consuming. There was nothing beyond it. So it seemed.

Then we heard a loud hail above the infernal racket.

"Come out with your hands in the air. Come out with your hands in the air. You are surrounded. Repeat, you are completely surrounded."

It seemed as if the copter was moving slightly away and then slightly back, and the voice issued the same command over and over again. Then the loud hailer fell silent. The noise had seemed eternal, but the pause seemed even longer.

"Lay on the ground with your hands behind your head," the loud hailer shouted. "On the ground! Hands behind your head!"

"Do not move. Repeat-do not move."

There was nothing again. Then the helicopter appeared above the road, rising and circling back.

I could see Jackson and the SWAT leader at the entrance moving impatiently on the spot, radios at the ready.

Our deputy had walked toward the scene. We could see him listening to his. Then he turned toward us, and held up his thumb.

"They've got him," he shouted.

Both of us started toward him, but he held up his hand to keep us back.

SWAT team officers began emerging from the track. In the middle of all that black, there was a splash of bright colour, a Hawaiian shirt.

He should have worn a jacket, I thought.

The Kern County deputy brought his car down, and the lengthy process of installing Russell in the back seat behind the metal grill began.

Finally, the SWAT leader announced that the prisoner was secure, and the car doors were closed.

In the general milling about and decompressing chatter, I moved forward. Russell had counted coup on me, three times. I wanted to look him in the face.

I walked up the edge of the right lane, under the rock face. When I was even with the patrol car, I could see Russell in the back seat, securely cuffed. He was looking directly at me.

I took off my cowboy hat, held it in front of me. Looking him in the eye, I twirled it, my finger through the hole. Then I carefully reshaped the crown and put it back on my head.

He grinned.

His face was tanned and dark with stubble, his black hair, pulled back into a short ponytail. Now he was just looking at me. There was no hostility in his expression, nor any other emotion. He was there, about to face charges that could earn him the death penalty, but he seemed unmoved.

He was a soldier, I thought, but then, who wasn't these days?

Russell and I had gone past the bravado of challenge and counter challenge. That was over. We were not even adversaries any more. For that moment, we read in each other's face what it is to be human.

THE BEAR CAME DOWN THE MOUNTAIN JUST AFTER DAWN. SHE WAS thirsty and she could smell the river. She broke through low pine trees and jumped onto the flat surface. Another man trail. She raised her nose. No man smell now. She could see nothing either way. The trail twisted out of sight both ways. She began to cross. Suddenly a distant roar began to grow louder. Not the river. She stopped and turned toward it. She was tired from her long trek northward and irritable without her cub.

She rose on her hind legs to face the menace.

A red man-machine sped around the blind corner. She roared back. The man-machine squealed in terror, tried to stop, flew up and over and was lost to sight. When the crashing sound stopped, she could smell blood, man blood.

Back on four feet, she left a scat to mark the place.

27

LUNCH AT LAST

By now it was after 1 p.m. and Jackson arranged with Guevara that we would be available at O'Brien's Restaurant.

Evie and I went into the restaurant first, while Jackson stayed behind at the CDFW truck. He said he would be right in.

When he joined us at our table, he said, "You wondered where my bear was. She's up the mountain a piece, making her way on up. She might be the bear that drove Greaves off the road."

It was Trantor who finally showed up to take our statements. She had traded in her plastic thongs for combat boots and her black skirt for black pants. She thumped down on the chair beside Jackson and dropped a lined, yellow writing pad on the table.

"Zach should be with his family by now," she said. "For that we are all grateful, but I cannot imagine why an officer of the law would fail to notify the Sheriff of his suspicions," she turned her head to Jackson, "and instead set off with his mother, an elderly friend and a picnic lunch."

"Who you calling elderly?" I muttered.

"Actually, we only brought beverages," said Evie.

Detective Trantor was waiting for Jackson to answer.

He shrugged. "I may not be cut out for law enforcement," he said.

Fred glared at him.

"Look, it was just a hunch. It could have been a wild goose chase," he said.

She sighed deeply, and pulled herself together. She rapped her pen on the writing tablet.

"So we have Morris William Russell in custody without bloodshed. The videos Warren Oliver left are strong evidence of first-degree murder in the deaths of Dietzen and Smith." She was scribbling a chart as she spoke. "The sniper rifle has also been recovered, having been sold at a gun sale in Orange County. We have eyewitness evidence to implicate Russell in the death of Mrs. King-he accessed the Cocci spores. The arson charge against him would be harder to prove, but the wounding of the young hunter has been linked to another of his guns. We may not proceed on the lesser charges, but Russell is wrapped up."

Now she printed 'Greaves' in large letters.

"Have they got Greaves up out the wreckage?" I asked.

"The wreck is up," she said. "The firemen are cutting the body out."

I thought of the affable fellow in the red top-down, and Clara beside him, waving as he drove off.

"Clearly, he was Zach's kidnapper, apparently to save the kid from being shot by Russell," said Fred.

"If they were at odds, why were they together at the ranch house?" I asked.

"Seems like payoff time. Oliver had a large amount of cash up there."

"But how could Zach ever have been released? He could identify them all," I said.

"Who says he was going to be? He had a new daddy."

Strictly speaking, he had never had an old daddy, although he seemed to like his step-daddy well enough.

"We had enough from Josephine to tie Greaves to the murders. Oliver's videos confirm that. The conspiracy charges might have been dropped. Josephine plea-bargained a five-year sentence, by the way, but she'll probably serve less. Greaves would have been convicted of first-degree murder at trial. Fate in the shape of the neighbourhood bear has saved the state the trouble."

"As for Warren Oliver..." she paused. "He was the mastermind. Dreamed up the whole eco-terrorist thing. Pretty ballsie involving his precious Halcon Village in the cover-up, but they say any publicity is good publicity. It was a two for one plan really. Get rid of a writer, who's about to blow your image, and bring your planning permission into disrepute, and at the same time, discredit ecologists, who are trying to block your real estate project."

"He didn't seem like the suicidal type," said Evie.

"Panicked," said Jackson. "Saw his life going down the tube. Caught red-handed with a kidnapped child!"

"Used a rifle?" Evie asked.

Jackson nodded. "Classic toe shot. That time we were all up here, the others well lubricated, we got to arguing was that even possible. We unloaded one of the guns, took off our shoes and tried it. Oliver was the best at it. He had these prehensile toes."

"Russell, the only one who still presents a danger to society, is under lock and key," said Fred, "so, all in all, I call that a good result."

"Now, I understand," she continued, "that you three took advantage of Officer Jackson's day off to enjoy an outing, and that your goal was to end up here at O'Brien's for lunch. I assume that you checked online to find out it was open mid-week because of Thanksgiving. Ordinarily, it isn't in November."

The three of us sat for a moment, eyes on Fred. Finally, we all spoke at once.

"Yes."

"Exactly."

"True."

"Not," said Fred, handing Jackson the writing tablet.

"I need you to write down exactly what led you to come up here-hunch or not, when you left home, when you saw the skid marks, what you did subsequently, etc. When you agree you've got it right, let me read it. When it's complete, we'll all sign it. While you're writing, I'm going to get some lunch. I'll have them bring you something, and make it clear you'll need the table for some time. Hamburgers and fries, all round?"

We nodded. Salad was not fortifying enough for the job ahead.

"You should take a pass on the 40 ounce steak," advised Evie.

Jackson handed the writing pad and pen to me. "You seem college educated," he cracked.

So we began the painful process.

It was getting dark by the time we started down toward Kernville. I was in the back seat behind the cage. We all needed extra room at that point, and we were talked out.

I was half asleep, when I heard Aunt Mae's voice in my head. "How're they doing, Joey?"

I didn't have to ask who.

Greaves was standing where the Jeep had leapt the guardrail, saying "What the fuck!" Oliver was still sitting in the blood spattered ranch kitchen. He was not astonished like Greaves. He was grief shattered.

Neither of them showed any sign of guilt.

Before I could put my question into words, Mae chuckled, "Things are different here, Girlie. It took Rod a good few years to figure it out. You helped him over."

"I cared about him," I thought-argued back. What I did not care for was the feeling he was sitting on the back seat next to me.

"We're all in this together."

It was no longer Mae's cackling voice, but my own.

"Did you say something?" Evie asked from the passenger seat.

I didn't reply. I was busy pushing Greaves and Oliver toward the light.

28

HOME

I woke late the next morning, the day before Thanksgiving, and lay listening to the plastic sunflower below my window turning and ticking in the wind. I tried to orient myself. Where was I? What was there to fear today?

Clara's house in Bear Mountain Place and we had brought Zach home to his mother and his grandmother and his two surrogate fathers.

I had fretted much of the summer about being homeless. Now it occurred to me that a nomad is never homeless. I had lived in twenty-five different buildings, great and small, deep in the mountains, in a country hamlet, in small towns, in sprawling suburbs and in two great cities. To each, I had carried a few treasures as the desert nomads carry their rugs, their hidden wealth. The only necessary hearth was the heart.

When I emerged from my bathroom into the kitchen in my robe, I was greeted by a delicious hot sugar and caramel odour.

"Bear claws heating," said Clara. "No dieting today for our sleuth extraordinaire. And I got you chai. We're going to sit at the dining room table and hear the whole thing end to end."

We had not eaten at the table in the three months we had lived here, so this was an occasion.

Julia and Colin arrived just as we were sitting down, bearing more pastries, and car cups with their beverages. Jazz was shooed into Clara's room, and the door was shut. Julia was much more allergic than me.

"Okay," said Clara, "we're ready for your tale, but I'd just like to say that I regret I wasn't much help at the end."

"You were my anchor," I said. "You were even ready to turn ghost buster."

That was good for a laugh, and then I began the story.

When I got to the end, a sombre mood descended. Such a waste of lives.

Then Colin said, "I saw Zach riding his bike with the other kids at the bus stop. He seems like nothing bad happened. Oh, did you hear about the deer hunters? Killed a deer right here in town."

(Two flatlanders, in a moving SUV, shot a deer on the front lawn of a BMP home. Residents drove them off when they tried to claim their prize. The following week, Sydney Akerman published their car licence number, and the registered owner's name in the *Prospector*.)

In the afternoon, Camille phoned from Douglas Peak to say she was back at home. She had finally been sprung from an FBI safe house in Austin.

Both Julia and Colin overhearing my half of the conversation, mouthed, "Ask her for dinner." So I did.

Le Petit Breton would be closed for the Thanksgiving, except for pickup of pre-ordered turkey dinners. We all had an invitation there, for coffee and desert at 7 P.M. Jackson and Evie were coming. Lori had said it would be a chance for Zach to thank us properly. I wasn't sure about that, but I was looking forward to seeing little Julia Ann.

The mood in the village was buoyant. The weekenders were arriving and catching up on the news.

"Now, we only have to worry about being shot by hunters," I heard one of them laugh at the General Store.

The big news was Zach's return. He was pictured exiting Kern County Medical Centre with his mother, Ben and Julien. Rescue details remained vague, although a Sequoia ranch was mentioned.

That heart-warming story led to more detailed reports that all the major ecological groups had signed on to the Halcon Village preservation offer. The Village was a go. Invariably, the news was appended to the news of Warren Oliver's sudden death at a ranch in Sequoia National Forest. It seemed as though the détente was Warren's last great achievement. Completion dates were so far in the future that I would probably not live to be offended.

The arrest of Morris William Russell in Kernville, on many charges, including two counts of first-degree murder, one of which was that of the renowned novelist, Arta Dietzen, was still mostly a separate item. It was, however, linked to the accidental death of Arta's husband Matthew Greaves. The Kern County Sheriff promised a press conference on Monday.

News outlets plumped up their otherwise lean holiday offering by replaying the tributes to Arta, including the public funeral at the Hollywood Bowl. Copies of her books were being snapped up once again as women sought solace on a lonely weekend. *Love in Peoria* had hit the stands two weeks earlier. *Love in Qatar* would be out by spring.

It was warm enough to have drinks on the deck on Thanksgiving Day. I stood at the rail with my glass of *Veuve Cliquot*, looking down through the trees.

The hawk's cry pierced the air. Over and over. She was just there at the top of a pine, but out of sight.

Behind me, Leo, Evan, Clara, Camille, Julia and Colin sat chatting over their champagne.

Next door at the King's, smoke rose from the barbecue on the lakeside deck. I could hear children laughing.

Families had been made and remade and were still in the making. Even my father had been changed. "These are pearls that were his eyes," I thought, remembering *The Tempest*, but I was not entirely convinced.

I left the others talking, and went in through the sliding door. Colin was taking the glazed ham out of the oven.

He put a pile of cutlery on the breakfast bar, and I began to set the table.

High on the mountain the bear settled herself into her den. It was a hollow beneath a fallen pine, well carpeted with brown needles. She had gained back the weight she lost on her long trek. There were fish now that she knew how to find them and good browsing along the stream. The water was delicious. It was time to rest and let the new cubs grow inside her. She would teach them many things, most of all, to stay off the man trails.

Footnotes

Journal of the History of Biology #37 557-583, 2004 Alagona, Peter. "Biography of a Feathered Pig: The Californian Conservation Controversy"

Vanity Fair.com/news/2000/05/Hitchens, Hitchens, Christopher. "The Road to East Egg"

Author's Note

Please consider posting a review on Amazon.

For other mysteries set in a fictionalized Pine Mountain Club go to mar-preston.com (*Payback, The Most Dangerous Species*) Mar also writes mysteries set in Santa Monica.

About the Author

Joyce A Howe's (Hood's) life is rooted in the oral culture of the northern-most Blue Ridge mountains, a 19th century way of life preserved into the 1930's; deeply influenced by oral reading of the *King James Bible*, which led to a love affair with Shakespeare; an oldest sibling plunged into mothering early; determined to go to university in spite of poverty; chose teaching over acting for stability (always front and centre anyway in classroom); put children before career, but ended up teaching English, media and creative writing for over 30 years; has lived in more than 20 homes; constant reader and avid fan of mysteries; lover of the Blues; author of an unpublished body of poetry and an e-book *Never Tell: recovered memories of a daughter of the Temple Mater* (Alternately *daughter of the Knights Templar*)

Hour of the Hawk is the first of a series of Joanna Hunter mysteries.

available at Amazon, Kindle Select

joycehowe.com

joyceahood8@gmail.com

ALSO BY JOYCE HOWE

NEVER TELL

Recovered Memories of a Daughter of the Knights Templar

88,000 words

What has no name does not exist. The cult had no name. What was done to the child had no name. "Don't tell," she was told. "Never tell." Tell who? Everyone she knew turned up in a ceremonial hood eventually. She knew by their voices.

In her thirties Joyce came across her father's pin bearing the words, "Knight of the Temple Mater". What was this? Why was it a secret? Was it Masonic or was it Knights Templar?

Not until Roy was dead could she remember.

She was a special child, like her little sister, trained to listen and remember, her personality split into separate parts. She had hidden selves but there was a deep, secret part only Aunt Mae, who had saved her life, knew about. This part was the spy.

Never Tell, like *Angela's Ashes* and *The Glass Castle* demonstrates the resilience of the human spirit. The narrator's voice, warm and darkly humorous, assures us of the redemptive power of love.

69264745R00210

Made in the USA
Middletown, DE
05 April 2018